A DENAZEN NOVEL

TOXIC

BOOK TWO

A Denazen Novel

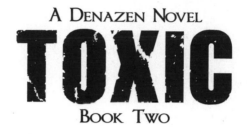

TOXIC

Book Two

JUS ACCARDO

Entangled Publishing, LLC
2614 South Timberline Road
Suite 109
Fort Collins, CO 80525
Visit our website at www.entangledpublishing.com.

Edited by Liz Pelletier
Cover design by Liz Pelletier

Print ISBN   978-1-62061-016-9
Ebook ISBN   978-1-62061-017-6

Manufactured in the United States of America

First Edition October 2012

For my best friend…
I love you, Mom.

1

Most people probably wouldn't advise downing Jell-O shots before racing to the top of a thirty-foot crane.

Me? Well, it sounded like a good idea. Plus, Jell-O shots? My fave. The slimy glob of vodka-infused jelly—strawberry banana—went down nice and easy. Probably due to the sweet Jell-O-y goodness…or possibly the four that came before it.

I set the empty plastic cup down in the dirt and scanned the crowd. My new group of friends. Sixes. Every last one. Not that there was anything wrong with my old friends—I actually missed them like crazy. My antics weren't nearly as impressive when there was a guy in the crowd who could walk on water. Or a chick that could breathe underneath it.

But this was safer. For now. These kids all knew about Kale's ability. They knew to keep their distance, while at the same time, doing their best to make him feel welcome.

There were about twelve of us scattered around the construction site. From the base of the crane, I could see our own personal lightning rod—David, I think his name was—starting some of the construction vehicles by simply touching them. His ability drew off electricity, allowing him to receive and channel it through his body. The electric current spitting from his fingers brought the engines to life, accompanied by a round of enthusiastic applause.

What the hell was it about guys and big equipment?

Squealing metal filled the air as one of the dump trucks tipped its bed, sliding debris onto the lot. A few seconds later, a large chunk of concrete rocketed into the air. A blue-white ball of twitching light followed, leaving a shimmering trail in its wake as it shot across the night sky. The two objects collided with a deafening crack, and the concrete shattered, raining tiny bits and pieces over our heads. There was a chorus of cheers, followed by hysterical laughter.

Six or not, *all* drunken teenagers found destruction an epic source of amusement. At least some things in life were static.

Good thing Paul was with us, or someone might have heard all the noise. With his ability to cloak stationary people, places, and things, the rest of the world could only see the future home of the new Parkview strip mall. A silent, empty construction site after dark.

Yep. Nothing going on here.

There were a million and five things I should have been doing at that moment. Obsessing over my meager wardrobe of suitable school outfits. Looking over my shoulder for stick-up-the-ass men in Armani knockoffs just salivating to snatch me. Worrying about the fact that I had roughly five months—possibly less—of sanity left.

It was a new and vicious trend. Worry, worry, worry.

What *was* I doing? What I did best. Crazy shit.

"Last chance to step off, Dez," the girl on the other side of the crane said, waving. She had brown eyes and long purple hair that twisted down her back in an intricate braid.

Step off? Someone had been sniffing some serious glue. I gripped the bars of the crane and arched my back. Snap, crackle, and pop. "Not a chance, baby."

Kiernan was a fairly new recruit to Ginger's Six mafia. We found her over the summer by following the list my cousin Brandt had given me before he left town. Her gift allowed her to blend into the environment, creating a bubble that rendered her pretty much invisible and silent. It was something Dad was drooling all over himself to get.

He'd tried, too. In an attempt to win her trust, Kale and I had taken her along on an amusement park trip. Dad's men used the opportunity to try snagging all three of us. It nearly ended in disaster, but in the end, we more than proved which side of the good versus evil fence we stood on, and Kiernan came back to the Sanctuary with us. She was crude and abrasive, and there was a good chance she was even crazier than me—and I kind of loved her.

Kale cringed beside me as I arched my back again to get rid of a stubborn kink. He hated the sound of my joints cracking. His eyes darted between me and the top of the crane. "What's this called again?"

"Craning."

"And *why* do you do it?"

"Because we're not supposed to? That's what makes it so damn fun."

Instead of stepping back to join the gathering crowd, he took position beside me. "I'm going up, too."

"I'll be fine," I insisted.

Above us, thunder boomed, and a blast of cool wind blew through the lot. A shiver ran through me. I prayed the rain held off because Kiernan had won the last race. I wanted a chance to even the score.

Kale rolled his eyes—a fairly new thing for him. "Of course you will. But you said it was fun. I'd like to try."

My heart gave a little squeeze. Deep, dark voice. Check. Soulful eyes. Check. Well-muscled arms that could make a girl's legs go rubbery—and a penchant for the dangerous. Check frigging plus. Could *any* guy be more perfect?

"You both goin' up?" Kiernan kicked the crane twice, and it gave an echoing rattle, sending vibrations up the bars. "Remember, no cheating!"

"I don't need to cheat," Kale called to her. He flashed me a lopsided grin and stepped through the metal rungs to the inside hollow. Poking his head back through the bars, he kissed me. Not a quick peck on the cheek, either. No, kisses from Kale were enough to make a porn star blush.

Just part of the *awesome* that was my boyfriend.

My über hot, strangely innocent-yet-could-kill-you-with-a-bar-of-soap boyfriend.

"We'll see about that, Ninja Boy." Kiernan laughed. She'd been calling him that since the day she met him, and it'd kind of caught on. Last week she'd even bought him a black *I'm a Ninja* T-shirt. Kale pretended to be irritated by it, but secretly, even though it was short sleeved, I was pretty sure he loved the thing.

Hands ready, she turned and nodded to Kirk—a small guy with the ability to manipulate wood—and nodded.

"GO!" someone screamed.

Kale winked. "See you at the top."

And he was gone. There was actually a moment of stunned stupidity as I watched him glide from rung to rung like a monkey-man on steroids. No normal guy should be able to move like that.

Oops. Kale wasn't a *normal* guy. When the smallest brush of your skin could obliterate a WWE wrestler, you left normal behind pretty damn fast.

"Crap," I spat as he disappeared from sight. Climbing. I was supposed to be climbing.

Fingers gripping the cool metal, I began my ascent.

At first my progress was impressive. Twice I caught sight of Kale, and Kiernan was way below. But the higher I went, the more tired my arms got. The wind wasn't helping, either. It'd picked up to the point that I had to stop and yank the hoodie over my head because the flapping material was so distracting.

About halfway up the tower, things started getting sloppy. Several times I misplaced my foot, almost slipping, and my fingers were starting to get numb. Kiernan still trailed behind—but barely, and Kale was now nowhere in sight.

Hooking an arm around the closest bar for balance, I stopped to catch my breath. Someone below screamed something that was followed by a symphony of laughter. I heard my name, but a cacophonous clap of thunder drowned out the rest.

Then, because I'd obviously done something to piss Mother Nature off, it started to pour.

"Oh, you've gotta be shitting me." At that point, a normal person would have given up. Not me. This was the kind of thing I lived for. Swiping a hand across my forehead, I pushed rain-soaked bangs back and continued to climb.

"Ready to give?" Kiernan shouted over the thunder. I couldn't help smiling. Judging by the slight tremble in her voice, *she* was the one ready to *give*.

"Not a chance," I yelled back.

She said something else—it didn't sound happy—but her words were lost to the howling wind.

When I finally reached the top, Kale was there, each leg

hooked through a metal rung for balance. He flashed me a wet but devastating smile. "You're slow," he said, extending a hand.

Our fingers laced together, and instant warmth spread throughout my entire body. Funny how just a single touch could do that. I let him help me up the last few inches and followed his lead, threading my legs through the closely spaced bars at the top. "I think Kiernan gave up."

He sighed and flicked a strand of dripping black hair out of his eyes. The rain had let up, trickling to nothing more than a light drizzle. The storm wasn't done, though. In the distance light blazed across the sky, with an occasional boom still splitting the air. "The weather conditions weren't optimal for climbing."

Anyone else would've earned a *duh* or *ya think* with a statement like that, but not Kale. The guy could've informed me that apples tasted like apples, and I'd be livin' large on cloud nine if for no other reason than hearing his voice.

"So, give it to me straight. You're part monkey, right?"

He blinked. "Of course not." A few moments later, his lips turned downward. "You're referring to my climbing skills, aren't you?"

"Yep. That was pretty frigging awesome."

He smiled, but it was only a shadow of his normal grin. "I can scale a building, if necessary. It's part of my training."

His training. Of course it was. That explained his less-than-enthusiastic reaction.

"Is there a name for it?"

"It's called Parkour, I believe."

Parkour! That was it. "I've seen videos on YouTube." I grinned and leaned closer, nipping lightly at his bottom lip. "Seriously hot."

It was all the motivation he needed. With one arm still wrapped around the crane, he circled my waist and pulled me close as his mouth covered mine. There was something incredibly hot—in a scorch-the-sun kind of way—about a toe-numbing kiss while balanced high in the air during a thunderstorm.

Warm fingers slipped under the bottom edge of my tank top and skimmed the line of my spine.

Incredibly, incredibly hot.

Kale's feather-light touches did more for me than any adrenaline rush ever could. I worked an arm free and ran my index finger over the thick scar hidden beneath his T-shirt. It went from collarbone to shoulder. Four inches below was another. The result of a training session gone *wrong*, he'd once said. I knew each and every one by heart—a map of the days and events leading to his eventual freedom. He'd told me about most of them, but there were still a few holdouts. Some stories he refused to share. I never pushed—even though I wanted to. He'd tell me when he was ready.

With his fingers tracing fiery paths up and down my spine, the whole world faded away. There was no storm. Denazen didn't exist, and our new friends below weren't waiting for us. There was no pressure about senior year, no hard knot churning in my stomach every time I thought about the Supremacy project and what might happen when I turned eighteen. It was just me and Kale at the top of the world.

Electrifying each other.

The kiss built slowly, all-consuming and raw. I was flying. The warm sensation creeping from my stomach to my spine and through my limbs was like mainlining pure adrenaline. It stole my breath while somehow breathing new life into me.

"I like the feel of your skin when it's wet," Kale whispered into my mouth as the rain kicked up again. He pulled back a bit and caressed the outline of my jaw, then let his fingers drop to the neckline of my tank top. "But wet clothes are annoying. They make it hard to *get* to you."

I nodded and tugged on the shoulder of his dripping T-shirt. Leaning forward a bit, I nuzzled his ear and whispered, "I think the best way to fix that is to lose the clothes."

He leaned away and, in a flash, had his shirt pulled over his head and tucked safely through one of his belt loops. "Okay."

Not exactly what I'd meant—but no complaints from me. Kale was *ripped*. I opened my mouth to tell him we should head back to the hotel, but he kissed me again, and all coherent thought evaporated.

Every inch of me was alive and humming—and then, suddenly, in pain.

Like someone had wrapped a rubber band around my chest, it was impossible to breathe. I struggled to fill my lungs with air but ended up choking instead, a series of body-wracking coughs lodging in my throat. Each fingertip burned like it was pressed against a red-hot stove burner, and every muscle felt ready to snap. It was hell.

Holy shit—we'd been struck by lightning.

It would have been logical if David hadn't been on the ground below, attracting electricity. But maybe he'd left? I pulled away with a gasp, heart nearly freezing as my legs almost untangled from the bars.

Blue eyes wide and confused, Kale reached for me. "Dez, what happened?"

"I don't know." Even though the early September air had a definite chill, sweat beaded across my forehead. My heart thundered as every muscle twitched. Everything felt hollow and raw. After a few seconds, my breath finally returned to normal, and the air cooled a bit.

I leaned against the cold metal and closed my eyes as Kale pulled me close. With both his arms wrapped tight around me, I took a deep breath. "All of a sudden it was like—"

An entirely new feeling—an intense wave of vertigo—came out of nowhere, accompanied by the sensation of rushing air. I slipped backward on the slick metal, legs unraveling from their perch like they were made of pudding. My knees caught the bar for a fraction of a second before the entire world flipped upside down. In a flurry of misty rain and bright ribbons of light across the sky, Kale disappeared.

And so did the crane.

For a brief moment, nothingness. The world spun into blackness as my arms flailed, trying to grasp something—anything—solid. Once my fingers brushed the side of the crane, but thanks to the rain, they slipped effortlessly off.

A sudden stop jarred my body, the halt of momentum slamming me violently against the side of the crane. My head connected with the metal in a deafening *clang*, and everything blurred and stretched before finally snapping back into focus.

"I got you," Kale huffed from somewhere over my head. He'd stopped me from falling, strong hands clamped like a vice around my wrists, and started to pull me up—but his foot slipped. The squeak of rubber against metal threatened disaster. A low curse escaped his lips as we dropped several inches, and in that moment, I was sure we were going down.

When my body stopped swinging, I turned to the side and peered over my shoulder. It was a *long* way to the bottom—which didn't bother me as much as the sudden stop it ended with. I hoped Kiernan made it down all right. The voices of everyone below drifted up—an occasional hoot, followed by roaring laughter. They had no idea what was going on up here.

"Hang on. I need better footing," Kale called. He sounded completely confident as he wound his leg between the two nearest rungs, then bent his knee and wedged a foot under the one below.

I didn't share his confidence. The constricting feeling was creeping back, making it increasingly difficult to take anything more than short, shallow breaths. My muscles burned, and my throat was sore. Like I'd been screaming.

Something horrible nipped at my subconscious. An unthinkable thing that turned my blood to ice.

"Kale," I said, trying to keep calm. There was a noise—an odd hum—that kept getting louder. It was making things spin a little and had started drowning out all the ambient noise. "I think—"

His face appeared over the edge, the rain from his hair hitting the top of my head in soft *plops*. "I have you, don't worry. Get ready. I'm going to pull you up."

He adjusted his grip on my wrists, and the fire spiked—then exploded. The pain trickled up each finger and to my shoulders. From there, it leaked into my chest and crept down my legs. It was like someone had ripped me open, lit a bonfire, and stitched everything back up with a rusty needle. I kicked out, trying to hook the edge of my sneaker around the closest bar so I could grab the crane, but it kept sliding off.

The movement jarred us both, causing Kale's grip to shift just a little.

"Dez, stop moving!" There was a slight trace of panic in his voice. That in itself was enough to freak me out. Kale didn't panic. He was *Mr. Stone Face* in a crisis. Another part of his *training*.

Normally he wouldn't have had an issue holding on—those muscles weren't all for show—but with the brief rain and my insistent squirming, his right hand slipped past my wrist, over my thumb, and then free. Instantly, the fire in my limbs cooled a little. Not enough to stifle the pain but enough to be noticeable.

Enough to confirm the unthinkable.

"Kale, let go!"

A flash of lightning darted across the sky. Close. The hair on the back of my neck sprang up like I'd jammed my finger into an electrical socket.

Another surge of pain. The humming grew louder. The wind went quiet, and the raindrops lost their tiny plinking noise as they pelted the metal. Our friends below quieted, and distant traffic seemed to come to a standstill. Even Kale, whose lips were moving frantically, was silent.

Desperate, I tried again to brace my feet against the metal, but it was useless. My sneakers kept sliding off.

"Please," I begged, wondering if he could even hear my voice above the strange hum. "Let go."

When he didn't, I let my fingers go slack.

Another inch.

Horrified, he readjusted his hold and made a swipe with his free hand, but the rain made it impossible. Without my help, his fingers glided past my wrist. He managed to grab my other hand with both of his, but they were already slipping. His lips began moving again, and I thought I saw him say my name.

I forced a deep breath. The pain was worse than anything I could have imagined. Like trying to breathe through broken glass. I couldn't take it anymore.

"Kale, you're *killing* me. *LET GO!*"

He did.

Part of me was relieved, while another part couldn't believe he'd let me fall. No way was I walking away from something like this. Crap. What was the first rule of taking a fall? Relax! Relax your muscles, and go limp. It wasn't unheard of for people to survive a major fall. Off buildings and out of planes. It'd happened before. I closed my eyes, braced for impact, and—

The air stilled. My hair, seconds ago a mass of tangles lashing all around, fell to frame my face. I held my breath and twisted to see the ground—it was only a few feet away—but I wasn't rushing at warp speed to meet it anymore. A few moments of weightlessness ticked by, and then I was falling again, only the sudden, bone-crushing stop you'd expect after a thirty-foot free fall never came. Instead, I landed with a barely there jar into strong, warm arms.

"I have to say, Dez, this is taking the adrenaline high to a whole 'nother level…" Alex set me down as the others crowded close.

I couldn't respond. My mouth was dry, and every nerve ending was singing and hopping spastically like my celebrity crush, Spider One, onstage.

A boom of thunder, then seconds later, a bright flash. All the tiny hairs along my arms and at the back of my neck shot up again. The lightning silhouetted Kale's bobbing form as he hopped down from the crane and darted forward to close the distance between us—thankfully with his shirt back on.

Someone poked my shoulder. Alex. "Dez? You okay?"

"You—what are you doing—"

He looked at me funny. "Why would you jump off the crane, Dez?"

"I didn't—"

Kale's scream cut me off. "Dez!" Carelessly he ran at the crowd, people clearing a narrow path just in time for him to crash through. He stopped a few feet away and neither of us moved.

"What happened?" Kiernan demanded, pushing to the front. She stood with her hands on her hips, glaring from Kale to me.

Alex answered. From the corner of my eye, I saw him point up. "For some reason, Dez decided it'd be a good idea to jump off the top of the crane."

Everyone started talking at once, but I couldn't hear them. Not really. It was gibberish. A mishmash of background noise. Whistles of approval and whispers of insanity all faded into white noise. The universe had finally stomped in and taken payment. I knew it was coming. Daun, the Six that had saved Kale after the battle at Sumrun, warned us over and over again. *Don't get complacent*, she said. *It will show up when you least expect it*. She'd been right.

Kale stepped forward.

So did I.

We stopped inches apart, neither reaching for the other. I

could see it in his eyes. Anguish. Guilt.

Understanding.

"Dez—" He made a move to lift his hand but stopped, fist clenched tight.

Daun's voice raged inside my head. Unwelcomed but persistent. *A side effect. An exchange. There is no telling what it will be.*

Along with my response. *I'll give anything for him.*

I took a step back and nearly tripped over thin air despite the fact that I was suddenly, painfully sober. "Don't. We knew it would happen. Fair is fair. I got something—I knew I'd lose something in return."

Kale's jaw tightened, and he took a single step back. "Nothing is lost. This is temporary. We can fix it. I can learn to control it—Ginger said so." His voice wavered a bit, and I wasn't sure if he was trying to convince me—or himself.

I couldn't help it. I laughed. It was a bitter sound—so unlike me. That kind of maniacal cackle that rides along with madness. The one that comes right before you lose it in line at the post office. Everyone had gathered in a semicircle around us— watching. Staring. None of them understood what was going on. They didn't know what I did. I skimmed their faces. The full gamut of emotion was there. Everything from genuine concern to irritation, all aimed my way. The weight of it all was too much.

Without a word, I turned and ran.

For a few moments, there were footsteps sloshing in the mud, trying to keep up. They were too heavy to be Kale's—if it'd been him, I wouldn't have heard them—so I guessed it was Kiernan. Luckily, she gave up when I made it to the edge of the lot.

I crossed the street and hesitated at the corner. Where the hell was I going to go?

The hotel—but that was probably the first place Kale would look. I couldn't see him right now. The look of guilt in his eyes had been like a steel knife jammed into my windpipe.

I could wander around for a while—but that seemed like a bad idea. My name was at the top of Dad's bag-and-tag list. I'd never made things easy on him. No reason to start now.

It was the last official night of summer. School started up again in the morning and that meant the party scene would be hopping. There would be at least three major raves—one at Curd's, since his parents were in Paris again, one in the woods by Putnam Mountain, and one in the fields behind Brandt's old place.

Normally any one of those would have suited me, but being around people didn't seem like the best bet at that moment. I wanted to be by myself.

So where did I end up? The one place I'd always been alone. Home.

The key was still duct taped to the underside of the loose siding panel at the corner of the house. I was betting the only reason it survived there was because Dad never knew about it. I'd hidden it last year during my *lose everything* phase. Somewhere in Parkview, there were four house keys just waiting to be found. Well, three. One ended up at the bottom of Milford Lake after a tire swing stunt went horribly wrong.

The door opened with ease—for once it didn't stick—and I stepped inside. Part of me wondered why it'd taken so long to come back here, while another part wanted to back away and never return. So much had happened, but the truth was, no matter how bad things got between me and Dad, this was—or had been—home. A part of me missed it.

Memories were memories regardless of the good or bad.

I closed the door, frowning. The place had been completely cleaned out. The big leather couch Dad was always telling me to get my feet off, the fluffy beige armchair I'd spilled rum punch on the night I threw my first party—even the carpet in the hallway had been pulled up. All that remained were the dirty wooden tack strips around the edges of the room and some dust.

The air smelled funky. Not like mold, really, but stale. Like it'd been closed up for months—which it probably had. With me out of the picture, Dad had no reason to keep up the charade. His domestic life had been nothing but bullshit from the beginning. He and Mom had never been married. Hell, I was nothing more than an experiment. Part of the new generation of Denazen's Supremacy project. An operation with the sole purpose of producing stronger, *more gifted* flunkies for Denazen to pull the puppet strings on.

I'd mimicked—changed one thing into another—my first thing at the age of seven. Even then, I knew I was different. Not right. At least by society's standards. So I kept it hidden.

As it turned out, that'd been a good plan. A few months ago, on top of finding out Dad was an assassin monger who used people like me, Sixes—called that due to an abnormality in our sixth chromosome—to do some really bad shit, I'd also learned he'd dosed my mom with some funky chemical while she was pregnant to *enhance* my gift. I wasn't the only one, either. Somewhere out there, there were a handful of kids my age on the verge of turning eighteen—and possibly going nutzo—with über powers.

That chemical they used? Yeah. It had some seriously *bad* side effects.

I shook off a chill and rounded the corner. One at a time, up the stairs to my old room. Even though I knew Dad and his endless dickhead potential, I still hoped some of my things had been left behind. A shirt or book—hell, even a shoe. Anything that had been *mine*.

Should've known better.

All my memories, all the sentimental things I'd collected

and saved over the years, gone. There wasn't a hanger left in the closet or a dust bunny hiding in the corner. The antique dresser Brandt helped me drag home from a garage sale several years ago, the headboard Alex and I carved our names into, even the Powerman 5000 bumper stickers I'd plastered to the wall just to piss Dad off—all gone.

It was like my entire life had been erased.

"This blows camel ass." I kicked the corner of the door. It bounced away and slammed against the wall with an echoing *thud*.

The whole thing shouldn't have bothered me. It was just stuff, after all, but it made my stomach turn and caused a sick lump to rise in my throat. It'd been *my* stuff. Pieces of *my* life. I let out a hair-curling scream. "Bastard!"

I might have started smashing something—something being the window, since that's all there was—but a noise downstairs stopped me.

Not a loud crash or a thundering boom, but something small. The tiniest creak. Like someone *trying* to be sneaky and channeling the fail whale. I'd done enough sneaking in this house over the years to know all its groans and whines by heart. This particular one came from the kitchen door.

Someone else was in the house.

For a second, I wondered if maybe Kiernan had followed me, after all. But I dismissed that pretty fast. She would have called out. No way would she be skulking in the dark. Three weeks ago she'd surprised me from behind, and I'd given her a fat lip. Lesson learned.

Flattening myself against the wall, I peered around the corner and into the hallway to listen. Nothing. I started to relax and chalk it all up to paranoia when, on the landing below, two figures drifted past the stairs, casting distorted shadows against the wall.

I slipped back into the room, heart thundering against my ribs. Of course Dad would have someone watching the house. What kind of an idiot wouldn't realize that?

Me, obviously.

Bile rose in my throat, and a wave of icy fear barreled through the room. Where to hide? The closet was out. Even if Dad hadn't removed the locks several years ago when he'd caught Alex hiding in there, they'd still just bust the door down if they wanted in.

Bolting for the front door was out of the question. There was no way I'd chance sneaking down the stairs. For all I knew, there were more than two of them. Even I wasn't *that* good. I scanned the room and decided there was only one viable option.

The window.

I crept across the floor and unlatched the lock. Sliding the glass up slowly, I cringed when it squeaked in protest. A high-pitched whine and subtle creaking noise. I sucked in a breath and held it, listening for signs I'd been discovered. No screaming or footsteps pounded the stairs.

Swinging one leg over the sill, I let it dangle over the edge—and hesitated. It would be easy to drop to the ground below and take off, but that wouldn't tell me anything. I wanted to know who these people were—to know for sure that they were working for Dad. The house had obviously been empty for a while. They could be squatters or something. Or party scouts. My friend Curd sent people to check on abandoned locations for upcoming raves all the time.

The other leg over, I grabbed the edge of the oak tree for balance, scrunching down and closing the window almost all the way before they walked into the room. The branch was thick enough to allow me to slide sideways and move past the window.

If they peered out, they wouldn't see me.

I hoped.

"Are you sure you saw—" a guy's voice started. He sounded young, but it was hard to tell without getting a look. I pressed my ear closer to the sill.

"Her come in? Yeah," another finished. At least, I thought it was the other. They sounded almost the same.

The window was still open a few inches. I could hear their voices getting closer. A moment later, one of them tapped on the glass several times. "Cross knew she'd come back—"

"Eventually? Yeah. But where is she?"

"Doesn't look like she went out the window. It's possible—"

"She slipped past us? Yeah. Doubt it, but let's check out front to be sure. Cross will kick our asses if he finds out she was here and we let her get away."

Okay, so that confirmed the Dad theory. And that back and forth? Seriously irritating.

After a few moments of blessed silence, I took a chance and moved closer to the window, daring a peek over the sill. The room was empty again. Since I didn't know where they'd gone, I decided to get the hell out of Dodge. Dad had sent them. Sticking around any longer might give me a personal account of what they wanted—and I wasn't interested.

Leaning forward, I held my breath and scanned the yard to make sure the coast was clear. So far, so good. Gripping the tree, I eased myself to the grass below. The sturdy oak had aided my social activities and secret nightlife for the last several years. Its spindly branches and woodsy smell were comforting in a way I wouldn't forget.

My feet hit the wet grass with a slight *slosh*, sending tiny prickles up my legs. I gave the tree one last look, running my fingers over the uneven bark. I'd probably never come back here again. No reason to. This place was nothing more than a shell. An empty dust jacket that had once contained a complicated work of fiction.

As I turned to leave, a strong breeze blew through the yard. Goose bumps skittered up my bare arms, and I tried not to shiver. As if saying good-bye, the oak tree's branches shimmied and shook, several leaves fluttering to the ground. I picked one up and twirled it between my fingers, sending droplets of rain flicking off in every direction.

Something crackled, like shoes crushing dead leaves, and I froze. A set of strong arms clamped on my shoulders before I could turn. There was no thinking. Only the reaction of a brain sent into panicked overdrive. I jammed my foot back with perfect aim and spun around.

A string of curses and spiky, bleached-blond hair. "Dez—what the fuck?"

The sight of Alex caused me to fumble. He'd caught me when I fell from the crane, and even though I should have felt grateful, anger bubbled in my stomach. Now that my head had cleared—a little at least—I wanted to bash his face in.

We hadn't seen each other since the night of Sumrun. He'd been standing over Kale. The bloody blade slipping from his fingers…the noise it made as it hit the ground…the look on his face…the rage…the betrayal—all came flooding back. It hit me like a semi falling out of the sky.

"You have serious nerve coming within two feet of me." I shoved him hard. He stumbled but didn't try to stop me. "What the hell are you doing here?"

He opened his mouth to answer but instead pointed over my head toward the house. Two identical guys glared at us from my window. "There's a more important question. What the hell are *they* doing here?"

"Shit!" Heart kicking into high gear, I sprinted across the lawn and rounded the corner of the house, skidding sideways as my left leg slipped out from beneath me. Balance gone, I went down on one hand as my Vans slid in the mud and wet grass. After several frantic attempts, I managed to right myself and keep going without wiping completely, but it'd slowed me down.

Footsteps hammered the ground at my heels.

Close. *Much too close.*

I dared a look over my shoulder. It took a second—not even, more like a fraction of a second. A huffing and puffing blur of blond and black—Alex—then back to the front. But that fraction of a second cost me the head start.

With a brain-jarring stop, I collided with something big and dark. One of the guys from the house.

"Silly thing. She was trying to—"

Alex crashed into the other. "Get away? Yeah."

Backing up, I forced a smile and hoped to hell it hid the *piss-*

yourself-stupid terror I felt. Normally I didn't scare easy, but after getting a first-person look into the hell that was Denazen? Let's just say I wasn't looking to take another tour.

Swathed in black from head to toe and blocking every inch of our path were the creepy Wonder Twins from the window. Goth carbon copies, down to the smudgy eye liner and scratchy black nail polish. They were both odd-eyed—one iris blue and the other brown—in opposite order.

I gestured between them. "Do you get many dates that way? 'Cause seriously, I wanna rip my ears off."

The first one flashed me a tight-lipped smile and tipped an imaginary hat. "I'm Aubrey, and this is my brother—"

"Able. Yeah, that's me," the second finished. Up close, I could hear the slight difference in their voices. Able had an odd, almost accent. He didn't quite pronounce his Ss right. They almost sounded like Zs.

Alex gave them a side-glare once-over. The guy's version of checking out the competition. "You work for Cross?"

Able nodded like a dashboard bobblehead. He circled Alex, eyes narrow, but to my surprise, didn't try to restrain him. "You're not 98."

"Sorry, no number here. Name's Alex Mojourn."

Aubrey frowned and folded his arms. No attempt at restraining me, either. Their lack of aggression made me nervous. It wasn't right. "That's—"

Able didn't seem to share his brother's disapproval. He smiled, winking at me like we shared some big secret, as a crack of thunder sounded above. "Disappointing? Yeah. Could be fun, though."

"I'm guessing you're Sixes. Is that your gift? Annoying people to death with your yapping?"

Alex rubbed his ears and scrunched up his nose. "Dudes—

she's got a point. The whole freaky exchange? It's getting old."

For a moment, no one said a word. The four of us stood there, simply staring at one another. The calm before the storm. The last few, tense moments before the birds hit the building. My heart hammered, and my muscles itched to run. The fact that they still hadn't made a move had me tweaking like a junkie, and I knew it wouldn't last. Something was about to go down. I could see it in their eyes.

They had the advantage because we had no idea what they could do. My gift was non-aggressive, and I'd bet nine of my ten toes they knew that. If you wanted an apple and had an orange, I could help you out. Beyond that, I was pretty useless. At the moment, anyway. Supposedly I would develop mad skills as a result of the Supremacy drug, but other than a few weird occurrences—things I'd been writing off as figments of sleep deprivation—there hadn't been any signs of uberness.

Alex, on the other hand, wasn't as useless. He was a telekinetic—meaning he moved things with his mind. That might present the twins with a bit of a challenge, but probably not enough to be of concern. They had to be packing serious mojo if Dad sent them in hopes of snagging someone like Kale.

After what seemed like forever, Alex was the one who made a move. I didn't have time to be annoyed because he grabbed my arm and steered me around them. "We're leaving. Tell Cross to suck me, will ya?"

He got four steps before turning on his heel and bolting toward the street, almost ripping my arm out of its socket in the process.

Behind us, one of the twins let out a high-pitched scream, followed by a double dose of creepy laughter. Oh, yeah. Leave it to Dad to find the crazies.

Crashing through the gate and into the front yard, we raced

across the street. The motion sensor light next to Old Man Philben's mailbox flickered to life, shining a spotlight on our path. He'd put it in right around the time he started telling the neighborhood about his alien abduction. Apparently, E.T. was interested in the contents of his red-white-and-blue bird-shaped mailbox.

Alex waved his hand in a frantic motion. Behind us, several of the neighbors' garbage pails flew toward the corner of the old house where Able and Aubrey were rushing the gate. The pails collided with the twins and knocked them to the ground in a symphony of clattering metal and stinky garbage.

I tried to stop, but Alex nudged me forward. "Won't stop 'em for long. Keep going!"

We rounded the next corner and ran like hell. By the time we made it halfway down the third block, it hit me. Something about this was wrong. I stopped short and ducked behind the side of Marlow's Jewelry Store, dragging Alex with me. "Why were you at the construction site?"

"*What*? Why the hell does it matter *now*?"

"Why were you there? I haven't seen you in months—smart move, by the way—then you just show up? Better yet, why did you follow me?" I poked him hard in the chest. Those creepy twins had approached the whole situation much too casually. Like they had an ace in the hole. An Alex-shaped ace. "Are you *with* those guys?"

He peeked around the side of the building. When he pulled back, his eyes were wide. "Are you asking me if I'm trying to snap you up for Daddy? Are you high? I'd never hurt—"

Fists curled tight, I decked him. My knuckles clipped the edge of his bony jaw, sending a thousand prickles of pain shooting through each finger, but it was worth it. He'd been about to say he'd never hurt me. So he thought watching him gut Kale wouldn't hurt? Still, after all that, the possibility that he was working with Dad—*for* Dad—made me sick. We'd had our differences, an even mix of lies and misunderstandings, but we'd meant something to each other once.

Then he had to go and try to kill my boyfriend.

He shook his head in surprise and touched his face. "Fine. I deserve that. But right now—"

"Screw you." Now wasn't the time to lay into him, but my mind kept coming back to what happened at Sumrun. The image of Alex standing over Kale was burned into my brain, and no amount of time would wipe it away. Plus him showing up the exact moment I fell from the crane? Way too convenient. A small, logical part of my brain told me it'd be impossible for him to have known I'd lose my immunity to Kale—much less the moment it would happen, but I didn't trust him. There was more to this. Had to be.

"This part of the plan? Steer me into a dark alley and wait for them to come along and scoop me up?"

He threw his hands in the air and kicked the side of the building. "*You* pulled *me* into the alley."

I glared at him but said nothing.

"I'm trying to *help* you." He looked like he might explode. I'd seen Alex lose his cool several times, and it wasn't pretty, but this screamed borderline unhinged. His face turned scarlet, and each fist, balled tight to the point his knuckles almost glowed in the dark, shook in frustration. "Ginger told me to go to the construction site, okay? She said you needed me."

"Bullshit," I snapped. "Why would she ask you for anything? You tried to kill her grandson."

"For fu—that *wasn't*—"

Something moved at the other end of the alley, followed by a duet of dark chuckles. Alex didn't wait. Without apology, he shoved me toward the street. No need to tell me twice. I might not have wanted him within forty feet of me, but if it was a choice between that and visiting with Dad—he won hands down.

"Head for Parker Avenue—the business district," I huffed. "We can lose them there."

We raced across Mill Street and cut through the Food Smart parking lot to Parker as the sky opened up again.

"Move!" Alex snapped in between gasps. "Faster!"

Because I wasn't already moving as fast as I could? *Moron!*

I hadn't been to the heart of the business district all summer. A bunch of the old crew used to come down on weekends and jump the buildings. The ones on the edge of the district—the few remaining low-rent apartment complexes and office buildings— were right on top of each other. Easy to jump. Starter flys, we'd called them. The ones in the center—the factories and warehouse distributors—were slightly farther apart. More of a challenge. Last time we'd all been out here, Gillman swore he was going to jump one of the buildings in the center. I wondered if he ever actually went through with it.

I stopped at the edge of the Janseck factory to catch my breath, but Alex wasn't having it. He yanked on my arm and shoved me in the direction of the tall, familiar building across the street. "Come on. My old apartment building usually keeps the door on the roof open. We can slip in and hide."

After dark, the traffic was minimal—not that the business district made the top ten hot spots of Parkview any time of day. We raced across the road and around to the back of Alex's old apartment complex.

The ladder for the fire escape wasn't down, and we couldn't reach it, but that was easy enough to fix. A simple wave of Alex's hand, and it came crashing toward us—complete with clanking metal and an echoing scream.

Why not just send up a flare or use a megaphone to announce our presence? Starting up the ladder, I hissed, "Be a little *less* stealthy, why don't ya?"

I pulled myself over the edge and climbed onto the roof. The wind whipping across my shoulders sent an icy chill down my spine, making me sorry I'd tossed my hoodie on the way up the crane.

"There." Alex flew across the roof and pulled up on the door handle. "Um…"

"'Um' doesn't sound good. Why are you 'um'-ing?" I took a step forward. "*Don't 'um'!*"

Someone had pissed in karma's cereal and blamed it on me. Tonight nothing seemed to be going right.

Alex gave one last, violent yank on the handle. "It's locked."

A metallic clatter behind us caught my attention. I didn't dare peek over the edge. "Gotta go." I took off across the rooftop, Alex on my heels, as Able's voice rang out.

"Hide and go seek, yeah?"

"Woo-hoo!" His brother let out a chilling cry as footsteps thundered behind us.

"Jump!" Alex screamed as he sprinted ahead and leapt from the ledge.

I stopped short—just in time to watch him sail through the air, over the gap between the two buildings, and slam against the edge of the one next door. But he caught the rim of the ledge and managed to haul himself over the side.

Acid bubbled in the pit of my stomach as I backed up to gain some momentum.

"Come on! Don't you wanna—"

Alex was stronger and taller. Longer legs. If he missed the roof, there was a good chance I would, too.

"Play? Yeah," the other finished.

They were almost across the roof and moving fast.

Too fast.

Screw it. I'd take my chances with gravity. Pushing off with my right foot, I sprang forward. The rain-slicked surface caused me to slip, hampering my speed. As the tip of my sneaker curled around the rim of the ledge, I shoved off as hard as I could and soared over the gap. The chill of rain-soaked clothes and cool September air against my skin was replaced by a healthy coating of nervous sweat.

I knew halfway through the jump that I wasn't going to make it. There just hadn't been enough power behind my push-off. Not nearly enough speed in my sprint. Instead of zooming closer to the rooftop, I started sinking down. Under different circumstances, I'd rag on myself. It'd been a seriously lame jump, and I could have done way better. Now, though? There was a scream building as my pulse thundered between my ears. This made twice in one night I'd taken a header from high up. Either fate was trying to tell me something, or the universe had a really sick sense of humor.

Thankfully, telekinetics weren't without their uses. One second, the edge of the building was going up—as I went down. The next, it was going down—as I flew up.

The air expelled from my lungs in a single, painful whoosh as I crashed onto the tar-coated roof at Alex's feet. Gasping, I let him drag me upright and forward as the first of the twins landed behind us with annoying grace. Seconds later, the other touched down beside him.

There was no time to freak. Like freighters, they charged before we had time to blink, scattering us apart. One of them—I had no clue which—hauled Alex back by his neck and tossed him into what looked like a giant air conditioner. There was a sickening crack and an audible wheeze as the breath was knocked from his lungs. A well-placed knuckle to the stomach, and Alex crumpled like wet tissue paper.

Something stirred in my gut. There were no leftover feelings for him, but seeing someone toss Alex around like a Frisbee made me slightly ill. Possibly because in the back of my head, *I* wanted to be the one doing it.

The other brother stood over me, smiling. Odd thing to notice, but he had a chip in his front tooth, and his nose looked slightly out of joint. He must have broken it at some point. Bones were like paper. Once you crumpled it up, no matter what you did to smooth it out, it was never quite the same. Might be the only way to tell Tweedledee and Tweedledum apart when they weren't speaking, which didn't seem to be often.

"Not sure what the fuss is about. You're a tiny little thing, yeah?"

Cold tar and gravel dug through my jeans, sending prickles throughout my entire body as I scooted backward on my butt until I hit the ledge.

Able—*yeah*, it was Able—leaned forward, smile growing wider. With one hand braced against my right shoulder, he pinned me back against the ledge and chuckled. "You're gonna love this."

Bringing his other hand up, he extended a long, black-tipped finger and placed it at the edge of my collarbone. There was a look in his eyes—like he'd checked out and someone else—*something* else—had checked in. Something insane.

I wriggled, trying to slip free, but it was no use. His hand against my shoulder locked me securely in place. With a twitch of his lip, he moved his finger over my bare skin, tracing the outline of my shoulder and making several small semicircles before stopping just above the armpit. Even though I was already soaking wet and freezing, his finger sent chills through my body—*not* the good kind. They dove deep into my core, numbing my insides.

His touch was wrong. *Sick*. It left my stomach churning and sent an army of goose bumps marching up and down my arms. A wave of nausea hit me, followed by a strong blast of vertigo. In front of me, the outline of his face grew watery, then snapped into extreme focus. Like someone had over-sharpened the entire world around him. Everything was too vivid—almost painful. Another flash, along with a sharp jab of his finger into my soft skin, and everything boomeranged back to normal.

The pressure on my right shoulder disappeared as Able straightened and snickered. "Was it good for you?"

I blinked and flexed my fingers. "What—"

He squatted in front of me and blew an exaggerated kiss. "I'm a little disappointed. You don't look like troub—"

I rocked back and to the side, kicking up. Jamming both Vans into his stomach, I shoved hard. "Trouble? *Yeah*. I kinda am."

With an *oof*, he stumbled back and cursed, almost recovering his balance just before toppling over. His glare tinted with the promise of payback, he sprang to his feet and lunged for me.

I rolled to the side, and he missed, grasping only a handful of air as Alex's voice rang out. "Dez!"

A second before Able attempted another swipe, he flew sideways and crashed into the pillar a few feet away.

Alex was on his feet and leaning against the side of the building, clutching his right arm. The other twin was nowhere in sight. We didn't argue or wait to see if he'd come back.

We ran like hell.

"You wanna tell me what happened at the construction site?"

Technically Alex had saved me not once so far but twice. Funny thing was, I didn't feel the least bit grateful. "You wanna go the hell away?"

"I mean it, Dez. If I hadn't been there, you'd be dead. What the hell happened?" He stopped in front of the Blueberry Bean window. The inside of the coffee shop was dark. They used to be open twenty-four hours, but last month, they started closing at midnight. Crap. Was it really that late?

We were about three blocks from the Sanctuary, and all was quiet. I leaned against the glass. The rain had finally stopped again, and it seemed like the twins had given up.

If only Alex would do the same.

Begging probably wouldn't help, but I was desperate. I didn't have the energy to hit him again, and I felt a headache the size of Mars coming on. "*Please* go away?"

Arms folded, he glared at me. Fred—the name we'd given

his happy-face labret bead—wobbled as he poked at it with his tongue. A dead giveaway that something was bothering him.

Was it too much to ask to be left alone? Maybe I did have some energy to spare. There was an itch bubbling to punch him again if he didn't go away. With my luck, I'd end up breaking a finger on his thick skull, thus completing one of the worst nights of my life.

To top this all off, I was going to get my ass handed to me by Mom and Ginger. Kale and I were under strict curfew because of Denazen. We were forbidden to attend the nightly parties, but I'd never let a little word like *forbidden* stop me from doing what I wanted. I might not be able to go to the official Six-only raves, but once in a while, like tonight, one of the kids planned a little field trip. I wasn't one to turn down an invitation.

Really, it was nice to know *some* things hadn't changed.

The worst part was Kale didn't quite get the concept of sneaking out. Without me, he'd waltz right in the front door without a second thought and get us both busted.

Alex cleared his throat.

He was still here. Apparently I needed to spell it out.

Fine.

"Are you really that dense?" I snapped as a bolt of lightning skittered across the sky. Obviously the storm wasn't quite done with us yet. "What kind of a *jackass* would stand here and try to talk to me after what you did?"

"After what I did? I saved your ass!"

I took a step forward and poked him in the chest. "Are you *serious*? Are you *seriously serious*?"

"I don't know what to say, Dez." He swiped a hand through his damp blond spikes. "Sorry won't cut it, and that's cool. I get it. But I wasn't *trying* to kill him."

"Sure as hell looked like it from where I was standing."

"Of course it did. 'Cause you're *never* standing in reality," he growled. "Do I hate him? Yeah, I do. He's in the way of something I want. That night at Sumrun, he was in the way of your freedom, and that's all I cared about."

I had to tell myself to close my mouth. *You're going to let the flies in*, Brandt used to say—ironically most of the time when Alex was involved. "My *freedom*? Because Dad would've really let me walk out of there with you?"

"He promised he would."

"I'd smack you stupid if someone obviously hadn't beaten me to it."

I started walking again, furious. The cool breeze, combined with my wet clothes, was giving me the shivers, and judging by the increasing thunder and lightning, it was only a matter of time before the rain came again.

"How was I supposed to know he was lying?" Alex grumbled, following me down the sidewalk.

Could anyone really be that dense? Alex knew about my dad even before I did. He'd lied to me for years. Hell, he'd done better than lie. He'd started *dating* me to keep tabs on Dad. Even if he hadn't tried to slice open my boyfriend, that right there would be enough of a reason to use caution approaching me. Cheating was something I might have been able to get past—someday—but using me? Not a chance.

Alex, never one to let things go, stopped short and grabbed my arm, hauling me back. "I know you care about the freak, and I'm sorry I stuck him—but you have to understand *why* I did it."

I yanked my arm back and shoved him away as a particularly loud crack of thunder sounded above our heads. A second later, the sky opened up. "I know *exactly* why you did it," I yelled over the sound of the rain. "'Cause you're a selfish bastard who can't stand the thought of not getting his way."

Proving just how immature he was, Alex stomped his foot, sending water from a rapidly gathering puddle shooting out in every direction. "I—you—impossible!"

He gave up and lunged, arms locking around my waist and dragging me close. As the storm raged around us, he smashed his lips against mine before I could even think about what he was doing, much less try to stop him. Fred's cool metal surface pressed into my chin as the rain poured down my face and Alex's lips moved over mine. Warmth and a familiar, slightly spicy taste locked my limbs in place.

For a half second.

I curled my fingers—I'd actually had the opportunity to grow my nails a little over the summer—and dug them into his forearms while bringing my knee up as hard as I could. He doubled over and stumbled away, gasping as someone behind us made a *very* angry sound.

I spun to see Kale surge toward us, soaked and furious. Impossibly fast, he covered the short distance in the blink of an eye.

"Stop!" I screamed, spreading my arms wide in front of Alex. Not for his sake, but for Kale's. No matter how mad he was, he'd still feel guilty if he killed someone.

Maybe…

His reflexes were sharp. Kale stopped with about two inches to spare, droplets of water flying every which way. "What is he doing here?" The venom in his voice matched the angry twist of his lips and barely contained rage in his eyes. Instead of flicking his fingers—the Kale equivalent of a nervous twitch—his fists were balled and ready to go.

Maybe he *wouldn't* feel guilty.

Carefully, I placed the palm of my hand against the material of his sopping T-shirt and pushed back. He resisted at first, cool blue eyes filled with hate and affixed to Alex. But after a few moments, the pressure on my hand lessened, and he stepped back. "Explain before I touch him."

So much for getting somewhere warm and dry. Kale wasn't budging from that sidewalk until he knew what was going on. Thankfully, the downpour was starting to ebb. "He followed me when I left the construction site."

Kale's expression faltered. "He was the one who caught you."

He'd been so wrapped up in what'd happened on the crane, it hadn't hit him at the time that Alex was even there. Which was probably a good thing. Alex might not have made it off that construction site.

As it was, he might not make it off the sidewalk. I just didn't know who would be the one to kill him.

Kale—or me.

"Good thing I *was* there, Reaper. Someone had to keep her from falling. You obviously couldn't."

Something exploded behind Kale's eyes. Rage, yes, but it was more than that. Guilt. He flinched like Alex had landed the mother of all blows. It only lasted a few seconds, though. After that, a twisted smile spread across his lips. The stiff set of his shoulders relaxed a little and he folded his arms. "She needs *nothing* from you."

Alex met his smile with an even darker one. "Seemed like she needed something from me tonight. I wonder what else she needs? Maybe something you're not giving her?"

Pressure against my hand. Kale pushed forward, fingers curling tight again. If anyone was likely to test his limits, it was Alex.

"He's not worth it," I said, standing my ground. I was determined to keep them apart. The last thing I needed right now was to get stuck in the middle of two raging, testosterone-drunk guys. "Not even close."

Kale didn't look entirely convinced. "I saw him *kiss* you."

Reaching out, I grabbed his hand. Contact. Connection. It was one of the few things that soothed him—and me. It was second nature. I never even thought about it.

My fingers brushed the top of his knuckles, but the comforting, familiar warmth I'd come to associate as home, as *safe*, was gone. In its place was something painful and constricting. A growing pressure, accompanied by a slowly increasing warmth in my stomach and a head full of fuzz. I tried but couldn't bite down in time. A small gasp escaped my lips as my shoulders and arms went rigid.

Horrified, Kale pulled his hand away and knocked me back—right into Alex.

"What the—" Alex caught me before I toppled to the ground. Shocked, he helped me right myself as I gasped for air. The pressure eased, and the humming in my ears melted into Kale's agonized apologies.

"Dez, I'm sorry!" The pain in his voice made the corners of my eyes sting. *He* was sorry? He hadn't done anything. I was the idiot who'd tried to touch him. Tried to touch my own boyfriend.

"*You* made her fall…" Realization rang in Alex's tone. He stepped around me until he and Kale were nose to nose.

Even though I knew it was the remnants of the storm, I could almost imagine the lightning overhead as sparks rising from the shoulders of each boy. Clashing Titans ready to fight to the death.

"You can't touch her anymore, can you?"

I coughed, still trying to fill my lungs with air. Gripping Alex's sleeve, I pulled as hard as my fingers would allow, but it was a feeble attempt. I barely jostled him. "Alex, knock it off."

"You almost got her killed," he continued, ignoring me. His voice held a slight hint of horror, but more than that, there was amusement. Satisfaction. He didn't care that I'd almost died. All he cared about was pointing out that it'd been *Kale's* fault. So typical!

Kale was silent, but I could see it in his eyes. He was counting. One by one each finger flicked in and out. We'd practiced it over the summer. Any time he felt the urge to *punish* someone, he'd count to ten. Most times he'd calmed down by eight. In this case, he might need to count to twenty. Maybe fifty.

One hundred might not be too much of a stretch.

Usually it was little things that set him off. Well, little to everyone else. Big to him. He still didn't understand the need for things like white lies and secrets. Kale saw the world in black and white—there was no room for gray. But this was different. Personal. A new emotion for him.

When Kale finally spoke again, his voice sounded calm, but I knew better. If anything, it was laced with more hate than before.

"You're correct. I can't touch her for the time being—but neither can you."

Alex's lip twitched. He folded his arms and puffed out his chest, standing a little straighter. I knew that stance. A challenge. "Wanna bet?"

"I do," Kale responded coolly. "Because if you try to do it again, I'll touch you. Then the only thing you'll be touching is the wind as you're scattered across this world."

Alex didn't reply. He did, however, have the intelligence to back away a few steps.

I wrapped my arms around myself and tried not to shiver. This had been a perfect ending to the worst day in history. The only thing that could make it worse was an alien invasion sent to gather probe victims. "Get out of here, Alex."

"Are you sure? I could—"

Kale growled.

"Go!"

He gave me a quick nod and started backing down the sidewalk as one final, roaring crack of thunder split the air. With a wink, he said, "I'll see ya soon, Dez."

There was a spring out of place. It protruded through the couch cushion, jabbing me in the back of the thigh. Kale sat on the small love seat across the room. He hadn't taken his eyes off me since Mom brought us into the common room.

"You know you're not supposed to leave the hotel after dark," she said. Sitting on the edge of the coffee table between us, she kept looking from him to me. She played with a pen left over from the dental convention that met here last week. Flicking the point. In and out. In and out. It reminded me of Mercy, the stuffy Denazen interviewer that tricked me into thinking she was on our side.

I responded with a wordless shrug and glanced toward the ceiling. There was a hairline crack that started right above my head. I followed it down the wall and saw that it pretty much cut the room in half. Right between me and Kale. Wasn't that ironic? If I were superstitious, I'd consider it a bad omen.

"You're both all right?" she tried again. There was a twinge in her voice that I'd come to associate with stress. Mom didn't deal with everyday situations as well as Kale.

I wanted to scream. Hell, no, I wasn't all right. The worst possible thing that could happen *just happened*. There was no way to make it *right*. Instead, I nodded.

"You're sure?" she prodded. I couldn't blame her. One look at either of us, and anyone with eyes would know it was a lie.

Kale looked like a guitar string ready to snap. His right hand wrapped around the arm of the chair, while the left clutched the edge of the cushion, knuckles white. The only sound coming from his end of the room was the soft dripping noise the rainwater made as it ran from the hem of his jeans and *plopped* to the floor.

I probably didn't look much better. My muscles ached from touching Kale, and my head pounded like a heavy metal drum solo. Every inch of me was soaked, and already a dark patch on my left arm—a souvenir from crashing into the rooftop—had started to bloom. By morning, it'd be one hell of a bruise. My right shoulder hurt where Able's hand had been, and the left one felt…odd. Not sore, but tingly. Kind of a mix between that pins and needles feeling you get when your leg goes to sleep and sunburn.

When Mom realized she wasn't getting either of us to talk, she settled for shooting nervous glances between me, Kale, and the door. It was probably no more than five minutes—even though it felt like three hours—but by the time Ginger, Kale's biological grandmother and the Granny Don of the Six Mafia, as I liked to call her, came through the door, I was about to crack. She was usually flocked by a horde of young, shirtless men, but tonight her entourage was a little different. This escort, with springy red curls, dangerous curves, and a smile made for an Orbit gum commercial, was considerably curvier than the others.

Ginger stopped in the middle of the room, plastic cup filled with the usual red liquid—fruit punch—in hand, and smiled. "I have a gift for you, Kale."

The redheaded girl strolled from behind Ginger, head held high. Her eyes immediately found Kale. And stayed there.

I didn't like her.

"This is Jade." Ginger drained the contents of her cup, then pointed to me and said, "This is Deznee Cross, Sue's daughter. And this," she said, nodding to Kale as he rose from his chair, "is Kale. He's the reason you're here."

"Okay, stomp the brakes and back the hell up," I said. "You're giving my boyfriend a redhead as a gift? That's uncool— not to mention illegal."

Kale looked from Jade to me, frowning. "You don't like her."

It wasn't a question—he was stating the obvious. Or, what he thought was the obvious—which in this case just *happened* to be the truth. We were still working on the right and wrong times to say things. It was one of the bigger hurdles. Kale didn't believe in hiding anything. If it was on your mind, you said it. If it was the truth, you went with it. Social acceptability was a lost cause with him.

"I don't *know* her, so I can't dislike her." There was an overwhelming urge to add *yet*, but I kept my trap closed. My personality made me easy to get along with—unless you were looking at my guy like he was a big, juicy slab of prime rib with a side of mint chocolate chip ice cream.

Which, just in case there was any confusion, she totally was.

"I've brought Jade here to help Kale learn to control his gift." Ginger frowned. "And considering tonight's events, it isn't soon enough."

Jade came forward and, while I tried to pick up the pieces of my jaw, reached for Kale. He stumbled away, knocking over the small card table beside the love seat in an attempt to put some distance between them. With a panicked look in Ginger's direction, he said, "Is she trying to kill herself?"

"It's fine, Kale. Trust me."

Jade, who still had that annoying smile plastered across her face, stepped forward again and shook Kale's hand—without shriveling up and blowing away. "It's very nice to finally meet you, Kale. I've been looking forward to this for months."

He said nothing, only stared at her small hand clasped in his. An itch I hadn't felt in a long time started worming in my gut. I was a bottle of soda that had just bounced down ten flights of stairs. Open me up, and I was going to explode. Ka-frigging-boom.

I wanted to wipe the smile from her face, but more than that, I wanted to pry their hands apart. Because they were still holding on to each other—something they should *not* be able to do.

Until this moment, there was only one human alive to ever touch Kale and live to talk. Me. Well, until a few minutes ago, anyway. Now Little Miss Sunshine comes along and just lays it on?

Forget not liking her. I freaking hated her.

She giggled and chewed the corner of her bottom lip—a move not many chicks could have pulled off without looking stupid. Unfortunately for girls everywhere, Jade nailed it. "You seem surprised."

Kale didn't answer. His hand was still attached to hers.

Okay, this was getting annoying. Someone had to step in because if they didn't let go soon, there was a good chance I'd implode. Or start ripping limbs off. I turned to Ginger. "How can she touch him?"

"Jade is very special." Ginger waved Mom over.

She had tears in her eyes and looked at Kale like he was some mythical creature she'd never seen before. "I've been waiting your whole life to do this." There was another shock to my system as Mom wrapped her arms around Kale and squeezed—with the same result Jade had. Nothing.

After a few moments of stunned silence, Kale's arms tightened, and he squeezed back. "How—"

Ginger wore a smug smile. "Jade is able to ground harmful gifts within an approximate fifteen-foot radius."

"Plus I can do this." Jade took the pen from Mom—thank God—and jammed it hard into her neck. For a moment, no one said a word. Tiny bits of plastic and droplets of ink trickled down her neck and fell to the floor. When she moved her hand, her annoyingly creamy skin was unmarred. No broken skin or red mark where the pen made contact.

Okay, so *that* was kind of cool. I was starting to feel a little inadequate. All I could do was mimic things—mostly small things—into something else. Apple to a pear. Dime to a penny. Ordinary paper to cash—all right, that came in kind of handy when eyeing a new pair of kicks. Sometimes I could mimic myself. I even did it to someone else—but that had been a disaster. Plus the whole thing came with a nasty, painful side effect.

"Jade is impervious to harm," Ginger said. "But she also gives off an aura that stifles harmful gifts. The only drawback is that it has an individual, diminished effect."

"Diminished effect?" Kale asked, looking at me. I knew exactly what he was thinking, because I was thinking it, too.

"Based on previous encounters, as long as Jade is near, she will restrain Kale's gift and enable him to walk safely though a crowded room. The diminished effect comes into play on a person-to-person and encounter-to-encounter basis. The more physical contact an individual has with Kale, the less Jade's aura affects them." She turned to me, frowning. "This shouldn't be an issue for *most* people."

Kale looked a little pale. "So after a while, the aura won't allow Dez to touch me at all?"

"That won't happen." Ginger looked from Jade to me. "We don't think."

Jade took his hand again and squeezed, and I had to bite my tongue to keep from saying something colorful. Kale chose that exact moment to look up. He blinked several times, then pulled his hand out of Jade's with a look of apology. I couldn't really blame him. To discover a way to have finally have the thing you'd always wanted had to have been overwhelming.

Still, as sick as it would have sounded out loud, I wished he'd paw my mom instead because I wasn't thrilled with the shit-eating grin this chick wore whenever she looked at him.

Jade looked from him to me, rolled her eyes, and continued without missing a beat. "In the past, people who have essentially overdosed on my aura just need some space. After a day or so, it seems to work again just fine."

"So what happens if someone *overdoses* on your aura? They'd touch Kale and, what, die?"

"I imagine it would be extremely painful before it came to that. Hopefully the *person* touching him would be smart enough to let go. His gift is *very* strong. Even *I* can feel it." Jade giggled and flashed him a flirty smile. "It sort of tickles. I imagine anyone coming in contact with Kale's skin is going to feel *something*. Even if it's nothing more than a twinge." With a smug grin, she said, "Keep it brief, and you *should* be fine."

Every second we stood here with this bimbo, the room felt smaller and smaller.

Ginger turned to Mom. "Did you feel anything?"

Mom glanced at Kale and hesitated. He was statue still, waiting for her answer. If there was anyone besides me on earth that he would die before hurting, it was her. She'd raised him inside Denazen.

"I felt—*something*. But it wasn't pain." She rushed on. "More like a tingle. Similar to acupuncture needles."

"Excellent," Ginger said, crunching the empty plastic cup in her hand. She pulled Mom to the corner by the television, and the two spoke quietly. Normally I would have tried to eavesdrop, but my attention was on something else.

Jade flashed Kale a sympathetic smile. Oh, yeah. She was good. Guys probably went gaga for those long lashes and pouty lips. "I can't imagine what it must have been like to have no human interaction. How horrible."

He opened his mouth to say something, but I cut him off. "He *had* human interaction. He had *me*."

Jade flashed a mock frown. "Had—past tense. Ginger said you were just like everyone else now."

Jesus. Did they plan on making some kind of news bulletin? Taking out an ad in the *Six Weekly*? "Well, he *could* touch me up until an hour ago."

The smug expression on her face nearly drove me over the edge. It had me wondering where I could bury her body and how fast. We'd met a Six over the summer with the ability to manipulate the earth. Something like that would come in handy for an impromptu grave digging...

Jade folded her arms. "But he can't anymore, right? I mean, not without *me* around."

"You can teach me how to control my ability." Kale stepped between us. "So I can touch Dez again?"

"I can try," Jade said. "Who you chose to touch afterward is your choice. There's a whole living world out there besides the people in this room."

The people in this room. She meant *me*! I glared from her to the coffee table. She might be impervious to harm, but she still might feel pain. Slamming her face through the furniture might ease some of the tension I felt.

No. Bad Dez.

I took a deep breath. In through the nose. Out through the mouth. Beating her to a bloody pulp wouldn't help Kale. I just needed to establish an order. Stake my claim so her place—and mine—was crystal clear. "Well, now that you're here, he can." I turned to him, trying to push aside the involuntary hesitation at the memory of our final moments at the top of the crane. "Right?"

He inched closer. No one else would have noticed, but I did. The slight shake of his hand as he reached for my face. Restraint. Something he'd never needed to use around me.

Pushing past the doubt, his fingers brushed my cheek and left a trail of fire in their wake. Fire—and a slight sting.

He withdrew his hand. "Does that hurt?"

I shook my head and smiled. "Not even a little."

He let out the breath he'd been holding and fell forward. Arms circling my waist, he crushed me close and buried his face. Tiny prickles sprang to life where his face touched mine through the gaps in my hair.

He probably would have stayed like that, just hanging on, but I pulled away. Normally I couldn't have cared less. The audience didn't bother me, and it didn't bother Kale. This was how he felt, and that was that. Nothing to hide.

So why let go? Standing there with Kale holding on for dear life might convey to Jade she had no shot. He was taken and obviously happy to be so. But there was a small problem. The longer he held on, the worse it got. The pain became less like pins and needles and more like sharp jabs. It was nothing compared to what I'd felt back at the construction site, but it was still there.

A small part of me wondered if it was amping faster than it should. Could I possibly have overdosed on Jade's aura already? It didn't seem right. She'd just gotten here, and Kale and I hadn't had much physical contact.

I should have said something. Right then and there, I should have opened my mouth and asked how long it would take for the effect to diminish, but I couldn't do it. Kale looked so relieved. And it wasn't *that* bad.

Not really…

"And what about you?" Jade cooed. "Or—are you not a Six?"

I pointed to the delicate gold bangle on her wrist. "That's pretty."

She held out her arm and gave her wrist a slight shake. The bangle jiggled back and forth, catching the light from the ceiling. Beaming, she said, "It's from France."

I reached out and touched the cool metal, then with the other hand, touched the collection of black plastic Silly Bandz on my own wrist. Throbbing in my temples, and a wave of nausea hit hard, but it passed quickly. The more I mimicked, the easier it got. I'd been practicing over the summer. Mimicking at least two small things a day. The effects weren't as bad, and they didn't last nearly as long as they used to. When I looked down, the black plastic shimmered and changed until we were both wearing the same thing.

Admittedly, it didn't look as good on me as it did her. The bright gold was out of place against my too-pale skin. "Mine's from Target."

She laughed. The sound was like a thousand tiny bells ringing at once. Delicate, charming—and annoying as hell. "Isn't that cute!"

Cute? Oh, I'd give her cute…

Ginger must have glanced over at that exact moment and

seen my face because she stopped whispering to Mom and stepped between us—unfortunately before I could inflict bodily harm. "I think it's time for everyone to get some sleep. You all have a big day tomorrow."

"Big day?" I grumbled, stepping back.

"School starts tomorrow."

"School?" Kale said with a look of horror. "I can't go to school."

Ginger smiled. "It's all taken care of. I promise you we've worked out a plan that's safe for everyone, and Jade will be with you every step of the way."

I was wrong. *Now* the day had officially capped at horrific.

Fan-freaking-tastic.

I looked around the small hotel room and cringed. This *wasn't* going to work.

"Which bed did you want?" Mom asked me this every night without fail. Like it was going to change from one day to the next?

She emerged from the bathroom wearing a white tank top and pink pajama bottoms dotted with little blue penguins. Not exactly something you'd expect a cold-blooded killer to wear, right?

Mom, like Kale, had been a prisoner of the Denazen Corporation since before I was born. She'd been forced to do horrible things at their command. I'd grown up thinking she died in childbirth, wishing for only the chance to meet her—to talk to her just once. Now here I was, not only talking to her, but sharing a room.

A *really* small room.

The first few weeks at the hotel, Mom kept her distance from everyone. We shared the same room, but she kept to herself for the most part. She didn't eat with the rest of us and never joined us in the lounge for poker or movie night. She only seemed to be able to handle company for less than fifteen minutes at a time. Any longer, and she'd start fidgeting and make an excuse to leave. The only exceptions—in time—were Ginger and me. And of course, Kale. She'd spend hours talking to him. With everyone else, she was quiet, rarely speaking unless there was something important to say. After a while, she got a little more chatty, but I didn't think she'd ever be what Brandt would've called verbose.

I shrugged as if it didn't matter but staked a claim on the one closest to the window by flopping down beneath the hideous painting of an old barn. I didn't like being by the door. Too many nightmares about Denazen bursting in while I slept, Dad leading the charge to drag me away. "Ginger said they moved Kale's room. Do you know where? I was gonna go check on him."

And it was true, I did want to check on him. We'd had a hard night, me and him. I wouldn't be able to sleep unless I knew he was okay. But I also needed out of that room. I loved Mom. I was happy she was safe and in my life. However, this was bound to get awkward. There was no way I'd be able to sleep after everything that had happened, and sitting around eating a pint of rocky road and dishing about boys wasn't exactly an option. What did you say to someone who'd been locked up for the last seventeen years, treated like an animal, and used as a tool to lure people to their death? *Hey, let's watch a movie. There's a new Ben Barnes flick out. Wait…you don't know who Ben Barnes is, do you?*

We'd been getting to know each other since the summer started, but it was slow. On my first night back, we sat in our room for over an hour, trying to talk. Neither of us had any idea what to say—or where to start. We'd been separated my entire life.

It was proving to be a slow process. In a strange way, Mom was more screwed up than Kale. Like him, she had her quirks. Nothing red was allowed in the room, and each time she took a shower, she left the door open and made me swear to leave *every* light in the place on. She even made me switch on the flashlight app on my new cell.

But in addition to what everyone considered small quirks, she had some bigger issues, too. She wouldn't allow anything elastic within ten feet of her. Hair scrunchies, rubber bands, hell, she'd freaked when she saw my collection of Silly Bandz. She'd even gone as far as ridding all her clothes of anything elastic. On our second night together, right before Kale and I took off to warn the Sixes on Brandt's list, I'd come in to find her cutting the waistband from all her underwear.

Can you say *awkward*?

She turned to the clock on the nightstand between our beds. "It's almost one in the morning."

I started backing toward the door. "I know. Thank God it's still early, right?"

"Dez." She looked uncomfortable. Was nice to know it wasn't just me. "I think there are a few things we need to talk about."

"Talk about?"

"There are some things we should probably get out in the open."

This couldn't be good. She was going to rail me about sneaking out to the party. Hell of a time for her to put on the Mom pants.

"I know you and Kale have grown close—"

"This is about *Kale*?" I gave her a dismissive wave and backed up a few more steps. "Trust me when I tell you, that ship has sailed."

"Dez," she said again, this time sharper.

I froze. Her tone was like a sledgehammer to the knees.

"It's far too dangerous for you to be alone with Kale right now. How do you think he'll feel if something happens to you?" As an afterthought, she added, "Plus it's a school night. You can't go."

"I can't? Watch me."

I regretted the words immediately. I wasn't trying to give her crap; it was more out of habit. I wasn't used to answering to anyone. Dad hadn't taken much of an interest in my life, and the few times he had, it had been to forbid me to do something. I usually ignored him and went along on my merry way. "I'm sorry." I leaned against the wall. "Force of habit. I don't do authority."

"So I've heard," she said wryly.

"Look, don't take this the wrong way, but I've been taking care of myself for a really long time—without parental interference. Dad talked, I ignored. It's a little late in my life for someone to be telling me to do my homework, wash behind my ears, and be in bed before ten."

"This is a big adjustment for both of us. I may have raised Kale inside Denazen, but being a mother out here—" Mom looked around the room wearing an expression much like the one Kale had when he first came into my house. Dazed and confused didn't cut it. Leaning over, she picked up the can of Sprite I'd left on the nightstand and gave it a shake. "Everything is different. I know you can't understand—"

"You're right. I won't ever fully understand what it's like for you, but I've spent enough time with Kale to know the world must look like an alien civilization from your eyes."

"I'm your mother, and you're my responsibility." She set the can down and stepped forward, sounding unsure.

"Please, *please* don't take this wrong, but I haven't been anyone's responsibility for a long time."

I leaned close and kissed her forehead. She cringed a little—personal space issues.

"Promise I won't be long. Just wanna make sure he's okay."

There was no chance for her to object. I was through the door and down the hall without looking back. When I got to the bottom of the first-floor stairs, it occurred to me that Mom never said which room they'd moved Kale to. I made my way to the front desk where—surprise—Rosie was still planted in front of her small TV.

I waved a hand in front of my face and scrunched up my nose. "Hasn't anyone ever told you perfume isn't a substitute for soap?" Every day it was a new, disgustingly pungent perfume. I imagined Rosie's house was crammed to the ceiling with little bottles in assorted shapes and colors bearing designer labels and expensive price tags. Sometimes the smell was so bad that I wondered if she didn't experiment, mixing several together to create her own icky fragrance.

She shrugged. "It's sad that you have no taste. It should be a criminal offense."

I did my best to breathe through my mouth. Not that it helped much. I could *taste* the fumes. "Don't you ever sleep?"

"I don't need sleep," she replied.

I couldn't tell if she was joking or not. After all this time, I still had no idea what Rosie's gift was. "They moved Kale. Can you tell me which room he's in now?"

A normal Rosie response would have been ten minutes of avoidance, then five minutes of bargaining, followed by a multiple choice answer and a sneer that could scare small children. This time, a slow smile spread across her face as she toyed with the edge of the registration book. "Oh, sure. They moved him into the room right next to that sweet, redheaded girl. What's her name, Jade? And have you seen her? Really beautiful. That Kale's a lucky guy getting to spend his time with *her*. Room one sixty-two."

I swallowed a sarcastic remark. It went down thick, aided by the stench in the air. I refused to let her see that it bothered me. I nodded and was out of the lobby and down the hall in record time, the new information motivating me. Of course they'd put him next to Jade. She was like a cosmic off switch.

When the door opened, he looked tired, but the second our eyes met, his face lit up like the stormy sky outside. Just the sight of him standing there looking down at me like that was enough to wipe away the niggling bits of insecurity I'd felt over What's-Her-Name earlier. "Dez."

He stepped aside and hugged the wall to give me plenty of room. Closing the door behind me, I crossed the floor to the phone and said, "Fifteen feet, right?"

Lips slipping into a mischievous grin, he was next to me and punching in the room number next door in a flash. Through the wall, I heard it ring five times before Jade picked it up, her sleepy voice garbled through the receiver. "Stay in your room, please," he said. "I'm going to kiss Dez."

I couldn't help the laugh that escaped my lips. Bet that wasn't what she hoped he'd say when he called.

All smiles, Kale hung up the phone.

"That's going to get really irritating." I tried to look annoyed, but it was impossible with him right there, grinning.

He was quiet for a few minutes before he began to laugh.

"What's so funny?" Though to be honest, it didn't matter. As long as he kept laughing. I heard that laugh in my dreams every night. Deep and a little bit dark, it caused my heart to pound and sent the butterflies in my stomach into a hysterical frenzy. It was my favorite sound in the world.

"Did it feel this way when I was angry at Alex?" His mood was light, but the mention of Alex's name caused his eyes to darken just a little.

Jealous. I was jealous of Jade. "It was kinda nice," I admitted, then backpedaled. "But it's *not* the same thing."

He tilted his head, right eyebrow rising slightly above the left. "You're *not* angry because Jade can touch me?"

"I most certainly am not." Only half a lie. I was more angry— at the moment, anyway—that she had to be lurking around so *I* could touch him. I was all for putting on a show, but I drew the line at voyeurism.

He laughed again, pulling me to him. "I like this. It feels good."

"I bet this feels better," I whispered, leaning closer.

He grabbed the sides of my face, ensuring I couldn't move. A giggle rose in my throat. Like I'd move? Away from this?

Warmth exploded everywhere he touched. Greedy fingers skimmed bare shoulders, slipped beneath the still-damp straps of my tank top, and traced eager lines up and down my neck. Warmth—and something else. Tiny prickles. Like the ones I'd felt earlier with Jade around, only slightly more aggressive. A few moments more, and my head started to hum. A low sound that made my ears itch and my stomach turn a little. A ghost of what I'd gotten a taste of on the crane, but enough to throw things off balance.

I ignored it and pushed off the wall. This. This was what I came here for. Yes, I'd wanted to check on him. Yes, I'd wanted to get out of that room with Mom. But most of all, I needed to connect with Kale. My lifeline. My *adrenaline rush*. I needed to feel like I was still alive. Like *we* were still alive. I needed to know that Jade's appearance and her ability to be touchy-feely hadn't changed anything between us.

And it hadn't—because nothing ever could.

After a few blissed-out moments, Kale pulled back.

"What's wrong?" I asked.

"I don't want to hurt you." He was torn. I could see it in his eyes. Wanting so badly to touch me, but at the same time so terrified to cause me pain.

I wrapped my arms around his neck and pulled him close again. "I wasn't feeling anything but happies," I whispered between kisses. "I promise."

A few more seconds of internal debate, and he caved. Backing up slowly, lips still on mine, he maneuvered us to his bed. We collapsed on the mattress in a tangled heap, never breaking contact.

With each touch, the humming in my head grew louder. The subtle prickles grew to a constant throb as the pain flared to life, starting at my fingertips and working its way throughout my body. Still, I ignored it. It didn't matter. Nothing mattered except this.

Except us.

"I don't want this," he breathed between kisses. "To go too far. If it hurts—"

Pulling him forward, I gripped the edge of his T-shirt—he'd changed out of the wet one—and pulled it over his head. Without missing a beat, he reached for the hem of my tank top, but I grabbed his hands and twisted them around my back. "Trust me, I'm feeling something, but it's not pain."

"Everything with *you* is better." Ice-blue eyes stared straight into mine. When Kale looked at me like that, it was easy to forget the rest of the world. Fingers knotting through my belt loops, he used them to drag me close again "*Only* you, Dez."

It wasn't run-amok teenage hormones or what he'd said— sure, those things were awesome, but that's not what did it for me. It was Kale's intensity. The almost feral and somewhat possessive spark in his eyes. The deep, dark sound of his voice.

It drove me over the edge.

I pushed the little nagging voice aside, peeled back my wet shirt, and let it fall to the floor. Hands, lips, and hips. Everything was a jumble of limbs on fire. One minute his kisses were tracing a soft line down my jaw, the next his fingers were tugging furiously at the button of my jeans.

I tried to giggle at his enthusiasm, but it came out wrong. Not a giggle so much as a gasp. Followed by another.

Heaven and hell. Light and dark. There were a million purpley ways to describe it. None of them would come close to the actual feeling, though. The humming in my head flared, and this time it wouldn't be pushed aside. The rubber band determined to squeeze the air from my lungs at the top of the crane was back—and it'd brought friends. Lots of them.

Still, I couldn't push him away. If I pushed him away, I'd never have this again. I couldn't accept that.

I bit down hard on the inside of my lip to keep from crying out, but it was useless. A small noise escaped my pursed lips. Kale faltered, and I wrapped my arms around his shoulders.

Tighter.

Closer.

I wouldn't let go. I wouldn't lose this.

Couldn't lose this.

"Dez?"

Shaking. I was shaking. Trying so hard to fight the painful sensation building inside me—to keep him from seeing the effect his skin had—but it was pointless. There was no way to hide it.

"I—" I pulled away from him and scooted back across the bed. The instant we separated, the pain began to ebb, and it was like a breath of fresh air in an otherwise stifling room. "I can't…"

Kale's expression fell. "I hurt you, didn't I?" He sat up and eased himself off the bed. Crossing the room, he didn't stop until he'd backed against the opposite wall—as far away from me as space would allow.

I opened my mouth, then closed it. No matter what I said, it would make things worse.

He caught my gaze, and for a long moment, all either of us could do was stare. This was hell. It was like someone was waving the one thing we both wanted, the one thing we *couldn't* have, in front of our faces.

Kale was the one who broke the spell. "You should go."

I flinched as though he'd hit me. This wasn't happening… "Go? As in, you're asking me to—to leave?"

He turned away, fists balled tight at his sides. The physical pain I'd been in was nothing compared to the look on his face. This was killing him, which in turn was destroying me. "You being here is…dangerous. I wouldn't be able to live with myself if something—" He turned to me. "You should go back to your room."

I slid off the bed, pulling my shirt back into place, and left without saying another word. I'd gone to make things better. I'd only made them worse.

• • •

We were back at the construction site. Kale and I were at the tippy top of the crane, wind whipping our hair in every direction. It wasn't raining anymore, but occasional flashes of lightning still danced above our heads.

"What would you do if I kissed you, Dez? Would you let me?"

I smiled, but it felt stiff. Forced. "Of course."

He leaned in a little closer. "Do you like it? When I kiss you?"

My tongue felt like it was heavy and coated in glue. I knew the words were right, but somehow they *felt* wrong. "You know I do."

"You shouldn't let him kiss you," a voice said from across the crane. I turned to see my cousin Brandt—currently residing in the body of Sheltie, the guy who'd killed him.

It seemed like an odd question, but I asked it, anyway. "Why?"

He only shrugged.

Kale's knee nudged mine. "So I can, then? Kiss you?"

I turned away from Brandt. "Since when have you ever needed to ask?"

Leaning in, Kale's lips brushed mine. They were cold. Not like Kale at all. He didn't smell right, either. The air filled with something stale. Like decay. Still, I didn't push him away.

He trailed icy kisses down my chin and along my neck. Brushing the strap of my tank top aside, he lingered at my left shoulder as a chill raced down my spine. "Time's a-tickin', girly."

I jerked back, nearly losing my balance. Kale was gone, replaced by one of the creepy twins from the old house. The one with the crooked nose. Able.

"Have a nice trip." He cackled. Arm shooting out, he tapped the corner of my shoulder. It was all the momentum my precarious balance needed. The bottom dropped out from my stomach, and the world zoomed by in a colorless blur.

One minute I was falling. Speeding toward the bottom and certain doom. And the next I was standing on the ground next to Brandt-as-Sheltie.

"Jesus!" I stumbled back, eyes glued to the top of the crane. My pulse thundered in my ears, and sweat beaded at the back of my neck as I gripped the edge of the crane to steady myself.

"Told you not to kiss him."

"Thanks," I responded wryly, after catching my breath.

"Hey, don't be like that. It's *your* dream."

I took a good look at him. He was wearing the same faded jeans and Strokes T-shirt he'd had on the last time I'd seen him at the Sanctuary. He'd been waiting in a room to tell me the truth about who—and what—he was before skipping town.

"Is that what this is? A dream?"

He shrugged. "Sorta."

"Sorta?" Typical Brandt answer. "Sorta isn't very helpful."

Again, he shrugged.

"Are you really here?"

"Sorta?"

"Br—"

His brow furrowed in concentration. "Layne Phillips."

"Huh?"

"Layne Phillips." He looked like there was more he wanted to say, but instead he stomped his foot into the mud and pointed to the top of the crane. "Things are happening. Pay attention, Dez."

"Attention?" I followed his finger. All I saw was the top of the crane. There was no one up there and nothing else around. "To what?"

Suddenly he was in my face. Fingers digging into my shoulder, he repeated, *"Pay attention."*

White-hot pain exploded under his touch, bringing me to my knees. Everything turned watery as the ground dipped and swayed.

"Pay attention," Brandt's voice screamed one last time. An insane echo that bounced off the walls of my brain.

I shot up, gasping, and found myself wrapped in a blanket

and curled around my pillow as the annoying country music twang of Mom's radio alarm clock filled the air.

A dream. Brandt had been trying to tell me something. It all came rushing back.

Something sharp prickled beneath my skin. The fabric ripped in my haste to pull it aside.

"Pay attention."

And I hadn't been. There on my left shoulder was an angry red splotch. It was warm to the touch and itched like crazy. Able. It's where Able touched me on the rooftop of Alex's old building. It's where Able's lips had lingered in the dream.

"Time's a-tickin', girly."

Shit... I was in trouble.

I shed the blanket and slammed my hand down on the alarm to silence the music. It was one thing to wake up feeling like I'd just been put through the puree stage of a blender—it was another to wake up feeling like I'd just been put through the puree stage of a blender to *country music*.

If this continued, Mom and I weren't going to cohabitate well. A quick scan of the room told me I couldn't even rail her for it. She was nowhere in sight.

I jotted down the name Brandt had given me, doing my best to ignore the elephant in the room. My shoulder. If I told everyone, they'd freak. That had disaster written all over it. Plus as nervous as he was about being out in a crowd, I knew Kale would love going to school once he got there. The guy was like a sponge when it came to new information. I couldn't take that away from him. If Mom and Ginger found out about my shoulder, there was no way they'd let us go.

No. I'd wait for a little while. Who knew what would happen

for sure, anyway? There was no reason to overreact just yet. Maybe this was as bad as it'd get—an allergic reaction. A little pain and some itching never killed anyone.

Pulling out one of the few new outfits I had to choose from—dark blue jeans and a stretchy black T-shirt with a close-to-dangerous V neckline, I showered and dressed.

I pulled back my long hair—still brown from my *memorable* stint as Lara Croft at Sumrun's costume theme—and began a quick braid, securing it with a scrunchie from my secret stash. I'd need to fix the color soon because cow brown so wasn't going to cut it. That, and after an entire summer without dye, blonde roots were starting to peek through. I'd meant to do it last week but kept getting sidetracked. If I wasn't so distracted by all the other crap going on in my life, I would have been too mortified to even consider going to school looking like this. Dad once told me priorities changed as you got older. It was the only bit of truth he'd ever given me.

I applied makeup and gave one last look in the mirror at the finished product. Part of me was horrified. I'd never been able to roll out of bed, hop in the shower, and be ready to go in less than an hour, but I didn't have much of a choice. Halfway through the shower, I remembered it wasn't just me and Kale heading to school.

His clingy new BFF would be tagging along, too.

I made it to the lobby exactly forty-three minutes after turning off the alarm. A new record. Not one I was proud of, either. Kale and Jade were already waiting. Red hair hung loose down her back, and thick curls bounced when she moved like some slow-motion montage from a Pantene commercial. An oversized black sweater was cinched at the waist with a loose-fitting belt and hung just below her thighs, almost meeting the high black suede boots. A swell of jealousy hit again. Obviously, *she'd* woken up on time.

"Hey," I said, looking only at Kale. I'd ignore her and act like nothing was up, and maybe she'd go away. Play with the stuff under the sink or something.

"Dez…" He sounded surprised.

Why did he sound surprised?

Jade was kind enough to answer. "Are you feeling better? We thought you were staying in bed today." She leaned a little closer, making a big show of putting a hand on Kale's arm. "I heard what happened. *So* sorry. Sounds like you overdosed on my aura already."

She *heard* what happened? As in, he'd told *her*? Since no one else had tried to wake me up, that meant he told them, too. They really expected me to stay home from school? And let Kale go with *Jade*? Ms. Touchy-Feely? They had to be frigging high.

I reached for Kale, but he stumbled away. It was understandable after what happened last night, but that didn't make it hurt any less. "I need to talk to you."

I'd prepared a whole upbeat, *we'll get through this* speech while in the shower, but standing here with him staring at me, the whole thing melted away. All I could think about was reaching out and taking his hand.

Another swipe and I got him by the sleeve, pulling off to the side and around Rosie's desk. "You heard what Jade said. In a day or so, I can touch you again."

He didn't answer right away. And when he did, his words made the room spin. "I don't know if that's a good idea."

"What?"

His voice was low. Sad. At his side, fingers began to flick. Pointer, middle, ring, and pinky. "It happened very fast, Dez. We didn't touch that much last night, and you *overdosed*, as Jade calls it."

I forced a flirty grin. "If I remember, we were touching a lot last night…"

He didn't return my smile. "I broke the door."

"Huh?"

"After you left… You were in so much pain. At first I thought she—the door connecting our rooms—I thought Jade left the room, and that's why it got bad so fast, so I broke it—"

"Whoa." Wrong. That had to be a mistake. "*Connecting* doors? Are you frigging serious?"

From the look on his face, he didn't see the problem. Of course not. Because using the door to go see Jade would have never occurred to him.

Bet it occurred to *her*, though.

He took another step back and slipped around so the corner of Rosie's desk was between us. "I'm sorry I hurt you last night. I didn't know—"

I held up my hand. The thought of him apologizing made me sick. "It wasn't your fault. I knew better and pushed it anyway."

He paled, and his knuckles went white as each hand tightened around the edge of the desk. For the longest minute of my life, he simply stared at me. "You knew it was getting worse, and you didn't stop?"

I went to grab his hand, but he jerked away. Scowling, I said, "It was my choice. *Mine.* You're worth a little pain."

"No," he said, pushing away from the desk. For the first time since we'd met, he actually looked annoyed at me. "I won't allow you to do something that causes you pain. *I* won't be the *cause*."

The look on his face. That tone. He was flashing back to his days at Denazen. To how things were before we met. Their *unique* methods of motivation. Pain was something Kale knew quite a bit about.

I was set to argue, but Jade cleared her throat and made

a show of strutting across the lobby and reaching for Kale's shoulder. He didn't brush *her* away.

"We don't want to be late. Are you sure you're feeling up to it, Dez?"

Scratch acting normal. This bitch needed to know where she stood. I forced a smile and squared my shoulders. "I'm fine, Jade. Thanks for the concern."

She went to turn away, but I grabbed her other arm. The one *not* groping my boyfriend. Reiterating what Kale had told Alex last night, I said, "And just for the record, I can't touch Kale—*for the moment*—but I *can* touch you."

With a flip of her hair, she swung her overpriced-looking bag over her shoulder. "Green looks good on you, Dez."

I bit down on my tongue and followed Kale to the front of the lobby. I had one foot out the door when a sharp whistle cut through the air. "Freeze."

When I turned, Ginger was standing in the middle of the room, striped purple housecoat and matching slippers blaring from the middle of the red-and-gold lobby. She had an armful of papers and a canvas bag that looked ready to topple her to the ground. "Where the hell do you think you're going?"

I stepped back inside and let the door close. "Is this…a trick question?"

She scowled and whirled on Rosie. "Did you forget to mention something to them, Rose?"

Rosie, without looking away from her TV screen, shrugged and mumbled something incoherent.

Ginger sighed and readjusted the bag on her shoulder. "With everything we learned at the beginning of the summer, along with some new information, it was agreed that it wouldn't be safe for you to return to your high school."

I balked. "Agreed? *Who* agreed? When was there agreeing?"

The room started to spin, and suddenly the Sanctuary felt very small. "'Cause I know no one asked me."

"Last night you said we were starting school today," Kale said. The disappointment in his voice was unmistakable. I'd been right. He was worried but still looking forward to it. "You said you'd worked something out."

"We did." She smiled and waved for us to follow. "This way."

Back through the lobby and down the hall, we finally ended up in the small conference room, not that the hotel had many. Two to be exact. And even though the other was larger, because of its location next to the kitchen, it always seemed to smell like bad cheese. No one could figure it out.

Ginger ushered everyone in one by one and motioned for us to take seats around the large oval table. Thumping her bag down, she said, "Welcome to the first day of senior year."

"This is a joke, right? Some kind of lame-ass underground initiation thing?" This wasn't happening. I could not be stuck behind these walls twenty-four/seven. "What about my old school? My friends?"

Older, grandmotherly types were pushovers. Nurturing, friendly—sympathetic. They gave you smiles and candy.

Not Ginger.

She slammed a hand down on the table and shot a patented *Ginger death-glare* my way. "I'm curious, Deznee. How much of your friends do you think you'll see from one of Cross's cages?"

I opened my mouth, then closed it. I didn't know what to say because she was kind of right, and it pissed me off.

"I'll be right back." She turned to the door, then hesitated. "And Deznee, *stay put*."

I feigned insult. "As if I'd try to leave." If I didn't know better, I'd say the old woman was a mind reader on top of everything else, because I'd planned on grabbing Kale and bailing at the first opportunity.

"It won't be so bad," a voice said from the door. "At least the company is good—most of it, anyway."

Kale was on his feet and around the table before I could blink. "What are you doing here?"

I rushed to get between them and held up my hand. "Don't." Turning to the new arrival, I said, "Alex?"

"I've decided I want to make something of my future." He placed a hand over his heart. "To do that, I need a *proper* education."

What crap! "Since when? You dropped out two years ago."

"I've seen the error of my ways."

"Okay, well, congrats," I snapped. "You know where the high school is, right? Do I need to draw you a map?"

He frowned, taking a dramatic step back across the threshold, and I contemplated slamming the door in his face. "Is that *really* how you wanna thank me for saving your ass last night?" He was staring at Kale now. "'Cause I can think of more imaginative ways."

Kale inched closer. "We have something to finish," he growled. I couldn't tell if he was talking about what happened at Sumrun or the kiss last night. Either way, when it came to Alex, Kale's view of right and wrong was seriously screwed.

Alex ignored him, stepped back into the room, and took the seat directly across from mine. Nodding to Jade, he asked, "Who're you?"

"This is Ginger's *expert*," I sat back down. "Supposedly she's here to teach Kale control."

One eyebrow up. The Elvis. Alex leaned back in the chair. "*Supposedly*, eh? What makes you so qualified?"

Glad he asked because I was wondering myself. Other than making a great target-practice dummy with overdone lashes and nullifying Kale's ability, I hadn't seen anything that would make Jade qualified to help.

Jade gave him a dismissive glare, then turned to Kale, smiling. "I'm *qualified* for all kinds of things."

Oh. Yeah. We *were* gonna come to blows.

"You're the ex, right?" Jade leaned back, grinning at Alex. "You and Dez make a cute couple. I can totally see the sparks between you two."

"Yeah," I said, letting my head fall to the table. "And hopefully they'll set Alex's head on fire."

"Ouch," he gasped, banging a fist against the tabletop. "Brutal, Dez."

Kale's lips twisted into a snarl. "There is nothing between Dez and Alex."

Maybe I should have stayed in bed. The four of us locked in the same room for six hours, five days a week?

This was going to be a disaster of epic proportions.

By what would have been fifth period, my concentration was shot. All I could think about was Kale. And Jade. And Alex. Our weekdays were going to make one hell of a soap. And probably a messy bloodbath.

"You can take a thirty-minute break. Stretch your legs, grab a drink." Ginger pointed to me. "But stay *inside* the hotel."

Crap.

Obviously, I was stuck here. Turning to Kale, I said, "I'm gonna grab a coffee from the kitchen, then meet you in the common room?"

He hesitated but nodded and turned to Jade, who was trying desperately to get his attention by chattering about the thing he was most interested in. Gaining control over his ability. She couldn't wait to get started and knew he'd pick it up right away. Blah blah blah.

Lingering in the doorway, I watched the two of them for a moment. Tabs. I was keeping tabs on my boyfriend. When the hell did I turn into one of *those* girls? On one hand, considering the situation, I could argue that it was for safety's sake. Something about Jade didn't sit right with me—and not just that she was hot for my guy. When she wasn't eye-humping Kale, her eyes darted every which way, almost like she was casing the place. Or committing the hotel's layout to memory.

On the other hand, it was obsessive. Sparked mainly because of Jade and her obvious drooling. Seriously. The girl needed a damned bib and bucket.

Jealousy. I'd never been *jealous* of anyone before. There'd been that girl with Alex at Roudey's, but that was more hurt than jealousy. Jealousy stemmed from insecurity, and that had never been me.

I left before I could do or say something stupid. When I passed the lobby, Rosie was standing by her desk, arms folded. She gave me a quick shake of her head and pointed toward the kitchen. What, did they think I was going to try to bust my way out? They had to guard the exits? Jeez. Talk about trust issues.

Then again, I *did* have a reputation.

Ignoring her, I made my way toward the kitchen. Rosie smelled like something from the deepest recesses of a cheap department store perfume counter and might not be the most personable human on earth, but the girl was a coffee addict. The good stuff, too. She kept a stash hidden in an old Folgers jar under the sink. When I got to the kitchen, I couldn't help smiling. For all her bristling and bitchy demeanor, there was a pot of her secret stash waiting for me, my XtreamScream 2010 mug sitting next to it as if in invitation. I poured the coffee, inhaling its calming aroma, then fished my cell out.

"O.M.G. I heard the news before I left for class this morning. Rosie told me. She was in total Bitch Heaven," Kiernan gushed into her cell before I could even speak. "She went on and on about how Kale had finally met a nice girl."

I leaned against the counter and dumped the sugar shaker over my cup, trying hard not to snort. Rosie knew damn well Kiernan would tell me what she'd said. "Tell me about it. Total nightmare. This expert Ginger brought in? She's all over Kale."

"Are you serious?"

"Oh, yeah."

"Please tell me she's a woofer."

"So not. Total hottie."

"Ouch."

"Yeah."

"So she was, what, dribbling on him right there?" Kiernan whispered into the phone.

"Drooling," I huffed. "Like a damn faucet."

"Not cool! What're you gonna do?"

I eyed the doorway, eager to get down to the common room, but I needed to vent. If I kept this bottled up, there was a chance Jade wouldn't survive the day. "What *can* I do? She's here to help Kale."

"Sure she is. And I'm Ke$ha."

"I trust him."

"Oh, no disagreement there, chickie. That boy thinks you invented *air*."

I knew Kale only had kisses for me, but hearing someone else say it made me feel a little better. "I'm just gonna have to suck it up."

"Well, you know I got your back, girl. Right?"

"I know." I lifted the cup to my lips and took a small sip. Not enough sugar. I tipped the shaker over again and sighed, watching a stream of white grains disappear beneath the dark liquid. "It gets worse. Alex is here."

"There as in, at the hotel?"

Satisfied with the sugar content, I made my way into the hall and out to the lobby. "Here as in, he made up some bullshit excuse to finish high school, and Ginger is letting him sit in on *classes*."

"Wow," she whispered. "Even after everything that happened at that party in June? How's Kale taking it?"

I passed Rosie's desk and threw myself into the couch near the door. "It's so not going to end well."

"Shit!" Kiernan hissed. There was a clanking noise and rustling paper.

"Where are you?"

"I saw it was you calling. I slipped into the only working bathroom on campus," she groaned.

I chuckled. "College life not all it's cracked up to be?"

"This campus blows chunks. Back home the professors were way hotter. I haven't seen one yet that I plan on begging for a little *extra credit*." There was more rustling. "I hate to bail, Dez, but I'm gonna be late for class."

"Yeah, go. No worries."

"Be careful with Alex, okay? I don't trust him."

"That makes two of us."

I downed the rest of my coffee and said, "You comin' home right after school? I'm gonna need to get out of here for a while."

Voices. She must've gone out into the hall. "Sorry. Signed up for the paper. We're meeting after three."

"The paper?" I laughed. "Must be a guy."

She snickered. "Hey, like I said. Slim pickins. I gotta jump on it while the jumping is good. We'll hang tonight. Promise."

The line went dead.

Sighing, I set the empty mug on the table in front of me as something zoomed past the front doors. For a second, the entire lobby went dark. "Did you see that?"

From her desk, Rosie mumbled something I didn't quite hear but never took her eyes off the television.

I stood and made my way to the glass doors. Nothing but sunshine and a large, empty parking lot. If I was imagining things this soon, how was it going to be after a week had passed? Confinement and I did not go hand in hand.

Dismissing it, I headed to the common room. Alex was sprawled out on the chaise lounge chewing like a cow—sloppy burger in one hand, TV remote in the other. He was chain-channel-flipping, and I debated grabbing his soda and dumping it over his head. It used to drive me nuts when he did that, and he knew it.

Jade and Kale were at the card table across the room. She was listening intently to whatever he was saying, complete with the occasional hair flip and batting eyes. Every so often she'd bend forward a little and give a good, shoulder-shaking laugh. Please. I *invented* those moves. Some fifty-cent, out-of-town skank wasn't going to dethrone me with a few shakes of her *obviously* padded puppies.

Deep breath. I stepped into the room, shoulders squared and head held high. I was reigning queen here, not her. She wasn't going to swoop in and toss me without a fight. "So what'd I miss?"

"You were gone awhile." Kale stood but didn't come any closer. This was getting ridiculous.

I pulled my sleeve down over my fingers and reached for his hand, but Jade batted my arm away.

"Don't get too close," she said to Kale. "You're toxic to her at the moment. Don't take any chances."

Behind me, Alex muted the TV and stopped chewing. Everything went silent.

Toxic? What a stupid, stupid thing to say! Didn't this idiot realize Kale was extremely literal? "No matter what his skin does, Jade, Kale is not toxic. To *anyone*. Are we clear?" The ice in my voice could have frozen hell over.

It didn't seem to faze her, though. She just shrugged and flashed me her sweetest smile. "My bad. You know what I mean."

"Whoa," Alex said, turning the volume on the TV back up. "Check this out."

I sank onto the couch, and Kale followed. Sleeve still pulled across my fingers, I took his hand. He resisted at first but relaxed after a moment when nothing happened. On the screen, the newswoman was standing outside a small Victorian. The print under her name said "Morristown." One town over from Parkview.

"I'm coming to you live from Stanton Street in Morristown, New York, where we're just an hour away from the vigil for Layne Phillips."

The woman's lips kept moving, but the words were lost. The only thing I heard was the name of the girl. *Layne Phillips.* The name Brandt had given me.

Jade gasped. "Oh, my God. I remember hearing about this like a month ago. It made national news. Her parents found her in her bed in July, shot between the eyes. Right in the middle of her birthday party."

At Sumrun in June, Dad told us the first of the second generation of Supremacy kids would turn eighteen in July. Was Layne the first? Is that what Brandt had been trying to tell me? That it'd begun? I didn't know where he was at the moment—we'd initiated relative radio silence—but he'd obviously heard about her death and somehow connected it to Denazen. That was the only explanation for him giving me her name. "How old was she?"

Jade scrunched up her nose and snorted. "Not like it *mattered,* but she'd just turned eighteen."

Bingo! She had to be one of the Supremacy kids.

Alex stuffed the rest of his burger into his mouth. "Total waste—the chick was a hottie."

Jade's eyes widened. "You *knew* her?"

"Not personally or anything." He turned to me. "She was at that river rave a few years back. You remember her. She was the one with all the tattoos. Had that killer bitch badge. The one that wound around her waist and wrapped around her tits."

He was right. I *did* remember her. She'd flashed everyone at the party showing off that creepy tattoo.

"She had that barcode tattoo, too. 'Member?" he said with a smile. His head swiveled until he was staring at Kale. "We used to joke that she was someone's *property*."

"Alex," I warned. Anyone could see where he was going with this.

He ignored me. Nodding to Kale, he asked, "What about you? Do you have a Denazen barcode?"

Kale's fist was a blur as it shot across the couch. No counting this time. The blow landed square on Alex's jaw. He rocked back and, just like in the cartoons, flew feet over head off the chaise.

Kale was off the couch, a look of horror on his face. From the other side of the chaise Alex rose, rubbing his face and looking just a little pale. It took me a minute to realize why. He didn't know what Jade could do. The only change he was aware of was that I wasn't immune anymore. Last he heard, Kale's touch meant instant death.

From the look on Kale's face, he hadn't been thinking about Jade's presence. He'd lost his temper. Slowly, though, it dawned on him. He looked from Alex to his hands. The sleeves of his new black hoodie had ridden up to reveal long, pale fingers. Jade was there. He'd touched Alex.

Alex was still alive.

I saw the realization just a second before Alex did. Something sparked in Kale's eyes, and a twisted smile—twisted, but *so, so* hot—slid across his lips. His voice was low and dangerous. It sent chills up and down my spine and made my breath catch. Part of my brain was screaming at me to do something, but another part was just too enthralled to look away.

"I owe you."

And if I'd blinked, I would've missed it. Right hand flat on the arm of the couch, Kale propelled himself over in a single swoop.

He landed in front of Alex, who'd taken a step back, still a little confused, just as Jade and I scrambled to our feet. "How the hell—"

"It's me. My ability mutes his," Jade said, inching her way around to the edge, but she was too slow. Kale's fist shot out again, this time catching Alex in the gut. He stumbled back, coughing, and for a minute, it looked like he was about to go down.

It was an act. A second later he launched himself forward. Kale turned and ran in the other direction. Alex fumbled for a second but followed, determined to ground him. Kale leapt at the wall by the door. Right sneaker hitting about two feet high, he pushed off in an amazing back flip and landed behind Alex.

I couldn't figure out why Alex looked surprised. He knew all about Denazen and what they'd made Kale into. This whole thing was pointless even with the use of his ability. But Alex wasn't giving up.

Things were flying. Couch cushions, a lamp, the cordless from the corner table. All zooming above our heads and chasing Kale around the room. He dodged them with ease like some weird live version of the *Matrix* movies. Some missed by a wide margin, while he narrowly avoided others.

"You need to try harder. I'm getting bored." Kale laughed. He was enjoying this much too much, but who could blame him? A showdown with Alex—a proper one—was something Kale deserved. Even if not for the events at Sumrun, it was the natural order of things for the new boyfriend and the old one to throw down. Especially if the old one was a dick who refused to take no for an answer.

Twirling to avoid the porcelain lamp, Kale's feet did a fancy sidestep, and the lamp crashed into the wall behind him. Darting forward, he grabbed a fistful of Alex's hair and slammed his head against the wall as Rosie appeared in the doorway.

"What the heck is going on in here?" she screeched as Alex crumpled to the floor. He ignored her, as did Kale, and she disappeared—probably rushing off to find Ginger.

A feral growl escaped Alex's lips as he jumped to his feet, regrouping. "I'm just getting started, 98."

His hands jutted out, and the couch surged forward. But the look of smug satisfaction on Alex's face didn't last long. Without turning, Kale leapt into the air and, in an astonishingly perfect backflip, landed safely on the other side. Alex wasn't so lucky. With Kale not in its path, the couch collided with him, knocking him back into the wall.

Jade watched the whole thing go down with a stupid grin on her face. "Kale is totally rocking the Fight Club vibe!" she squealed as Alex climbed to his feet and threw himself back into the fray. Once in a while she'd try to step in, but every time they'd swing close, she jumped back with a tiny yelp and hide behind the couch.

Frigging moron.

Allowing Kale a few minutes to kick the crap out of Alex was something he deserved, but it was time to end this before someone started to hemorrhage—that someone being Alex, of course. He'd landed a few blows using his ability, but Kale had maintained the upper hand most of the fight. Enough was enough. It was a miracle that the entire hotel wasn't down here with all the noise they were making. What the hell was taking Rosie so long?

"Knock it off," I yelled.

Of course, my commanding voice and fearsome reputation got their attention right away. They froze in place and whimpered apologies, properly cowed.

Not even.

"You're not a good person," Kale growled as he dodged a flying plate. It crashed against the wall behind him, bits and pieces exploding in all directions.

"And *you* are? Least I've never *punished* anyone." Alex laughed and swung out with his own fist. The blow landed in midair beside Kale's shoulder. He straightened and rolled his shoulders. "Tell me something, *Reaper*. Did you keep count? Have a score sheet, maybe? You can tell me the truth. You *liked* it, didn't you?"

Any lingering control Kale might have had evaporated.

Alex saw it, too. He smiled and inclined his head toward me. "You can't hit that anymore, eh? No worries, brother man. I can step up to the plate in your place."

Kale threw himself forward, knocking them both down. They crashed into the wall, bumping the TV from its stand and sending it crashing to the ground. Bits of plastic and glass exploded, bouncing across the floor, making tiny plinking sounds.

Kale jumped up and hauled Alex to his feet. "You are no better than me. And you're going to stay away from Dez."

Alex shoved him away. "Or what?"

Kale grabbed the front of his shirt. "Or I'll come find you. Alone."

And that's when the shit really clipped the fan.

Ginger came hobbling into the room—finally—screaming at the top of her lungs. Kale, momentarily distracted, turned. Alex had never been above a low blow and used this to his advantage. He brought his head back and slammed it forward into Kale's. I heard the crack as though it'd happened to me. Both boys stumbled back a few steps but managed to stay on their feet.

I shoved Jade aside and stormed between them before it went any further. Kale shot forward to make another lunge for Alex, but I'd gotten in the way. He had just enough time to knock his bare-knuckled punch harmlessly to the side.

They both looked at me like I was crazy.

"What the hell is wrong with you?" Alex snapped, shoving my shoulder.

He didn't push hard, just kind of touched my shoulder and nudged, but it was enough. Kale elbowed me aside and flew at him again. Only this time, Jade actually did something. Grabbing a handful of Kale's hoodie, she yanked back. But it didn't stop him. In one fluid twist, he bent at the knees and shimmied, leaving the hoodie hanging in her hands—sans him.

He was about to take another swing, but a scream sliced through the air, stopping everyone cold. It was laced with fear and sounded like it came from the lobby.

Even worse, I knew that voice.

"Mom!"

Kale screamed for me to wait, but I didn't listen. How could I? Mom was in trouble. Back through the door and around the corner I ran. The hallway seemed longer than usual—each step moved me back instead of forward. I reached the lobby in record time and found Rosie standing in the middle of the room, a bewildered expression on her face.

"What happened?" I snapped, scanning the room. It was just us.

She shook her head and pointed toward the door. "I—I'm not sure what—"

Time came to a screeching halt. Just beyond the glass doors, a dark blue van was squealing to a stop. The door slid open, and three men in Denazen's patented blue monkey suits were wrestling Mom inside.

I heard Kale yelling behind me again, but I didn't stop. Through the doors, across the lot, and over the bushes that bordered the property. *Nonono.* "Mom!"

My heart slammed into overdrive, brain demanding my legs pump faster. Cover more ground. A few feet ahead, the men finally managed to maneuver Mom into the vehicle as it jerked into motion. There was nothing really coherent going through my head in that moment. I acted on pure instinct. With a quick prayer, I dove for the still-open doors on the van. I dove for Mom.

For once in the last few days, something went right—sort of. My speed was perfect and my aim exact. I sailed through the opening and straight into Mom. Actually, I sailed *through* Mom. Why? Because Mom wasn't really there. I realized my mistake a second too late. A pair of strong arms circled my waist and yanked me further inside as I tried to squirm back through the opening.

I resisted, clinging to the edge of the door as one of the men tried to pull it closed. Fighting harder, I managed to slip one leg over the edge and out of the vehicle, blocking the door track. Something in the back of my mind raged. If they closed that door, it was over. Good-bye, sunshine, good-bye, world. Good-bye, freedom.

One hand still curled around the metal rim, I groped the floor for the blanket sitting inches away. The second my fingers gripped the itchy material, I closed my eyes and held my breath.

A string of curses filled the air, accompanied by the increased cool September breeze and a flood of light. I opened my eyes in time to see the door-turned-blanket peel away and flutter from the side of the van. One of the men had been leaning against the door in an attempt to block my path. The door now gone, he lost his balance and toppled over the side and out into traffic. Good. One less to worry about.

"Bind her hands! She can't do her little switch-a-roo tricks if she can't touch anything," the one holding me yelled.

I squirmed and shimmied, but his grip was too tight. "How would you like to spend —" I slammed my head back like I'd seen Kale do once. All I hit was air. "—the rest of your life as a seventeen-year-old girl?"

That got him to let go. Only problem was, he shoved me toward the other side of the van and away from the door.

A familiar chuckle drifted back from the driver's seat. "Careful, Wayne. That little girly has some kick to her, yeah?"

Able.

I opened my mouth to comment that *he* knew all about my kick, but a deafening clatter sounded above our heads. The van swerved, and Able cursed. "What the hell—"

His answer came in the form of Kale, who swung in through the doorless opening and landed between the two remaining suits. Lips twisted, a low growl rose from his throat. He lunged for the first man without a word, right hand locking around the man's uncovered wrist. There was a moment of terror in his eyes and then nothing.

The remaining suit stepped between Kale and me as Able jerked the wheel hard to the right. Squealing tires and blaring horns filled the air, and Kale lost his balance, sliding sideways— dangerously close to the edge. Aubrey was out of his seat and shouldering the suit aside before I could speak. He hauled me up as Kale righted himself.

"Watch it, 98," Aubrey growled. "It would suck if you lunged for me and she accidentally slipped out of a moving vehicle."

I could see the frustration in his eyes. Aubrey was right. We were all balanced too close to the edge now. If Kale came at us, Aubrey would try to avoid him, and things could get messy. At seventeen, I had no desire to become roadkill.

From the driver's seat, Able snickered. "I gotta admit, girly, I was wrong. I told them you'd never fall for it, and here you go proving me wrong, yeah? I just lost twenty bucks because of you."

"Carley," Kale seethed. He was poised and ready to pounce, expression grim. "You used Carley to make us see Sue."

"Carley?" I asked, trying to twist free of Aubrey's steel grasp.

He smiled, tightening his grip on my arm. If he didn't loosen up, the circulation was likely to stop. "One of the Residents. She can beam an illusion straight into your brain." He stomped his foot. "Boom! Just like that. You'd swear on the air in your lungs it was real. She was in the lot around the side of the building."

Kale inched forward as the van's speed decreased. We were coming to the intersection in the middle of town. The light was notorious for taking forever. Maybe if we timed it right, we could use it to our advantage.

Of course just as we came to a stop, the light must have changed, because the van jerked forward, listing slightly to the left as we turned onto Daughten Avenue. The vehicle picked up speed fast—Able obviously wasn't worried about traffic infractions. As Aubrey and the Denazen suit faced off against Kale, I watched as Parkview zoomed by in a blur.

"Step away from Dez," Kale snapped.

"Why don't you just come and get her?"

We were fast approaching the town limits when a low curse came from the front seat, and the horrific sound of grinding gears and screaming metal filled the air. Everything shook, tilting sideways, and gravity disappeared. Something knocked me down and to the left, and sharp pain exploded at the base of my neck. For a moment, everything went watery. Hollow sounds—yelling and something else. Scraping. Like twisting metal—which, when everything cleared, I found was exactly what it was. The van had somehow ended up on its side, bodies strewn around the cabin like discarded trash.

The first thing I became painfully aware of was the brain-numbing pain in my right knee. I'd dislocated it once after a particularly nasty round of bumper surfing, so any injury was always ten times worse. The next thing I was aware of was the smell.

Smoke.

I tried to sit up but couldn't get more than halfway. "What the—" The duct tape the Denazen agent had wrapped around my wrists snagged on something that prevented me from getting up. I gave it a few good tugs, but it was no use. I was stuck.

To my right, the agent hung from the opening where the door used to be. My guess was he'd toppled sideways on impact, then got caught in the door track when the van flipped onto its side. A thin trail of red dripped from the corner of his mouth, and I shuddered. If the van had flipped the other way, we'd probably all be dead.

Kale lay beside me, and my pulse surged when I realized how close he was. Another few inches, and his hand would have hit my cheek. He was still, eyes closed, but the subtle rise and fall of his chest told me he was in way better shape than the agent— for the moment. The smoke leaking in from the back of the van fanned into a small flame, and as I watched, crept closer.

"Kale." I coughed. The acrid smell was getting stronger, and my eyes and throat were beginning to sting. "Kale, you have to move!"

From the front of the van, one of the twins moaned. I craned my neck to see Able, still in the driver's seat, slumped against the window. He wasn't moving. On the floor between us, Aubrey was getting to his feet.

Back to Kale. The tiny flame was getting bigger—and closer—and Kale still wasn't moving. Something sharp broke the skin on the back of my hand as I stretched to twist sideways. Taking a deep breath, I bit back a scream and thrust out my right leg out, bracing it against Kale's shoulder. I was able to nudge him out of the path of the flame and closer to the door.

"Able?" Aubrey mumbled from the front, trying to reach his brother. He lost his balance, tugging Able's still form down with him.

I yanked on the tape again with the same results. Kale was safe from the creeping flames, but that put me next in line. Panic coated the inside of my throat like syrup. Of all the ways to go down, burning to death was last on my list next to being crushed. "Kale!" No answer. I turned to the front. "Aubrey, get up! I'm stuck."

He ignored me, still trying to rouse Able with no luck.

Kale stirred. "Dez…?"

"Kale! I'm stuck. Hurry!"

He struggled up and stumbled across the cab, going down on his knee twice as he tried to maintain balance. "Lean forward. I need to see."

I leaned as far as I could to give him room to work. After a moment, Kale cursed softly. He was trying to hurry and not touch me at the same time. It wasn't working. A few feet away, Able stirred. Aubrey was desperately trying to wrestle the passenger-side door open and shove Able up and through, but without his brother's aid, he wasn't having much luck. "Hurry…" I prodded.

I could feel Kale trying to pull the edge of the tape up. Each time his fingers came close to touching my skin, I couldn't help flinching. Unfortunately, this only made things worse. Each time I tensed, Kale would freeze, terrified he'd come too close to making contact.

He let out an anguished scream as the flames crept closer. "Your bindings are caught under a piece of bent metal. I can't get it without touching you!"

With Jade not here, we couldn't take the chance. It had

started as intense pain on the crane, but what if I was exactly like everyone else now? If he touched me, I'd be dead. Dissolved in a pile of dust. Though at this rate, if he *didn't* touch me, I'd burn to a pile of dust. Talk about your double edged swords.

I swallowed the lump crawling up my throat as a shadow fell across the cabin. When I looked up, for a moment all I saw was a male form outlined and illuminated by the sun. The way the light hit him, it almost looked like there was a halo around him. An angel, come to save the day.

Alex said nothing as he pushed aside the dead agent's body like it wasn't even there and dropped into the van. Once out of the sun, I saw he looked horrible. There was a fresh gash across his right cheek, and above his forehead, a large chunk of blond hair was red and dripping, leaving a trail trickling down past the corner of his left eye, which was nearly swollen shut. I knew he'd taken some damage during his fight with Kale, but it wasn't nearly this much.

For a second, the sight of him was so startling that I forgot about the twins, the fire, and the fact that we were probably turned over in the middle of the road. "What the heck happened to you?"

"Move!" he snapped at Kale. He had the tape free and off my wrists in seconds—just before the flames kissed the spot where I'd just been. "Are you okay?"

I let him pull me up, cringing just a bit when I put weight on my left leg. A quick scan of the van, and I saw Aubrey and Able were gone. "I'll live. What happened to you?"

Alex nodded to the front of the van as he dragged me toward the door, lips hinting at a smile. "Dude doesn't know how to drive."

Ginger glared at us from the front of the room. Sliding a box of tissues across the table at Alex, she said, "Don't drip blood on my damned floor."

The twins hadn't followed us—they'd actually disappeared, which I thought was kind of odd. Between the three of us, we probably couldn't have battled roadkill.

The remnants of Alex's fight with Kale—a bloody nose and split lip, along with the shadow of a bruise coming out across the entire right side of his chin—made him look like he'd gone ten rounds with a stampeding elephant. His T-shirt was torn at the collar, and his left eye was swollen almost shut. But it was the other things, the nasty-looking gash and still-bleeding head wound, that kept me from throttling him for the crap he'd started with Kale.

When we climbed from the van, I'd nearly thrown up. Alex's car was sideways in the road, the entire passenger side smashed in. The glass was shattered and the front tire flat. He'd driven past the van and cut in front to stop it from getting away. It was heroic—in an epically *stupid* way—and if I hadn't run off like an idiot, he wouldn't have done it.

Compared to Alex, Kale looked like he'd barely broken a sweat. His bottom lip was swollen but not split, and a faint bruise had started to bloom across the bottom of his chin where he'd hit the van floor when we'd collided with Alex's car. In the chair across from Ginger, Kale watched Alex with an even mix of satisfaction and annoyance.

"Does anyone want to tell me what started that fiasco?" Ginger glared at me. "The one *before* you ran from the hotel like a brainless idiot?"

"Idiot?" I snapped, even though I knew she was one hundred percent right. "I thought they were taking my *mom*! Ask Rosie. She was there. She saw the same thing I did." I gestured to Kale, Alex, and Jade, all seated around the table. "And everyone heard her scream."

"Whoa," Jade said, waving both hands in front of her face. "Don't bring me into this. I didn't see or hear anything."

"You really believe it would be that easy to get into the hotel? Don't you think I have this place locked up tighter than a frog's ass?" Ginger narrowed her eyes, shooting me another one of her famous glares—this one we'd named *Ginger's glare of duh*. "Sue isn't even at the hotel. She's been gone since early this morning."

"Locked up how?" I pressed, stopping short of pointing out that when you cared about someone, you didn't over think things. You just acted. But pointing out how she'd sacrificed her family for what she believed was common sense didn't seem like the best bet right then. Plus she was right. I'd acted impulsively, and if I had it to do over again, well, I'd do the same thing.

But I'd still be sorry about it.

Ginger cackled and slammed her cane into the ground. "Just because you don't see something doesn't mean it's not there. This hotel is the safest place on earth for any Six. No one is getting in here without being let in on purpose." She cleared her throat. "Now. One last time. What the hell caused all that chaos?"

No one said a word.

"Well?" Ginger pushed. "Don't make me start swinging this damn cane!"

Kale sighed. He wasn't defensive or apologetic. Just matter-of-fact. "I don't like him."

Looking from Kale to Alex, Ginger said, "I don't like cabbage. Do you see me taking on the produce section of the food store?"

I couldn't help the giggle that slipped from my lips. A mental image of Ginger beating down a horde of cabbage as a swarm of carrots parachuted down from planes circling above popped into my head.

Kale narrowed his eyes. "He's *irritating*." He stood and started to pull up the hem of his shirt. "*And* he stabbed me."

Alex rolled his eyes. Grabbing another tissue, he dabbed the corner of his forehead. "And you're still alive. Time to get over it."

Kale held his hand out to Ginger. "Fine. Give me something sharp. If I stab him, then we'll be even."

She closed her eyes and took a deep breath. "I'm not dealing with this anymore. Detention. All four of you."

"Four?" Jade whined. "I didn't do anything. I never even left the building!"

"Detention? This isn't even real school!" I cried.

Ginger ignored Jade and glared at me. "Oh, it's real," she said. "And so is detention. As for you—" She turned on Alex. "I allowed you to be here as a favor. So far, you've made me regret it. I suggest that for the rest of the day, you remove yourself from my hotel so I don't beat you *bloodier* with my cane."

Alex didn't argue. He stood, flicked the bloody tissue into the trash next to Kale, and stormed out the door without a word to anyone.

Jade snorted. "Nice going, Dez. Can't you get through one day without causing trouble?"

I stared. Was she kidding? "You've been here, what, like twenty-four hours? Already I wanna kill you."

"Disappointed to find the world doesn't revolve around you? I'm here, and I'm *not* going anywhere. Deal with it."

I took a step toward her. "Wanna bet?"

"Enough!" Ginger boomed. "Do I have to chain you each to a different corner of the room?"

After a few moments of silence, she asked, "Was anyone hurt?"

"Sadly, no," Kale mumbled. He folded his arms and looked toward the door with a sulky expression. "I'll have to try harder next time."

• • •

I was sitting in the dark when Mom came into the room.

"Ginger told me what happened," she said, settling on the edge of my bed. "What were you thinking?"

"Please don't lecture me. I—"

"No lecture," she said, voice low. The lights flickered on, and I cringed against the sudden brightness. "Just a set of simple instructions that you are to follow no matter what."

I blinked as my eyes adjusted. Her tone was a little scary, and the look on her face? If Dad had ever pinned me with an expression like that, I would have thought twice about stepping out of line.

"Listen carefully because I'm never going to repeat this. You are to stay away from all things Denazen. That means obeying the curfew Ginger has set for the hotel, staying away from all unknown Sixes, and most of all, no more stupid rescue stunts."

It took me a moment to find my voice. Granted, we hadn't known each other long, but I'd never seen this side of Mom. All business with an undertone of something else. Something dangerous. "I thought it was really you. I couldn't just stand there—"

"Yes. You could. And next time, you *will*. It doesn't matter if it's me, or even if it's Kale."

I sucked in a deep breath and held it. It'd be way too easy to say the wrong thing here. On one hand, Mom was naïve. On the other—and I loved her no matter what—I still wondered when she might snap. Living free from Denazen's iron thumb didn't sit as well with her as it did with Kale. She became easily stressed and moody over seemingly insignificant things. Suzie Homemaker one minute—last week she'd tried to get me to make cookies with her—then pacing the hotel room like a caged cheetah on crack the next. And her nightmares? Let's just say we'd had the nightstand between our beds replaced three times already.

"Why were you sitting in the dark?"

"Seemed like a more productive use of my time than teaching goldfish to swim."

She tilted her head, confused.

"I was told not to *interrupt* Kale and Jade." It was going on eight p.m., and I hadn't spoken to or seen Kale since I left him in the conference room with Jade. At dinner, Rosie left to bring them their food, cheerfully stating they were *too busy* to stop.

"Oh." Mom hesitated, fidgeting with the corner of her bedspread. "Do you want to talk?"

"Nothing to say, really."

The look of relief on her face almost made me laugh. Mom wasn't in to the whole express your feelings thing. "So I think I'm supposed to say something here."

"Something?"

"About fighting?"

"*Technically*, I wasn't fighting."

Her expression hardened. In a single beat of my heart, she was back to danger Mom. "Cut the crap, Dez. I'm trying to be serious."

I sat up straight and flinched. "Ouch."

Her expression softened just a bit, but her voice held its hard edge. "Give me a break. I have a long way to go for Mother of the Year, and you're not making it any easier."

"I'm sorry about today. It was a stupid thing to do, but I saw you and…" It was hard for me to put my feelings into words. We were several steps above being strangers, yet I loved her with all my heart. Sometimes when I caught her looking at me, expression so full of confusion and fear, I wondered if she felt the same way. "Plus I'm on edge because of this Jade thing, and —"

"Jade thing?"

"You know—her frigging existence? She's all over him and…"

"And you're jealous?"

"I guess so. I went from being someone special, the only person on earth he could touch, to being just like everyone else."

She stood. "You're still special. That boy is crazy about you. If for no reason other than that, he'll learn to control this. Things will be fine in the end. You'll see."

I slid off the bed and pulled on my sneakers. A situation like this called for a good sulking session. Not a pep talk. "I need coffee. You want?"

She made a face. No hot drinks. Another quirk. "No."

"Your loss. I'll be back in a little."

I took the elevator to the first floor. Kale refused to set foot in the things, but when he wasn't with me, I was free to use them. My feet appreciated it.

After I'd downed one cup and fixed another for the road, I started back to the room. At the last minute, I decided to detour. The idea of sitting up there with Mom made me squirmy. Going from no Mom to all Mom, all the time, was proving to be a bit much.

I hadn't seen Kiernan at dinner, and when I'd texted to remind her of her promise to hang, there was no reply. She usually hit the hotel gym before bed each night. I was hoping to find her there tonight. Age-appropriate company I could bitch to over a pint of mint chocolate chip ice cream sounded like a good plan. But instead of Kiernan, I found Kale.

And Jade.

Still in the hall, I stood off to the side so they couldn't see me. Kale was sitting on the edge of one of the treadmills, and Jade was standing in front of him, holding out a plant.

"It's really all about focus and control. Clear your mind and think about the plant. Don't over think it. Picture green and pretty."

Kale scrunched up his nose and cringed away. "It's not pretty. It looks like a weed. And it smells bad."

She giggled. "Big baby. Just take it."

He hesitated but finally reached for the small pot. It didn't escape my notice how she leaned close and let her hand *accidentally* skim across his knuckles.

It didn't escape his, either. "I still can't get over that," he said, looking down at his hand with wide-eyed wonder. It reminded me of the way he'd looked at me in Curd's basement the night we met. A million different emotions swirling around, each vying for attention.

"Touching people, you mean?"

"It's extraordinary," he responded.

Jade smiled. A beaming grin that probably would have caught the attention of any male in a five-mile radius. "Go ahead and try again. I'm letting my aura down. Keep concentrating and touch it."

"Letting it down?"

"Didn't I mention that? It's something I can control." She smiled, playfully punching his arm.

Kale watched her for a moment, deep in thought. When he spoke again, his voice was nearly as dark as his expression. "You can control it? And did you let it down? The other night when I was with Dez?"

"No!" she said quickly. "Not at all. Kale, I would never do that." The look on his face softened just a bit, and Jade rushed on. "I know Dez and I don't mesh, but I'd never physically hurt her. I know it would only hurt you…"

"Okay," he said slowly, and a part of me wanted to smack him upside the head. Really? He was going to believe her that easily? Then again, I didn't know why it surprised me. Kale's biggest hurdle to date was understanding when and why people told lies.

She nodded to the plant, still in his hands. "Shall we try?"

Finger extended, Kale touched the tip of the plant with an unsure expression on his face. For a second, nothing happened, and hope swelled. But it was quickly dashed when the leaves shriveled and turned to dust. In seconds, the only thing that remained was a small plastic pot filled with dried-up, graying dirt.

Jade took the pot and handed him another live one. "It's your first night. Don't get discouraged. Try again." She squatted so she was at eye level with him and rested a hand on his knee. "Really clear your mind. Picture green. Think about *life*. This is all just mind over matter."

Sighing, he touched the new plant and got the same results. He brushed the dust from his jeans and let the pot fall. It bounced once, then rolled away, dirt spilling from inside. "Why did Ginger pick you to help me? Your gift doesn't need to be controlled."

She sighed and sat down on the weight bench across from him. "Mine doesn't, but my little sister Gabriella is sort of like you."

I could see his expression from here. Shocked, and a little sad. "Like me?"

"*Sort of* like you," she corrected. "Gabi's gift wasn't deadly like yours is, but it *was* a problem when I wasn't around. Whenever she got nervous, or scared, or angry, she would burn things. The older she got, the worse it was." She picked up the remnants of the plant Kale dropped and set it straight. "My mom tried everyone she could—no one could help. Gabi ended up living like a prisoner, only being able to leave the house when I was with her."

"That's sad." The sympathy in his voice made my chest clench just a little. I'd bet good money he was thinking about Denazen.

She shrugged and picked up a clump of dirt from one of the destroyed plants, smushing it between her fingers. "I didn't start out trying to help her—I mean I wanted to—but I never thought I could do anything. After a while we started experimenting. I'd drop my aura and let her touch me. Her gift—and Ginger believes yours as well—is fueled by emotions. Learn to keep them in check, and you can control it."

"How long did it take?"

"With Gabi?" There was a moment of hesitation. Her lips tilted downward, but I could tell it was all for show. The kind of frown you force to cover up a shit-eating grin. "Eight months."

"That's a long time," Kale said, eyes wide.

But Jade didn't seem concerned. "Not really. But don't worry. I'll be with you every step of the way. You'll get this eventually."

"Hey," I said. Coffee still warm in my hands, I stepped into the room. Watching them from the hall felt weird. Like I was doing something wrong. Plus I didn't want to hear anymore about Jade's sad, pathetic family. I wanted no part in feeling sorry for her.

"Dez." Kale's face brightened instantly. He stood and crossed the room in three fluid steps, stopping a foot or so away.

"Needed coffee." I waved the cup. "Just thought I'd see how things were going."

Without taking his eyes from me, he pointed to the door. "Go away now, please, Jade. I want to be alone with Dez."

Jade's face turned scarlet. *Poor thing* didn't know what to say. Here she was, pouring her bleeding heart out, trying so hard to make a connection, and he boots her. Kale wasn't trying to be rude; he just didn't know how to pad his requests with polite. In this case, it was some serious win.

She wiped the annoyance from her face and flashed a sugary smile as she passed. "Don't get too *close*. I'm going upstairs."

"I really don't like her." I closed the door with a snap and slid down the wall.

Kale did the same—only several feet away. My brain knew he was worried about hurting me. Emotionally, though, all my heart felt was the sting of rejection.

"Tell me why."

I stared at him. "Are you serious? She's just waiting for the chance to jump you."

His eyes widened. Expression serious, he leaned forward. "That's what you're worried about?"

"Well, yeah. She can—"

He chuckled and scooted just a little closer. "That's ridiculous. She has no training."

Training? For crap's sake. Sometimes I wanted to beat my head against the wall when talking to Kale. "That's not what I meant." I shook my head. "Ya know what? Never mind. How do you feel?"

"You're referring to my fight with Alex."

I nodded. "And it looked like you dinged your head pretty hard in the van."

"I'm fine." He thought about it for a moment. Flexing his arm, he said, "I would have been burned for that at Denazen."

My stomach turned. "Burned? For what?"

"Before the van. My fight with Alex. As punishment. Those of us who misbehaved were sometimes forced to hold scalding metal to our skin."

I wanted to throw up, but I refused to let him see it affected me. One of the reasons he kept most of his time with Denazen a secret was because he didn't want to upset me. I was determined to prove I could handle it.

"Losing control is not something they allow." He gave a small laugh. "I've never felt like that before. I'm trained to be aware of my surroundings. Careful. But earlier I couldn't see anything but my anger for Alex. It clouded everything."

I leaned back against the wall. "Sometimes we lose it. That's just the way it is."

"No, thank you. It felt good at first, but in the end it was…"

"Exhausting?"

He gave me a sad smile. "Yes."

"Sounds about right."

A few moments of silence passed before he spoke again. "It won't take that long. I won't let it."

"What won't take how long?"

"Jade teaching me control. It won't take eight months like it did with her sister."

He'd known I was there.

Of course he did. Nothing got past Kale. "How come you didn't say anything?"

He tilted his head, confused.

"You knew I was standing outside the room."

"You didn't want to come in. You had your reasons."

"I know it won't take that long," I said, hoping the words sounded more convincing than they felt. "You're brimming with control."

His hand twitched. "I have powerful motivation. I want to kiss you."

"I know how you feel."

"But for now, I really should avoid being near you." Expression torn, he said, "I don't like being this close knowing I could hurt you…but the idea of staying away is—painful."

I pushed off the wall and turned. On my knees, I crawled until I was sitting in front of him with my back against one of the treadmills. "Close your eyes."

And without question, he did. I'd seen firsthand what Kale's skin could do. From the first moment back at Curd's house when he'd touched a Denazen employee so we could escape, to the plant a few minutes earlier. I knew exactly how deadly it was.

But I just didn't care.

"Just keep them closed." Pulling my sleeve over the tips of my fingers, I brushed the side of his face.

He froze. "Dez, don't…"

"Shh." There was a funny tickle in my stomach. It was a monster contradiction to the painful lump in my throat. "Just pretend. Imagine it's my fingers against your skin. Just for a little while."

A soft noise escaped his lips.

My covered hand glided across his cheek and down his neck. Eyes still closed, Kale reached down and tugged at the hem of his shirt. In a fluent movement, it was over his head and clutched between the fingers of his right hand. The other was tangled in the denim of his jeans.

I figured I'd already overdosed on Jade's aura, making Kale's skin painful, if not deadly, to me even when she was around, but after hearing what she said about controlling her ability, and regardless of her denial, I was sure she'd done it deliberately. According to Ginger, it would essentially *reset* in a few days, and until then, I had no choice but to take her word for it. But to not be alone with him until then? I couldn't do it. Wouldn't do it.

Down the side of his neck and skimming lightly across the planes of his chest, I traced the scars there, one by one. His reaction kept me going, even though I knew I should stop. Small noises in the back of his throat, he tugged in desperation at his denim-clad leg. "Dez—"

"Shh," I whispered again, leaning just a bit closer than safe should allow. This is how it was with Kale. So easy to lose myself. Let all the walls down and forget about everything. He really was everything to me. My beginning and end.

Lower and lower, I traced my way down to the waist of his jeans. A surge of adrenaline pumped through my system. When I let my sleeve slide up so I could undo the button, I knew I'd gone too far.

11

Kale's body went rigid. His eyes shot open, and his hand clamped around my sleeved arm. "You have to stop."

He was right. Still, though, I couldn't. An adrenaline junkie through and through, this was the ultimate high. Kale plus danger. The enticing combination short-circuited my common sense—not that I had much according to some—and made rational thought a thing of the past.

Carefully, I gripped the tip of the zipper and pulled it down a fraction of an inch. The door wasn't locked. I could tick off at least a half dozen names. People that hit the hotel gym before bed. At any moment, someone could walk in and find us. I'd made out in public at a few parties, but this was something entirely different. A new kind of rush that sent my heart hammering and took my adrenaline to new levels.

"It's okay. I—"

In a half beat of my heart, I was on my back, and Kale was hovering just above me. I could *feel* the warmth radiating from his skin. Skin so dangerously close to mine.

Shocking blue eyes stared as the tips of his dark hair tickled my cheeks. "This is dangerous," he growled. "To push further would be insanity."

"I know."

To my surprise—and the slightest hint of something akin to fear—he didn't move away. "But—"

"I know," I sighed.

"It feels strange." He pulled back just a bit. I could see his whole face now, not just the mesmerizing blue of his eyes. He looked confused.

"Strange?"

"Sometimes I can't breathe when I'm near you. Knowing we can't touch steals the air from my lungs. It hurts, and it's all I can think about. But this…" He leaned in again, and a wicked smile spread across his lips. He was closer this time. I could smell the soapy remains of shampoo and the lingering scent of chocolate on his breath. "This makes me forget. It makes my head spin. Like beer."

Some girls might've been insulted at the comparison, but not me. Kale associated beer with losing control. A large part of me loved that I could do that to him. "I know how you feel."

"So this is what it's like? To be a junkie?"

I tried not to laugh when Kale said things out of context, but sometimes it was impossible. "An *adrenaline* junkie," I corrected with a slight snicker. "And yeah. That, and being in love."

His expression sobered. "But it's dangerous for me to lose control around you right now. The risk is far too great. It's painful."

I swallowed the lump forming in my throat. "Sometimes love *is* painful."

He scrunched up his nose, brows rising slightly. "That doesn't make sense to me."

"It makes sense," I assured him. "From day one we had the deck stacked against us, but we got through. We'll always get through. Wanna know how I know?"

"How?"

Until I met Kale, I had no idea it was possible to fall so completely in love with someone. To not know where they ended and you began. It was something that grew more and more with every passing day, and I knew in the deepest parts of my soul that it would continue to grow. We'd always have obstacles thrown in our path. Denazen, Kale's past, Jade… But it would never change things. There had never been anything I was more sure of.

"Because what we have is *epic*. It's the kind of thing they put in books and movies. The epic ones are always hard, Kale. They're blood, sweat, and tears, but they're worth it."

He was quiet for a moment. "And yet you still worry I'll fall in love with Jade because I can touch her."

With someone else this would've been tricky. The truth would make me look desperate and pathetic. But not with Kale. He didn't operate on the same frequency as everyone else. On one hand, he was more dangerous than anyone I'd ever met. He could slip into a room, kill you with a spatula, and be out of town before anyone knew about it. On the other, he was the most pure, untarnished soul I'd ever come across. It was an odd mix so uniquely Kale, and I wouldn't change it for anything in the world.

He was the one person I was completely free to be myself with. With Kale, there was no chance anything I said would be construed as needy or pathetic. I'd never get an eye roll or dismissive wave. One of the things I loved most—I never had to hide anything—

Only I was. My left shoulder chose that moment to twitch, sending a dull ache down my arm. Crap. I'd been trying to ignore it in hopes it would simply go away.

Who was I kidding? I had to tell him. He'd figure out something was wrong, anyway. Kale knew me better than anyone. Better than I knew myself sometimes. I opened my mouth to come clean, but when the words spilled out, they weren't what I'd planned. "In my heart I know that would never happen, but it's always been my worst fear."

He hesitated for a moment, blue eyes nearly boring holes through mine. This was it. He'd call my bullshit and force me to tell him what was up. A large part of me was relieved. After a moment, though, he sighed. "It's a silly fear. You have to understand that."

A strand of his hair fell into my eyes. Slightly disappointed, I blew it away and frowned. "Says the guy who can't touch his own girlfriend."

"This is *temporary*."

Twisting, I nodded to the row of dead plants lining the other side of the gym. A defeated army of greenery. An image of Kale and me, old and gray and sitting on a porch swing with Jade standing behind us, bound and gagged, popped into my head.

"I know…" But I couldn't help wondering what kind of damage would be done before we got it all straightened out…

• • •

The next few days went by without serious issue. Kale, Jade, and I continued to go to *school*—and detention turned out to be code for slavery. Ginger must have saved all the manual labor chores around the hotel for a rainy day because there was no end in sight. We'd done everything from washing windows to scrubbing out the stove.

Alex returned but stayed in the background. He left the hotel on lunch break and was giving me the silent treatment.

It was possible he'd realized Kale's threat was serious, or he'd learned his lesson—don't screw with an ex-assassin. Either way, it was peace, and we needed that.

I needed that.

The blotch on my shoulder hadn't gone away. In fact, it'd actually gotten bigger. It itched like hell and ached at random, inconveniently timed intervals. I woke up almost in tears most mornings, throbbing pain and occasional flashes of heat demanding attention, but I chose to pop pills and ignore the whole thing.

The longer I put off telling everyone, the more it seemed like a bad idea, until finally, the thought of coming clean scared me almost as much as Denazen. They'd flame me for waiting so long, and in the back of my mind, there was still the lingering hope that this would all go away on its own. It was stupid, and a part of me knew that, but I couldn't do it. I'd tried. The words just never came.

Jade and Kale grew closer. At least that's what it seemed like to me. Anytime I looked, they were whispering to each other. Twice I'd entered the room, only to have them go silent. Kiernan swore it was my imagination, insisting Kale spent so much time with Jade because he wanted to learn and get back to me. Still, something in the back of my mind whispered dark things.

Ginger gave them an hour to practice control each day, right before break. They'd slink off to the common room and practice with meditation and plants. During this time, she'd send Alex and me to the kitchen to make lunch. Her twisted idea of home economics.

On the third day, Alex finally broke his silence. "So what's up with the redhead?"

I slathered one piece of bread with extra mustard and set it on the counter. "What do you mean, what's up?"

He handed me the cheese. It was the same routine every day. Next I'd spread a thin layer of mayo on the other piece of bread, and then put three pieces of cheese between them. Kale had a thing for cheese.

"Seems like her and Reaper are getting a little friendly."

I pinched the bridge of my nose. He knew that name bothered me and used it whenever possible. "Stop calling him that, please."

One slice of bread on a plate, followed by a chunk of turkey slices, then exactly three pieces of pepperoni and a dollop of mustard. Alex's eating habits had always turned my stomach. "So he dumped you for her?"

Acknowledging the verbal poking would only make it worse, but I couldn't help myself. "We're still together," I said, gritting my teeth.

He waved a piece of pepperoni in my direction and feigned astonishment. "It's, like, an *open* relationship? You were never the type to share, Dez. I'm surprised."

"They're just *friends*." This time it came out a little sharper. If I squeezed the mayo any harder, it was likely to explode. "She's helping him learn control."

He waggled his eyebrows at me. The thin silver barbell above his right eye danced. "Control? Is that what the kids are calling it these days?"

"You're an ass," I said, flicking the loaf of bread across the counter at him. Making me do work around the hotel was cruel. Making me do it *with* Alex was just inhuman. I knew the silent treatment would never last.

There was a commotion at the door, and a second later, Kale walked in with Jade.

"And you're a blind idiot," Alex mumbled, grabbing his sandwich. "I'm outta here."

In his haste, he almost ran Ginger over on the way out. "Watch it," she snapped. "And make sure you're back *on time* today—with all the items on that list I gave you."

"How was practice?" There. See? I could be civil. The question hadn't even sounded sarcastic.

"Never mind that," Ginger said, handing me a package. "I need you to run this down to the post office. Now. Make sure to send it out first class."

"Me?" I took the small box from her and gave it a good shake. It felt empty. "You're letting me leave?"

"I don't have a choice. I need this mailed. Kale needs to practice, and Alex is already running an important errand for me."

"Rosie?" I knew I should shut my mouth. This was totally ironic. A few days ago I would have done anything to get out of the hotel, but now it seemed fishy. I mean, come on. She'd had Rosie guarding the exits, and here she was opening the door and pushing me out?

"Rosie had an errand of her own to run. She won't be back till later this evening."

"Aren't you afraid I won't come back till tonight?" I said. "Or that Denazen will snap me up the moment I walk out the door?"

Ginger looked from me to Jade and smiled. "Something tells me you'll be back as soon as possible. As for Denazen, I can assure you nothing bad will happen to you."

Nothing bad? It was the closest Ginger had ever come to revealing something she'd *seen*. It probably should have set my mind at ease—but it didn't.

Ginger pointed to the plate of sandwiches Alex and I made and said to Kale, "You and Jade, use the extra time to get in some more practice. You need it." To me, she said, "Get moving."

I bitched about it the entire way to the car—which was

kind of funny. Now that the opportunity for some semblance of freedom had been presented, I was pissed. On top of all that, my shoulder was killing me.

I'd popped more Advil in the last twenty-four hours than I had all year, but it wasn't helping much. A nagging feeling was telling me to take a look, but I couldn't bring myself to do it. I wasn't normally an advocate for avoidance—charge things head on, that was my motto—but acknowledging an actual problem meant I had to deal with it. And not only wasn't I ready, but I had no idea what to do.

A tiny, whisper-light voice in the back of my head said, *tell Kale*. Keeping this a secret from him was stupid, and more than that, selfish. He'd never keep something like this from me. It wasn't fair for me to keep it from him. I resolved to pull him aside and 'fess up as soon as I got back to the hotel.

The post office was across town, so Ginger had given me the keys to her Toyota. A bucket of blue-tinged rust and unidentifiable fetid odor, the car miraculously started. I had Kiernan on the phone before I even pulled out of the parking lot.

"I swear. She's trying to hook them up."

"So she's sending you to the post office? To mail a package? What is it—medication for some poor, dying kid in Canada?"

"I know, right? Why the hell did I have to go *now*? And why is she so eager to let me out on the building? A few days ago she practically had the doors barricaded."

"Maybe she's trying to avoid issues with Alex?"

"No way. He hasn't even been spending lunch break with us. He leaves and goes God knows where."

"Well, then why couldn't *he* mail the stupid package?"

"She said he was already running an errand for her."

"What kind of errand?"

"That's a great question. One I probably won't get a straight answer to." I sighed. "I should go. It's lunch. There's gonna be a sick line. Come see me after school?"

"You got it, babe."

"And don't flake on me this time," I added right before hanging up.

Traffic was a nightmare. It ended up taking me almost twenty minutes to get to the post office. Then, when I did, I found the line out the door.

"You've got to be kidding." I slammed the driver's-side door closed and trekked across the lot, package in hand.

Despite its length, the line moved quickly, and in no time I'd made it past the first set of doors. The woman in front of me held the second door open and stepped through. I let it close and waited for her to move farther up. The stench of her perfume was giving me a headache, and on top of the dull aching in my shoulder, I didn't need that.

Through the glass, I could see a reflection of the parking lot. A dark sedan pulled in and swung into the newly vacated spot next to Ginger's old clunker. The driver stepped from the car and made his way across the lot, casual as could be. Other than the shape, it was hard to make out the details of his face, but the perfectly pressed suit and dark sunglasses stood out like a flashing neon sign. The door gave a small squeak as the man stepped through.

Or it might've been me.

"Hello, Deznee."

Determined to play it cool even though my heart rate had jumped to about three beats past critical, I nonchalantly said, "Dad. Love to say it's good to see ya, but..."

"I'll be happy for both of us. You're looking well. I see life with your mother is agreeing with you."

"I doubt you're here to spew compliments. Flattery is *so*

not your style." I glanced around him and saw the dynamic duo climbing from the backseat of his car. One settled against the passenger-side door, while the other made himself comfortable on the steps just outside.

"I'd like to talk to you about Denazen." Dad said, keeping his eyes front and center. "I think you and I got off to the wrong start."

The only explanation for what I *thought* I'd just heard was insanity. That, or a supreme wax build up in the inner ear canal. "Wrong start? You're an animal."

Dad removed his sunglasses and tucked them into the inside pocket. "98 is more an animal than I am. I don't think you quite understand what it is we do at Denazen."

Was he serious? Trying that whole *we're out to help mankind* bit? On me? "Kale, jackass. His name is *Kale*," I snapped. I'd stayed on the other side of the double doors so no one inside could hear our conversation, but someone had joined the line behind Dad. The woman made an irritated noise of disapproval at my choice of wording and covered her small son's ears.

Great. Now I was corrupting children. I pushed past the woman and her son, flashing her an apologetic smile, and hurried down the steps. "And I totally understand what Denazen stands for."

As I passed, the twin seated on the steps rose and fell in step with Dad, who stayed right beside me. Ahead, the one by the car winked and pulled open the back passenger's side door.

Oh, hell, no.

I changed direction, Ginger's stupid package still in my hands, and veered to the right. Unfortunately, that put me around the overgrown, darkened side of the building. Out of view of the parking lot.

Dad flashed me his sweetest smile. One I once thought was

constructed to put clients and judges alike at ease. "You may think you've tamed him, but it's best to remember 98 is a killer. He needs to be controlled. You really have no idea what he's capable of."

"I think you're confusing him with yourself." Trying to be discreet, I surveyed the immediate area for something I could use as a weapon if need be. Ginger's package was feather light and would be useless for defensive purposes.

"We're not the enemy, Deznee. You have a chance to be a part of something monumental. Something that matters. If you come back with me, I can show you."

Behind Dad, the twins stood, both with their arms folded and eerie smiles on their faces. That's when it occurred to me the weapon wouldn't be necessary—and why Ginger knew it'd be safe for me to come. They weren't here to snag me. If they'd wanted to, it would have been easy to lie in wait beside my car and simply ambush me. This was something else.

And that didn't make me feel much better.

"I'm not one of those brainless twits you have running around the building like trained mice." I remembered the conversation with Flip, the guy I'd met in the cafeteria on my first day at Denazen. "I already know the truth. You can't brainwash me into thinking otherwise."

Expression cold, Dad stepped a little closer and said, "You may want to rethink your decision. Three members of the Supremacy group have already been put down. You might have heard about the latest on the news. Layne Phillips?"

"You're telling me the girl in Morristown was a Six?" I'd already figured this out because of Brandt and the story we'd seen on the news, but I wanted to hear him say it.

He simply smiled. We were around the side of the building and standing under an overgrown tree. The small amount of light that got through made Dad's features look almost inhuman. Fitting. "And you remember Fin, right?"

My stomach convulsed. "Fin is dead?" It was bad enough hearing about the others, but because I knew Fin—we'd gone to kindergarten and up through high school together—the whole thing seem more real. Closer.

"Not yet," Dad said. "The others started showing signs four to five months out. First it was a surge in their gift. Several months before they were rendered completely irrational, they all showed signs of advancement. Then, as their eighteenth birthdays grew near, they became unstable. Violent. They saw and heard things that weren't there. Grew paranoid and delusional. Fin's birthday is in a week, and four days ago, he started showing signs. It's much later than the rest—a week is the closest we've ever come—so we can't be sure what will happen. We're still hopeful, but only time will tell."

A nagging thought stirred. I remembered the nail color change outside of Vince Winstead's house at the beginning of summer. I'd mimicked it without pain—or even trying to. It hadn't happened since, and it wasn't what I'd considered a major surge, but it was enough to make me uneasy. "Has *anyone* survived?"

Seconds ticked by. Just when I was sure he wouldn't answer, he said, "As a matter of fact, yes. One. A very unique girl with a gift I think *you'd* find very appealing. Especially in your current situation."

"Well, what's—wait…my situation?"

The twins both snickered and continued standing guard.

Dad's smile widened, and he clucked his tongue in mock sympathy. "Yes. Very sad. I heard about your *issue* with 98."

"How did you—you know what? Don't care. What about this girl? What's different about her? How far past eighteen is she?" I couldn't believe I was trying to have a rational, civil conversation with that same man who'd drugged my mom, then locked her up for seventeen years. I should have been trying to choke him. Instead, we were playing Twenty Questions.

"She was given a vaccine. Something developed in hopes of a cure."

I almost dropped Ginger's package and lunged forward to shake him violently by his overpriced lapels. "And it worked? Why the hell haven't you given it to the rest of them?"

"It's made from a very rare component that we've recently discovered. There isn't much, and we have no way to get more at the moment. I saw no reason to waste it." His fingers drummed a steady beat on the doorframe. "Tell me, Deznee, what would you be willing to sacrifice for a cure?"

And there it was.

"We done? 'Cause I know, sure as shit, you didn't expect me go along with this." I attempted to brush past him, but he stepped into my path.

"Actually, I did." He reached for me.

I'll admit it. I panicked. The Devil of Denazen, Kale had called him once, and it was the truth. The man had no soul and wouldn't think twice about shoving his own mother in front of a speeding train if it got him where he needed to go.

Grip like a vice around my forearm, he gave a brutal squeeze. With a nod over his shoulder toward the boys, he said, "You've met the twins before, correct?"

Goose bumps skittered along my skin, but I played it cool. Brandt's words, *pay attention*, echoed in my ears. I peered around him and fixed my best badass glare at the twins. "Tall, annoying goth boys with a tragic sense of style?"

One of them—Able, I think it was—flipped me off, while the other blew me an exaggerated kiss.

"A pathetic replacement for 98, I'll admit, but handy nonetheless. Tell me, Deznee. How have you been feeling lately?"

The temperature dropped. Screw that. It plummeted. Suddenly I felt like a ham hock hanging on a meat rack. I became acutely aware of the throbbing ache in my left shoulder and how it sent tiny prickles across my skin, causing the muscles in my fingers to twitch every now and then.

Don't say it, my brain begged. *Don't tell me*. If I didn't know, I could continue to ignore it.

He smiled. My expression had given me away. "Aubrey and Able are interesting specimens. Not as interesting as 98 but still very handy. One's touch can poison you. Slow and painful, the venom creeps through the bloodstream and effectively liquefies you from the inside out. I've seen it. It's quite nasty."

"Sounds charming." Score one for me. I managed to say it without my voice shaking, but I had to tighten my grip on the package. Trembling fingers probably would have made it obvious.

"As simply as one can poison you, the other can heal you. All it takes is a single *touch*."

"And you're telling me this why?"

Before I could stop him, he yanked back the neck of my T-shirt with his free hand, exposing my shoulder. "Because your clock is officially ticking. Think it over."

He released me and stepped back, straightening his jacket. The twin who had blown me a kiss waved.

"One cure when you return to Denazen with me, and the other when we have 98 back in custody."

And then they were gone.

After I forced myself to move, I'd mailed Ginger's package and then proceeded to drive around for a while in a daze. I had to get back to the hotel, but the thought of facing everyone—of facing Kale—now that I *knew* the truth was like a string of bricks around my neck, dragging me under. Soon to be six feet under, if what Dad said was true. I needed to think for a minute. Decide what to do.

I pulled into the coffee shop a block from the hotel and made a beeline for the bathroom. With a deep breath, I angled myself in front of the mirror and brushed aside my shirt.

One of the things I was best known for was my iron-coated stomach. Even in school, when they showed those films about drunk drivers—mangled cars tangled with decapitated corpses and gore—I'd held it together. Pig dissection? No problem. I even survived Sloppy Joe Day. Now, though, seeing the angry red patch and its new additions—spindly black lines that snaked out in all directions—I was about to lose my lunch. And last night's dinner.

Maybe everything I'd eaten for the entire week.

The irritated red, bruise-like patch I'd woken up with a few days ago was now inflamed and deep purplish. The center was darker—not quite black—but close, and the tiny tendrils that crept out seemed to throb with a life of their own. Twice I had to blink because I was sure they'd twitched and squirmed underneath my skin.

Suddenly I was having a hard time catching my breath. I fixed my shirt. *Don't look.* Out of sight, out of mind. Another deep breath, and I turned to the door. I needed to get back to the hotel before they started to wonder. The most important thing was to not make a big deal out of this. Keep it hidden. Stay chill.

Game face. Out the door and past the counter, I left without ordering coffee. Hands in my pockets as I walked to the car, hiding all evidence of a freak-out. Having everyone spaz over this wouldn't help. They were already freaking about the Supremacy thing. Adding something else to the pile might topple everything like a bad game of Jenga. I'd been prepared to tell Kale everything. The plan had changed.

Turn the key. Start the engine. Foot on the gas. Pull the car onto the road. Nice and easy.

Think. I just needed some time to think. I could figure this out on my own. I was a resourceful chick. This was *not* a death sentence. Dad was lying. He was a liar—it's what he did. That whole show at the post office was a scare tactic. An attempt to bully me into walking right through his front door. It wouldn't work.

Pull the car around back. Get out—keeping hands in pockets. One foot in front of the other. Left. Right. Left. Right. In the front door and past the lobby. Act normal.

I stepped through the conference room door. The three of

them had their heads in a book, and Ginger was nowhere to be seen.

Jade looked up, grinning. Was it my imagination, or was her chair even closer to Kale's than when I left? "Didn't expect you back so soon."

And with those words, it was like the universe slapped me upside the head with a cosmic bat. I froze, shoulder momentarily forgotten. *OhmyGod.* I knew something was off about her. Dad somehow knew about Kale and me, and he didn't show up at that post office by chance. Someone told him where I'd be.

Jade told him where I'd be.

The timing would be tight but doable. All she'd have had to do was slip away, make a quick call, and boom. A visit from Dad.

I leaned forward on the table. "Expecting me not to come back at all, maybe?"

She tried for a casual shrug but failed. Our eyes met, and she grinned.

"Where did you go to mail my package, Deznee? Chinatown?" Ginger hobbled in and thumped another book down, sliding it across the table. It landed in front of me.

"Lunchtime," I said, still watching Jade. This was going to take finesse. I could out her now, but there was no real proof. More than likely they'd write it off as jealousy. No. I needed cold, hard facts. Something to prove it was more than a case of love triangle blues. Plus if I said something now, they'd find out about my shoulder. That was a bad plan. I took a step back and turned to Ginger. "Line was out the door."

Sinking down into the seat across from Jade, I opened the book. It all made sense. Dad knew he needed someone to keep tabs. He wanted to get his hands on me, and he wanted Kale back. He also wanted Ginger and the rest of the underground out of the picture. I couldn't figure out how, but somehow he'd managed to throw Jade in Ginger's path.

"Enough chatter," Ginger snapped. "Read through chapters two, three, and four, and write up a four-page summary." She paused for a moment at the door, almost like she was waiting for me to object. When no one protested, she disappeared around the corner and into the hallway.

I let my head thump against the cool surface of the table and ignored the open book. Dad was lying. I was sure of it, but a small voice in my head said consider all the options *just in case*. My options were sadly limited. Really, there were only three. Taking Dad up on his *offer*—out of the question. Even on the off chance he was telling the truth, it wasn't something I was willing to do. I didn't know half the things Denazen did to Kale over the years, but the little bit he had told me, coupled with what I'd seen up close and personal, was enough to make me seriously consider digging my own grave before handing myself over.

I could tell Kale like originally planned—which would lead to Mom, Ginger, and the rest of the underground finding out and would just cause everyone's stress level to skyrocket. Plus what would Kale do if I told him Dad could fix this? I'd bet all my fingers and toes—hell, I'd throw in a lung—that he'd march himself into Denazen and demand a trade. Himself for the cure. Dad asked me to come back first, but something told me he wouldn't refuse if Kale offered. In fact, knowing Dad, he was probably counting on it.

The last option, the one that looked the best, was to just leave it be. I'd seen the intricate lies Dad could spin to get what he wanted—hell, look at my entire life—this was exactly that. Another fabrication to get what he wanted. I'd keep an eye on it. If by some chance it got much worse, I'd have to consider telling someone.

For now, one hour at a time.

There was a dull pounding in my head, and the throb in my shoulder had progressed to a moderate stabbing pain. I closed my eyes and did my best to block it out. When I opened them after what seemed like hours to peek at my cell again, only five minutes had passed. Around the room, everyone else was lost in their own method of passing time—none of which included the reading Ginger had left us. Jade had a bottle of glaring-pink nail polish out and was touching up her tips. Alex stared at the ceiling while picking at the loose rubber sole on his right boot.

When I twisted toward Kale, he was looking right at me.

"Something's wrong," he said.

I held my breath and picked my head off the table. "Didn't sleep last night. Just tired. Plus reading about the French Revolution?" I tapped the book in front of me. "Serious snoozefest."

After a moment, he said, "Okay…" And a smile slipped across his face. "Will you go to the homecoming dance with me?"

"You're asking me out on a *date*?" I wasn't sure how he knew what homecoming was, but he got bonus points for doing it in front of Jade and Alex.

"How the hell is that even going to work?" Alex snapped. He winged his pen across the room. It crashed into the wall behind me and bounced to the floor. "One touch and he'll vaporize you. Even *you* can't possibly get off on that."

Jade tried to hide her smile—and failed. "I have to agree with Metal Face. It's not like you can dance with each other or anything."

"Not like it matters." I turned to Kale. "Technically this isn't a school. There won't be a homecoming dance." To Jade, I snapped. "And really? Could you be more of a bitch?"

"Not my fault you can't deal with reality," she said, standing. "Face it. He's toxic to you. Get over it."

"Yeah. See, that's the second time you've said that." I said, standing as well. "One more time, and I'll lay you out."

"What are you gonna do? Copy my outfit?" She flipped me off. "Go ahead. It'll still look better on me."

"Oh, chickie. I hope you're not implying I need a gift to kick your ass. I prefer the old-fashioned way."

Hands on hips, Jade snickered. "I'm invincible. Go ahead and give it your best shot."

"I wonder how invincible you'd be if I shoved an M-80 up your ass?"

From across the table, Alex coughed to cover up a laugh.

"Dez, please," Kale said. "I need her help. To fix things."

I looked at him. His expression made my breath catch. It was the same Kale as always. Intense and hot as hell. But there was something else. Something I'd only seen once before.

Fear.

"Whatever," I spat, sinking back into the seat. "I don't trust her, though."

Jade flashed me her sweetest smile. "You don't have to. *Kale* does."

•   •   •

After Ginger dismissed us for the day—which was fairly early due to another almost death-match between Alex and Kale about looking at me—I pulled her on the side to ask about Jade.

"You're going to have to deal with her for the time being. She's here to help Kale."

I snorted. "I keep hearing that, yet I'm not seeing any progress."

She sank into the chair. I'd followed her to the common room. Someone had cleaned it up and replaced the television. Every afternoon, Ginger liked to watch reruns of some weird show called *Jake and a Fat Person* or something. She wasn't happy I was cutting into TV time. Any second she was liable to start swinging her cane.

"It's only been a few days." She glared at me. "I know this is a foreign concept to you, but have some patience."

"Fine. Then just tell me how you found her."

"Found her?"

"Yeah. Did you, like, know her family? Her parents? Did she take out an ad in the paper? How did you find her?"

"She was referred to me."

I blinked. "*Referred*? By who?"

"By someone I trust. By someone *you* trust." She leaned sideways, trying to see the TV.

"Okay." I folded my arms and moved an inch to the left. "*Who*?"

She narrowed her eyes.

"Why are we even having this conversation? I mean, seriously, you know why I'm asking. You know *what* I'm asking. Why not cut the crap, and give it to me straight? I don't like leaving her alone with Kale. I don't trust her."

She gave up on the TV and sighed. "I know you think I'm being cruel. But it's not that simple. Yes. I know things. I know the answer to the question you're asking. But as I've told you before, I have learned from Miranda Kale's—"

This again? "Oh, please! You learned from her mistakes? The chick's been dead for over a hundred years. Her only mistake was trusting the wrong guy. Believe me, it happens all the time." I pointed to the door. "Even happens with girls. Perfect example—Jade. Trusting her is a bad idea. I can feel it, Ginger. She's *not* here to help."

Ginger shook her head. "I understand why it looks that way to you, but that's not so. To interfere in someone's path causes an unnecessary ripple. I refuse to be responsible for that. Look what happened when Miranda interfered."

According to Ginger, her ancestor Miranda Kale—the one she'd named Kale for—was the first visionary. She interfered in her husband's path and prevented his death, which brought about the chain of events that created Denazen—supposedly. Ginger used this knowledge to create a set of unbreakable rules. Rules she lived by no matter what. It was those rules that allowed her to step aside, letting her own daughter die and her only grandson be imprisoned and treated like an animal for the first part of his life.

I'd asked Kale once if he had any hard feelings. He'd looked at me like I was crazy, stating Ginger did what she believed was best. And it was true, she *did* truly believe it.

But that didn't make it right.

"And how do you know that's not what was meant to happen? Maybe she was meant to save his life. Maybe Denazen was *meant* to be. And you interfere with people every damn day!"

I was getting louder and louder, but Ginger didn't seem to notice. "I don't," she said calmly. "Everything happens exactly as it should,"

"You do," I insisted. "By simply housing Sixes, or giving us orders to do this and that, you're interfering."

"Everyone who comes to the Sanctuary was meant to be here. It is a stop along their own personal path, as the very creation of the sanctuary was a stop along my own personal path. The detention you earned yourself—the chores—they are part of *your* personal path."

She placed a hand on my shoulder, and I had to bite my tongue from calling bullshit. There was no way she was getting me to believe clearing out the dryer vents for detention was part of my *path*.

"When I look at you, I can see the key events in your life, from birth to death. I know this is nearly impossible for you or others to understand, but had you not been meant to be here, I would have refused you solace. I don't interfere. I simply work with the plans that I'm given. The things I see."

I shook her hand off and stepped away. She was right. I didn't understand. "It sounds like a really long-winded excuse to me."

"I'm sorry, Deznee." She stood, placing a wrinkled hand on my shoulder. "Interfering in someone's path is not an option. The key events shape us into the people we were destined to be. Changing them changes the person."

Without another word, she turned and left the room—and her stupid show.

The rest of the afternoon dragged by painfully slow. Kale and Jade were shuffled off to a private corner of the hotel while I was instructed—twice—to let them be. Of course, knowing they were down there, and I wasn't even allowed to sneak a peek, played serious havoc on my brain. Something was up with that girl. I could feel it with every fiber of my being. I imagined every scenario from her tranqing him and dragging his unconscious body out to a waiting Denazen van, to him ripping her clothes off with his teeth.

By the time ten p.m. rolled around, I was tired but too keyed up to sleep. I didn't feel like roaming the halls and didn't want coffee. Rolling over, I held my hand out to examine the rush job I'd done on my nails a few nights ago. It was a coppery gold that looked ridiculous against my pale skin. Now was as good a time as any to get rid of it.

It wasn't long ago that the idea of spending a Friday night alone, *doing my nails*, would have been unheard of. There was always a party, always a thing. Now look at me. Holed up for safekeeping. There was a good chance I'd suffocate long before the Supremacy crazies set in.

I sat up and pulled open the nightstand drawer. The only things normally in there were a brush, some Silly Bandz I'd hidden from Mom, and the nail polish remover—the latter of which was nowhere to be seen.

"Crap." Now that I'd looked at it again, I *really* wanted the stupid polish off. I'd scrape the damn stuff off if I had to. Ugly flake by ugly flake.

Then I got an idea.

In the corner of the room was a small pile of Mom's clothes. Think the country music was bad? Try sharing a small room with an adult slob. At least if I left my crap lying around, there was an excuse. I was seventeen.

Sitting at the top of the pile was one of Mom's T-shirts. Moss green. I closed my eyes and pictured the shirt, then focused on my nails. After several moments passed, I opened my eyes. The putrid coppery color had been replaced—perfectly—by moss green. There was a slight twinge at the base of my neck and a tiny wave of vertigo but other than that, no pain.

My mouth was dry. Maybe under different circumstances, this would have been the coolest thing in the world. Not only had I just mimicked something by simply looking at it, but I'd consciously changed a part of myself. Without any pain! The possibilities were pretty much endless. But with Supremacy hanging over my head? My elation didn't last. When a pounding sound filled my ears a few minutes later, I was sure it was my heart. Cardiac arrest. I'd subbed the blinding headaches for heart trouble. Par for the course lately.

It took me a second to realize it was the door.

Taptaptap.

Padding across the room, I saw Kiernan through the peephole. "'Sup?" I asked, pulling the door open.

Bouncing past me, Kiernan threw herself onto Mom's bed. "Whatcha doin'?" She looked around. "Your Mom still not back?"

"Haven't seen her at all today."

She kicked her feet onto the bed and tilted her head to the right. "So…?"

"So what?"

"You didn't answer. Whatcha doin' up here all alone?"

"Homework."

Kiernan spread her arms and frowned. "Where are your books?"

"I put them away when I heard the door."

Eyebrows raised, she said, "So, Pining 101?" Before I could manage a comeback, she was off the bed and had my sneakers in her hand. "Here. Put these on, and let's go. Fast."

I obeyed, hopping from one foot to the other as I tried to keep my balance. "Why?"

"'Cause you're way too young to be sulking in your room over some guy."

"I'm not—"

"Whatever. You need a pick-me-up. And I just so happen to know a great one."

"This is going to get us in trouble, isn't it?"

She hooked her arm through mine and flashed me an impish grin. "Only if we're lucky."

Kiernan was a girl after my own heart. Her pick-me-up turned out to be a party downtown. After she successfully snuck me out the back door by creating a diversion Rosie couldn't ignore—telling her someone broke her television—we were on our way.

The last house on Shannon Lane had been abandoned for over four months. Foreclosed and forgotten, it was the perfect place to throw a back-to-school bash. A dairy farm on one side and the edge of Memorial Park on the other meant there wasn't anyone around to call the cops. At least, not for a while.

When we arrived, I was surprised to see Luke, one of the people staying at the Sanctuary, perched on the bottom step, cigarette dangling from his lips and beer in hand. He'd come to the hotel during the summer after a group of Denazen agents raided his apartment. He was a nice guy, quiet, and had the ability to communicate with animals. It'd actually come in handy. The Sanctuary's basement was currently vermin free as a result of Luke directing the mice elsewhere. Like, to the burger joint a block over.

"Hey," I said as we climbed the old Victorian's steps. The wood creaked beneath my feet as I avoided a suspicious-looking puddle with pale white chunks at the base of the first step.

He gave me a nod and took a swig from the bottle. "You're not supposed to leave the hotel at night."

I looked around. When I didn't recognize any of the other kids, I asked, "Is this a—"

"Six bash? Hell, no. Ginger doesn't do residential. This one's all Nix."

"You came here instead of the usual party?" I could understand my reasons—I was under house arrest. But Luke? He loved using his ability. A few weeks ago, I'd heard all about how he'd called in the local wildlife for a makeshift petting zoo to keep some Six kids entertained.

He shrugged. "Sometimes it's interesting to see how the other half parties." He looked from me to Kiernan and winked. "So where's your usual cohort—not that I'm complaining about the present company…?"

I opened my mouth to answer but didn't get the chance.

"Ah, there he is." Luke whistled. "And who's the hottie?"

When I turned to see what the fuss was about, I nearly threw up. Waltzing up the path, arm in arm, were Kale and Jade.

"Dez," she said, saccharine smile firmly in place. "What are you doing here?"

Kiernan, true to her *I've got your back* statement, elbowed me aside. "What is *she* doing here?" She turned to Kale and poked him hard in the chest. "Did you follow us?"

Kale's brow furrowed, obviously confused by Kiernan's tone. He opened his mouth to answer, but Jade ran him over.

"Follow you? We didn't *know* you were here—whoever you are."

That's right. Jade and Kiernan hadn't met yet. Now didn't seem like the ideal time for introductions, though. And if I had my way, Jade wouldn't be staying in town long. I pushed past Kiernan, moving dangerously close to Kale. The words tumbled out before I could clamp my mouth shut. I knew how bad they sounded. How pathetic. But for some reason, I couldn't stop. "If you didn't follow me, why are you here?"

Again Kale opened his mouth, and again Jade was kind enough to speak for him. Poor guy couldn't get a word in. "Your friend Curd called to tell you about the party. I thought since I'm going to be here *for a while*, I should make some friends."

"Curd called the hotel?" I hadn't spoken to Curd since Sumrun. When things went down, I thought it'd be best to steer clear of everyone until I knew things were safe. Curd had been hurt when I brought Kale to his house. It hadn't been bad, but still. "He doesn't even know where I'm staying."

"Oh, he still doesn't." She reached into her pocket and pulled out a cell phone. "You left this in the conference room."

I patted my front pocket. When I found it empty, I snagged the cell from her hands. "You *answered* my phone?"

She flashed an innocent smirk. "Was only trying to be helpful. When I told Kale about the party, he was kind enough to escort me."

"Escort you?" I glared at Kale. My head was starting to pound, and the ache in my shoulder intensified just a little. Things had to get worse before they got better, I told myself. The increase in pain only meant whatever it was, it was healing. With a deep breath, I said, "You snuck out of the hotel to bring this bitch to a party?"

"That was wrong?" He looked genuinely confused. "But you snuck out? Jade wanted to see the party."

"Yeah, Dez," Jade said in a singsong voice. "*You* snuck out.

Why is it okay for you and not for Kale? You can't control him. He's a free agent."

I opened my mouth, then closed it. Anything else I said would just give Jade more ammo. Turning, I stalked up the steps, past Luke and Kiernan, and into the house.

Someone had gone a little crazy with the glow toys. The place was pitch black, but you could see the bobbing and thrashing forms outlined by glow jewelry and paint. Next to the entryway, a small Coleman lantern sat by a large cardboard box. There were a few glow bracelets left in the bottom, so I snatched them up and moved into the room.

The thumping beat pounded as people bounced and shimmied in the center of the room. It made the headache a little worse, but I didn't care. It was a nice distraction from the anger bubbling in my gut. Beyond the dance floor, the hallway was packed with neon-wrapped bodies. Squinting against the dark, I spied a couple kissing in the far corner. Even though a party raged all around them, their only focus was each other. Jealous, I turned away. Across the room, a large white cooler and a table full of pink drinks sat in the corner. Score.

I downed one, then swiped another and headed to the dance floor. A drink in each hand, I made my way to the edge to wait for Kale. No way he'd let me just walk off.

Only he did.

Ten minutes and two drinks later, someone tapped me on the shoulder. I turned, expecting to see Kale, but found Curd, bright pink drink extended in greeting. "Dez, baby! Glad you got my message. Where ya been?" He threw his arms around me, drops of his drink splashing down the back of my shirt. It might have irritated me if I wasn't so happy to see him.

"Spent the summer with my aunt." As far as everyone in my old life knew, my mom had died when I was born. Telling people

I spent the summer with her might raise a few eyebrows. We'd agreed that if anyone asked, for now at least, Mom was my Aunt Sue.

A couple walked by, each holding a drink. Curd reached out and snatched the one out of the guy's hand. "Don't look at me like that. You're headed upstairs. You won't need it." Turning back to me, he said, "Some chick started a rumor you were doing homeschooling. Say it ain't so."

"'Fraid it is."

"Serious suck. You still with that guy? The weird one?"

I hesitated for a second before tipping the cup up and downing the entire thing. "Curd! You gave me an empty cup."

He winked and held out his arm. "We can remedy that."

When Kiernan finally found me, Curd and I were sitting at the bottom of the stairs in the middle of an off-key duet of the Pine Man—a local tree-cutting service—jingle.

"Been looking for ya," she said, nudging herself between Curd and me.

"We've been right here." I poked Curd in the shoulder. "Kiernan, this is Curd. Curd and I go way back."

"Hey, baby." Curd said. He was plastered. In the time we'd been sitting there, he'd collected quite a pile of plastic cups. He kept trying to wear them on his head, but they always fell off. "Love the hair. How wicked would it be if the carpet matched the drapes? We could go upstairs, and you could show me."

Kiernan stood and rolled her eyes. She was used to dealing with overzealous guys. Morgan, a Six that had briefly stayed at the hotel during the summer after she arrived, had insisted she was his soul mate. That was, until he met Lisa, a Six with the ability to mimic other people's voices.

"Or I could take Dez and leave." She grabbed both my hands and pulled hard. Unsteady at first, I struggled to my feet as the room spun just a bit.

He waggled his eyebrows and made another attempt at his cup-hat. It failed. "Gonna show her?"

Kiernan winked and slipped her arm around my shoulder. "Of course."

"I think I'm in *love!*" Curd exclaimed, thumping a hand against his chest, over his heart.

She grabbed my shoulders and pushed me up the stairs, giving Curd a final, dismissive glance. "Jesus, Dez. How many have you had?"

A little wobbly, I missed the top step and almost went backward. Kiernan caught me in time. "Not *that* many, but I didn't eat tonight."

She pushed open the first door we came to and shoved me inside. It was early, so no one had claimed the room yet. In a few hours, there'd be people going at it like rabbits in here despite the icky smell and army of dust soldiers gathering in the corners.

"Why?"

The muted beats of a new song started, and someone downstairs screamed. "I forgot?"

"Forgot? Girl, you need to stop obsessing."

"What am I gonna do?" I leaned against the door and slid down to the dusty wood floor. There was a few pieces of furniture left in the room—a broken dresser and an old mattress on the floor on the other side of the room. It was dark, but it looked stained in several places and had springs poking through the side.

"About what?" Kiernan joined me. "Jade? Or Kale?"

I blew at a stray hair. My bangs had grown out over the summer. They were at that annoying in-between stage. Too long to leave alone and too short to do anything with. "Have you seen them? Is she sticking her tongue down his throat yet? Has she tried to hand him over to Denazen?"

She sighed. "Of course not. She's busy playing social butterfly. The worst thing she's doing is dragging Kale around like a piece of meat."

"But he's *my* piece of meat," I whined as something loud crashed downstairs.

Kiernan's eyebrows rose.

"You know what I mean."

"It's fine, Dez. He's totally not into it. If it'll make you feel better, he started to come after you when you stormed off, but she wouldn't let him."

"Wouldn't *let* him?"

"She sold him something about it being proper procedure to let the girl storm off. He totally bought it."

Proper procedure? Oh. She *was* good—using Kale's lack of in-the-know against him—against me! "I *hate* her." The pounding in my head surged, and a moment later, so did the throbbing in my shoulder. I made a decision. "And I have a confession to make."

"Please tell me it's a juicy one and does *not* involve that walking pot factory from downstairs."

I flexed the fingers on my left hand. Sharp needles of pain shot up each one. "Curd? Um, no. It's about my dad and Denazen."

From the corner of my eye, I saw her watching me. Oh, yeah. I had her attention. "Really..." Disappointment—and fear. When it came to Denazen, Kiernan was a little traumatized.

I opened my mouth, but something slammed hard against the door. Kiernan and I both jumped about a foot into the air, as a second later, a guy with a blond goatee and spiky black hair poked his head through the door.

"Fudge!" he screamed at the top of his lungs before slamming the door in his own face and continuing down the hall.

He must have opened the door next to this one, because I heard him scream again.

I sighed. "I saw him today—my dad."

Her eyes went wide. "Are you serious? Where? *When*? And you didn't tell anyone?"

I shook my head. My buzz was starting to clear, and for a second, I contemplated grabbing more of whatever that pink stuff had been. The clearer my head got, the more my shoulder hurt. "He showed up at the post office. And no. I didn't tell anyone. I couldn't—I was afraid because—"

I trusted Kiernan and had started the conversation with the intention of telling her about my shoulder, but second thoughts were creeping in. I didn't want her telling the wrong people— meaning anyone—in a misplaced attempt to help me. In the end I chickened out and settled for the least damaging thing. Supremacy.

"The Supremacy kids are—well, they're not doing well." I couldn't say it. Couldn't tell her they were all dropping like flies. Or, more accurately, *being dropped* like flies. "Dad says they found a cure, and he'll give it to me...if I turn myself over."

"Are you shitting me?" she said as someone downstairs let out an excited scream, followed by a chorus of insane laughter. A second later, a girl—her voice was slightly familiar—screamed for them to turn up the music.

The new song started, and I found myself feeling a little bitter. It was one of my favorites to dance to. Instead I was up here in the dark. Hiding. It was a perfect example of how my life had changed over the last few months. "I wish."

She thought about it for a minute, then shook her head. Strands of wispy purple hair fluttered free from her braid. "No way."

"Huh?"

"He's totally playing you."

Maybe I hadn't lost the buzz after all. "How is he *playing* me?"

"How do you *know* there's a cure? How do you know they're even dying? And really, Dez. If he gave you the cure, you'd live, right? Why would he let you go free? Wasn't the purpose of that Supremacy thing to make super soldiers or whatever?"

She had a good point. A few of them, even. "I guess I don't know there's a cure for sure, but I do think they're dying. There was this girl on the news. Layne Phillips."

"That's the girl in Morristown that was found dead in her bedroom, right?"

"I'm pretty sure she was Supremacy. Dad said they *retired* her."

"'He said'? I'm gonna chalk this up as the alcohol, 'cause no way are you this dense."

As if on cue, someone downstairs screamed, "More beer!"

"Huh?"

She punched me lightly in the shoulder—thankfully the right one. "Think about it. Of course he said that. It got you thinking, right? Got you worried? Mission complete. He's taking credit for some other whack job's kill to freak you into doing what he wants. Totally classic bad guy move."

I opened my mouth, then closed it. I didn't believe it was a scare tactic for one second. Brandt had given me the name first, and my gut told me he was right.

"Maybe," I said, unwilling to give her the rest of the information. Brandt stayed out of conversations. It was safer for him. As far as the world was concerned, he was dead and buried, and if I had any say in it, it would stay that way.

"What about that hippie chick? Have you tried her?"

"Who?"

"That Daun girl. The one that saved Kale. Maybe she could help you?"

Holy crap. Daun. I'd never even considered going to her. Chances were she couldn't do a damn thing about the Supremacy thing, but I bet she could help with Able's poison! While I still didn't believe it was fatal, it was painful. "You're a genius," I said, pulling her in for a hug.

"And I've got killer hair, too."

I nodded to her long purple braid. "Kale would love this color. I was thinking about streaks."

Kiernan didn't say anything. Instead, she pulled away, eyes wide.

"What?" I looked behind me, worried we weren't alone anymore. There were footsteps in the hall, and I could hear the faint sound of a girlish giggle, but it was just us in the room. "What's wrong?"

She was bouncing up and down like a two-year-old with a box of sugar cookies. "*OhmyGod!* That is so frigging cool! How come you didn't tell me you could do that?"

"Do what?"

She grabbed my shoulders and twisted me toward the dust-covered mirror on the far wall. "*That!*" Someone knocked on the door. "Occupado!" Kiernan screamed, eyes still trained on me.

Through the dust and dim lighting, I saw my reflection. Something wasn't quite right. Leaning closer, I saw my hair, previously in its boring cow-brown incarnation, was now streaked with brilliant purple.

"Um…"

"That is *so* awesome. Think of the cash you'll save on hair dye!"

Kiernan continued to gush, and a block of ice formed in the

pit of my stomach. Dad's words echoed through my head.

The first sign was a surge in their abilities. Several months before they were rendered completely irrational, they all showed signs of advancement.

I thought back to the moss-green-shirt-turned-nail-polish. I'd mimicked it without touching it, but I'd been *trying* to do it. This time it'd happened completely on its own without so much as a head twinge or muscle cramp—exactly like the polish at Vince Winsted's—and that scared the crap out of me.

"Think of the wardrobe possibilities," Kiernan continued. "You'll never have to spend cash on clothes again. Walk in to a store, check out the merch, and BAM. Insta-wardrobe. Oh! And catalogs! You can totally stock up on fashion mags and be Parkview's own runway diva." She tugged at the end of her shirt. "Try this."

"Try—"

She rolled her eyes and gave an exaggerated sigh. "My shirt. Try mimicking *your* shirt into *my* shirt."

For a brief moment I had a Denazen flashback. That tool Rick commanding me to mimic on cue. Meaty, sweat-covered fingers on my skin as his greedy eyes all but ate me up.

Deep breaths. In and out. That was over.

Eyes closed, I concentrated.

I didn't need to open them to know it worked. It wasn't the slight, drained feeling that overcame me or the cool, welcome breeze tickling my now bare midriff. It was Kiernan—who was obviously way more excited than I was.

"Oh-my-frigging-God."

"I think you're right," I said, trying to cover up the sick feeling in my stomach. "This could be epic for my wardrobe."

Suddenly there was a loud bang. Seconds later, someone screamed. It was garbled and frantic, but when the wail of a police siren sounded, I had a pretty good idea what they'd said.

"Shit!" I scrambled up, the last of the pink liquid buzz gone, and raced to the window. Pulling up in front of the house were four patrol cars. "Not good…"

Kiernan threw open the door and froze, shoving me back inside as I tried to peer around the corner. "No good! They're already in the house." Frantic, she slammed it closed. "We have to go."

She made a move to grab my arm, but I stepped out of reach. "Not a chance. Kale is here! I'm not leaving without him."

With a growl, she pointed to the window on the other side of the room. "Go out there. I'll see if I can find Kale."

And before I could make an objection, she disappeared. A second later, the door opened and closed again. Kiernan was almost as impulsive as me. We should have used her ability to sneak past the police and right out the front door, but that would have meant stopping to think for a second. We were cut from the same cloth. Act first and think later.

I was able to drop to the patio awning just below the window. On the front lawn, a flood of people streamed from the house as the wailing sirens drowned out their panicked cries. The cops had a few kids in cuffs by the cars. They were trying to grab the stragglers as they ditched the party.

As soon as the coast looked clear, I lowered myself to the ground. But I'd underestimated the height. My feet buckled as I landed in the dew-damp grass. I jarred my shoulder, which sent a dizzying wave of stars dancing into my field of vision. No time to think about it. I shook the pain off, cursing, and was about to get up and make a run for the woods, but a pair of worn, black shit-kickers came into view.

"Not leaving, are you? Party's just getting started, yeah?"

14

"What a surprise." I got to my feet and brushed off my jeans. The cops were busy with the front door and weren't paying us any attention. "Slumming?"

Able grinned. "Is it so hard to believe I came to see you?"

It was believable, all right. Should have known that crap Dad spouted about having a *choice* was bullshit.

Able took a step closer. "Since *I'm* here, and *you're* here, how about we go somewhere? Together, yeah?"

He reached for me at the same moment Curd came barreling out of the house and around the corner, followed by a very shirtless Vicki Donnor. She bounced like runaway Jell-O, nearly popping out of her zebra-striped bra, and knocking over anyone unfortunate enough to get in her way. I could understand her hurry. After the last party, her father threatened a nunnery if she got caught again.

Able was focused on me so he didn't see them come around the corner. I took a small step to the side to avoid collision. Vicki, determined not to get snagged by the cops, slammed him from behind. The surprise blow knocked Able off balance and sent him stumbling sideways. She muttered an apology as she zoomed by, and Able cursed, but I didn't wait around.

I sprinted around the corner to the front of the house. The lawn was out of bounds because the patrol cars were still there. The backyard was a no-go. I couldn't make a run for the woods because Able was blocking my path. The only choice was the house.

There were a few partygoers still trying to bail. They trickled from the house, some from the front door, others trying to sneak around the side from the backyard. Luckily, the cops were so busy rounding them up that they didn't see me slip back inside. I pulled out my cell and pointed the glowing screen toward the ground so I could see where I was going. The stereo was still blasting, the opening beats of the song familiar.

In the corner, the keg had been knocked on its side. Small droplets of golden liquid formed an expanding puddle underneath it. The folding table that once held the mixed drinks was also on the floor, a pool of pink creeping toward the center of the room. Scattered glow jewelry lay everywhere, making the room look like a tiny neon graveyard.

I hesitated at the stairs, listening. All quiet. It seemed like everyone had gotten out. Pointing the cell into the hall, I used it to light my way to the kitchen. There was still noise coming from outside. Faint voices and car doors slamming. The Parkview police were on a mission. A few weeks ago the local paper had done an article about the party scene and how the Parkview PD wasn't doing enough—aka *anything*—to stop it. Now, they were determined to prove themselves. They'd chase you through the woods all the way to the next town from what I'd heard. I had no intention of testing that theory.

I brushed the old lace curtains aside to check the backyard. If the coast was clear, I could make a break for it and find Kale and Kiernan. But unfortunately, the coast wasn't clear. Thin material aside revealed Able on the other side of the glass, grinning like a cat that'd just eaten an entire flock of baby birds. I nearly toppled backward out of surprise.

My hands shot out to fumble with the lock, but he was too fast. He slammed the door open and pushed inside. "Thought you lost me, yeah?"

Running was my first plan, but it didn't pan out. I tripped over a fallen metal folding chair and went down hard. Breath caught in my lungs as my left elbow slammed against the floor. Thousands of tiny tingles shot down my arm and up my neck.

Able was on me, and there was no time to run. Time for plan B. Scrambling upright, I took the folding chair and backed away several steps. No way was I going to make this easy for him.

He chuckled. "You're gonna hit me with a folding chair, yeah?" He stopped and spread his arms wide. "Go for it. I'll even give you a free shot."

No need to tell me twice. Fingers tightening around the legs, I swung the chair at his head as hard as I could. At the last second, I mentally crossed my fingers and pictured one of the heavy wooden chairs in the lobby of the Sanctuary. Cherry wood, deep red velvet seat cushion, and an ornate back. Tacky as hell, but seriously heavy. The sudden weight change knocked me slightly off balance but not before the chair collided with Able in a satisfying *thud*. He and the chair crashed to the ground, and I took off toward the door.

I made it to the stairs and was about to slip back out the front door, but Aubrey stepped out from the dining room and into my path. There was only one way to go. Up. I changed direction, skidding on the drink-soaked floor, and took the steps two at a time. When I got to the top, Able's scream split the air. Any sense of humor he had was gone.

Really, coming *back* into the house was one of the more brain-dead things I'd done recently. I'd backed myself into a corner.

"Hey!" someone whisper-yelled as I passed one of the rooms. I knew that voice. It was like nails scraping against a blackboard.

Jade was standing by a sliding glass door that lead to a small second-story balcony. There was just enough light from the moon filtering through the dirty glass to make out her annoyed expression.

"What are you still doing here?" A quick glance down the hall. Still clear. They had to be regrouping or something, or they would be here by now. "More important, where the hell is Kale?"

"We got separated by the crowd."

I stared. "You got *separated*? Are you crazy? In this kind of chaos, do you know the damage he could accidentally do if you're not with him?"

She rolled her eyes. "Relax. When we heard the sirens, I told him if we got split up to head back to the hotel."

"And he *agreed* to that?" I was relieved but also a little annoyed by the idea he'd leave without knowing I was safe.

Jade read my expression like a book, lips curling into a cruel smile. "Of course. You just have to know *how* to ask." She leaned closer. "Weren't you wearing a different shirt? And what's up with your hair?"

"Never mind. Why are you hiding up here? You could have easily gotten snagged by the cops."

She nodded at the sliding glass doors. "I was in the bathroom when the cops came in. I ran in here to hide and was going to go out and climb down, but it's stuck."

Pushing her aside, I reached for the handle and yanked. Yep. Stuck.

"Up here, yeah?" Able's voice came from down the hall. "In one of these rooms. She didn't get far."

I tiptoed back to the door and peered around the edge. Aubrey and Able were making their way down the hall, peering into the rooms along the way. There were two rooms between them and us. Only one choice left. "I'd love to say I'm sorry about this, but really, I'm so not."

Jade scrunched up her nose and folded her arms. "Sorry? About wha—"

I ran at her with as much speed as I could gather in the short distance. Grabbing her shoulders, I propelled us into the sliding glass door. It shattered into a thousand tiny pieces, some skimming my neck and cheeks, but most missing me, thanks to my handy-dandy human shield.

Could we have found another way out? Maybe. At the very least, I probably could have kicked the window to break it instead of tossing Jade through it like a volleyball—but that wouldn't have been nearly as satisfying. Or as much fun.

The plan was for us to land on the small patio, then climb to the ground below, but I'd underestimated the balcony's size. It was much smaller than it looked from inside.

And way less stable.

We crashed into the handrail—then through it. Jade yelped as we tumbled over the edge and plummeted to the ground. It wasn't a long fall—ten feet, maybe—but it still could have ended badly for me if Jade hadn't been kind enough to cushion most of the impact with her body.

"You *bitch*," she seethed and shoved me off.

I rolled away, gasping for air. The fall had knocked the wind from my lungs and jarred my good shoulder. For a moment, I was sure it was broken. Unresponsive fingers and sharp pain from neck to elbow made me panic. Broken bones would be more than a simple inconvenience at the moment. But when the pain started to ebb and my fingers began to wiggle, I knew I was in the clear.

I glanced to the window in time to catch a blur of black. The twins. They'd be down the stairs and around the house in no time. Up. I needed to get up and away. I stumbled upright and wobbled as a wave of vertigo hit.

"What the hell is wrong with you?" Jade squealed. She was on her feet and obviously in better shape than I was.

What the hell was her problem? It wasn't like she'd gotten hurt.

Unfortunately.

From the right corner of the house, the twins stepped into the moonlight, and our eyes met. Aubrey flashed a wicked grin as they started forward.

"Shit," I cursed, whirling in the other direction.

"Don't move!" someone yelled.

To our left, two police officers were rounding the other side of the house. When I glanced over my shoulders, the twins were backing into the shelter of the tree line. Within seconds, they'd blended into the darkness—but I knew they were still there. Watching and waiting for their chance.

The toxic twins or a nice, bumpy ride in the back of a squad car. It was no contest.

"Over here!" I called, arms flailing. Nodding to Jade, I called, "She's underage—and drunk!"

As they hauled us to the squad cars, Able stepped out from the darkness. His head was bleeding where the chair had hit him, and his expression was full of fury. His lips were moving, and even though it was dark, there was enough moonlight for me to get a pretty good idea what he'd said.

"*This isn't over.*"

"I cannot frigging believe you. You throw me out a window *and* get me arrested? Taking this jealousy thing a little too far, don't you think?"

I tucked my feet up, cringing, and rested my head against the wall. The throbbing in my left shoulder had doubled since our impromptu swan dive from the window, and the itching was driving me insane. I had to sit on my hands to keep from scratching at it. Then there was Jade's voice. Each word was like a knife slicing my head in two. I tried to ignore her, but she wasn't deterred.

"That was totally selfish."

The police were gallant enough to escort us from the party in the back of their squad car. To take their hospitality one step further, they even provided us with our own *special* waiting area as they called Mom and Ginger. It stank like week-old puke, was decorated with pretty metal bars, and had several gruesome-looking stains on the floor.

I closed my eyes and gnashed my teeth into my tongue. "What the hell are you whining about?"

"Instead of going to make sure Kale was okay, you try to kill me. When that fails, you get me arrested as payback for showing up at the party."

"You're invincible, remember? I *can't* kill you—no matter how much I'd like to." I opened my eyes and snorted. "And ego much? That had nothing to do with petty crap and revenge. In fact, I did you a damned favor."

She balked. "A favor? You're a *lunatic*. What person in their right mind throws someone through a window? Or *tries* to get arrested, for that matter? You're a seriously damaged individual! I don't know what he sees in you."

Standing, I took a deep breath. We were in a cell. Alone. There was no one to stop me from kicking the crap out of the little twit. I couldn't actually hurt her, but there could still be some serious enjoyment in trying.

"One with good survival instinct. We were about to get raided."

"Um, duh? The cops were already there."

"The cops? No. I mean by *Denazen*. While you were busy trying to throw Kale in my face, a group of Denazen flunkies was coming toward us. Or maybe you already knew that."

She scowled and turned away.

I took a step forward. "And how is it they found their way there? Any ideas?"

Shoulders stiff and cheeks flushed, she turned to glare at me. For a minute I thought she might actually take a swing. Or *try* to. "*What* is that supposed to mean?"

"It means, you pop up at a party, and then Denazen shows right on your heels? You don't think that's odd? Especially after that post office stunt?"

Her eyes were wide, and she flashed me a look of mock surprise. "Post office stunt? You are truly certifiable, you know that?"

"Don't play that innocent crap with me. I know what you're all about. And come on! You drag Kale out of the hotel to a party that Denazen crashes? How's that supposed to look?"

"Like I wanted to hang out with the guy I like?"

"The guy you like?" My mouth fell open. Had to give her credit. It took some serious balls to say that. That, or stupidity. "The guy who made it clear he already has a girlfriend? *That* guy?"

Her annoyed expression melted into smug satisfaction. "In case you haven't noticed, Kale *likes* spending time with me. Maybe your girlfriend status isn't as solid as you think."

"Kale is being *forced* to spend time with you. There's a difference."

She folded her arms and sat back down. With a flip of her hair, she said, "It didn't feel forced earlier. Ginger gave him the choice to do something else or hang out with me and practice. Thousand guesses what he picked."

I snorted. "Practice. *Of course* he chose that. Ginger told him you're here to help, and he actually believes it. He wants to learn to control his gift and be done with you, so things can go back to normal."

I heard the words and even managed to make myself sound totally sure of them, but a little tingle in the back of my brain started poking. They always looked so cozy. Close. Maybe Kale did enjoy spending time with her.

No. That was crazy thinking.

"Hey, whatever you need to tell yourself. Seems to me he likes the new normal just fine."

"Jam a sock in it," a cranky voice snapped.

When I turned, Ginger was standing in front of the cell doors with one of the officers that brought us in. Her lips were pressed in a thin line as she slammed her cane into the ground twice, then banged it against the bars.

The officer unlocked the door and pushed it open, stepping aside.

"Thank you, Larry. Give my regards to Lillian, will you?" Turning to us, Ginger snarled, "Get out to the car. Now. Someone my age is supposed to be in bed by seven p.m. Instead, I'm dragging two trouble-making kids out of *jail*."

Without a word, I slipped past her and all but ran for the door. Ginger was mostly bark, but there was enough bite in the old woman to have even someone like me worried. She wasn't the kind of person you wanted to piss off.

"It was Denazen," I said after Sira—another one of the Sanctuary Sixes—pulled the car from the police lot. "I saw them. Betting they called the cops as a distraction."

"Which would be exactly why you were all told *not* to leave the hotel after dark." Ginger twisted in her seat. "Does that sound familiar?"

I sighed. Normally my first instinct would be to tell her she was overreacting. It was a party. What harm ever came from a teenager sneaking out to a party? But with everything going on, I should have used more caution. Should have known better. I didn't know if Kiernan had been caught, so I didn't ask, but Kale was a different story. "Is Kale okay?"

"He's back at the hotel." She whirled around to glare at Jade. "Did you stop to think what might happen if you got separated?"

Jade paled. "He didn't—"

"Nothing happened," Ginger snapped. She held the redhead's gaze for a moment before turning around in her seat. Over her shoulder, she mumbled, "But this whole thing could have easily been a disaster."

We drove the rest of the way in silence. The car pulled up in front of the hotel as Alex's friend, Dax, Mom, and Kale came bursting from the front door.

"What's wrong?" Ginger asked, slowly extracting herself and her cane from Sira's front seat. I hadn't noticed at the police station, but the tips of her light blue slippers ended in a pair of beady eyes and a bright yellow beak. The smallest of the Angry Birds.

Dax hesitated and shook his head, eyes on me. "Just got a text from Alex. He was at that party." He clicked a button on his key fob, and the white Chevy on the other side of the lot flashed its headlights and beeped twice. "They chased him into Memorial Park."

A lump formed in the pit of my stomach. "They? Who, the cops?" Alex had a bad rep with the local PD. One more infraction, and he was going to land in serious hot water.

"They as in Denazen."

Kale sat up front with Dax, while Mom, Jade, and I squeezed into the backseat. I'd expected an argument from Ginger when I flew across the lot to Dax's car without so much as a word, but she'd stayed silent and disappeared inside the hotel. I bet it was because of something she'd seen. We were all *supposed* to be at that park. If we weren't, we would have never gotten out of the parking lot. It would have been comforting if I didn't know her so well. Even if one of us was slated to bite the big one, she would have let us go simply because it was meant to be.

When we got to the park, Dax rounded us up. He looked at Mom, brows raised, but said nothing.

It was weird. She nodded and tapped her hip as the smallest hint of a smile shadowed her lips.

We split up in hopes of finding Alex faster. Mom went with me and Jade, while Dax took Kale. I was pretty sure if it was anyone other than Alex, Dax might have suggested he and Kale go separately, but I think he was worried about what Kale would do if he found Alex first.

I was a little surprised at first that we'd split. Of all of us, Kale had the only offensive ability, and it made more sense to stick together. It might have made searching slower, but it would be safer. One could argue that Jade was invincible, and Mom was nearly as big a badass as Kale, but it seemed like we'd gone off to battle without any weapons—until I saw the subtle bulge beneath Mom's shirt. She was carrying.

Always alert, Mom scanned the woods off to the right of the path as we went. "You didn't see him at the party?"

I hadn't even known he was there. "I wasn't there long, and it was dark."

"*OhmyGod*," Jade whispered, panicked. She grabbed my arm and yanked, almost knocking me off balance. "Something moved in those bushes."

I shoved her off, pointed to the ground, and smiled. From under the bush, long ears attached to a tiny brown speckled head peeked out. "Yeah. That bunny is a Denazen suit in disguise. Where do you suppose he's hiding his gun? Or maybe he doesn't need one. Maybe he's a martial arts master trained in the art of kickassery."

"Bitch," she mumbled, turning away.

We walked for a good ten minutes without seeing any sign of Alex, the others, or Denazen. Unfortunately, Memorial Park was exceptionally huge. There were seven hiking trails, two lakes and a pool, and basketball, tennis, and racquetball courts. Without a clue from Alex about where he was hiding, this could take all night.

"I'll bet you a million Metal Face made a break for it and is long gone." Jade stopped walking and folded her arms. "We're wasting our time."

"No," Mom said, stopping beside her. "Dax told him to stay put."

"So that *must* mean he did it, right?" Jade snipped with a dramatic roll of her hand.

Mom squeezed her eyes closed and sighed. "Dez is right. You're extremely annoying."

It was something I'd expect from Kale, not Mom. She was usually quiet in her opinions and tended to stand back and watch rather than get involved. "Okay, it's official. I have the coolest mom in the universe."

Jade opened her mouth—assumedly to shoot off another snipe—but froze. Arm flailing, she gave a small shimmy and squealed, *"Notabunny. Notabunny!"*

Just past the West Lake gate at the head of the path, four suits were charging toward us. Mom reached behind her and yanked out the gun, dropping to her knees and taking aim. One shot. One agent down. The bullet hit him in the knee and he let out anguished scream.

"Get back," Mom spat. I hesitated, not wanting to leave her, but she screamed, *"Now!"*

I didn't argue. Grabbing the back of Jade's shirt, I took several steps away and tucked us behind a large pine tree. More shots rang out, and Mom cursed. One of the agents yelled something, followed by a moment of silence, then the appearance of Mom around the other side of the large tree.

"I got three of the four. The last one ran off, so we should be—"

The moon was nearly full and the night sky clear. The agent thought he was being sneaky, coming up around behind Mom while we were all distracted, but his shadow announced him right before he reached the tree.

I yanked Mom forward just as his arm shot out to pull her back. She shoved me away, but I didn't take it personally. I'd seen her in action during the battle at Sumrun. She was a lot like Kale.

Completely immersed and focused on the task at hand. At the moment, that task was beating down one of Denazen's not-so-finest.

I poked my head around the tree. There were two more approaching. "Company's coming."

Mom ducked a swing and retaliated with one of her own, catching the agent squarely in the gut. "Head for the woods," she huffed. "I'll be right there."

We scattered. I ran for the woods as instructed while Jade took off in a different direction.

I stopped at the tree line, trying to decide if I should attempt to follow her, but one of the approaching agents said, "Grab the redhead. I'll get Cross's kid."

Cross's kid? What the hell? Was there a milk carton picture going around? These freaks knew me on sight? In the dark? Feet pounded the concrete trail close on my tail. There was no time to wait for Mom or go looking for Jade. I had to shake him.

Or at the very least, gain some ground.

When he was closer, I stopped short and dropped to the dirt. I jarred my knee, which was already sore from the window incident, and both wrists. It was less than graceful, but effective.

Unable to stop in time, the guy stumbled over my back and crashed to the ground. I didn't wait. As soon as he was down, I was up and sprinting toward the tree line.

But I changed my mind at the last minute. Instead of heading for the woods, I veered toward the playground. Through the sand and under the monkey bars. Over the seesaw. Around the slide. Finally back on the path, I made my way into the picnic area. It was heavily wooded. It'd be a safe enough place to stop and catch my breath.

I ducked behind a thick maple and stretched out my left arm, wiggling each of my fingers. With every movement, I had to bite down to keep from crying out. The pain was getting worse. The gunfire had stopped, and now the park was silent except for the occasional cricket and rustling leaves. Mom and Kale could take care of themselves—Dax and Alex, too—but I was still worried. And Jade... Unfortunately she'd be fine. I was willing to bet she was working for Dad, so there wasn't any real danger for her.

After a few short moments and a somewhat lower heart rate, I stepped out from behind the tree. Karma, continuing the *Screw Dez* kick it seemed to be on lately, had a Denazen agent walking into the picnic area at the exact same moment. Our eyes locked. I bolted but wasn't fast enough.

He leapt, tackling me against the nearest tree. I hit the trunk hard with my right arm at an odd angle. There was no gentleness as he pinned both arms behind me, elbow jabbed into the hollow of my back to keep me under control.

Biting down on the inside of my lip, I sniffled. The way he had me against the tree allowed no movement. I was pinned awkwardly beneath all his weight. Even if I struggled with everything I had, I wouldn't get free. Time for a different tact. "Please..."

"Hold still," he mumbled, tugging my arms tighter. There was a chance he intended to rip them clean off.

I did exactly as he asked.

Another sniffle and a soft whimper—a real one that time. My left arm was on fire. I let my shoulders shake slightly and inched my right hand out from under me. It hurt like hell, and I had to gnaw on the inside of my lip to keep from screaming.

"Oh, cut the crap, kid. I didn't hurt you." He didn't sound sure.

Perfect.

I shook a little harder and for good measure, added some more sound effects.

The guy seemed to buy it. "Hey, look, everything will be fine. No one wants to hurt you." I wasn't sure if he actually believed it, or he was just that good a liar, but it didn't matter. He was distracted, and that's what I was aiming for.

Right arm free. There was a branch to the left next to my hip. Just a few more inches, and it'd be in my hand. "You wanna kill me," I whined. "Do all sorts of experiments to see what makes me tick."

I must have stumped him because he hesitated. "Experiments? Um, we're not like Area 51, kid. We're trying to help."

Help. Yeah. And I was the Dalai Lama in drag. More sniffles. "You—you swear?"

One.

More.

He loosened his hold. "Yeah."

Inch.

My fingers closed around the branch, and I twisted hard. The wood broke free from the trunk, and I focused on the memory of the metal piping in the hotel basement Ginger had Alex and me scrub as part of our detention duty. The rough bark smoothed out and evened, becoming cool to the touch. The moon danced from behind the clouds, and the stick-turned-thin-metal-pipe gleamed in its light.

"Liar," I spat, twisting. The pipe flew up—a projectile with all my strength behind it, aimed at his head. I had to bite my tongue to keep from yelping when something stretched in a way nature hadn't intended, and a sharp pain shot from my elbow to my neck. The metal connected with an echoing *zing*, sending Mr. Clueless stumbling backward.

He would have hit the ground if someone hadn't been standing there to help him.

Kale caught the man, bare fingers wrapping tight around

his neck. In one graceful turn, he slammed the suit into the tree behind them. Crumbling on impact, the body dissolved into a billion ash-like particles that scattered away in the breeze.

Kale brushed the dusty remnants of the man from his hoodie and closed the distance until there was only about half a foot separating us. Maybe less. Icy blue irises filled every inch of my vision. "Did he hurt you?"

His voice was calm, but there was an edge to it. Tension. Shoulders taut, he kept his arms board straight and his eyes on me. Twice I could have sworn his fingers twitched.

"I'm fine," I whispered, dropping the pipe. The metal clattered against a rock and rolled before falling silent on the ground between us. It ended up in a perfect horizontal line, and I couldn't help admiring the irony. Lately the universe seemed intent on throwing things in our way. "You?"

He moved closer. "They're ill-equipped to deal with me. None of them are wearing safe suits."

I swallowed. In my mind there was a flashing neon sign above Kale's head that said, *Do Not Touch*. Still, I almost did it, anyway. For a second, I didn't care what would happen. I just wanted to feel his skin against mine—even if it was the last thing I did. "Dax?"

Sleeve pulled over his fingertips, he brushed the hair from my face. "Being away from you made me uneasy. I left him to find you."

I wanted to argue that leaving Dax alone to find me wasn't the right thing to do, but it was pointless. If I wanted to be totally honest with myself, had I been with anyone other than my mom, I would have done the same thing.

Something moved in the brush beyond the picnic tables. Sleeve still secured over his skin, Kale took my arm and started walking down the path toward the cliffs. "We should find Alex and the others. There are seven Denazen men in this park right now. More are likely on the way. If they know I'm here, I have no doubts they'll come better prepared."

"Seven? Are you sure? How do you know?"

He shrugged. "I saw them. There are seven."

Someone stepped onto the path in front of us. "Seven Denazen men. That's not including—"

Then another someone. "Sixes, yeah?"

"I swear," I mumbled, stopping short. "I must have been Jack the Ripper in another life. I'm being punished."

"Nice to see you again, girly," Able said. The gash on his head had been cleaned and left to the open air. It went from the tip of his ear and disappeared under his hairline just above the right eye. A swell of pride filled me—I'd gotten him good. He saw me looking and tapped the side of his head. Without his usual, taunting smile, he said, "I owe you for this."

Kale stepped in front of me, the corner of his lip curling up. He looked between them, eyes falling on Able. There hadn't been much time before the accident for Kale to study the twins, but somehow he could tell them apart. "You were driving the van."

Able winked. "Finally. The famous 98, yeah? We didn't have a chance to meet properly earlier. You remember—when you crashed my van?"

I tugged back on Kale's hoodie, but he resisted.

"I only dented the roof. The real destruction came from Alex. I would be happy to supply you with his address," Kale stated calmly. "If I wasn't about to touch you," he amended with a slight chuckle. Sleeve pushed up past his elbow, he reached for Able.

Goth Boy raised his hands in dramatic surrender. "I wouldn't do that if I were you, 98. I think it would *upset* your girl. Besides, we're not here to bust your balls."

He stepped back, making room for Aubrey to take his place.

Kale's eyes narrowed. "Why are you here?"

"Just wanting to check in." Aubrey grinned and nodded toward my shoulder. "See how our friend Dez is doing."

Both twins stared, their eyes daring me to say something.

Aubrey made a move to grab my hand. Kale's reaction was instant.

"NO!" It didn't occur to me that Kale could accidentally touch *me.* All I could think of was Kale touching *Aubrey.* I wasn't protecting him, I was protecting myself. If what Dad said was true—still a big if, in my opinion—Aubrey was the only way to cure the poison. If he died, I died. I shoved past Kale and got between them.

The three of them watched me. Aubrey and Able wore amused expressions while Kale's was confused. His gaze lingered for a moment before turning back to the twins.

"She doesn't seem to want you dead. If you don't leave now, I will reconsider."

"Don't go all rebel commando on us, yeah? We'll go."

Aubrey snickered as they turned and started back up the path. Over his shoulder, he called, "I'm sure we'll run into each other again *soon.*"

Once they were out of sight, Kale turned back to me. Suspicion was written all over his face. "The one with the wound—you hit him?"

He'd been unconscious for a short time, so I'd taken my chances. Should have known better. "I hit him in the van while you were out."

He was quiet for a moment. "The wound was fresh."

I knew the look I'd get but said it anyway. "It's complicated."

"Dez," he warned, taking a step closer. "There is something you're not telling me."

"I—"

"What the hell are you two doing standing out in the open?" Dax emerged from the shadows of the trees. He stalked across the field, cell phone in hand. Jabbing it at Kale, he snapped, "And where the hell did you go?"

Kale didn't even blink. "I went to find Dez. You were fine on your own."

Dax, normally impossible to ruffle, looked like he wanted to scream. "Everyone was supposed to stay with their partners!"

"You're not my partner," Kale said. There was no argument in the tone of his voice. Only a simple, static logic that was all Kale. "Dez is.."

Dax might have argued, but his phone began to vibrate. He stared at the screen for a second before waving us forward. "It's Alex. He's in the maintenance house on the south side of the park. He's hurt."

"Hurt? What do you mean, hurt?"

Dax looked worried. He pocketed the cell and nodded to the path leading up to the pool area. "We should hurry."

17

Mom, who we found halfway down the hill, had shifted into one of the Denazen suits once we reached the bottom. Dad, to be exact. There was something eerie having Mom-as-Dad standing there with us. I didn't know whether to laugh or scream.

Or run.

Jade found us as we came through the south gate. She seemed fine but kept looking over her shoulder like she expected someone to come bursting from the woods at any moment. Together again, we'd made our way to the maintenance house where Alex was holed up and were now crouching behind the bushes several yards from the building. Two men stood outside, one blocking the main door, and one in front of the window with a cell phone glued to his ear.

"What's the plan?" I asked, peering over the top of a large bush. Dax still hadn't told us what *hurt* meant, but I imagined it had to be bad if Alex got himself cornered in the first place.

"Shanna will go in and create a distraction. When she has

their attention, Kale will move in and take them out."

Shanna? Dax had a nickname for my mom? What the hell…?

He turned to her and winked. "Ready, Shanna?"

She flashed him a flirty smile—disturbing considering the body she was currently wearing—and stepped out from behind the trees.

"What's going on?" she demanded in Dad's deep, impersonal voice. The sound sent chills up and down my spine. It was a sound bite from my darkest nightmares.

"We've got the telekinetic cornered inside, Sir," the one by the door said. "We called for backup and transport."

"Backup? It's a telekinetic, for Christ's sake. Tranq him, and let's move."

The man held out his tranquilizer gun. "We're out of ammunition. He was evasive. Every time we enter the building, we're assaulted with flying objects."

Mom-as-Dad growled. "*Evasive?* Your incompetence is unacceptable."

Man, she was good. Even though she'd spent the last seventeen years locked away at Denazen, she knew Dad better than I did. She had his mannerisms and tone nailed perfectly. Even his movements and the way he held himself. If I didn't know it was her, I would have never seen the difference.

"He's wounded," the one by the window piped up.

The man by the door was quick to respond. "Bieder shot him, sir. We don't know how serious it is, but he's been in there for a while now."

The suit by the window—Bieder, if I had to guess—cringed.

"You use a deadly weapon to take down a Six we can use and then can't even move in and capture him?"

"In my defense, he *is* a telekinetic," Bieder said. "He'd already taken out Barnes and Farber." He stepped up to Dad, holding out his cell phone. "Take a look at this, sir."

Mom-as-Dad reached for the phone. Her mimics weren't the same as mine. Where I changed the structure of things on a molecular level, hers were illusions and nothing more. All it would take was the tiniest brush of his hands to undo the whole thing.

Which is, *of course*, exactly what happened.

"What the—"

Mom swung as Kale jumped up and exploded from the brush. He charged forward like a speeding Mack truck and crossed the field to where she was. The guy by the door saw him coming and tried to take off, but one well-placed kick from Mom had him grounded. Dax made a beeline for the guy that had been on the cell as he tackled Mom to the dirt from behind.

With everyone's attention elsewhere, I ran like hell for the building and slipped inside. The air was musty, and there was a faint odor of chlorine.

"Alex?" I called, poking my head around a tall stack of boxes. The building was more of an oversized shed and was dimly lit by the moonlight shining through the single, grime-covered window. Hard pressed for space, the park had stuffed an ungodly amount of junk inside, and the whole place was cluttered as hell. Three steps inside, I had to maneuver between two large shelving units covered in dusty boxes and sidestep a lawn mower that looked like it'd been sitting there since the sixties. Once past, I noticed dark puddles on the floor trailing to the back. "Crap. Alex?"

I followed the trail and found him hunched in the corner, wedged behind a stack of plywood, eyes closed. He was bare-chested, having tied his T-shirt in a knot around his upper thigh to stanch the blood flow. I dove forward, grabbing the sides of his face.

"Alex!" I snapped. "Open your eyes. If anyone is going to kill you, it's going to be me!"

The little voice in the back of my head was at war with the sick, sinking feeling in the pit of my stomach. This was Alex, my stomach said. *Alex.* While the little voice reminded me of what he'd done to Kale at Sumrun.

What he'd done to me at Roudey's.

A groan and a flash of hazel. "Dez?"

The sound of his voice lifted the two-ton weight that had settled on my shoulders. "What happened?"

"Was worried they got you," he said, eyes closing. "I saw—saw you and Kiernan go in. Backtracked to find you and…"

"Is he okay?" Kale came up behind me. Jade was right on his tail—as usual.

"I dunno," I said. "It looks really bad."

Blood pooled beneath his leg, creeping outward in a small semicircle around him. His right side was covered, jeans and T-shirt soaked through.

With clinical interest, Kale moved Alex's hand—without vaporizing him since Ms. Annoying was present—from where it clutched his thigh. "The human body can lose much more blood before it begins to shut down. It appears the bullet missed the femoral artery. He'll live."

"Don't sound so excited," Alex mumbled. His head lolled to the side as he opened his eyes a slit.

Kale shrugged. "Disappointed. This would have been a convenient resolution to the problem."

Alex tilted his head, a tiny smirk on his face. "Problem?"

Kale's expression was stony. "You."

"Let's get out of here before anyone else shows up," Dax said, charging through the door. He brushed me aside and grabbed both Alex's hands, hauling him to his feet. "Can you walk?"

Out of the corner of his eye, Alex glanced my way. Taking a

deep breath, he nodded. "I can walk."

• • •

By the time we made it back to the hotel and got Alex patched up and situated, it was Saturday morning. While everyone had been busy fussing over Alex—the bullet passed clean through, and the bleeding was finally under control—I'd slipped into the lobby and looked up Daun's room number on Rosie's computer. Coffee in hand, I went to find her.

"Deznee," she said with a smile. Stepping aside, she held the door open and waved me in. "It's very early. Is everything okay?"

"Oh." Wow. I felt like an ass. With all the chaos and lingering adrenaline of the night's activities, it had totally slipped my mind that it wasn't even seven a.m. yet. Normal people were still sleeping. "I totally spaced on the time. I'm so, so sorry!"

Daun only smiled and held the door open a bit wider. "Come in. Please."

This was a huge risk, but I was out of options. "I need to ask you something. A favor. But first I need to be sure what I say stays between us. No matter what."

If she was suspicious, it didn't show. In fact, nothing showed with Daun. She was easygoing and mellow to the point that you wanted to check her pulse once in a while to be sure she was still alive. She rarely spoke and hardly ever mingled with the other hotel guests. "I'm leaving in two days. Whatever you say will leave with me."

"Leaving?"

She smiled and ran a hand along the edge of her comforter. "It's time to move on. What can I do for you?"

I knew my first request was a no before I even asked. Mom and Ginger would have already thought of it. Still, in order to get it out of my head, I had to hear it for myself. "You know about the Supremacy project, right?"

Understanding bloomed in her eyes. Frowning, she gave her head a slight shake. "I'm sorry. There is nothing I can do for you."

I nodded. Well, at least I knew for sure now. I'd never been one for *what ifs*. "I figured. Didn't hurt to try, though. There's something else."

She'd expected the Supremacy question. The fact that there was something else had caught her off guard. "Oh?"

"This is where the secret part comes in." I rose from the chair, cringing, and pulled aside the shoulder of my T-shirt. "Is there anything you can do for *this*?"

She did her best to hide her surprise but failed. "What—"

I fixed my shirt and sank back into the chair. The last few hours the pain had changed a little, and it was making me nervous. Now instead of a dull ache or stabbing sensation, it was hot and cold. One minute I had the chills, like I was standing in the middle of the Arctic shelf, and the next I was on fire. Every limb burning to the point I was sure I'd combust. Currently the chill was setting back in. I was starting to consider that Dad might be telling the truth.

I wrapped my arms around my shoulders and sighed. "It's some kind of poison. I did something stupid, and one of Dad's employees did this to me."

"This is from a Six?"

I nodded.

She stepped forward and brushed my shirt aside, placing her hand against my bare skin. Her touch was surprisingly cool, like the stethoscope at the doctor's office, and I jumped a little on contact. "Stay still," she whispered, closing her eyes.

Several moments passed before she opened her eyes. "Give it to me straight, Doc," I joked. I had to. The look in her eyes? So not encouraging.

"I'm sorry, Dez. I can't do anything for you."

"At all?"

"This is beyond my abilities—and it's serious. Possibly life threatening."

I felt like a balloon had popped inside my chest. As if mocking me, a rush of heat and a sharp pang skittered down my left arm to my fingers. Possibly life threatening? That was not something I wanted to hear. Standing, I said, "I understand. I had to at least try."

"May I ask why you aren't telling the others?"

"My dad's got these two Sixes—one poisons with his touch and the other heals. He says he'll give me the cure if I turn myself over to him."

She frowned. "And you're afraid Kale will offer to go in your place?"

Again I nodded. "I can't let him go back there. Especially since it might be a moot point, anyway. So far all but one of the kids from the Supremacy project that hit eighteen are dead." There. Dead. I'd finally said it out loud. It wasn't even as hard as I thought it'd be.

Dead. Dead. Dead. I was as good as dead.

"Your situation is not an enviable one. My advice is to tell them."

"You won't—"

"No. But I believe you should. Maybe there is a path you've not thought of. An outside perspective might unveil an answer previously hidden to you."

"No offense, but you sound like a fortune cookie on crack."

"That," she said with a smile, "is the first time anyone's ever said that to me. I do believe I'll remember it for the rest of my life."

18

After leaving Daun, I refilled my coffee and went back to the room to crash. By eight thirty, I gave up and switched on the TV. Mom must have been watching it because it was turned to forty-two, the local access channel. Markus Clamp, a local journalist and conspiracy theorist, had a show she found enthralling for some reason.

I was lucky enough to tune in right at the beginning of yesterday's rerun.

"I'm talking with Sid Fenton, boyfriend of the late Layne Phillips."

Markus Clamp might have been an über tool in my book, but for once he officially had my attention.

On the screen, Sid squirmed in his seat.

"I, like so many others, believe there's more to this story than we're being told. Tell me, Sid, was there anything odd in the days before Layne's death?"

Sid hesitated, and Markus went in for the kill.

"Okay. You're nervous, and I understand that. But you agreed to come on this show, so you must have something to add. Something you want the public to know."

"It wasn't a *random act of violence* like the cops said," Sid spat after a few moments. His expression had gone from nervous to pissed. "And it wasn't drugs like her parents insisted. Yeah, Layne was messing around with some stuff, but she was going through something."

"I don't suppose you care to elaborate?"

Sid just glared at him.

Markus nodded. "Fair enough. How about we try something a little different. I'll say a word, and you tell me if it means anything to you and what. Sound good?"

Sid could tell he was being set up, you could see it in his eyes, but he nodded anyway.

I tucked my feet up and got more comfortable.

"Gang."

Sid actually laughed. "No way. Layne wasn't in a gang, and what happened wasn't *gang* related. This is Parkview, for Christ's sake."

"Unstable."

At this word, Sid faltered. "I wouldn't say unstable. The last few months were hard for her, but she wasn't as cracked out as her parents are making it seem. They tried to tell the cops she was into some weird shit. They tried to head shrink her. It was all bullshit."

"What about...Denazen."

On the screen Sid froze, and I almost toppled off the bed.

Sid didn't say anything, but he didn't have to. The horror was written all over his face. And it didn't escape Markus's notice. "What is Denazen, Sid?"

Sid recovered and straightened in his chair. "It's that law firm that burned down at the beginning of the summer. What's that got to do with Layne?"

Markus gave him a knowing grin. "I was hoping you could tell me."

Sid shifted in his seat.

Markus leaned back. You could tell by the cat-that-inhaled-the-canary grin that he knew Sid was hiding something. Hell, anyone watching knew. Sid didn't know crap about keeping a poker face. "I've got a source that says Layne mentioned keeping a diary to her parents. Maybe there's something in there that could shed some light on things. Any chance you know where it is?"

"Layne didn't keep a diary," Sid said quickly. "She thought they were lame."

"I think you're lying, Sid. I think that diary is the key to connecting your dead girlfriend to Denazen. This source—"

"Who?"

Markus waggled a finger. "A good journalist never outs his source."

Sid stood. His face was bright red as he took a menacing step toward Markus. The vulture didn't even flinch. "You're a hack looking to cause trouble, not a journalist." He flipped Markus off and stalked away from the camera. This wasn't anything new. The few times I'd had the displeasure of catching bits of his show, I'd seen plenty of *guests* stalk off. In fact, it was pretty much his thing. Push people till they snapped and make fun of the resulting explosion.

"Well, there you have it, folks. What *really* happened to Layne Phillips, and what does the Denazen Law Firm have to do with it?" Markus stood. "And where is that elusive diary?"

The rest of what he was saying was drowned out by the little voice in my head. The one that frequently got me into more trouble than it helped me out of. A diary. If she wrote about Denazen, then maybe there was something useful in it. Something about Supremacy or the cure.

It was a long shot. But I had to find out.

• • •

With some help from Google, I knew where I was going and was ready by ten. My mood wasn't sunshine-y. I was sore, not to mention black and blue from my daring attempt to fly, and my shoulder wasn't letting up. A deep ache that intensified each time I moved had set in to keep the constantly oscillating cold/hot wave company. On top of that, every once in a while a wave of nausea would hit. It never lasted long but made me think twice about attempting anything more than water. Even coffee seemed like a bad plan—and *that* was depressing.

My current temperature was elevated by what felt like a thousand degrees. I'd peeled off my hoodie, stripping down to my tank even though the weatherman said it was only in the fifties. The constant back and forth was threatening to drive me insane.

Rosie wasn't at her desk, so there was no one to monitor the front door—which struck me as odd. Rosie never left the desk. But maybe this meant my luck was changing for the better. I was certainly due. I'd be able to slip out and be gone before anyone knew it.

"I thought you'd be sleeping."

Or not.

When I turned around, Kale was leaning against Rosie's desk. An entirely new pain—an aching deep in my chest— washed over me.

"Could say the same about you." I looked around. It was just the two of us. "What, no shadow?"

He pushed off the desk and crossed the lobby, stopping a safe distance away. "Where are you going?"

"Why do you care?" The words spilled from my lips before I could think twice, and I blamed the pain in my shoulder. It was affecting the connection between my brain and my mouth. Mostly.

His eyes went wide. "You're angry. At me?"

"No," I said, stepping away. "Yes. Sort of." Backing up to the door, I leaned against the cool glass. The heat was fading, cold settling in. I pulled the hoodie over my head and tugged the sleeves into place. "Look, I'm sorry. I'm not feeling great, and the whole thing with the party last night—"

"Because I came with Jade."

"That, and you left. *Without* me." The truth was, I *was* angry at him. I wanted to tell him what was going on. With Dad. With the twins. But I was afraid. If he'd been there with me, he would have found out by default, and there'd be no more hiding. The logic really wasn't solid, I was blaming him for something he had no control over, but I didn't care. Not right then, anyway.

"Jade said—"

I held my hand up and pushed off the door. "Do *not* finish that sentence."

"You threw her out a window?"

My rational mind heard a simple question. My emotions, however, heard a bitter accusation, and I snapped. "I saved her ass—and mine!"

His eyes narrowed. With careful, measured steps, he came a little closer. "From what?"

I bit my tongue. Shit. Open mouth, insert entire damned leg. What the hell was wrong with me today? There was no way he'd let it go now.

"Dez," he said, inching closer. "Saved her from what? Tell

me what happened last night. It has something to do with those Sixes in the park. That's where you hit him, isn't it? He was at the party?"

I backed toward the door.

"Dez."

"Yeah, he was there. I think the cops were called as a distraction so Denazen could slip in."

He blinked. "How would they even know we were there? It wasn't one of Ginger's parties."

"Exactly, Kale. Think about it. How did they know?" I waited. When he didn't say anything, I continued. "Because *someone* told them."

"Someone?"

I rolled my eyes.

"You think it was *Jade*?"

"Duh."

He shook his head. "No. You're wrong."

That pissed me off, and I couldn't be sure if it was the poison making me go borderline bitch or the fact that he was actually defending her. "Whatever. I gotta go."

He went to grab my arm but froze. Stepping back, he asked, "Where?"

I shrugged, trying to play it casual. "Stuff to do."

"I'll come." He sidestepped me and pulled the door open.

"No need."

"I'm not stupid." Arms spread wide, he said, "This is still very new to me, but I have eyes—and I know you. I know you're hiding something. You're avoiding me. You never avoid me."

"Not you. I'm avoiding your shadow." He started to say something, but I cut him off. "I can't deal with her, okay? Not now." My voice rose, and I struggled to keep it together. "Everywhere I turn, there she is. With you. All over you. In order for *me* to touch you, *she* has to be there."

"She's not here now."

"And I guess that means I can't touch you. Not without agonizing pain and gut-wrenching nausea. Or, ya know, *death*."

He flinched but said nothing.

I looked around his shoulder, expecting to see her pop out from behind the desk or around the corner. She had the inconvenient-timing thing nailed. When the lobby remained silent, I sighed and kicked at the carpet. Snapping at Kale was stupid. This wasn't his fault. "I'm sorry."

"I want to go with you."

"You don't even know where I'm going."

"I don't care." He pulled his sleeve down tried to take my hand, but I jerked away. The gesture was sweet, and somewhere in the back of my mind, a tiny voice raged. *Why are you so angry? What the hell is wrong with you? This. Is. Kale!*

Sighing, I pulled out Ginger's keys and dangled them in front of him. "Have it your way, but be advised you're now officially guilty of grand theft auto."

"You haven't told me where we're going."

I pulled Ginger's ancient car up to the curb two blocks from the Phillipses' house. The whole ride over I'd been debating what to tell Kale. Keeping secrets from him was hard enough, but actually making up a lie? No way. He'd see right through me. He already knew something was going on with Able.

I settled for getting as close to the truth as possible.

"We're here to search Layne Phillips's place."

He unbuckled his safety belt and shifted in the seat. "The girl from the news?"

I nodded.

"Why?"

"I think she was Supremacy. I think Denazen was behind her death."

"What makes you think she had anything to do with Denazen?"

"Gut feeling," I said, pushing the car door open. "We should hurry. Her parents both work down at the town hall. They're only open till one on Saturdays."

I could tell he wanted more of an explanation but thankfully didn't push. A few months ago, I could have gotten away with simply saying I'd gotten an anonymous tip. Kale was newly free, and as far as he knew, stuff like that happened all the time. Now, though? Now he'd question it. He'd see it as a total *Dez thing*— his explanation for the things I did that everyone else on the planet seemed to find incredibly stupid—or inexplicable.

We walked for a few minutes before either of us spoke.

He pulled his sleeve down and took my hand. "I'm looking forward to Monday."

"Me, too," I said. My fingers twitched, enclosed in the thick material of his hoodie.

When Kale asked me to the homecoming dance, he'd been disappointed to find out that without an actual school, there was no actual dance. He felt like it was his fault I was missing my senior year and was determined to make it as authentic as he could. He'd done hours of research, according to Rosie, and eventually went to Ginger for help. In honor of homecoming, she'd made reservations at Flavour, Parkview's own dinner and dance club, and also extended the invitation to all the Sixes that lived at the Sanctuary. That meant Kiernan would be there. Knowing Jade would be all over Kale—probably wearing some slutty dress—I was thankful.

Someone had to keep me from killing her.

The rest of the way passed mostly in silence. A few times I shot Kale a sideways glance. Shoulders stiff, he kept his eyes straight ahead and said nothing. Twice I caught him flicking his fingers and saw the barest hint of lip movement as he counted. I knew it was my fault, but there was no way to fix it—at least not yet.

"This is it," I said, stopping in front of the dark gray ranch. The lawn was meticulously trimmed, complete with an obnoxious pink flamingo and matching babies. A large pine tree shaded the entire front side of the house, reaching to the edge of the lawn.

"You're sure no one is home?"

I pointed to the empty driveway and made my way around to the back of the house. "No cars."

"How will we get inside?"

I stopped and waved him ahead. "I'll leave it to the expert."

Kale being Kale, I assumed he'd scale something in true ninja style or pick the lock. It's what he did. Super stealthy with a side of infiltration awesome.

Instead, he walked up to the back door and put his elbow through the glass.

"Oh, my God!" I held my breath and shot a quick glance over my shoulder. Tiny plinking sounds filled the air as bits of glass bounced against the walkway. This was a quiet neighborhood. The houses were all relatively close together. It'd be easy for someone in their backyard to see or hear something and scamper off to call the neighborhood watch or whatever they had here. "Are you crazy?"

"There's no one around. It's safe." He reached through, unlocked the door, and pushed it open.

I followed him inside. "There could have been an alarm."

"There were no indications."

I followed him through the door. "Indications?"

He rolled his eyes.

God. I loved when he did that.

"There are no stickers on any of the windows, and there were children playing on the front lawn several houses over. This is a quiet neighborhood. Low to no crime rate. They wouldn't have need of an alarm."

I closed the door behind me and pointed to the steps. "Come

on. We only have a couple hours till Mr. and Mrs. Phillips get home."

We found Layne's room at the top of the stairs. Judging from the condition, I guessed her parents hadn't had the heart to come back in after the night of the party. Clothes littered the floor, and half a sandwich sat on the corner of the desk. Several flies circled above, waiting for their chance to swoop down and grab dinner.

"You take that side," I said, pointing to the half of the room with the window. A large coffee mug in the shape of Road Runner's head sat balanced on the sill. There was a dresser and cedar chest against the wall with a small shoebox in the corner. I wanted the closet and desk for myself. "I'll take this one."

"What am I looking for?" Kale leaned forward and peered into the mug.

"There was a rumor she kept a diary. I'm hoping she has it hidden in here."

Kale didn't look convinced. "Wouldn't someone have found it? Wasn't she killed here? The police would have searched the room."

I shrugged. "Depends on how well she hid it."

We went to work, searching in silence for what seemed like hours. Every once in a while I'd look up to find Kale watching me with an odd expression on his face. He'd open his mouth to say something, but I'd quickly turn away. He didn't push it.

When I checked my phone again, it was almost twelve o'clock. I kicked an empty shoebox across the room and sighed. I was almost through the closet and hadn't found crap. "This blows."

Kale pulled his head out from beneath the bed. "I don't believe she'd leave a written statement confessing Supremacy involvement."

I shoved myself away from the closet and stumbled upright.

My leg had fallen asleep, so I teetered, almost losing my balance. Grabbing for the closest item—a hanger full of large, tacky purses—I tried to keep myself upright. I failed, taking the hanger full of bags along with several of the surrounding sweaters to the floor. I knocked my head against the doorframe and pulled a muscle in my good arm, but it was worth it.

"Wanna bet?" I untangled myself from the pile of clothes and leaned forward. On the wall of the closet, there was a poster of an M.C. Escher painting. The first and most obvious thing that made me suspicious was the fact that it was in the closet. Escher was epic. Why the hell would someone hide him in the closet? The second was a tiny red smudge on the wall at the corner. The poster would have covered the stain, but when I fell, one of the sweaters had come off the hanger and caught the corner, pulling it down.

Holding my breath, I reached out and tore the paper from the wall. Written in what looked suspiciously like dried blood was the word "Supremacy" over and over. Big letters. Small letters. Letters done in squiggles and zigzags. "That is seriously freaky."

Kale came up behind me. He didn't seem fazed. "But it doesn't do much more than confirm your suspicion."

A good point. Big deal? We knew for sure she was Supremacy. That didn't give me anything useful.

Kale inclined his head and knelt down beside me. "Maybe there's something in the panel behind the wall."

"Huh?"

He reached around, grabbing one of the wire hangers off the rod. Unbending the hook, he leaned into the closet and jammed the metal into the wall. A few sharp pokes, and I saw the smallest hint of a seam. A few more jabs, and it separated from the wall, revealing a small cubby hole.

"This might be something," Kale said, picking up a small

leather bound book.

I took the book from him and flipped it open. The first word on the random page I hit was "Supremacy." "Score! Was there anything—"

Kale stiffened. "Shh!"

Muffled voices, then one clear as a bell. "I want a clean sweep of the bedroom. No one leaves till we find that diary."

"Shit!" I started for the window but Kale beat me to it.

"Stuck." There was the tiniest hint of panic in his voice. "We're—"

"Screwed," I said as three men in Denazen's trademark blue monkey suits barged into the room.

20

Kale stepped in front of me, and for the longest second, no one moved.

"This makes my job a whole lot easier," the one in the front said. He eyed me like a supersized golden goose egg that someone had just tossed his way. "I bet Cross promotes me for bringing his *baby girl* home."

Kale chuckled and shrugged out of his hoodie. The sound sent a thousand tiny shivers down the back of my neck. "You know I'll kill you if you come closer."

The man sighed and stepped aside. His colleague had a tranq gun—standard issue, Kale told me once—aimed right at us. "Which is why *you* won't be coming any closer."

I heard the tiny pop as the dart left the gun, followed by a muffled grunt as Kale shouldered me aside. The dart hit the window, and the glass cracked but didn't break.

Kale flew at the men, scattering them apart like a bowling ball headed for the perfect strike. One went down right away.

Eyes wide, he tried to scramble out of the way but wasn't fast enough. Kale's bare hand connected with his face. He shoved hard, and the man stumbled, disintegrating just before colliding with the wall.

One of the others kicked out, catching Kale across the middle. He wobbled and fell to the ground—but he didn't go alone. Twisting at the waist, he kicked his legs around in a circular motion and, with a graceful sweep, caught the man behind the knees.

Meanwhile, the last one charged me. I scooped up the dart from the floor below the window and ran to meet him. He managed to grab me around the throat, but not before I sank the sharp point of the dart into the soft skin of his neck. His fingers flexed once. Twice. Three times—before he let go and staggered away.

He ripped the dart from his neck and threw it to the ground with a growl. "You'll pay for that," he swore.

"I hear that a lot," I said with my sweetest smile, then dodged him as he came at me again, though this time with a lot less grace. The meds on the dart were starting to take effect. I just had to keep him hopping until he went down.

He took another swing. The force behind it threw him off balance and sent his body lumbering sideways into the desk. The chair wobbled to the left and crashed to the ground just in time to trip the agent Kale was dealing with. I made the mistake of watching him go down, ignoring my own guy and giving him the chance to gain the upper hand.

But it was only a halfhearted attempt. The agent's grip was lethargic, and his movements were slow. I was able to buck him off and move away before he even knew what'd happened.

He opened his mouth, but no words came. Eyes rolling back, his body collapsed to the pale blue carpet.

I took a few seconds to admire my handy work. Big mistake. I heard the soft *pop* of the gun again and out of the corner of my eye saw the pointy blur zooming toward me. It would have been impossible to move from its path. Yet somehow I did.

Or *someone* did. Kale.

He crashed into me from the right, sending us both careening sideways. The impact was so hard, I stumbled and collided with the far wall, well out of his reach. He was on his feet again in the blink of an eye, facing off against the remaining Denazen guy.

"This is silly," he said. "You *can't* touch me, and you *won't* be touching her."

The man said nothing, only smiled and reached around to his back. A moment later, he produced a small knife. It made an audible *whoosh* as he sliced it through the air in front of Kale, who avoided it with ease and reached for the man—only he wasn't like the others.

He ducked safely out of reach, whipping the blade in intricate circles. Kale pivoted and spun while the man attempted to carve him into more manageable bits, spinning and swinging the knife with exquisite expertise. Kale advanced as the man skated out of reach. It was like watching an exotic dance. Poetry and grace hiding deadly intent. Once I tried to move forward to help but thought better of it. Kale was focused and deadly. I couldn't take the chance that I'd accidentally get in his way.

A low curse spilled from Kale's lips. The knife had caught his shoulder. At first it was nothing more than a rip in his T-shirt. A few moments later, the edges of the tear began to darken as the wound started to bleed.

Kale, slightly shocked, turned to examine it.

That should have been a huge red flag. But it wasn't until the man relaxed, folded his arms and chuckled, that I saw the reason. Protruding from the back of Kale's other shoulder, was the dart the man shot at me.

Kale must have seen it at the same time I did. His eyes got impossibly wide as he yanked it out. It fell to the floor, bounced twice against the carpet, and lay still at his feet. "I'll kill you long before the effects kick in."

But he didn't sound so sure. In fact, his voice kind of fluttered. I was betting the man hadn't noticed—most people weren't as hyperaware of Kale as me—but it was unmistakable. He might have had the biggest, most badass training Denazen could offer, but in the end, he was only human.

And humans didn't do tranq darts very well.

The man shot forward, foot sweeping the back of Kale's knees. Hampered by the tranquilizer pumping through his system, he didn't move in time and crumpled to the ground. I rushed forward to help him but froze when the man pointed the gun at me.

"Stay put, kid." Turning back to Kale, he wedged a shoe under his chin and laughed. Waving the gun, he said, "Cross is right. You're nothing but an animal. Easy to contain with the right tools."

Groping the ledge behind me, I searched for the Road Runner coffee mug I'd seen when we came in. When my fingers brushed the cool, oddly shaped porcelain, I breathed a sigh of relief. I'd been worried it might have gotten knocked down in the commotion.

Fingers threaded through the handle, I stepped forward and smashed the mug against the man's temple. He dropped the gun and stumbled back. I'd debated mimicking the mug into something more useful—the blow was helpful but had only dazed him. Something like a pipe would have done a bit more damage. But I didn't want to take the chance that Kale was coherent enough to notice. He had no idea my ability had gotten stronger.

The agent groaned and took another step back, rubbing his head. I didn't let up. Following him, I kicked at his gut, sending him off balance and tumbling into the open closet. I slammed the door closed and pulled the small nightstand in front of it before rushing back to Kale.

He was trying to sit up but dazed. Definitely not the super alert guy I was used to. I tried slipping my arms under his shoulders, but he pushed me off.

"No," he mumbled. "Don't touch me. You'll—"

The closet door rattled.

I ignored his protests and snatched the hoodie from the carpet behind me. Wrapping it around his bare arm, I pulled up. But I didn't make much progress. I wasn't a weakling by any stretch, but Kale was a big guy. With a lot of muscle. It translated into a ton of dead weight. "Help me out here, Kale. We gotta go. Now." The closet door rattled again. It wouldn't hold much longer, and I didn't want to be here when the suit got out. "Five minutes ago, actually."

Kale managed to get to his feet, but staying there was harder. Two steps toward the door, and he was down again. I grabbed hold of him and yanked up, but his sleeve rode up, and my fingers brushed against his bare skin. This time the effect was instant. It skipped the pins and needles and shot right for the mind-numbing pain and shortness of breath. I went down beside him, seeing stars and struggling to move the air in and out of my lungs.

As if that wasn't bad enough, the closet door picked that moment to explode outward in a splinter of paint chips and wood. The man snarled and, hands extended, flew at us. Kale, unable to pick himself off the floor, made a grab for the man's ankle as he passed. Suit guy went down with a *thud*.

I moved away, stumbling up and attempting to go around so

I could drag Kale out of the room if I had to, but I didn't make my pass wide enough. My foot caught something, and like the man, I went down again. Hard. I tried to scramble to my feet, but something yanked me across the floor. More like someone. My shirt rode up slightly, the rough carpet biting into my skin. Not the most fun way I could think of to get rug burn...

"Dez..." Kale moaned, rolling onto his side. It took a few tries, but he managed to get on his knees as the man made a swipe for my arm.

A few feet away, Kale was tugging on the hoodie. That was fine. I only needed a tiny bit of skin.

Kicking out with my other foot, I caught the man's shoulder. He let go of my ankle, and I dove for Kale. So did the man.

I reached him with about a half second to spare, grabbing his cloth-covered arm and yanking up the sleeve as I thrust out his bare hand. The man had built up too much momentum. He couldn't stop. The tips of his fingers rammed into the top of Kale's hand. There was an agonizing second where the man's eyes went wide, and then he was gone. Nothing more than a shower of dust clogging the air.

On my feet, I grabbed Kale and pulled him up. He wobbled but stayed upright. "We have to go."

• • •

The rest of Saturday passed slowly. We made it back to the hotel with the diary and no further signs of Denazen, even though I half expected them to be waiting to ambush us on the way in. Ginger swore the hotel was safe, but I wasn't feeling it.

Luckily, when we'd gotten back, there'd been no one around. I helped Kale up to his room, and he crashed. While he was sleeping, I curled up on the chair next to his bed and went through the diary.

Layne Phillips knew she was adopted at an early age. As far as I—and she—could tell, her parents had no idea about her gift or connection to Denazen. At the age of ten, she discovered she could manipulate water. Five months ago, her gift changed. Not only could she manipulate water but its temperature, too. There was entry after entry of experiments logged—all with disastrous results. She'd tried to freeze a bathtub full of water and ended up freezing the water in the pipes of her house. Then, without realizing what she'd done, she'd tried to heat the water, causing the pipes to explode and the entire house to flood.

Another time, she turned on the outside hose and tried to use the water inside to control it, breaking four windows and smashing in the side of her mom's car. The decline in her mental facilities was apparent at the end.

The experiments got stranger and less thought out. In one, she filled her dresser drawers with water. When it leaked out, she tried using her ability to put it back in, becoming frustrated when it leaked out again. Her last noted experiment detailed how she'd gone to Memorial Park after dark and tried to remove the water from the pond.

The more I read, the less sense the pages made. Layne became more paranoid. As far as I could tell, she'd never even been officially contacted by Denazen.

Early next morning, I abandoned Kale's room in favor of food. I'd dozed for a few hours here and there, but nothing much. Things inside my head were churning and wouldn't allow for peace. The nausea seemed to have let up, and having not eaten anything substantial in the last few days, I was feeling peckish.

I pulled my hoodie tight around my shoulders and sank into the kitchen chair to try and get a bowl of cereal down. I'd been starving when I started, but after a few bites, the sugary puffs in the bowl were unappetizing and tasted stale. I shoved it to the side and eyed the diary, then the door. Twice Jade had poked her head in to see if Kale was there. If she did it again, there was a good chance I'd try to strangle her.

Kale was still out like a light, and I was getting fidgety. The diary left me a little confused. Wasn't Denazen supposed to be raising these kids to believe in their glorified bullshit? From what I'd read, Layne Phillips seemed to have no idea who they were or what they were about. She did, however, know about Supremacy. That kind of stumped me till I'd gotten to the end of the journal. Three weeks before her birthday, she started having nightmares. A man appeared, telling her she was destined for great things. He told her all about the Supremacy project and that she'd been *chosen*. The poor girl had been convinced she was headed for the happy house.

"Hey."

I pushed the diary aside and looked up. Kale was standing in the doorway, hair mussed and eyes bleary. For someone who'd gotten a lot of sleep, he looked beat.

"Hey, yourself." I stood. "How do you feel?"

He stepped into the room, rubbing his head. "Fuzzy. Like I hit my head. Did I hit my head?"

I smiled and held out the uneaten bowl of cereal. Kale took it. "It's the drug they use on the dart. It'll go away. Promise."

He took a bite and made a face. Not enough sugar. Kale was the only person on earth I'd ever met to use more sugar than me. He poured it over everything. I'd even caught him sprinkling it on toast a few weeks back. "Are you okay?"

"I'm fine."

He pushed the bowl away and leaned forward. "You're holding your shoulder."

Crap. The pain was pretty much a constant now. The temperature shifts still came and went, but they'd subsided in frequency and strength. I wanted to feel good about this—hoping it proved Dad was lying, and I *was* getting better without help. "Oh. Yeah, slept wrong. Spent the night in the lounge chair in your room."

For a second I was sure he'd call bullshit, but he nodded. "Did you find anything in the book?"

I snorted and grabbed it from the table. "Nothing useful." Waving it back and forth, I smiled. It was Sunday. I was feeling crappy. Some Kale time might make things better. It technically couldn't be *kissy Kale* time, but anything was better than nothing. I'd been thinking about it last night, and I'd finally worked up the guts to tell him what was going on. I wanted to do it before I lost my nerve. "Let's sneak out and hit the hiking trails behind the hotel. I'm restless and could totally go for blowing off some steam. We can talk…"

He didn't answer right away. When he did, it was with a frown. "I'm meeting Jade in a few minutes."

"Meeting Jade?" I couldn't stop my voice from rising. It was a stupid question, I already knew, but I asked, anyway. "What the hell are you meeting her for?"

"Ginger wants us to put in more hours of practice."

"Of course she does," I said. "Ya know, for someone who swears she won't interfere in people's lives, it looks like she's doing enough of it from where I'm standing."

"Am I interrupting something?" Jade appeared in the doorway looking like a teenage boy's dream. Tight denim skirt, strappy sandals, and a top that looked like it belonged on a kindergartener. Someone hadn't checked the weather outside.

"You're always interrupting something," I mumbled. Stepping up to Kale, I said, "Good luck with practice. Come see me after?"

He smiled. "You know I will."

I wrapped my arms around his shoulder and pulled him

close. He was watching me with a mix of hunger and fear. He knew what I was about to do. Part of him wanted it, and part of him was afraid. I knew, because it was exactly how I felt.

The instant our lips touched, I felt a sting. It started small—nothing more than a funky pins-and-needles numbness—but with each second I didn't pull away, it grew sharper and harder to ignore. After a few seconds, his arms wound around my waist, fingers digging in to draw me closer.

I hoped Jade was getting this. Getting that *she'd* never be getting *this*.

It was Kale that broke the kiss. "That hurt, didn't it?"

I wanted to tell him not to go, that I wanted to talk, but I couldn't do it. The resolve I'd felt moments ago about coming clean about Able was already vanishing. There was a part of my brain that knew this was wrong. I'd never been an indecisive person, but I was bouncing around more with this one little thing than a rubber ball.

"Not at all," I lied. To prove my point, I traced a line from his cheek to chin. "See? All good."

The corner of his lip twitched and he smiled—but it was forced. He knew I was lying.

As he turned to follow Jade from the room, I clenched my fist and bit down on the inside of my lip to keep from crying out. It was almost as though Jade's presence was barely affecting me at all anymore. How long before touching Kale meant instant death—even with Jade in the room?

21

I didn't see Kale again that night. When Mom came up to the room, she told me not to wait up because Ginger was making them work overtime.

Ginger was starting to piss me off.

The next day didn't get any better. I was late again and woke to a loud country crap alarm. Mom was nowhere in sight. By the time I made it to the conference room, Alex, Kale, and Jade already had their noses buried in the books, and Ginger was giving me the *if-you're-late-again-you'll-be-scrubbing-toilets* glare.

It wasn't until that evening that my mood improved.

I smiled at the girl looking back at me in the slightly steamed-up bathroom mirror. Her long blonde hair, streaked with deep burgundy chunks, hung in loose ringlets past her bare shoulders. The dress she wore, off-the-shoulder spaghetti straps with a fitted-lace bodice and slightly flared skirt that ended just above her knees, matched the streaks perfectly.

I couldn't wear the dress like it was, but I wanted a minute to appreciate it as it was meant to be. Simple. Stunning. And allowing for some eye-popping skin candy to show.

Pushing my arms through the simple cotton shrug I'd bought along with the dress, I thought about my favorite shirt. A black satin peasant blouse I'd bought last year after falling in love with the sleeves. The shirt was long gone. Taken God knew where along with the rest of my things, but I could still picture it perfectly in my mind.

With a deep breath, I closed my eyes and concentrated. Really, I should have tried this before tonight, but getting a moment alone had been impossible. To keep me out of Kale and Jade's hair, Ginger kept me hopping after *school*. I'd had chores and errands coming out my ears for the last week.

The skin on my shoulders and arms tickled as the fabric of the shrug shifted and twitched. When I dared open my eyes, I couldn't help smiling. It wasn't ideal—I was used to showing way more skin—but it was *definitely* pretty in a sweet, understated sexy kind of way.

My gift was now more visual then sensory. As long as I'd seen it, I could mimic it. This enabled me to change the shoulder straps, meshing the simple black shrug into an extension of the dress. The boring sleeves of the shrug now looked like the ones on my favorite peasant blouse, only in deep burgundy.

This covered my arms—and more importantly, my shoulder. No way would I be able to explain away the ugly, angry blotch Able had left. It had doubled in size, and the lines creeping from the center had thickened.

The neckline of the dress was still dangerously low—there were just some things I wasn't willing to compromise for safety—and the length was still short, but the sleeves would make Mom feel a little better.

When she'd heard about our faux homecoming, she was

more than a little concerned. She said bluntly that Kale's and my obvious inability to keep our hands off each other would result in disaster. I'd assured her we'd be fine, but I could tell by the look on Kale's face at the time he was worried, too.

Slipping a pair of strappy heels to my feet, I fluffed my hair and pulled open the door.

Mom was waiting on the other side.

"I still don't like this," she said, eyeing the dress. I tried to be careful not to show it to her when I'd brought it into the room. Other than Kiernan, I hadn't told anyone about my newly improved mimicking skills. It probably wouldn't worry them that much—I'd never told them about Dad's visit to the post office or what he said about the advancement of Supremacy's Sixes—but why invite trouble?

"It'll be fine. We'll bc careful." I did a little twirl. "What do ya think? Awesome, right?"

She frowned and took several steps back. "It's red."

"Nah. Burgundy. Totally different color." It was my mission in life to cure her of her aversion to red. It was one of my favorite colors, and I wasn't willing to give it up.

There was a knock on the door.

A moment later, Mom was ushering Kale into the room. He stepped forward, eyes glued to mine, and held out an armful of deep purple roses. "Curd said these will seal the deal."

I took the flowers, trying hard not to laugh at the expression on Mom's face. "Since when are you taking dating advice from *Curd*? More importantly, *why* are you taking dating advice from Curd?"

He frowned at the flowers. "Is this wrong?"

I glanced over my shoulder as Mom took the flowers and backed away. She busied herself with finding something to put them in.

"They're perfect," I said with a grin. "So, Curd?"

"We spoke at the party. He asked me if he could have Jade."

I snickered. That was *so* Curd. "And what did you say?"

He looked kind of puzzled. "I told him of course. As soon as I was done with her."

I should have been mad, but really, he had no clue what he'd said. "I'll bet my right arm you've earned the respect of Parkview's most renowned letch."

"He did seem pleased." He held out his hand, and I saw he was wearing black gloves. "You look really nice."

"You, too."

"Curd told me to say that, too." He frowned again. "But I don't like his way of saying it."

"Oh?"

With his free hand, he brushed a gloved finger across my cheek. The satiny material was cool and smooth against my skin, and it made me ache for the warm, calloused touch of his bare hand. "Beautiful. You look beautiful."

"I like your way better."

His frown disappeared, blooming into a very satisfied smile. "Good."

And just like that, all the Jade-tension melted away. How could I second-guess his feelings? The *no-touching* thing was no big deal. It was temporary. Trivial. Something like that couldn't come between us. Especially not with him looking at me like he was. Like I was the only bit of light in a world full of dark.

There was another knock on the door. Against my will, I let go of Kale's hand and pulled it open. Standing there, looking amazing in a strapless, shimmering green gown complete with dangerous slit, was my least favorite person on earth.

"Is Kale here?" She smiled and batted her overdone eyes. Red hair swept into a loose up-do with tiny tendrils artfully escaping, Jade looked like she belonged on a runway in Paris rather than the streets of Parkview. I looked good, but necessity had me stepping out in something way more conservative than usual. She had me beat in the drool-worthy department.

"Where *else* would he be?"

"He was supposed to meet me in the lobby five minutes ago." She leaned around me as Kale came to the door. "Ready?" She beamed at him.

I whirled so fast that my head spun a little. "What does she mean, *ready*?"

Jade answered for him. "Reservations? The reason I'm wearing this killer dress?" Then, as an afterthought, she said, "Yours is *cute*, too. Sleeves are safer, huh?"

Then it hit me. "You're bringing another girl on our first official date?"

For a second, Kale looked confused. Then he frowned. "That's bad, isn't it?"

I *understood* why Jade was tagging along. Really, I did. In fact, I should have seen it coming even before she showed up. It would be disastrous for Kale to go without her. All it would take was an accidental brush or a simple misstep, and someone's life could easily be over. Still, even knowing that, I was annoyed.

I took his hand and pulled him out the door. "Let's just say it won't win you Boyfriend of the Year."

The car ride was weird. Like something out a junior high first-date nightmare. Rosie drove us to the restaurant in her minivan. As if that wasn't bad enough, Jade made a big stink about seating. She stated—in an annoyingly rational manner— that I should take the front seat. I didn't want to start building up my resistance to her aura before the dance. It was safer that way.

Yeah. *Her* safety, maybe. Before the night was over, there was a very real chance I'd kill her and bury the body behind the restaurant.

We entered Flavour to find the place packed. Couples were crammed on the dance floor, swaying to the soft music of the band at the front of the room. Elegant, but not exactly my idea of a party.

I gave our name to the hostess, and she led us through the crowd, heading for the back of the room where Kiernan was already sitting.

She saw us and stood. "Hey, can I talk to you for two seconds?"

I glanced back at Kale and Jade, who'd already settled at the table. Next to each other. "I guess," I grumbled.

Kiernan led me to the corner. Her face was flushed, and she looked ready to freak. "I have a favor to ask."

"Why do I get the feeling you're not about to ask for help moving furniture down a narrow set of steps?"

"I met this guy a few days ago on campus. We kinda flirted and, well, he was shy, so I asked him out."

"So this is why you've been scarce lately, you little vixen!" At least that explained her ditching me. It didn't help that she hadn't told me, but at least there'd been a reason. "So you asked him out... Out as in here, tonight, out?"

"Yeah. Since Ginger invited me to your little homecoming stand-in, I thought I'd use it as a dry run. Hope that's okay?"

"That's great! Where is he? Is he hot?"

"He ran to the bathroom just before you guys came in. Should be back any second now."

"So what's the favor?"

"Just try to make him feel comfy? I think I really like him. We've talked on the phone for hours, and we have a ton in common. This is, like, one of the best things that's happened since..."

Since we'd convinced her to leave her home and everything she'd ever known. A pang of guilt washed over me. Kiernan was a little rough around the edges, so we all sometimes forgot how hard all this was on her. The one thing I'd learned fast was that she kept a lot hidden. She wasn't an emotional sharer, so for her to be coming to me about this guy like this, it had to be pretty big.

I grabbed her hand, resolving to make her crush feel like a rock star if at all possible, and started back toward the table. "Of course. Start talkin'. What's his name? What's he like?"

Her cheeks flushed, and she beamed. Pointing to the door, she said, "Look. There he is."

I followed her gaze, and all the air left the room.

She tugged me past our table and maneuvered us through the thickening crowd, eager to get across the room to her date. With each step, my legs threatened to give out.

When we got to him, he was all smiles. A six-foot bundle of charm and hotness.

A total illusion.

"Dez, this is Able."

"Able," I repeated. There was a possibility everyone in the room could hear my pulse pounding. The temperature plummeted, but I was positive I was starting to sweat.

His previously wild, longish hair was slicked back, and the black, chipping polish on his fingernails was gone. Erased without so much as a speck. There were no dark smudges under his eyes, and tonight, both irises were an unremarkable brown color. Contacts. The bastard had gone as far as getting contacts to lure her in. Kiernan was a sucker for guys with *sweet brown eyes*.

"Nice to meet you, *Dez*."

His grin widened like he intended to swallow me whole as he reached for my hand. The memory of our encounter on the roof, and of the dream that followed, his cold lips skimming across my shoulder, sent a chill down my spine. I jerked away before he had a chance to touch me.

He chuckled and winked at Kiernan. "Don't worry. I'm not contagious—unless I wanna be, yeah?"

I opened my mouth, but the words just wouldn't come. He was watching, eyes daring me to say something.

"Hey," I managed, throat dry. This was beyond bold. How was he going to explain himself to Kiernan when Kale recognized—and attacked him? He couldn't possibly think he'd get away with being here.

I did a quick scan of the room. There was no sign of Able's creepy other half. Dad couldn't have sent him here to bring me in. He'd know better than that. Maybe this was just a scare tactic. A mind fuck. Definitely something Dad would do to keep us hopping.

"Shall we?" Kiernan hooked her arm through Able's and flashed me a brilliant smile. "We're going to step out and get some..." She winked. "Fresh air."

What could I do? Stop her? That would cause a scene—and something told me that was what Able wanted. "Sounds like a plan."

They turned and wove through the crowd. She'd be safe. He wasn't here for her. It was me they were after. And Kale. When I got back to the table, Kale and Jade were having an animated conversation about the importance of salad forks. She was smiling and nodding, but I knew for sure that she wasn't paying attention. The giveaway? When I got close, she leaned in and put her arm around his shoulder with a smirk. She knew I was watching.

"This song is perfect. Want to dance, Kale?" Jade asked, standing. She made a show of adjusting her gown, rearranging the slit so most of her leg showed, and tugging down the bodice so there was enough cleavage visible to block out the moon.

He smiled at her, and my heart cracked just a little. To see him light up for someone other than me was almost more than I could take.

But instead of swinging Jade around the dance floor, he turned to me, gloved hand extended and fingers wiggling several times. "We'll stay close to the table."

Close to *Jade*, he meant.

He didn't wait for me to respond. Lacing his fingers with mine, he pulled me to the edge of the dance floor just as the band began the slow, sugary beats of the Rolling Stones's "Wild Horses." Wrapping one arm around my waist, he pulled me close.

"You look beautiful."

I smiled. Possibly even blushed. Standing here with him was almost enough to forget about Able being outside with Kiernan. "You said that already."

He shrugged. "It was worth repeating." Brushing a stray hair from my eyes, he said, "You changed your hair."

Standing so close to him, swaying on my uncomfortably high heels, was the perfect time. He'd just given me a golden opening to tell him about my gift and its wonkiness with the hair comment, but something stopped me. "Yeah. I know you said you liked the brown, but—"

"I like it." He smiled. Leaning in, he placed the softest of kisses across my forehead. In my ear, he whispered, "I miss you."

When he pulled back, all I could focus on were his eyes. Icy blue beams of intense zapping my heart into oblivion. "I'm right here," I said.

With his other hand, he tilted my face up. "Are you?"

"Of course." I almost added, *And so is Jade*, but didn't. I could feel her eyes on me. If looks could kill, I'd be twelve feet under with a condo over my grave.

A few feet away, an elderly couple danced, the man spinning his wife out, then dipping her dramatically. It reminded me of the first time Kale and I danced.

He started to lean close again but hesitated. "I feel like…"

I held my breath, hoping for—something. I didn't know what. Maybe I wanted Able to walk in. It could have been that I wanted Kale to flat out call my bluff. Really, the short of it was, I wanted to be forced into telling him the truth. Deep in my gut, I knew that was the only way I'd get it out. "Feel like what?"

He shook his head. "I don't know. Something is off. You're distracted."

I sighed. Of course I was. My new BFF was currently in the parking lot, possibly sucking serious face with a killer, I was months away from losing my shit and going bonzo, oh, and there was that pesky little poison working its way through my system— all while keeping it to myself to protect the ones I loved.

Distracted? It was a miracle I hadn't had a coronary yet. If I did somehow manage to survive, I'd be gray by the time I was twenty. The song faded, then melded seamlessly into the next, this one a smidge faster.

I tightened my grip on Kale and took a deep breath. "Things are kinda screwed up right now."

"There's something you aren't telling me."

Yes!

No.

Crap. "No, there isn't."

"There is," he insisted, leading us to the right a bit. We'd gotten too far from the table and drifted onto the dance floor. "You're so far away from me all the time. Evasive. I feel like I can't find you."

"Maybe if Jade would get out of the way, you could." I regretted my words immediately. Way to sound like a five-year-old.

"She's trying to help."

"Herself, maybe," I said under my breath.

"You should give her a chance. She's nice. I like her. She's my—friend."

My mouth dropped open, and I had to consciously force myself not to let go and step away. I couldn't help it. "Your *friend*? Kale, she doesn't want to be your *friend*. She wants more than that."

"You still think I'll want her because I can touch her."

"She can be something I can't right now—a lifeline to a normal life—and you're only human." I glanced out over the dance floor. It was full of couples, embraced and entranced by each other, uninhibited, and it made me jealous.

His expression hardened. "Only human? Is that what you think? That my feelings for you can be overturned by something as simple as physical contact?"

There was really no way for me to answer without sounding like a complete bitch. In some ways that was exactly what I thought. I hadn't had much luck in the love department. Alex, my dad—I'd always gotten shafted.

And then I'd met Kale. I fell—hard. But in the deepest recesses of my mind, I waited for the inevitable. For that point where he realized I wasn't what he wanted or wasn't good enough. I would go from being Ms. Right Always to Ms. Right at the Time.

He pulled me just a bit closer, eyes on mine, as we swayed to the music. "You are my lifeline. My normal life."

"So you're saying you're *not* crushing hard on the fact you can paw people without killing them while she's around?"

His eyebrows went up.

I sighed. "You like being able to touch people, right?"

He tore his gaze from mine and surveyed the room full of people with a look of wonder. This was really his first time out in a crowd when he didn't have to worry about accidentally hurting someone. "Oh. Yes, I do." When he turned back, he was smiling.

"But I won't need her for that. I'm going to learn to control it."

"Have you considered the possibility that you won't?"

"Of course not." He stopped swaying as the song faded, the DJ announcing an anniversary, and pulled me to the side. "You don't believe I can do it?"

It wasn't so much the look on his face—a *you just ran over my puppy, then stole all my candy* expression—as the tone of his voice. Hurt. Rejected. I was making it sound like I had no faith in him, and that wasn't it. I had more faith in Kale than I did any other person on earth. What I lacked faith in was nature. The universe. Maybe there just wasn't a way to fix this. Deep down, I kept wondering even if he did learn control, would the universe let me back in? I'd gambled for his life and won, but there had to be a price to pay. There was *always* a price.

"I'm sorry," I said. "If anyone can do this, it's you. This whole thing just has me tied in knots."

He took my hand and spun me around slowly as the music started again. "Knots?"

"It's an expression. Confused. I'm just confused." I made a decision. This thing with Able was starting to really scare me. I'd been convinced it was nothing more than a ruse to force me in the direction Dad wanted, but after talking to Daun, I wasn't as confident. I needed Kale on my side. By my side. "Look, this has gotten really compli—"

"My turn," a voice said from behind us. Jade was standing there looking gorgeous in her barely there emerald dress. "It's impolite to let a girl sit alone at a table. I believe you owe me a dance."

Kale looked from Jade to me. I could have said no. Kept him all to myself and pushed forward with the damn confession. That would have been the intelligent thing to do. But it would also make it seem like I felt threatened by her. And I didn't.

Not really.

Plus I still had Able to deal with. The longer he stayed out there with Kiernan, the more nervous I got. "It's fine," I said with a forced smile. "I need a drink, anyway."

Kale nodded and took her hand, and my stomach turned just a little. A part of me was hoping he'd refuse and stay with me on his own, but that wasn't fair. I told him I didn't mind. I'd *lied*. That wasn't something Kale really understood, so how could I blame him?

I watched them float onto the dance floor, weaving farther out than we'd dared go. Why should they stick to the edge? With Jade wrapped around him like a boa constrictor, everyone was fairly safe.

Beyond them, I saw several familiar faces. Barge was dancing close to a girl his own age, a slight brunette in a purple cocktail dress and kitten heels. They looked cozy. Every once in a while she'd giggle, and he'd light up like the sun. A few feet away, Panda was there with Sira, who seemed uncomfortable with the whole situation. I'd bet Ginger had tapped her to chaperone. Panda, being the gentleman, must have asked her to dance. All in all, the whole scene screamed of blah. I was about to turn to the door—I needed to check on Kiernan—but someone tapped me on the shoulder.

"I can cut in now, yeah?"

I sucked in a deep breath and looked around, frantic. Kale was with Jade, swaying to the music on the farthest edge of the dance floor. I could barely make them out through the crowd. "Where's Kiernan?"

Able flashed me a wicked grin. "She ran to the bathroom, then was heading out to show Aubrey a *really* good time in the backseat of my car."

"You're a sick shit."

He took my hand and dragged me onto the dance floor. "Aww. You're too sweet."

His skin was cold and clammy. How the hell had Kiernan not noticed its wrongness? I fell in step with the music, determined to keep it together. Able wanted me to make a scene and attract attention. I refused to give him that.

"So who's that with your boy?"

I didn't answer, following his gaze to where Kale and Jade were dancing dangerously close. Kale kept glancing over his shoulder, searching for me, I assumed, while she tried to keep his undivided attention.

"They seem pretty cozy."

Poking. Able was just poking me to get a reaction. Two could play that game. "Cut the crap. I know about Jade—I'm not an idiot. She's keeping him on that end so he can't see you."

He chuckled. "You *do* have it all figured out, yeah?"

"Yeah," I snapped. "Wanna know what else I know? You're gonna leave Kiernan alone after tonight."

"Demanding little thing, yeah?" He chuckled and spun me around. "How 'bout you leave with me, and I'll never talk to Kiernan again? Then you can shield your friend from my *obvious* bad influence, and I can let my brother heal you so you don't die an agonizing, wasteful death. Everybody wins, yeah?"

"What about Kale?"

"Not worried about him. Soon as you're tucked away, Cross knows he'll come running." He paused, tilting his head to the right. With a grin, he nodded across the room.

The crowd parted slightly. Jade was pressed up against Kale with both arms wrapped around his neck. Their faces were so close that if you saw them from a certain angle, it might have looked like they were kissing.

"Then again, maybe you're not the beginning and end of his

universe anymore, yeah?"

Suddenly I changed my mind about wanting Kale to see him. *Look. Turn this way*. But the song came to an end, and Jade led him off the dance floor and back to the table. The waitress was just setting down our drinks. He followed her without so much as a glance backward. Apparently I'd been forgotten. With a sick lump in my throat, I watched as they each took a glass, weaving back through the crowd and to the door.

"I'm not going with you," I told Able.

"Your dad explained it, yeah? I was standing right there. You know what's going to happen?" He trailed his finger down my neck and nudged aside the shoulder of my dress. "Wow. Hit you *hard*, didn't I? You don't have much time, girly. Starting to feel it, yeah? Random chills. Flashes of heat. Dull, aching pain that increases until your eyes won't stop watering? He left out a few things. Have the hallucinations started yet?"

"If you don't remove your hand, I'd going to rip it off." I kept my voice even, but the truth was, his fingers on my bare skin turned my stomach. And his words? Even worse. He was scaring the crap out of me. Hallucinations?

"I'll take it from here," a voice said.

Able released my hand and stepped away. "No-number-Alex. How ya doin', man?"

Alex might not be my first choice for a white knight, but at that moment, I didn't give a damn. I would have taken Sal, the piss-soaked homeless dude on the corner of Fifth and Mesher.

"I've overstayed my welcome, yeah? No problem." Able turned to Alex and winked. "Ask her if the pain's set in yet." Giving me a long once-over, he sighed. Before I could move away, he clasped a hand down on my left shoulder and gave it a tight squeeze. Involuntary tears stung the corners of my eyes. "See you *real* soon, girly."

Once Able was out of sight, I turned back to Alex. The room erupted in applause as a live band began setting up in the corner. "What are you doing here? You don't live at the hotel."

"What am I doing here? What was *he* doing here?" He narrowed his eyes. "Ya know, this is becoming an annoying trend, Dez. I save your ass, and you act like a bitch."

"Did I look like I was in mortal danger? We were just talking."

"He was at your house waiting for you, and he works for Denazen. Oh, yeah, and he was driving the van from hell—or did you forget? He wasn't here hoping for a hookup."

"He's actually Kiernan's date."

"Her—"

"She doesn't have a clue who he is."

The singer, a willowy girl in a stunning black cocktail dress, announced they'd be taking requests for the next hour, then stepped back onto the stage as the guitarist struck the first chords of a new song.

"You have to tell her!" Alex snapped over the music. "You're putting her in danger by *not* saying anything." He glanced around the room, eyes falling on the table. "And what does Freak Boy say? How come he hasn't—"

"Kale hasn't seen him. Someone is keeping him conveniently busy."

Fred the labret bead wobbled on Alex's chin. "Kiernan is your friend! Since when do you bail on your friends, Dez?"

"Dad's not interested in her at the moment," I snapped back. Honestly, though, Alex was one hundred and fifty percent right. Not letting Kiernan know about Able was dangerous. Dad might be focusing on me, but if an opportunity to snag a useful Six came up, he wouldn't pass it by. I'd need to either come clean or think of a way to tell her to stay away from him.

"Just tell her the damn truth," Alex growled.

He moved a step back, never taking his eyes off me. I looked away—probably the worst thing I could have done. Unfortunately, Alex knew me too well. He'd been able to lie to me, but I'd never been able to slip much past him.

"You're hiding something," he said. "What is the—" His eyes went wide.

I should have moved. Backed out of his reach. Turned and ran like hell through the crowd and for the door. But I couldn't. His expression kept me rooted. I followed his gaze to my shoulder. The sleeve of my dress was just slightly out of place from where Able's fingers had been.

Before I could move my slow ass out of the way, Alex reached out and brushed the fabric further to the side. It shouldn't have been an issue. When I'd left the hotel, the angry red blotch and spiderweb black veins only came to the tip of my collarbone. But the poison was spreading.

And it seemed to be speeding up.

Before I could stop him, Alex grabbed my hand, pulling me closer. Too fast, he reached up and pushed the shoulder of my dress to the side, face pale. The black lines had crept past my collarbone.

"What the hell is that, Dez?"

I was tempted to walk away, but knowing Alex, he'd run straight to Ginger just to piss me off. "Remember that night on the roof of your old building? When Able touched me? It's some kind of poison."

Alex looked like he was going to be sick. He opened and closed his mouth several times, doing his best imitation of a fish. "Daun," he finally spat, twisting me toward the door. "We need to get back to the hotel."

I pulled away from him. "Daun's gone. 'Sides, don't you think I already talked to her? She tried. There was nothing she could do."

Some of the color returned to his face. "Jesus — the way you've been acting… For a second, I thought no one knew about this."

"They don't. The only one who knows is you. And well, Daun, but she's gone, so that doesn't matter."

"Are you insane? Have you taken a good look at that thing?"

"It's complicated, okay? There's a cure."

"Which you obviously don't have."

"Well, no. But I know there is one. That's good enough for now."

Alex could be a dick, but he was generally pretty sharp. "Your dad has it, doesn't he?"

"Pretty much."

"What happens if you don't get it?"

I rolled my eyes. "I'm not *sure*."

He slammed his foot down. Several people at the table next to us looked up. I recognized a few of them. All residents of the Sanctuary.

"You're not sure? Are you kidding?"

"Dad wants me to believe that it's going to kill me," I admitted.

"You're fucking certifiable, you know that? First, you let Kiernan go off with some guy who's working for your father, now you're hiding some killer rash? Lemme guess. He wants to trade that asshole for the cure." Alex took a step back, realization sparking like a wildfire behind his eyes. "Holy shit, Dez. That's why you haven't told them. You're protecting that freak. He doesn't know, does he?"

"No. And it stays that way. Besides, it's not about Kale anymore. Dad said he'd trade the cure if I turned *myself* over to him. Plus like I said, he wants me to believe it's going to kill me. That doesn't mean it's true."

Alex turned and started for the door. "This is crap."

I rushed forward, jumping in front of him. "*This* is my choice."

"You need to tell them. Tell Ginger. She can fix this."

"What the hell? Now all of a sudden you've got this creepy blind faith in Ginger? Since when?" I took a deep breath and grabbed his arm, pulling back with all my strength. "Alex, I'm asking you—begging you—don't say anything. Just give me a little more time. I need to figure this out."

He pulled away. "Doesn't look like you have a lot of time to think."

"Think about what?" Kiernan came up behind us.

"Where's Able?" I asked before Alex could answer.

She frowned. "He got a call and hadda bolt. Seemed funky, though. Like guy-code, ya know? Call me at such and such a time, and if things blow, I have an excuse to bail?"

"Might not be such a bad thing. Dez said the dude was freaky." Alex turned to me. "Right?"

Kiernan frowned. "You didn't like him?"

Great. Nice of Alex to put me on the spot. His way of forcing me to tell Kiernan, I guessed. Yeah? Well, no one was forcing my hand. I did things my way. On my own time. "It's not that," I said, placing a hand on her shoulder. "He was just—he was all over some chick at the bar when you ran to the bathroom."

Kiernan's eyes went wide. "Are you serious?"

I nodded, avoiding Alex's heated stare. "I know, right? She left a little while ago. Bet that phone call was an excuse to bail because of her."

"That bitch," she cursed.

I felt horrible for breaking her heart like that, but better safe than sorry. I needed to be sure she wouldn't try contacting him.

She threaded her arm around Alex's waist. "You came alone, right? Be my date for the rest of the night?"

He looked like he wanted to say no. But with a smile I knew was totally fake, he said, "Looks like it's my lucky night."

"Wow. *That's* a statement, Dez." Jade came up behind us. The grin on her face made me want to shove her in front of a moving truck. Of course they'd come back now. Able was gone. The coast was clear. It was safe. Kale was beside her, and I couldn't help noticing how his hand rested against the small of her back.

"Um," Alex said, looking around. He took my hand and started dragging me toward the door. "I think we should leave. Now."

I glanced over my shoulder at Kale. His expression was a mix of confusion and surprise. "When did you do that?"

"Do what?" I asked as Alex shoved me out the main door and into the hall. Dragging me to the end, we burst onto the outside steps and didn't stop till we'd made it around the corner of the building.

Kiernan and the guys stared at me like I had three heads, and Jade was grinning like the mean girl in school when the class nerd trips in the middle of the hallway.

"Feel free to tell me what just happened." I scanned their faces. Nothing. "Anyone?"

Kale reached for a strand of my hair, his head tilting to the left. "You dyed it?"

"Idiot," Alex snapped before I could respond. "When do you think she had time to *dye* it? Between when you left to go suck face with the super slut here and the last song?"

Kale turned away from me and stepped to Alex. "I know exactly what that means, and if you say it again, I'll touch you."

"Sorry, dude," Alex said, waving his hands. He flashed Kale a mock frown. "I don't swing that—"

"Focus here, people!" I yelled.

"Dez," Kiernan said, frowning. She reached up and pulled the clip in my hair free before I could stop her. "Your hair is, um, green."

"Matches *my* dress perfectly," Jade said with an evil grin. "I know I said it before, but really, you look *good* in green, Dez."

I knotted my fingers through the ends of my hair and pulled

them forward so I could see. Sure enough, the strands poking out were a really cool shade of emerald.

Alex looked smug. He didn't know about my newly improved gift, so I was betting he thought this had something to do with Able's poison. Because that made so much sense, right? Poison that turned your hair green? Moron… "So, any ideas how your hair changed color?"

I shot Kiernan a *help me!* expression, but she only shrugged, indicating I was on my own. "I—"

Alex folded his arms. "I've got a theory. Maybe—" A squeaky, chipped voice suddenly split the air, screaming for people everywhere to follow the sound of his voice and kill whoever was holding the phone.

Saved by Kiernan's cell.

As she dug it out of her purse, Alex glared at me. He was seconds away from spilling. I could see it in his eyes. This was the kind of situation where I wished my gift was something more useful than mimicking.

Mind control would have been awesome.

"We gotta book," Kiernan said, snapping her phone closed. She dropped it back in her purse and pointed toward the parking lot. "That was Rosie. Something's wrong at the hotel."

24

Thankfully Alex had come in his rental car—and alone. I'd suggested heading back inside to grab some of the others, but Kiernan insisted we didn't have time. She was freaked by whatever Rosie had said on the phone. The entire way to the hotel, her eyes darted back and forth as she fiddled with the straps on her shoe. When we pulled up in front of the main doors and he killed the engine, everything was dark.

And wrong.

From the car, we couldn't see much. The only thing visible inside were the red emergency lights above the door.

"The hotel lost power!" Kiernan whined as she climbed from the backseat. She slammed the door closed and stomped her foot. "*That* was Rosie's big drama?"

"What, *exactly*, did she say when she called?" I'd made sure to sit in the front seat. I didn't trust myself to sit in the back with Jade and not strangle her. The entire walk to the car, she'd made snide comments about my hair—which was still a funky shade of green. If it wasn't for the fact that everyone was watching, I'd have hauled off and decked her, not that it would have done any good. Kicking the ass of someone you couldn't actually hurt was pretty pointless. But I was willing to give it my all. I was nothing if not determined.

Alex pocketed his keys and came around to the passenger side of the car.

Hands on hips, Kiernan said, "Not much. This is Rosie we're talking about. Queen of the cryptic and annoying. She just said something was *wrong* and get back ASAP. She sounded scared though."

"Something's so not right about this." I pulled off my shoes. Kiernan had convinced me to wear heels, and with my swimming head and unstable equilibrium, it'd been a miracle that I hadn't face-planted yet. I wasn't taking any chances. The heels fell to the pavement with a subtle *clomp*, and I started for the door, but Alex stopped me.

"Don't you think you should wait out here?"

I looked around. Kale was glaring daggers at Alex, who was staring at me like I'd lost my mind. Jade was eye-humping Kale like a lovesick puppy while Kiernan looked ready to kick her ass.

Seriously. Worse-timed drama *ever*.

"Why the hell would *I* stay out here?"

"Maybe we should split up? A few of us go around to the back?" Kiernan turned to me. "Ginger gave you the compactor door key, right? You and I could try to get in that way while the others try the Dumpster door."

"Yeah, but—"

"We stay together," Kale said, taking the lead.

No one argued—including Alex. You couldn't dispute the facts. And the facts were, Kale was trained for this kind of thing. Breaking and entering. Sneak attacks. All-around ninja stuff.

Alex could name each member of every nineties alternative band ever formed. Kale could kick all their asses. It just was what it was.

We found the main doors open, which might have been simply odd anyplace else, but at the Sanctuary? It was freaking scary. Because Denazen was a constant threat, Ginger went to extreme lengths in regards to security, and I was pretty sure after the van thing, she'd beefed it up even more. The hotel was normally locked up tighter than Scrooge McDuck's money pit.

Kale stopped just inside the door, staying perfectly still.

"What is it?" I whispered.

After a few moments passed, Kale said, "Something is wrong."

"Wow," Alex hissed. "Figured that out all on your own, did you?"

"Where is everyone?" Kiernan grabbed my hand and squeezed. "Because this is seriously squicky…"

Kiernan's hand. That was it!

Although it irritated me to do it, I grabbed Alex's hand. "As cheesy as this is gonna sound, everyone join hands."

Alex looked from my face to our tangled fingers and smirked. "As much as I like this, I'm thinking now's not the time to sing 'Kumbaya.'"

Kale growled.

"Idiot. Kiernan can make us all invisible. We can move through the hotel and check things out without being seen." I turned to Kiernan. "Right? Or is it too many people?"

She winked at me. Since coming to the Sanctuary, Kiernan's ability had gotten a little stronger. When we'd first met over the summer, she could only blend in to her surroundings if she was still or moved slowly. Now she had much more range of motion.

"Nah. I'm awesome like that." Everyone's hands linked,

there was the slighted hint of a ripple in the air, and Kiernan smiled. "We're good to go."

As we made our way through the lobby, around Rosie's desk, and down the hall, I tried not to think about Kale holding Jade's hand. It was out of necessity—that was all. There were more important things to focus on. Like the complete and total lack of light and the eerie silence that filled the air.

Part of me wanted to think we were overreacting. Just a power outage. Rosie had just called to ruin our night. We'd find her sitting in the kitchen with a cup of coffee and a magazine, and she'd say, *Sorry. False alarm.* Happened all the time. She lived to find new ways to annoy me. Kind of like the way I'd loved to piss Dad off. It was more than a hobby. It was a way of life.

Another part knew better.

We reached the end of the hall where it opened into the common room and froze. Thanks to the emergency lights lining the ceiling, we could see it was a wreck. The TV was on the floor, shattered—again. This was crazy. At this rate, we would singlehandedly keep Samsung in business! The coffee table was broken, too, splintered bits and pieces all over. The lounge chair was tipped on its side, and the couch was knocked up against the far wall, cushions strewn around the room like discarded toys. It looked ten times worse than when Kale and Alex went at it—and that was saying a *lot*.

Kale sighed. "Dez?"

I swallowed. The dark in his voice made me nervous. "Yeah?"

"Get back, please."

And then hell broke loose.

Kale released Jade's hand, which broke the connection to Kiernan, rendering him totally visible. Diving for something on the floor—one of the severed table legs—he swung up into the darkness. The bone-crunching *thunk* echoed through the room as the wood connected with something.

Someone.

Alex was the next to let go. This sucked for Jade since she had his other hand, and now that he was visible, so was she. The enemy wasted no time, reaching from the darkness to make a swipe for her. With a wave of Alex's hand, the couch jumped forward, knocking into a dark figure. Jade screamed and jumped aside as he lost his battle with gravity and fell to the ground in front of us. The man tried climbing to his feet, but Kale was there in an instant with a perfectly aimed kick to the head. There was a grunt, and the guy went down like a hundred pounds of coffee.

Someone down the hall screamed. Seconds later, a loud boom shook the floor and rattled the large shelving unit against the wall. The cordless shimmied off the end table on the far side of the room. Everyone scattered.

I didn't see which way Alex or Kiernan went, but Jade ran toward the kitchen. Kale, still wearing his gloves, grabbed my arm and took off back down the hall toward the lobby.

"It's Denazen," I spat, flattening myself against the wall. I was glad I'd left my shoes by the car.

Kale turned to me, eyebrows raised. "Of course."

"Rhetorical," I snapped. Peering around the corner, I pulled my arm from Kale's grip and took a step into the main room.

"Wait," he whispered.

I ignored him and crept around Rosie's desk. The phone was in the corner by the television. Unfortunately, when I brought it to my ear, there was no dial tone. I set it back down, not bothering to return it to the dock. "Dead. They cut everything."

"Procedure. The first thing that's done before a raid."

"This is bullshit," I mumbled. "Our first date, and Dad has to screw it up. I seriously hate that man."

"We'll try—" Kale stopped. Tilting his head to the side, wisps of onyx hair slipping into his eyes, he turned away.

One minute he was standing there, statue still beside me, the next he was twisting as another figure lunged at us from behind. Graceful and quick, he dropped to the ground and whipped the table leg sideways. It collided with the man's knee in a sickening crunch. In a fluid move, Kale's right glove was off, and his fingers curled around the man's throat.

But nothing happened.

For a split second, I thought, *Huh. Go figure. Someone else like me.* What were the chances? But then I remembered…

"Jade." Kale settled for slamming the agent's head into the wall. The man crumbled to the floor, silent.

We scanned the room, but there was no sign of Jade. I was pretty sure if she were skulking under a desk or cowering behind a potted plant, she would have hopped out by now to lay a sloppy one on her big hero.

"Even when she's not here, she's in the damn way," I mumbled.

Kale either didn't hear me or ignored the comment. "She must be close."

I shook my head and backed away a few steps. "I guess it would be bitchy of me to say let's leave her here?"

The tiniest hint of a smile lifted the corner of his lips. "That would be a bad person move."

"Depends on your perspective."

A scream split the air, and the smile was gone, his expression darkening. "Jade," he breathed and sprinted toward the kitchen.

I followed, trying to focus on the actual disaster of Denazen hitting us at home base rather than the fact that my boyfriend had just dashed off to save the girl who had a mad crush on him. It wasn't easy.

We rounded the corner and saw another hooded figure

moving toward the door. Jade was slung over his shoulder, unmoving. As the man spun to face us, her hair whipped and bounced like a Barbie doll's, arms swinging daintily across his back. Like a damned fairy-tale damsel in distress. God. She was even annoying while unconscious. Somewhere in the world there had to be a law against that.

Kale sprang into action, charging the man like a runaway train. The guy dropped Jade and tried to sidestep the attack, but he was too late. Kale slammed into him, sending them both to the ground.

I took two steps forward, begrudgingly about to help Jade — even though a little voice was telling me to kick her body under a table and hope Kale forgot about her—when someone grabbed me from behind.

"Miss me, girly?"

That voice crept up my spine like an arctic chill, leaving goose bumps in its wake. One arm locked like a vice around my neck, Able used the other to clamp his hand down over my mouth as he jerked us sideways into the shadows. Out of Kale's field of vision. A distraction. Jade was playing possum to get Kale out of the way. Again.

Worked like a damn charm, too.

"Daddy sends his love," Able whispered in my ear. He smelled like Mountain Dew, and I had to force myself not to puke. Mountain Dew was the worst smell ever. Even worse than burnt popcorn.

"Maybe you'd like to send yours?" With each word, his breath disturbed my hair, strands fluttering back and forth to tickle my skin as he held me secure.

As if responding to his closeness, my shoulder began to throb, hammering an uneven rhythm of pain that sent pangs throughout my entire body. The sudden increase messed with my equilibrium and made my heart pump a little faster.

While I didn't have a license in badass like Kale did, I wasn't exactly helpless. I sucked in a lungful of air and stomped back, grinding the heel of my foot into the top of Able's. It didn't do crap to hurt him—he was wearing thick boots, and I was barefoot—but he *did* stop to laugh at me. And that was his mistake. While he was busy snorting over my pathetic attempt at freedom, I flung myself forward and threw him off balance. His grip loosened just enough for me to slip free and bolt across the room in Kale's direction.

Kale was a tornado, spinning through the room and taking out everything in his path. Deadly to confront but too amazing to take your eyes off. Even one of the agents had stopped to stare.

When the last guy went down, Kale crossed the room to where Jade was still playing dead. I wanted so badly to call her out, but now wasn't the time.

Heaving her over his shoulder, Kale nodded to the doorway. "We need to find the others."

No arguments from mc. The less time we spent hanging here in the dark with piles of Denazen trash scattered at our feet, the better. I glanced over my shoulder. Able was long gone.

We snaked back through the lobby and into the hallway around Rosie's desk. Through the door and into the stairwell. Everything was silent.

"We can't search the whole place with Little Miss Sunshine slung over your shoulder," I whispered. Leaning over the railing, I lifted my head and listened. You could have heard a feather hit the ground. Not a good sign—and creepy to boot.

There were Denazen men in the building. There should have been sounds of struggle. Of fighting. Could they have gotten everyone out already? Nightmare images of Denazen suits marching Sixes out the back door to waiting vans made me shudder.

I held my breath and listened harder. When all that came was eerie silence, I pushed off the railing and turned back to Kale. He was setting Jade down on the landing, taking care not to slam her head against the wall.

"I could slap her a few times." I said, wiggling my fingers. Half joking. Okay. Less than half. "Try to wake her up?"

He got down on his knee, bending close to her face. For an insane, drawn-out moment, it almost looked like he was about to kiss her. I didn't know whether to scream or cry. *My* Prince Charming off to wake up some other princess.

"I think she's waking up," he said.

I folded my arms and leaned back against the wall. "Maybe 'cause she was never asleep to begin with?"

Liquid chocolate eyes fringed by annoyingly long lashes fluttered open. Her head listed sideways just enough for several springy curls to fall across her cheek. "Wha—what happened?"

"You ran away to save your own ass, remember? Didn't make it very far. Then you got *captured*."

I swear to God, Kale rolled his eyes and sighed. He stood and held his hand out to help her up. "What's the last thing you remember?"

I pushed him aside. "I'm betting it was the phone call telling Dad to send in the second wave."

She did her best impression of surprised, but I wasn't buying it. "What are you babbling about?"

"This place is locked down tighter than a nun's chastity belt. No way is someone getting inside without help."

Her eyes went wide. She took a step toward me. "Are you're trying to say you think it was me? I wasn't even here! I was with you."

For a split second I might have believed her. That whole

wide-eyed, *but I'm innocent* routine could've been pretty convincing, except I knew better. Had some insider information. Something Dad said at the post office echoed in my head.

"Has anyone survived?"

"As a matter of fact, yes. One. A very unique girl with a gift I think you'd find very appealing. Especially in your current situation."

Jade was a spy for Dad. And not just any spy. *She* was the Supremacy survivor. Now that it'd all come together, it made total sense. Her invincibility. The immunity to Kale. Dad saying I'd find her gift appealing. So her plan was what? To charm Kale's ass off, then deliver him right to Dad? Such a *girl* move! Seduce and conquer. I didn't know if that made the way she was drooling all over him better—or worse.

I matched her step, fists tight. "I'm not *trying* to say anything. It was you. You're Supremacy."

"Supremacy? Is that some kind of lame-o skater slang?" She shoved me. "Like I said, I wasn't here. I was with *Kale.*"

"You set it up before the dance, then."

"You're a piece of work, you know that? You think flinging crazy accusations is going to get rid of me? You're the *only* one who believes this crap!"

Kale tapped me on the arm. "Dez..."

"Just because I'm the only one willing to see it doesn't mean I'm wrong. I *know* who you are."

"Jade..." Kale tried again. From the corner of my eye, I saw him looking up into the stairwell. For once, Jade didn't hang on every syllable like a groupie.

"Who I am?" she squealed. "Yeah. I'm the girl who's tired of your shit. It never occurred to you that someone else is leaking information? That maybe one of your buddies is a traitor? Are you really that insecure that you need to pin this on me?"

Insecure? Fingers stiff, I let loose. I did her a favor, though. Something I'd never done before. I slapped her. I'd kicked, bitten, kneed, hell, I'd even head-butted, but slapped? No way. Too much of a *girl* move.

She didn't as much as flinch.

Oops. Invincible.

"Bitch!" she snarled, letting her own fist fly. The blow struck my left shoulder, and, as a scream split my lips, I went toppling backward. In that moment, I actually wished I was dead. The spasm that spread from the impact point and out through my limbs was agony. Involuntary tears stung the corners of my eyes as I dragged myself up.

It was useless, but I would have lunged for her if not for the insane giggle that filled the stairway. We all turned at the same time. At the top of the stairs, coming down one step at a time, was Fin.

I'd seen some crazy shit since my life had detoured onto the path of *The Surreal Life*, but this took the cake. With every step, Fin left behind a smoking, charred patch. Tufts of gray drifted from his feet, which were bare, and the linoleum surrounding him on either side shriveled and shrank away.

He caught me looking and giggled again. "Checking out my tippy toes? Shoes have no love for me now. The air bites and bitches and bleeds until they run away screaming." Hopping down from the last step, he did a little twirl, ending with an elaborate shimmy. He tapped the side of his head, hopped forward, and said, "*Boomboomboom!* It's a mess in here. All fire and brimstone and creepy-crawly critters fighting to take a big bite."

"Jesus, Fin…" Obviously he'd passed the *showing signs* stage and had entered the all-out crazies. I knew we should be running, but my limbs just wouldn't respond. I was transfixed by the sight of him. Was this going to be me? Lost in a haze of power and insanity?

Was this where Layne Phillips had been heading? A small, sick part of me wondered if Denazen had done her a favor. If there was no cure once it got to this point, it would be cruel to leave it alone. Right?

"Jesus doesn't buy crackers, Dez. He doesn't even shop. You should know that. You of all people, with your weird hair and creamy skin. I'm where the hotspot is now. Take a bite of immortality and chew it up good." Fin lifted his right hand and waved it in our general direction. Tiny flames sprang to life, swirling up and twirling into a tight ball. With a flick of his finger, he sent it rocketing at us, scattering us apart.

Kale shouldered me aside, and Jade dove to the left. "Get down!"

The smell of acrid smoke and burning hair filled the small space. Jade screamed and swatted frantically at the strap of her dress. A tiny flame puffed out.

Fin giggled again and advanced several steps. "I used to want to nail you, Dez—now I think I'd rather watch you burn in the pretty, pretty fire." He stopped midstride and stomped his foot, hysterical laughter bubbling from his lips. "You're so hot, after all!"

From the middle of the landing where he stood, a brilliant light began to form. It flickered between his open palms and pulsed with a life of its own as it increased in size. We were at least four feet from him, and the building heat was enough to make me squirm.

"I have a present for you, Dez. It's gonna burn your britches and swallow you whole." He held the blazing ball out. "Nine lives won't save you this time, bitch, but you'll look pretty with charred edges!"

What would that blazing ball do to us if we were still here when he let go of it?

Kale dragged me by the sleeve of my dress, his other hand clasped in Jade's. We crossed the threshold of the stairwell door as the fireball touched down. The ground convulsed, and the wall behind us exploded. No time to look. Down the hall and around the corner. Into the lobby. Another boom, and a definite rise in the air's temperature. Shattering glass and a deafening roar. Then, for a few minutes, silence. Like someone had slammed the mute button but left the movie playing.

Five steps forward, and the floor shook again, sending us all off balance. The pressure of Kale's fingers around my arm was gone. I thrust my hands into the smoke to find him, but it was pointless. I was alone.

Like the fire safety movies they show you in grade school instructed, I dropped to my knees and followed the wall to what I hoped was the nearest exit. Several feet later, I rounded the corner of the lobby.

The smoke was everywhere, stealing all the good air away and replacing it with a foul, burning cloud. In the far corner, the edges of Rosie's desk were burning. The stacks of paper she kept so meticulously stacked and organized shriveled, bursting into mini infernos and creeping closer to the coffee pot she kept on her desk. There was a pop, the first sound since the explosion, and the glass pot shattered.

"Kale?" I screamed, but the word didn't quite make it past my lips. Coughing. There was too much coughing. Continuous spasms as my body shook and rebelled against the pungent air. For some reason, it brought the memory of my first drink to mind. The skin-searing burn as the alcohol slid down my throat. It'd been like swallowing sandpaper. A shot of Goldschläger at a warehouse rave. It was right before Alex and I became official.

He'd dared me to do it, saying there was no way I could handle it. I'd never been one to walk away from a dare.

Lost in the thick smoke in front of me, a girl screamed. Another voice—Kale's—I was sure of it, called out my name, but he was too far. Impossible to find.

Instinctively, I tried to take a deep breath. Major mistake. It resulted in another, more violent round of body-shaking coughs. My eyes stung, and my chest ached. Burning to death. Was there a worse way to die? I couldn't go out like this. It was weak.

Pathetic.

Hell, no.

I braced my hands against the wall and used it to pull myself upright, refusing to give up. Off the ground and running. The door. I was in the middle of the room. Safety was only a few feet away. I could find it with my eyes closed. What was a little smoke? Behind me, the flames roared, consuming everything. Like fiery parasites, they ate through anything in their path.

Gone. It was all just gone. Swallowed by gray.

Someone screamed. Just a garbled sound that was neither male nor female. Something cool wrapped around my upper arms, and I was moving again. Faster. Straighter. Out past the broken glass doors and into the night air.

The *clean* night air.

"Take it easy, miss," a voice I didn't recognize soothed. "Don't take panicked breaths. Nice and easy. That's it."

It took several attempts for the fire in my lungs to lessen. Deep, measured breaths slowly replaced the bad air with good.

"Dez!" Kale skidded to a stop in front of me. He went to reach for me, but Jade, always frigging in the way, batted his hand aside.

At least he had the intelligence to glare at her for it this time.

"Are you okay?"

I tried to answer, but the burning in my throat stopped me, so I just nodded.

Behind him, Ginger, Kiernan, Alex, and a small group of others watched as the firefighters battled the blaze destroying our home. I was glad Daun left. Would she have gotten stuck inside? How many didn't make it out? There were still so many faces unaccounted for.

So many unaccounted for...

Oh, God.

I scanned the crowd again.

She wasn't here.

"Mom!"

25

I was almost back to the building when one of the firefighters tackled me. Spinning me back toward the crowd, he said, "Is that who you're lookin' for, kid?"

Frantic and running straight for us was Mom.

We collided halfway. Her arms wound so tight, it made the smoke seem like easy breathing, but I didn't care. She was okay. I was okay. We hadn't lost each other.

We rejoined the crowd and watched in mournful silence. The Sanctuary hotel was nothing more than smoldering ash and hazy plumes of gray smoke by the time the firemen were done. Two bodies were pulled from the wreckage. Rosie and another woman whose name I didn't remember. I'd seen her around. She could shift into a tiger.

Four people were still unaccounted for. The firefighters assured us there was no one left inside the building, saying that in cases like these, people panic and run and usually resurface later. We knew better. They wouldn't resurface. They'd been taken by

Denazen.

"It was Fin. Had to be," Mom said as she settled behind me.

The fire trucks were pulling out, and Ginger was in the process of arranging everyone a temporary place to stay till we could get things sorted out.

"It was," I whispered, remembering the look on his face. He was completely unglued. Far past gone. They'd *retire* him soon, if he even made it out of the building alive. There was nothing I could do to help him.

"How do you know?" Mom blinked and backed away a bit. "And why is your hair *green*?"

I ignored the hair question—I really had no idea what to say—and focused on Fin. "We saw him. He's—"

"Dez?" Kale came up beside Mom.

One look at his face, and she beat a hasty retreat in an obvious attempt to give us some privacy.

"You let go of me. Inside. I lost you."

I took a small step back. "Technically, you let go of me."

He was looking at me funny. Not angry, and not sad, but somewhere in between. "Did you hurt your shoulder?"

"No?"

"You're rubbing it."

I froze. "Itchy. Where's your shadow?"

He ignored the question. Expression sad, he said, "You can't touch me like you used to. But you can still talk to me." He took a step closer. "I need you to talk to me, Dez."

I couldn't breathe. Every inch of me wanted to come clean. "Kale…"

"Something is wrong. With you. I don't understand why you won't tell me. You're hiding something."

But I couldn't. It would only make things worse. "I— sometimes there's just stuff people can't tell each other."

He folded his arms, not the least bit dissuaded. "We're a team. You and me. Everything together. That's what you said. You have to tell me. That's how it works."

"This is—" I scanned the crowd and found Jade standing by one of the ambulances. She was staring at us, lips twisted and expression angry. I could see the hate in her eyes. Hate my father had been able to easily manipulate. Hate that had destroyed the hotel and killed our friends. Had killed Rosie… It was easy to see she wanted to storm over and break up our conversation, but the EMT fussing over her refused to let her move from the tailgate.

I needed to distract him. "I know you think Jade is a good person and that you like her, but she's a *bad* person, Kale." I pointed to the remains of the hotel. "This is *her* fault. I know it. And I'm not just saying that because she wants to steal my boyfriend."

• • •

"How ya doin'?" Kiernan plopped down on the floor next to me.

I sucked in a deep breath and looked around. Ginger had gone with me, Kiernan, and Mom to her friend Meela's house. Mom and Ginger took the spare bedroom while Kiernan and I were bunking in the living room. "I'm a little freaked. Fin was…"

"That's the guy you used to go to school with, right? Kale told me what happened when you were talking to your mom. It was that bad?"

"It was way bad." I peeked at her through a curtain of hair. "As if I don't have enough to worry about with Jade skulking around, seeing the possible crazy that's my future is a little unsettling…"

Picking up her borrowed pillow, Kiernan sighed. "I could kick Jade's ass for you. Would that help?"

I forced a laugh. "I think that's something I'd like to do for myself. But first, I need to find proof that she was responsible for letting Denazen in to the hotel. Kale needs proof."

Kiernan frowned. "Dez, I hate the girl. You know that, right? But she *was* at the dance with us."

"It was all a setup."

"No offense, but I think you're reaching. You want it to be her, but hon…I don't think it is."

"It is," I insisted. "It all fits. She was the only one who knew I was going to the post office."

"Dez, I knew, too. You called me, remember?"

I blinked. I'd totally forgotten. "So *you* called Dad?"

She punched my arm, then threw her hands up in mock surrender. "Ya got me." Sighing, she leaned back against the couch. "All I'm saying is, maybe someone else knew. Someone you didn't realize. Maybe someone overheard Ginger telling you to go."

"No. It was only me, Kale, and her. I haven't figured out her plan just yet, but I know I'm right."

"Okay," Kiernan said slowly. "But Dez, she was with Kale the entire dance. It *does* give her an alibi. She can't be in two places at once."

"What about when Kale and I were dancing?"

Kiernan shook her head. "She was sitting at the table. Talking to Alex. What did she do, beam your dad a message from her brain?"

"Who knows?" I looked around. The living room reminded me of something from a Martha Stewart nightmare. There were doilies under everything and enough fake flowers to choke an entire herd of horses.

Meela was a Six that lost her son to Denazen. She'd jumped at the chance to help us when she'd heard what happened.

Supplied with clothing—out of style and ill fitting, but clean—she'd opened her home to us for as long as we needed.

Kale and Jade were sent with Paul and Panda to a nearby relative of Daun's. Alex had taken the others to Dax's apartment downtown. Thankfully, he hadn't been at the hotel but offered his place if we needed more room.

I didn't know where the rest had gone, but Ginger assured us they were safe.

I took a deep breath and tried not to gag. Either Meela spritzed the flowers with something, or the air freshener she used smelled like something Rosie would have worn. The thought stung. Our relationship had been rocky from day one, but Rosie had been my friend—even if neither one of us would ever had admitted it. And now she was gone.

I pushed my grief aside and focused on the facts. Jade would *not* get away with this. "I think Jade's Supremacy. Like me—in fact, I'm sure of it. That means she'd have some seriously epic abilities."

Kiernan looked skeptical. "I dunno, Dez. Brain beaming? So not. I kinda think you want it to be her."

"What I *want* is to nail the person responsible. And that person is Jade."

Kiernan shrugged but didn't answer. Instead, she grabbed the other blanket from the couch—a pink-and-white floral monstrosity—and spread it over her cot. "I'm on your side, Dez, but I think you're wrong about this."

I waited till she'd burrowed under the covers before I got up and slunk out to the backyard.

The crisp night air was like a slap in the face. The sun would be up in a few hours, and I'd still be awake. Thinking. Worrying. Plotting. Jade was going down. She'd be dragging Kale off to Denazen over my dead body. Which at this point, was a very real possibility.

The pain in my shoulder spiked again. Funny how that happened whenever I thought about Jade. It was a sign. I was willing to bet my fingers. Tugging aside my borrowed T-shirt— creeptastically a powder-pink, adult-sized *Hello Kitty Loves You* sleep shirt—I stared down at the mark Able had left behind. The original spot was hard to see now, the dark middle bleeding out in all directions.

The spidery lines creeping from the center were past the tip of my collarbone now. If it kept spreading this fast, they'd be down my arm and well past my elbow by the end of the day. Not to mention up the side of my neck. Time was running out. The poison would be out of the vial soon. I'd have to come clean, which meant I needed a resolution. Now.

The screen door creaked, and someone hobbled out onto the porch.

"You're up late," Ginger said from behind me.

I didn't turn around. If I ignored her, maybe she'd take the hint and go back inside. The last thing I needed was a speech on letting events take their intended course.

"Shouldn't you be asleep?"

"Shouldn't *you*? I mean you're what, like, ninety? You old folks need your shuteye."

She snorted. "That was pathetic. Merely a shade of your usual venom. Is something bothering you, Deznee?"

I sighed. "Why are you even asking? You already know the answer. Probably know the date and time I'm gonna buy it, too, right? Please at least tell me I go out in a blaze. Doing something crazy. None of that crapping out all peaceful-like in my sleep."

The bench behind me squealed in protest as she sat. "You know it doesn't work that way."

This time I turned around. "You obviously know what's

going down." I hated the desperation in my voice, but no matter how hard I tried, I couldn't hide it. "Tell me. Tell me if he ends up back at Denazen."

Tell me if I end up dead…

For a second I thought she might answer. Her expression softened, brows knitting together with a sympathetic frown. Her gaze flickered to my shoulder, then away. Oh, yeah. She definitely knew. She knew, and the sick part was, she was the one person I didn't have to worry about squealing. Not because I could trust her, but because if I was meant to die, she didn't intend on lifting a finger to stop it.

After a moment, she shook her head. "I know his purpose and path. Kale's road, like yours, has never been an easy one."

And Kiernan thought Rosie had been cryptic?

"You know who's responsible for burning down the hotel, don't you? The person who let Dad's people in."

"I do."

That pissed me off. I mean, I knew she did—at least I figured she did—but to hear her admit it really set me off. Jumping to my feet, I stomped forward. "I know you have all these stupid little rules, but people *died*. Good people. *Friends* of yours. You're just gonna let her rip us apart from the inside?"

"There is no interfering in things like this. They happen the way fate meant them to. To allow otherwise would be chaos. We've been through this many times now, Deznee."

"No, *chaos* is what we had tonight. A burning building. With people stuck inside. Something *you* could have prevented. *That's* chaos. There were kids in there, Ginger. Little *kids*."

"That's fate."

"*That's* bullshit."

She didn't answer.

"You know it's Jade, and you sent Kale with her."

Thoughtful, she lifted her head to the sky and sighed. "Jade is…in a unique situation."

"Unique situation? And that gives her the right to destroy us?"

"Perhaps you need to consider the possibility that you and Kale are not meant to be together. That clinging to each other could destroy you both?"

I just about fell over. "What?"

She didn't answer.

"Screw you," I spat. An icy chill had crept into the air. "This is where I draw the line. Is that what all this Jade crap has been about? You really *are* trying to push them together? 'Cause you have some fucked-up notion Kale and I aren't *meant to be*? And pushing him back to Denazen is your answer?"

Reality was starting to slip. It was like a bomb going off inside my brain. Everything from the tips of my toes to the edge of my nose…it all went numb. Everything, that is, except my shoulder. With a sudden flash, pain exploded.

"You're wrong…" I stumbled up, fighting to keep my balance. My voice sounded funny. Garbled and thick. "…if you think Kale and me aren't going to stick, you're *wrong*."

She got to her feet, knuckles white around her cane. Eyes sad, she said, "I'm sorry. I know this is hard, and you probably think me no better than your father."

"The thought crossed my mind several times," I admitted bitterly.

"I am on your side, Deznee. I know it doesn't look that way, and you think I don't love my grandson or care about these people, but that couldn't be further from the truth." She was quiet for a moment. The cool September air kicked up, fluttering the edges of her bright blue housecoat. "Everything is happening as it was meant to. And unfortunately, when all is said and done, I fear it will be you and Alex that pay the biggest prices."

I'd been right. No sleep for me. After Ginger finally went inside, I spent the rest of the night on the porch. Well, most of it. There was an hour stretch where I paced from one end of the lawn to the other, wet grass tickling my toes as I racked my brain to figure out a way to prove Jade was behind all this.

And that whole thing about me and Kale? I had no intention of paying attention to it. Never in history had there been a more wrong statement. Kale was the only thing that kept me sane sometimes. Nothing about him being in my life would destroy me. Not ever. As far as the Alex thing, well, I was choosing to look the other way concerning that, too. Alex made his own choices—usually bad ones. They were his responsibility.

I'd been doing that a lot lately. Ignoring things. A tiny whisper in the back of my head said that was wrong—unlike me—but I chose to disregard that, too.

By the time the sun crested the hills behind Meela's house, I crept back inside with an idea about how to get the dirt on Jade.

"You're pissed at me." Kiernan appeared in the doorway. In her hands was a steamy peace offering. Coffee.

I took the cup from her and did my best not to laugh. She was wearing an orange broomstick skirt and pink blouse with an obnoxious ruffled collar. Jesus. Meela was obsessed with pink.

"I figured you might be," she continued, gesturing to herself. "Which is why I did something only a true friend would. I spared you from *this*."

"It's—"

"Beyond words? Yeah. I know." She backed into the kitchen and pulled out a chair. "Meela? So not going to be working the runways any time soon. The other outfit isn't going to buy you a date, but it's not as bad as this one."

I sank into the chair across from her.

"And I figure if you forgive me, maybe you can fix it for me?"

"I wish I could, but how would we explain it? No one knows about the change in my ability yet…"

She frowned but nodded. "True. I see your hair is blonde again—though I thought the streaks were red at the dance? Now they're blue."

I reached up and fingered a strand of hair. Blonde mixed with deep blue highlights. In the chaos I'd totally forgotten about it. I never consciously changed it back. Then again, I'd never *consciously* turned it green, either. I was going to have to get a handle on that ASAP. "Huh. It's better than the green."

Kiernan tugged at the edge of her blouse. "So about last night… I wasn't trying to make it seem like I thought Jade was squeaky clean, I just thought—"

"Over it. Redemption is yours if you want it."

She eyed me, a smile spreading across her lips. "Oh?"

"I need you."

"No offense, but I'm not into blondes. Plus," she said waving her cup at me, "you're a little lacking in the muscle department for my tastes."

"Your gift. I need to do some digging."

"You wanna spy on Jade and Kale?"

"Not Kale. Just Jade. I know she's working for Dad, Kiernan. I *know* it. I just need to find proof so Kale and the others will listen to me."

"She never leaves Kale's side. Do you really believe she's going to drag him with her when she goes to chat up your dad?"

"She can't be with him every minute of every day. She has to leave him alone at some point. And I'm betting when she does, even if it's to make a phone call, I'll get the proof I need."

After finishing my coffee, I went to see what clothes Meela had scrounged up for me. Kiernan had been right. The second outfit wasn't nearly as bad as the first. Simple black sweatpants and a Marist College hoodie. I'd just finished changing when there was a knock on the door. I emerged from the bathroom and found Kale and Jade in the kitchen with Kiernan and Paul, and Alex and Dax were talking quietly to Mom in the hall.

"Wow," Jade giggled. "You guys look…great."

And that's the universe for you. Always there with a crappy sense of humor. Jade was still wearing her shimmery gown from the dance. You'd expect that after escaping a building fire—and assumedly sleeping in the damn thing—she would have shown up looking like a disaster. You know, like a *normal* person? Nope. She'd pulled her hair into a ponytail, and the dress, though slightly wrinkled with spots of ash, still made her look beautiful. Like a supermodel at a disaster photo shoot.

Kale was staring. He hadn't uttered a word since I'd entered the kitchen, and he hadn't taken his eyes off me. A few days ago, that would have made all things right with my world. This morning? It hurt more than my shoulder—which was getting close to insane.

I was a mess. My life was crumbling around me, and the only thing I wanted was to confess everything to him. But I couldn't. There was no way to tell him Dad had paid me a visit without sending him off the deep end. And there was no way to come clean about the new Supremacy information I had without 'fessing up about Dad's visit. And the whole thing with Able? *Yeah*. If I told him about that, he'd try to trade himself to Dad for the cure. Normally I was proud of the fact that I could stand alone, but for the first time in my life, being on my own was really starting to bother me.

"We have a lot to get done today," Ginger said, cane clinking against the kitchen tile. "There will be a meeting at tonight's party. Because of last night's events, the location will not go up on Craigslist."

My mouth fell open. "Seriously? We're having a *party*? The damn hotel just burned down. People are dead. *Rosie* is dead. And you wanna party?"

"There is a Six party every night, Deznee. To suddenly deter from the normal routine would only put people on edge. The last thing we need is a wave of panic. Things will continue as usual, and we will use the opportunity to regroup and plan."

She reached into the pocket of her blue housecoat. Out came a handful of small, colored slips of paper. "You will be notifying people in person. No one goes alone. I've split you in to teams. You are to stay with your partner at *all times*. Do not share your list or the instructions on it with anyone but your partner— including those in this room."

She turned to Mom. "Sue, you will go with Dax."

Mom nodded and took the folded piece of blue paper. Was it my imagination, or was she smiling?

Next, Ginger turned to Paul, who was standing in the

doorway. Handing him a small orange sheet, she said, "You and Barge take this one."

She continued handing out slips until all that was left was me, Kale, Kiernan, Jade, and Alex. Uneven numbers.

"Jade," Ginger said, handing her a pink slip. "You are with Kiernan." Turning to me, she said, "You and Kale."

Jade looked from the slip to Kale, frowning. "Is that a good idea? Kale could accidentally hurt someone if I'm not with him. He could hurt Dez."

Ginger grabbed the redhead by the shoulders and spun her toward the door. "He got along for years without you hanging all over him. I think he can manage."

"This is good! I can keep an eye on her," Kiernan whispered. With a wink, she followed a very sulky Jade from the room. A few seconds later, the front door slammed closed.

"What about me?" Alex said.

Ginger flashed a red-tinted smile. She'd been drinking the Mobol's fruit punch again. It was the only one that stained. "You're with me, Alex."

Without a word, they were gone, too, leaving Kale and me truly alone for the first time in days.

"You don't want to be with me." Kale took a step toward me.

Not be with him? That's all I wanted to be. "It's not that."

"But you don't want me with Jade?"

"Of course not!"

"Are you angry with me?"

"Why would I be angry?"

He looked genuinely confused. "I don't know. That's why I'm asking."

"We should get moving on this list." I took a step back and unfolded the paper. A few seconds more, and I'd end up spilling everything. Lying to Kale was one of the hardest things I'd ever had to do—not to mention I sucked at it.

"Okay," he said slowly. "But *we* aren't done."

"We're not done. Never." I let the hoodie sleeve cover the tips of my fingers and squeezed his hand. "First thing on the sheet says to notify Prias Sheen about the party location."

"Where is the location?"

"Um," I skimmed the paper. "Looks like it's in The Rockies."

"Rockies?"

"It was an indoor rock climbing place. Closed down a few months ago. It's on the very edge of town."

"How do you climb a rock indoors?"

"They're not really rocks you're climbing, more like plastic. They put a harness on you, and one of the guides is there to spot you."

He looked horrified. "Plastic rocks?"

"Forget it."

• • •

We gave Prias, a woman with the ability to manipulate vegetation, the information about the party's location and continued to move down the list. Seven names. By one in the afternoon, I was starving.

"Anything on that list about munchies?"

Kale stuffed the list into his pocket. "You're hungry?"

"Ready to eat a small horse."

For a second, he looked worried, then he nodded. "Expression?"

I smiled. "Expression."

"Ginger said don't deviate from the list."

We'd just gotten off the bus—Kale's *favorite* mode of transportation—and were standing on the corner of Main Street in front of Shaker's Pizza. There were a dozen places we could grab a quick bite. In and out and back to work in the blink of an eye. There were only two more things on our list. Check Ginger's post office box and notify one more person. We had time to eat.

"I'm sure she didn't mean to have us starve. What ya in the mood for?"

"Cheese sticks," he said, leaning close. There was a spark of hunger in his eyes—and not for fried cheese, either. He was remembering the last time we'd had them, if I had to guess. Right before all this started. He'd bitten one end, and I'd chomped the other. It was sweet. A very *Lady and the Tramp* moment that lead to, well, a not-so-*Disney* moment. An hour's worth of them.

My heart sped, and I had to take a step back to keep from touching him. I couldn't think straight when he looked at me like that. "Probably a better idea to get something fast and get back to the list."

He took another step closer. I took another back. We did this until I'd backed into the side of the building.

"This is worse than anything Denazen ever did to me. To be so close and yet have so much distance. To know I could hurt you—or worse—but still want so badly to touch you."

"I know how you feel."

He was inches away now. Warm breath puffed softly across my face. "I know there's something you're not telling me. It… bothers me."

I couldn't deny it. Not with him looking at me like that. Standing so close. "There are things you don't tell me," I said, breath catching.

He frowned. "That's not the same."

"Isn't it?"

"No. The things I don't tell you are in my past. They're unpleasant."

"In the past or not, they still affect you. They're still part of your life."

Spreading his arms, he placed a hand on either side of my head, palms flat against the wall. "I don't want you to think of me at that place. The things they did. The things they made me *do*. I don't tell you to shield you from that."

"In case you haven't noticed by now, I'm not the kinda girl that needs shielding." I gripped his cloth-covered arms and pushed him back a few inches. "And this thing I'm not telling you? It's something like that. Something I don't want to tell you so I can protect you."

"I don't like that."

"I'm sorry," I said. "How about a compromise? I'll tell you half?"

He looked skeptical but nodded. "Okay."

I tugged him around to the side of the building. Thankfully it was trash day, and the Dumpster had been emptied. When I was sure we were alone, I ran my hands through my hair, picturing the brown it'd been in the days just after Sumrun.

Kale reached out and fingered a small lock of hair. "That's why your hair turned green last night. You can change it now."

"You don't seem surprised."

He frowned. "It was green when you left last night. It was blonde with blue when I saw you this morning. As Alex so *helpfully* pointed out last night, you wouldn't have had time to dye it."

Um, duh. Of course he would have noticed. Which begged the question; who else had noticed? Everyone, of course. How could they not? Mom had asked outside the hotel last night. I ignored it and she'd let it drop, but she couldn't have been the only one who'd noticed. It was green, for Christ's sake. Seriously, what was wrong with me? I'd never been lacking in common sense before. Sure, it was a little odd no one had said anything, but I guessed with everything going on, changing hair color wasn't the most immediate thing on their minds.

"It's a little out of control, though, hence the green. I didn't do that on purpose—it just happened." I ran my hands through my hair again. Back to blonde and blue streaks. "It's not limited to touch anymore. It works through visual. I see it, I can mimic it."

"And you can't control it?"

On the street across from the alley, a large truck passed, and I had to wait for it to get to the end of the road so Kale would be able to hear me. "I can do it when I want to—so far—but sometimes it happens when I'm not trying."

"That could be bad."

"Tell me about it."

He was quiet for a moment, then frowned. "You can change parts of yourself?"

"You sound worried," I said as the bell above Shaker's door rang again. Even though we were around the corner, every time someone opened the door, the smell of pizza wafted out. It was making my mouth water.

"I like you the way you are."

That brought a smile to my face. Old-school Kale. Simple and to the point. "I'm not changing, I promise. My clothes, on the other hand…" I checked to make sure the coast was still clear. A couple was passing in front of the alley, pizza box in hand. I wanted till they were gone, then grabbed a handful of my borrowed black sweatpants. The fabric got stiff and tightened to fit snug around my thigh. The pair of jeans I'd tried on at the beginning of summer. They did awesome things for my ass. "Much nicer, ya think? And it's not just me I can change, either—I think."

I laid my palm flat against his chest. It felt good to touch him, even if there was a layer of cloth between us. Closing my eyes, I pictured deep purple. I didn't know if it would work, but it was worth a shot. When I opened my eyes, Kale's long-sleeved T-shirt had changed color. It was also a bit more snug. This *could* have its uses.

"Plus major win—no more headaches or brain-blurring nausea!"

He smiled for a moment, but it didn't last. "You didn't want to tell me that your abilities had increased? What does this have to do with that other boy? Able."

"Nothing," I said. I'd started to believe Dad was telling the truth about Able's poison, sort of, and that made me even less likely to tell Kale. I knew what he'd say and how he'd react.

I knew what he'd want to do.

"Then you haven't told me what I wanted to know. There's something going on, and it involves him."

"He's just another Denazen flunky that works for Dad. There's nothing *going on*."

"Dez…"

"You're gonna have to trust me, Kale. I have everything under control."

He backed up a bit and sighed. He wasn't buying it, but let it go.

And I felt like the worst girlfriend in history.

When we finished everything on Ginger's list, there was a note at the bottom that instructed us to be at Bella's, the newly opened Italian bakery, at exactly five-oh-five. We were to sit at the fourth table from the door and order coffee. Ten minutes later, Mom and Dax settled across from us.

"Any trouble?" Mom asked, looking between Kale and me.

"Nada," I answered. Reaching for the sugar with my left hand, I cringed.

Kale, never missing anything, saw. "I knew you hurt your shoulder last night." He twisted in his seat, eyeing me.

"Just a pulled muscle. Nothing to call the paramedics over."

Kale was going to argue, I could see it in the stubborn set of his jaw, but rescue came from the most unlikely source. Jade.

"So what'd we miss?" She pulled a chair from the next table and wedged it between Kale and Dax. Kiernan sat down next to Mom. They'd both changed clothes.

"We were just about to vote you off the island," I said,

stirring my coffee.

"You've got my vote," Kiernan said enthusiastically, glaring at Jade.

Dax pulled out a blue slip of paper. Sliding it across the table to Kale, he said, "You and Jade are going to head to this address. Work on your control. Someone will be by to get you when it's time to head to the party."

Grinning, Jade stood, looped her arm around Kale's, and practically yanked him from the chair.

I couldn't help my smile when Kale pulled free from her grip and leaned over my chair. "What about Dez?"

"Dez and Kiernan are supposed to head back to Meela's and lay low until the party. Shanna and I are heading out to meet Alex and Barge."

Kiernan glared at Jade. "Why can't Dez and I *lay low* with Kale and Jade?"

Mom pointed to Jade, then me. "You can't be in the same room at the same time for more than five minutes without attacking each other. A whole evening? No. We stick to Ginger's instructions."

"You'd just get in the way," Jade said. "All those longing, puppy-dog stares you throw at him all the time… It's amazing the guy hasn't suffocated."

"Dez doesn't throw dog stares at me," Kale said, coming to my rescue. "She just likes looking at me." He turned, pinning me with a stare that made my chest tight. "And I like looking at her."

Jade snorted. "Why?" she mumbled under her breath.

I started to stand, but Mom grabbed my arm. "And on *that* note, everybody scatter. Stay at your designated places until someone comes to retrieve you."

"Shall we?" Next to Mom, Dax stood and held out his hand. She took it without hesitating. Oh. Yeah. Definitely something going on there.

Lately, I'd noticed a slight change. I was starting to think Dax had a big part in it. There was a slight age difference between them, but if they made each other happy, then who was I to judge?

He narrowed his eyes at me. "Going to stay out of trouble?"

I nodded.

"Say it."

Looking him straight in the eye, I smiled sweetly. He'd know it was bullshit, but I hoped he wouldn't narc me out. I knew that while he didn't dislike Jade as much as I did, he also didn't trust her. "Absolutely."

He hesitated for a moment, and I held my breath. Finally, though, he nodded and left with Mom.

Kale sighed. "Please go straight back to Meela's."

I flashed him an innocent smile. "Of course. That's where they told me to go."

He hesitated for a moment before grabbing the sides of my face. Enough time had passed. With Jade there, the pain wasn't horrible, but it *was* there. When I didn't object—or more likely, pull away screaming—his mouth covered mine. For a moment, I forgot about the acid churning in my stomach and the increasing warmth where his fingers pressed against my skin. My lips were beginning to numb, and my jaw ached. The pins and needles danced—hell, they were moshing—just beneath the surface, determined to keep us apart. I deserved an Oscar for acting like it had no effect on me.

My arm came up, and I ran my fingers through his hair. If Kiernan hadn't kicked me, God only knows how far I would have taken it just to show him—to show Jade—I could.

I tried to pull way, but Kale stopped me before I got too far. "Are you okay?"

My heart was racing, and almost every muscle in my body throbbed, but I forced a smile. "Are you kidding? After a kiss like that? I'm better than okay."

He didn't smile. "Please be careful." Turning to Jade, he said, "Let's go."

As soon as they were out of earshot, I whirled on Kiernan. "Anything suspicious?"

She rolled her eyes. "Yes. She asked me to wait around the corner so she could chat privately with your dad."

"I'm serious."

"Nothing suspicious." Kiernan winked and nodded to the road. "But let's go see if we can dig something up."

"You read my mind."

• ¢ •

We were able to easily catch up to Kale and Jade because she'd insisted they stop for ice cream. What the hell did she think this was—a date? We watched her slip inside the ice cream place on Harbor Drive, dragging a reluctant-looking Kale behind, and hung back while they put in their orders.

"Showtime," I said, grabbing Kiernan's hand and dragging her toward the building.

They were sitting in seats at the very back of the room. Thankfully, the booth behind them was empty. Using Kiernan's ability, we'd be able to scoot up and listen to their conversation from right over their shoulders.

"Um, Dez, what happens if someone sits here? No one can see or hear us, but if someone sits on us, trust me, they'll know."

I gestured to the row of empty seats. "There are a few other seats open. What are the chances someone's going to sit *here*? Now *shh*. I wanna hear what she's saying."

"No one will know if we sneak a quick treat," Jade was saying with a giggle.

"Where I'm from, it's a bad idea to disobey orders," Kale said casually. He sat against the wall and alternated between looking from Jade to the front door. There was a steady stream of customers for takeout, but only a few stayed to sit.

"You mean Denazen?" Reaching across the table, she took his hand in hers. "What was it like there?"

What was it like there? Who the hell asks a POW how the food was in prison camp? This girl was a hell of a piece of work.

Kale's expression was sad. "Dez asks me that a lot."

"And what do you tell her?" Jade leaned back as the waitress returned to set a large metal cup in front of her, along with a spoon and extra-long straw. In front of Kale, she placed a soda.

"Not much. I don't like to talk about Denazen with her."

"Why not?"

Kale picked his hand off the table, Jade's still attached. "Your hand is smaller than hers. It feels different."

"Different? Is that a good thing or a bad thing?"

Kale smiled. A *kick-start-my-heart-with-a-car-battery* kind of grin. Warmth bloomed in the pit of my stomach—until I realized it wasn't me he was smiling at. It was Jade.

"Good different," he said, letting go so he could unwrap his straw.

I didn't have to see Jade's face to know she was beaming. "Mother—"

"*Shh*," Kiernan hissed, nudging me with her shoulder. "I can't hear."

"So was it really that bad? Denazen?" Jade asked, taking a sip of her shake. "And oh, my God. You have to try this!"

Kale, polite as always, refused when she all but thrust a spoonful of creamy brown ice cream in his face. "Why do you want to know about them?"

Finally. Some common sense. Maybe now he'd see she was fishing for information.

Jade sighed and stuffed the spoon into her own mouth. "My dad used to work for them. Not the one in this town. His was in Seattle."

Kale tensed. "He's dead?"

"Of course not. He quit."

His eyes narrowed. "No one quits. They're terminated. I've personally terminated four previous employees."

"He came home in the middle of the night, grabbed Mom and me and my sister, and we left. Didn't pack. Didn't say good-bye. Just left. He refuses to tell me why. I didn't even know what Denazen did until Ginger told me."

"Ha," I whispered as a child screamed by the counter. Apparently his vanilla cone was *too* vanilla. "See? I told you."

Kiernan rolled her eyes. "Told me what? This doesn't prove a thing."

"If I had been in Seattle, your father would not have gotten away alive," Kale said bluntly.

Maybe Jade made a face. Or maybe she teared up. Whatever her expression, it caused Kale to frown. "I apologize. That was… unnecessary. Dez says I need to be less blunt."

"Sounds to me like Dez wants to change you."

"Change me?"

"She doesn't like who you are. She wants you to act differently. Be someone you're not. That thing you told me about? The counting? Perfect example."

Kale took another sip of his soda, then frowned. "That's bad?"

"Not if you want to let her control you." She tilted herself forward, no doubt giving him a bird's-eye view down her low-cut shirt.

"No one controls me. Not anymore." His voice was even, but I heard the darkness beneath the surface. The danger. "Dez is trying to help me fit in here. Not control me."

"I'm just saying, I think you're fine the way you are." She waved her spoon in his direction. "That temper you're trying so hard to keep under wraps? It's who you are."

"No. It's not. It's who Denazen wanted me to be."

"There's nothing wrong with a guy having a bit of a temper. In my opinion, it's kind of sexy."

"Holy crap. She's practically licking him," Kiernan hissed. She adjusted herself in the seat to get a little closer.

Jade leaned back. "So you never said. Why don't you talk about Denazen with Dez?"

"I don't want her opinion of me to change."

The spoon made an annoying *clank* as Jade scraped the bottom of her cup. "Why would you think it'd change?"

I leaned forward, breath held. I should have felt guilty about spying—I was here to find out about Jade, not pry into Kale's life—but I didn't.

"I was a monster. I can't erase the things I did, so I must still be one. Dez says I'm not, but she's wrong. She doesn't know."

Scraping the last of the thick shake from the bottom, she pushed the cup aside and leaned forward on the table. "Why do you think you're a monster?"

Kale looked from her to the cup. He tipped it over, eyes wide. "You finished it already?"

Her shoulders shook, and an annoying giggle filled the air. "It was so delish! Besides, a healthy appetite is sexy, right?"

Kale nodded. "Over the summer Dez challenged me to a hamburger-eating contest. She won."

Jade's irritation at the mention of my name was obvious. She visibly deflated, shoulders stiffening. "So, monster?"

"I've punished fifty-two people since I turned twelve. Forty-three men. Eight women. One child."

"'Punished'?"

"Killed."

There were several moments of silence. She was probably trying to pick her jaw up off the floor. "Oh, Kale. Don't beat yourself up over what happened."

Don't beat yourself up? On top of being an annoying little skank, this chick was an idiot. He tells her he murdered fifty-two people, and that's what she says? *Don't beat yourself up?*

"They made you do it, right?"

"Their methods of coercion are—persuasive."

"*Ohcrapohcrap,*" Kiernan chanted, shoving me in to the corner of the booth.

All the empty tables in the place and a man the size of a Volvo has to wedge himself into this one? He crashed into the seat backing Jade's—the one Kiernan and I were in—and his two kids climbed in across from him. One had a can of soda, the other was waving a headless Barbie doll that looked like it'd been dragged through the mud.

We were squashed against the wall, a few inches of free space separating us from the booth's large new occupant. "Now what?"

Pounding the table and kicking the seat, the two kids screamed, demanding hot fudge sundaes.

"What's that smell?" Kiernan pinched her nose.

As if to answer, the man next to us leaned toward the aisle slightly and fired off the most foul-smelling butt burp ever launched.

"*OhmyGod.*" I gagged. Frantically waving my hand back and forth to clear the air, I tried to lean over the seat to hear what Kale was saying. With the kids pounding on the table, it was impossible. I could see his lips moving but couldn't quite make out the words.

"Move!" Kiernan pushed me up onto the table. "He's about to blow again."

She pushed past, knocking over the kid's soda can in her haste. It tumbled off the table and into the younger one's lap, inciting an entirely new crying jag.

"Quick! She's heading to the bathroom." Kiernan jerked me forward before I could dismount the table. I slipped in the soda and crashed to the floor, dragging her down with me.

Of course the chaos didn't end there.

The Six version of a classic Lucy and Ethel bit, Kiernan and I, sprawled across the floor, didn't have time to move. A woman in a pencil skirt and tacky blouse—something I might have expected Dad's flunky Mercy to wear—came rushing down the aisle. I tried to move my leg, but the area was too narrow, and there was nowhere for it to go. Since we had somehow managed to not break contact, we were still cloaked by Kiernan's ability. The woman's foot caught under my knee, and she went flying— right toward Kale, who'd just gotten up from his table. In an attempt to save herself, the woman made a grab for him, but he jumped back onto the seat and out of her way. She crashed to the floor with a shriek, skirt splitting up the side.

I didn't waste time. Hauling Kiernan off the ground, I steered us around the cursing woman and into the bathroom.

"Ugh. I don't understand it," Jade's voice growled. I should have had this wrapped up by now."

I gave Kiernan an *I-told-you-so* grin and scrunched down to see which stall Jade was skulking in. Last one on the right. "Come on."

Inside the stall, Jade mumbled something too low for me to hear, then said, "I swear. I'll get him."

Slipping in to the stall next to her, I carefully closed the door.

"Here." I braced my hand against the divider wall. One foot balanced on the edge of the toilet, I said, "Grab my leg."

"Grab your leg? You're going to what, watch her take a dump?"

I rolled my eyes. "She's on her cell."

Kiernan sighed and grabbed my ankle.

Hauling myself up, I lifted onto my toes. "Crap. I'm, like, an inch too short. Hang on." Twisting, I placed my right foot on the toilet paper dispenser and hopped up.

"Stop moving," Kiernan snapped. "I almost let go!"

I ignored her and wrapped my fingers over the edge of the stall, pulling forward. "Bet if I knew Parkour, this wouldn't be so damn complicated," I mumbled. I'd just cleared the edge, the top of Jade's red head finally in view, when something cracked.

"Um, Dez? What was—"

Under my right foot, the paper dispenser broke free from the wall and crashed to the ground. I went with it.

I hit the floor with a jar, knocking my head against the edge of the toilet. Something smacked me in the face. Fingers.

"Ow!"

Kiernan squealed. "Oh, my God. I think I'm sitting in *pee*!"

"Oh, my God," Jade's voice snapped from the stall next door. She pounded on the metal divider several times before sighing. "What are you doing in there?"

I reached for the coat hook and tried to haul myself up. "Relax. It's probably just water."

"I'm so not loving you right now," Kieran breathed, pulling herself up. She unlatched the door and pushed it open. "And stop wiggling. She heard us because I lost contact, like, twice already!"

Next to us, the toilet flushed, and Jade's door swung open. She straightened her shirt and walked across to the sinks. She shot a quick glance at the stall we were in, its door swinging open, then at the door, and shrugged.

"He might be weird," she said, turning back to the mirror. "But he's endgame material." She turned on the faucet and soaped up her hands.

My boyfriend was *not* weird. He was perfect. Dragging Kiernan across the room, I kicked hard at the pipe beneath the sink. It took exactly three blows for it to come apart, sending water shooting in all directions.

We left Jade battling water and squealing like a five-year-old.

28

"Are you okay?" I heard Kale ask when Jade finally emerged from the bathroom. Her hair was slicked back, and her shirt was soaked.

She mumbled something and paid the bill, then followed him out the door.

The address Ginger had given them wasn't far, so I was relieved when they decided to walk the rest of the way. It provided me with the freedom to walk next to Kale and really listen.

Not that there was anything to listen to.

Jade kept trying to engage him in conversation, but Kale being Kale, gave her simple, one-word answers. He wasn't trying to be rude or dismissive, he was just being himself. If she knew anything about him, she'd know that for him to be really chatty, she'd only have to talk about simple things. Things people like her took for granted. Thunderstorms and snowfall. Bike rides and zoo animals.

One of the people on Brandt's list, Andrea Durham, was an employee at the Bronx Zoo. We'd met her there over the summer to warn her about Denazen. And even though Kale wasn't happy at first about the animals being caged, eventually he sort of fell in love with the zoo. We'd gone back four times since. His favorite part? The bears, of course.

By the time they got to the house, Jade looked like she was ready to explode. Reaching under a small porcelain frog statue, she pulled out a silver key and ushered Kale through the door.

The place was empty. There was no furniture, and judging from the smell, no one had lived here in quite some time. I wondered if Ginger knew the owners, or if we were squatting.

Time passed slowly. Two hours of watching Kale work on his control while listening to Jade try to provoke a reaction—any reaction. She'd tried sexy—batting her eyes and rubbing against him. He'd responded by telling her how much he wished I was there. She hadn't been happy about that, scowling outright and sulking like a child.

She'd done concerned—further elaborating on her theory that I was only out to control him, just like my dad had. Kale simply thanked her for the concern but assured her that when she got to know me, she'd see how wrong she was.

And she'd tried bitchy—spouting off that Kale needed to open his eyes and move on. She even tried to tell him our inability to touch was a sign from the universe. That confused him just a little—which in turn confused her. The bitch was clueless about the inner workings of Kale's mind.

By eight p.m. all the potted plants someone had kindly supplied were lined up against the wall, shriveled and gray, and they'd gotten nowhere.

"Let's move out to the backyard," Jade said, taking Kale's hand. "It's a beautiful night, and there's plenty of green out there."

He was frustrated. I could tell by the stiff way he moved. Tense. Kiernan and I followed them out the back doors to the patio.

"She's lying to me," Kale growled as he stalked back and forth.

Jade bent down and picked a maple leaf from a low-hanging branch. Handing it to Kale, she asked, "Who?"

He took the leaf and crumpled it in his palm, the dust drifting between his open fingers. "Dez. There's something she's keeping from me. She told me earlier."

Jade let out an exaggerated sigh. "*This* is why you're making no progress. I told you, this is all tied up in emotion. You need to clear your mind. Let it all go."

"She said it was to protect me," he continued as though she hadn't spoken.

Jade rolled her eyes. "Protect you? Unlikely. Someone like *you* doesn't need protecting. Personally, I think it's something else."

That caught his attention. "Something else?"

"I'd be a really horrible *friend* if I didn't point this out, Kale. But really, don't you see the way she looks at Alex? They've got history together. He's obviously still got a thing for her, and I've seen the way she looks at him. She feels the same way."

"You're wrong. He hurt her."

Her expression softened. "And you did, too. You almost killed her."

He looked like she'd just sucker punched him, and at that moment there was very little holding me back. "I didn't—that wasn't my fault. I would never—"

She took his hand. I waited for him to pull away, but he didn't.

"There's no way he's going to buy this shit…" I hissed. Tugging on Kiernan's hand, I took a step closer. We were about four feet from them now. Every word, every expression, clear as day.

"I know you didn't mean it," Jade continued. "But Dez runs on pure emotion. She's an all-or-nothing kind of girl. She can't touch you, and maybe that's just too much for her. Alex is available, interested, and she can touch him."

"I'm gonna fucking kill her." I tried to let go of Kiernan's hand, but she held tight. Jade's crap until now had been dirty, but throwing *Alex* in Kale's face? That was an entirely new kind of low.

"Wait," she whispered. "I wanna see how far this bitch is gonna go. *Then* we'll kick her ass."

Kale was shaking his head. "You don't know her."

"She saved you from Denazen. I get it. It's totally natural to feel attached to her because of that—"

"I *love* Dez," he said. The ferocity in his voice eased some of the tension in my shoulders, but it also sent a chill trickling down my spine.

"Are you sure? Maybe you should take a break from the underground. Go out and see the world. Get to know yourself. I'm not trying to confuse you, but, Kale, if you've only been able to be with her, how do you know there's not someone else out there?"

He took a step back, and the breath caught in my lungs. I could see it. The understanding sparking to life in his eyes. "Dez said that to me once."

The look on Jade's face, the justification and smug satisfaction, made me sick to my stomach. "See? She knew it, too."

He didn't answer. Instead, he tilted his head to the sky. All the tension seemed to drain away. His shoulders, previously taut, his fingers flexed and flicking—all gone. He was the picture of relaxation.

Of acceptance.

It was like watching a train wreck in slow motion. You see it coming toward you. You have plenty of time to walk way. But you can't. You're just glued. Waiting for the carnage.

Jade took his hand again. "I think you need to consider—"

"Can I kiss you?"

And there it was. The train.

"Dez, let's go," Kiernan said softly. She tried to tug me backward, but I wouldn't budge. I couldn't. My feet were suddenly filled with ten tons of lead, and my heart was on the verge of stopping. I had to see this through.

A part of me laughed at the fear clouding my brain. This was Kale. He'd never do it. He'd never kiss someone else. Another part of me cheered him on. *Prove me right*, it screamed. *I knew this would happen. I told you so. I fucking told you.*

"What?" Jade's eyes were wide. She dropped his hand and stepped away.

"Can I kiss you?" he repeated.

"Dez," Kiernan tried again. "You *don't* need to see this."

I couldn't form coherent words, or I would have told her that yes, I *did* need to see this. I wouldn't be able to believe it—to accept it—if I didn't see it with my own two eyes.

Kale stepped closer and wrapped his arms around Jade's waist. He didn't linger for dramatic effect or caress her skin lovingly. He dove in for the kill, and the train rolled over me at full speed.

Dead. I was dead. Hollow. Cold. All I could hear was my own voice. Over and over. *Itoldyouso. Itoldyouso. Itoldyouso.*

It took a moment, but Jade threw herself into it. Giggling, she wrapped both arms around his shoulders, pulling him close. She had him now. No way was she letting go. The yard was eerily silent. Crickets, cars passing on the street out front, even the sound of my own heart pounding in my ears—it all disappeared. The only sound was Jade and Kale.

There's this whole romantic notion about kissing. In the movies, it's this mysterious thing back dropped by sweet music and fade-to-black moments. In reality, though, there're spit and suction and slurping noises. And Jade was either a really sloppy kisser, or she was just going to town.

There was a tiny voice inside my brain fighting for attention. It tried to spew logic. Jade wasn't into him. Not really. She was working for Denazen. For Dad. This was part of the plot to reel Kale in. And while that fact had consoled me each and every time I saw her shooting him the *fuck-me* eyes, it didn't change the fact that Kale had fallen for it. *He* kissed *her*.

I didn't mean to do it. It just sort of happened. One minute I was holding Kiernan's hand, the next minute I wasn't.

They didn't notice at first. Too wrapped up in themselves, I supposed. Jade saw me first.

"Oops," she whispered, pulling away from Kale.

Jade wiped her mouth with the back of her hand and at least had the decency to move away a few inches. I caught the barest hint of a smile before she looked in the other direction.

I laughed, a horrible sound that actually hurt my own ears. It was grating. Wrong. Broken somehow. "Some ninja, huh? I was standing here a whole twenty seconds."

At first Kale didn't say anything. He didn't even look surprised. Or sorry. Then it must have hit him.

"Dez, I—"

I held out my hands. He needed to stop. I couldn't listen to that voice. That voice I swore to myself would never lie. Never betray. I'd put him on a pedestal—which wasn't fair, really—and he'd fallen.

"No. Seriously. It's cool, right? You guys are great together. You know, 'cause you can grope each other without all the death and pain and shit."

I took a step back. Kale took one forward.

"Wait. Dez, it's—"

I laughed again. Even louder. And longer. In fact, I couldn't *stop* laughing. I'd snapped. Trauma had brought on the Supremacy crazies five months early because there was no other way I'd come unhinged like this. Not Dez Cross. Ms. Keep It Together. The whole thing reminded me a little of the way Fin had bounced down from that last step, giggling like a loony and spouting nonsense.

I didn't live by many rules, but I had a few. Never let anyone see you cry, and never, *ever* let anyone see you fall apart. I tried, but I wasn't able to hold back the tears. And since I'd broken rule number one, rule number two seemed like fair game.

"Not what it looks like? Is *that* what you were gonna spew? Did you know that's what Alex tried to say to me? Or maybe you were going to tell me this was all some kind of setup? An act played out to shield me from something big and bad? Guess what? *Alex* said that to me, too. Matter of fact, for all the bad blood between you two, you have a hell of a lot in common all of a sudden. You both screwed me over for some cheap-ass whore."

Jade snickered. "See? Notice how she keeps bringing up Alex?"

Everything turned red. I fell forward and struck out, putting all my weight behind the blow. Jade toppled back, losing her balance and hitting the dew-wet grass with a muffled *thud*. I knew she hadn't felt anything, but it gave me some small amount of satisfaction. I watched her for a moment, our eyes meeting in rage-filled challenge.

And then I was running. Somewhere behind me, Kiernan called out, but I ignored her. Space. Distance. Miles. I needed a huge gap between me and Kale. Cities. Planets. Hell, nothing would be enough.

I got about a mile from the house and stopped to catch my

breath. No stupid moves this time. Last time I'd run off, I'd ended up running into Aubrey and Able. Not that things could reach a whole new level of *oh, shit*, but why take chances?

So I found a dark corner and cried my eyes out. Five months ago my life hadn't been perfect by anyone's definition, but in my opinion, it'd been pretty awesome. I was getting ready for senior year, made a hobby out of driving Dad's blood pressure to new heights, and partied till dawn. I had friends, flings, and freedom.

Then I met Kale.

I'd never had so much faith in anyone before. In anything. Fierce. Loyal. Pure. That was Kale. He made me feel special. Whole.

Now I was sitting on the other side of the fence. Lost and alone. The poison was getting worse. It was getting harder to concentrate through the constant pain in my shoulder. Random waves of gravity-defying dizziness came and went in increasing increments. And the idea of food? Pass.

My time was up. I was going to have to come clean—if for no reason other than by morning, it'd be impossible to hide. From the time I'd seen Kale and Jade, to the time I'd arrived in the alley, the poison had almost reached my elbow. I was pretty sure it'd made it to the base of my neck. Kale might have noticed back at the house if the yard hadn't been so dark.

And you know, he hadn't been busy sucking Jade's face off.

Icy fear started wiggling in my stomach. Before, I'd had something to focus on to keep my mind busy. Proving Jade was working for Dad. Now that I had that proof—I hadn't seen her talking on the phone, but we'd heard the conversation just the same—all I could think about was the poison and how badly I wanted to run to Kale.

But that couldn't happen. He was holding on to Jade now, and the poison seemed to be spreading faster. There was one bright spot in all of this. The Supremacy crazies weren't going to get me.

I'd never make it that long.

But there was another option. One I'd originally thought was out of the question. Giving Dad what he wanted. Me for the cure. It was feasible now, wasn't it? On one hand, by no definition did I want to fork myself over to Denazen—I knew what they did to people like me—but on the other, one of my main roadblocks was gone. If Kale was falling for Jade, then maybe he wouldn't come after me.

A small whisper in the back of my mind tried to tell me again that something about this wasn't right, but I was able to push it aside. The kiss was fresh in my mind. The image had been permanently embedded into my brain. The sounds. The smells. The look in Kale's eyes. Pity. It had been pity in his voice. Everything was starting to make sense now. Kale had started falling out of love with me the moment Jade arrived. Ginger was right. We weren't meant to be together because he and Jade were.

The whisper tried again—*wrongwrongwrongwrong*—but the facts were too strong. Couldn't be denied.

I'd call Dad. Right after the party. Tell him I was ready to deal. Wasn't ideal, but it might be my best shot at seeing eighteen.

Might be my *only* shot at seeing eighteen.

I left a message on both Mom's and Ginger's voice mail telling them I'd split from Kiernan, and I'd meet them all at the party. After that, I headed for town.

Three blocks away, I slipped into the McDonald's on Fourth Street. Standing in front of the cracked mirror, I washed my face. My eyes were red and swollen, and my cheeks were flushed. Definitely not party perfect. Taking a deep breath, I held out my hand and wiggled my fingers. I *had* to be party perfect. This was my last hurrah. "Time to see what this baby can really do."

Touching the skin below my right eye, I focused on the magazine balanced on the edge of the sink. A Cover Girl ad with Drew Barrymore's bright eyes and wide smile. Her flawless skin. Creamy, even, and just a bit too pale. As I watched, the puffiness faded, and the redness seemed to sink away, replaced by a normal, healthy glow. Next, I tried something a little more experimental. Makeup.

Not as simple as I'd thought.

I flipped through the magazine, searching for something dramatic. Sure, I could mimic the same old routine I'd gone with a thousand times, but this was a special occasion. A going-away party—even if the others didn't know it yet. I had to be perfect.

I found an ad I really liked. The model had thick, black-rimmed eyes with dramatic, smoky lids and a dainty, lattice-like swirl at the corner of each eye. Slightly goth but seriously cool. Definitely something I could rock.

The experiment started with disastrous results. The first try, instead of eyeliner, I ended up turning my entire eyelid solid black. While it would have gone over pretty well with the hard-core goth crowd, it wasn't quite what I was looking for.

The next attempt was a little cooler but not quite right. The iris of my right eye. That would have been perfect for Halloween, but not tonight.

When I finally managed to get my eyes just right, I moved onto my lips. The top one blood red, while the bottom turned white. The next attempt yielded even freakier results. An almost tie-dyed effect in shades of brown and tan. Circus lips. Change the color and add a red nose, and I could have passed for the Bride of Bozo.

After I nailed the makeup, it was time to deal with the clothes. The black jeans had to go. They were cool but not the look I was aiming for. The model I'd used for the makeup was wearing a killer red leather skirt and some pretty drool-worthy boots, but I was in a pants mood. Easier to move around without the worry of having a Paris Hilton flashing fiasco.

I flipped to the end, disappointed, and closed the magazine. About to go with something from my old wardrobe, I saw it. The girl on the back cover. The ultimate party outfit. It was an ad for a place called *Shocking the House*. Placing my hands flat on my thighs, I stared at the page. The pants came in two colors—black and brown. I focused on the brown. Snug around the thigh and knee, then straight down with the tiniest of tapers. They closed in the back—laced over the curve of my butt and tied in an elaborate bow that hung down several inches. The front formed a deep V that came several inches below my belly button.

The next part sucked. Normally I'd go straight into heartbreaker mode. Something tight that showed a dangerous amount of skin—the corset top the model had on was perfect—but the poison was too noticeable now. I had an idea, but wasn't sure I could pull it off. If it worked, I had a killer future in fashion design.

I pictured my favorite red silk shirt, remembering the feel of the material against my skin. Smooth and slippery. How it draped my shoulders and fluttered slightly whenever I moved. It had a thin ribbon in the back that tied to make the shirt fitted. That ribbon had always been my favorite part. Now, with any luck, it'd become something even better.

I focused on the model's corset, pictured the ribbon tied by a thin string at my wrist and winding—slightly thicker—up my left arm. It thinned again at my neck, wrapping around like a choker before diving south and diagonally skimming the top of my chest at the perfect semi-cleavage-baring angle. On the right side, the ribbon thinned to the width of a shoelace, winding in an artfully intricate pattern down my arm, and tying to match the other side.

The bodice of the shirt fused with the ribbon seamlessly and ended just above my waist. The gap between the edge of the shirt and the waist of the low-cut leather pants showed just enough pale skin to be sexy but not enough to be trashy.

I smiled at my reflection in the mirror. One last thing. Touching the tips of my hair, I closed my eyes. When I opened them, I couldn't help but gasp. It was the opposite of when I'd met Kale. Black with blonde streaks. Other than the brown I'd gone with for Sumrun, I'd never dyed my whole head. I'd always been blonde with a splash of color. The change was drastic and a little bit of a shock to my system, but I liked it.

Dramatic with an almost tortured feel. Dark.

It suited my mood—and my future.

• • •

I'd used napkins on the way out to make some quick cash. The Rockies wasn't far, but I'd opted to go with a slight heel— nothing like the shoes I'd worn to homecoming—on my boots and figured my feet would appreciate the bus ride. That, and the pain in my shoulder had spread. I ached all over now. It sapped my energy and made simple things like walking harder than they should be.

"Ginger's not too thrilled with you," Paul said as I approached the building. The outside was covered in faux rock and had two mannequins scaling either side of the sign advertising The Rockies. I'd come here a few times with Alex and had always been afraid those stupid things would fall on me as I entered the building.

I shrugged. "Nothing new about that. Everyone here?"

"Sue and Ginger got here five minutes ago. Your boy's been here awhile."

I didn't correct him. Kale wasn't really *my* boy anymore, was he?

Paul grabbed my arm as I passed. His fingers dug into my skin, and I had to bite down to keep from crying out. "They're going to rip you apart to see what makes you tick."

My heart just about stopped. *"What?"*

Paul stood, yanking me closer. "Denazen. They're going to lock you up, then slice you open. Pull out your bits and put them on display."

I jerked myself free and stumbled back. "What the hell?"

He blinked. He was sitting back on the steps, his hands nowhere near me. "*I said*, are you okay?"

I swallowed the lump in my throat and forced a smile. The hallucinations had started. "'Course. Why?"

He shrugged. "Just look a little paler than usual. Must be the hair." He winked. "*Hot*, by the way."

I flashed him one final smile and pushed my way inside. Like always, the place was party heaven. Flashing lights danced across the walls as bodies packed the center of the room, swaying and thrashing to the beat. I'd never asked, but I wondered who set these things up. Every night it was a different location, yet each one was always just as awesome as the last.

"You never listen, do you?" Alex said, stepping into my path. Then he must've gotten a good look. His mouth fell open, hazel eyes roaming my body from toe to blonde tips. "You look—"

"Amazing? Of course. Sucks to be you right now, huh? Missing out on such amazingness?"

"I was going to go with awful." His gaze lingered for a moment before he stepped back and shook his head. Behind him, the dance floor was packed with bodies. Most familiar, some more so than others. "Ginger's ready to shit kittens."

"Overreact much? I needed some time alone. Back off."

He looked like he wanted to argue but held his hands up in a show of surrender.

"Where is she? I just want to tell her what Kiernan and I found out. Jade is working for my dad. I overheard her talking to him on her cell."

"When?"

"Few hours ago."

"Her cell was in the hotel. I heard her complaining. She doesn't have it anymore."

"Well, then she got another one. I heard her talking to Dad. Then she said Kale was endgame. She almost had him."

"Holy crap," he growled, surprised. Taking my arm, he started for the stairs. "We need to tell Ginger before she starts that meeting."

I nodded and started to follow, but the room picked that moment to spin out of control. Everything was a blur of garbled noise and color as I crashed to my knees. Hauling me to my feet, Alex spun us toward the corner and pushed me up against the wall. Everything was snapping in and out of focus. He looked pissed.

Seizing my left arm, he pushed the fabric to my elbow. "Fuck."

"It looks worse than it is," I tried.

"I doubt that." His expression went from angry to furious. "What the hell is wrong with you? You had your chance. Time's up. I'm calling Cross myself."

Surely I'd heard him wrong. I tried to push him away, but my arms were made of pudding. *"What?"*

His fingers brutally pierced the soft underside of my arm. A few feet away, someone giggled. The girl from Roudey's. The one he'd cheated on me with. She waltzed over, swinging her hips and licking her lips. With a wink, she wrapped an arm around Alex possessively and nodded. "Cross is the only one who can help you. He's the only one who cares enough to save you."

"You want me to—"

Fingers latching around my wrist, he pulled me away from the wall and toward the stairs. The room had stopped spinning, and by the time we reached the top step, everything was back in focus. The bimbo from Roudey's was gone.

When we burst through the door, Ginger was in the middle of asking how everyone did with their lists. Mom was on the far side of the room, standing suspiciously close to Dax. Kale was on her other side, arms folded and lips pressed tight. Jade, I noted, was on the opposite side of the room by the door. She was staring at him with a mix of anger and fear. When Alex barged in, me attached to his arm, everyone turned.

"So nice of you to finally join us, Deznee," Ginger said, glaring at me. "As I was saying, we've discovered a new problem on the Denazen front."

Beside me, Alex stiffened. "Dez," he said, trying to push me into the middle of the room.

Ginger continued. "Aside from hitting our home and taking our friends, a source says they've started working on a new project. A new Supremacy trial."

"Dez." Again, this time louder.

I shook my head, eyes begging him to be quiet. I'd made the choice to turn myself in, I just wasn't ready to tell them. I wanted to wait. Now Alex was going to ruin it.

"Dez," he screamed. It echoed off the walls, bouncing around the small room like a runaway racquetball. "Tell them. *Now.*"

When I still didn't move, he grabbed my arm and jerked me forward to the middle of the room.

From the corner of my eye, I saw Kale lunge for him, but Alex held up his hand. "Back off, asshole. I'm doing her a favor." The fabric on my sleeve tore as he shoved it up past my elbow. "She's dying."

I shot Alex a glare I hoped conveyed *I'm going to kill you* and sighed. Even though it was a lie, I said, "Dying is a little dramatic."

"What is that?" Mom breathed. The fact that I was wearing red seemed to go unnoticed. She pushed past Alex and grabbed my arm.

I'd been ousted. Might as well come clean. So much for enjoying my last party. "Poison."

"Poison?" she repeated, pale. "What kind of poison? Where did it come from?"

Just behind her, Kale was watching me, eyes wide. Icy blue laced with concern stole my breath away.

He still wanted me.

Of course he still wanted me. *Why* had I thought he'd give me up so easily? I remembered the moments after the kiss crying in the alley and standing in front of the bathroom mirror, but it felt like someone else's memory. Like I was watching it on repeat from the other side of the screen.

I answered Mom but kept looking at Kale. It was his presence that gave me the strength to say it out loud. An odd feeling, since only an hour ago, I was determined to leave him behind. I'd been convinced he'd willingly let me skip into Denazen's arms. The thought was ridiculous. I knew it was ridiculous—yet I'd *believed* it. Like, *the sky is blue and cats say meow* kind of believed.

"The night I fell from the crane, I went back to the old house. A couple of Dad's people were there. They were Sixes. One touched me."

"The one from the van," Kale said. His voice was low, and his fingers were flicking.

I looked away. "Yeah. Able."

"We need to call Daun," Dax said, arm around Mom's shoulders. He pulled her back several steps to give me some room.

Alex shook his head. "Dez approached Daun before she left. There was nothing she could do."

I swallowed. Might as well go full Monty. "There's more. When I went to the post office the other day, Dad was there."

I glared at Jade. She looked away. Why not put a neon *I did it* sign above your head?

"*Someone* told him I'd be there. He said there was a cure." Stumbling to my feet, I said, "For the poison—and the Supremacy side effects."

That got everyone talking at once. While I watched them argue with one other, I noticed two things. Kiernan wasn't here yet, and Jade was off in the corner, inching toward the door.

"Stuff socks in it," Ginger boomed after several minutes passed. "I can't think with you all yapping at once." She turned to me. "So Cross has the cure. I assume he offered a trade?"

Of everyone, Ginger was the only one not freaking about my revelation because she'd known about the poison all along. "If I turn myself over to him, he'll give me the cure for the poison."

Ginger nodded once. She'd expected as much. "And the Supremacy side effects? What of that cure?"

I kind of wanted to smack the old woman in that moment. Why ask questions when she probably already knew the answers? But instead of snapping, I turned to Jade. She was reaching for the door handle. "What do you think, *Jade*? Is there really a cure for the Supremacy side effects?"

She froze. "Me? Why are you asking me?"

I stalked to the door, fighting to keep the waves of nausea at bay, and shoved her back. "'Cause you're the only survivor." I poked her in the shoulder and said, "Jade is working for Dad. He says she's Supremacy. Over eighteen and alive. The only one to be given the cure."

A muffled squeal escaped Jade's throat. "He said that? I've never met the guy!"

"I heard you. At the ice cream place. You were in the bathroom talking on your cell."

Horror morphed into something else. Anger. "You. That was you and Kiernan, wasn't it? How dare you spy on me!"

She brought her hand up, and I smiled. "Go ahead. I'll destroy you. You ground harmful gifts—and mine isn't harmful. I'll mimic you into the fat, ugly midget that lives over on Fifth Street if you so much as swat air in my direction."

"Cut the crap," Ginger snapped. "Answer my question, Deznee. What did Cross ask for in exchange for the second cure?"

I opened my mouth but just couldn't get the words out.

Kale didn't seem to have the same problem. His fingers stopped moving. "Me. He told her once I was back at Denazen, he'd give her the cure."

He turned to me for confirmation, and I looked away.

"The second cure doesn't exist," Alex snapped. "Cross will say anything to get what he wants. Maybe Jade is one of Cross's people, but she's not Supremacy. No way."

"But the first cure, it does exist?" Kale asked.

Alex nodded.

"Then call him now. Tell him I will go back in exchange for the poison cure."

Ginger nodded and turned to Dax. "Would you mind making the arrange—"

Everyone had gone nuts. "Are you out of your senile, bat-brained mind? He's *not* going back."

"This is my decision, Dez," Kale said softly.

"It's really not. This is *my* life. It's *my* call, and I say no way in hell."

"Approach this logically, Kale." Jade stepped forward, pushing herself between us. "Let's say you go back, and this Cross guy keeps his end of the deal. He gives her the cure. Then what? She croaks a few months later because the Supremacy thing doesn't exist? Then she's dead, and you're back in hell for nothing."

"The Supremacy cure *does* exist," I said, grabbing her by the hair. I yanked her head around so we were eye to eye. "He gave it to *you*!"

She screamed, and Alex shot forward to rip us apart.

"This is my choice," I growled at them. "And I've made it. I'm going to turn *myself* in. I've got nothing to lose at this point."

Several seconds of silence—then chaos.

Mom and Dax were screaming, Jade was smiling, and Kale was in my face.

"You're not going," he said. Over and over.

"What the hell is going through your head?" Alex yelled, shouldering Jade aside.

He reached for me, but I knocked his hand away. "What? You just said I should call my dad!"

His eyes went wide. Like a cartoon character who'd gotten the surprise of his life. "I would never suggest—"

"You did," I insisted. Sharp pain flared at my temples, and I knotted my fingers through my hair to ease the pressure. "Just before! When we were downstairs. You said Cross was the only one who would help me."

His expression was stricken. "Dez, I'd never—"

A sharp whistle cut through the room. "Everyone, shut the hell up. This is my party, and I demand the floor."

Stunned silence filled the room. Ginger, happy to be the center of attention again, turned to me. "Deznee, you're telling us that Alex advised you to take Cross up on his offer? Please, tell me, what are the side effects of this poison?"

Alex had never suggested going to Dad. I'd imagined the whole thing. "Intense pain and…hallucinations," I replied a little sheepishly.

That's what Able had said at the restaurant. What else hadn't been real? Jade had already confirmed the ice cream place— thank God—but what about the kiss I saw?

Of course that'd *never* happened. Kale wouldn't do that to me. It all made sense. The fuzzy, erratic feeling I'd felt just before it'd happened. It was similar to the way things warped during my *conversation* with Alex. The whole thing had been one big, horrific hallucination.

Ginger nodded and pointed to the door. "Everyone out except for Kale, Deznee, and Sue."

Once the door closed, she turned to Kale. "You will not be going back to that place."

He started to argue, but she snapped her fingers and turned to me. "And neither will you."

Kale let out an audible breath and leaned back against the wall.

"We will arrange a trade. Deznee will tell Cross she is willing to go with him if he cures her, but he must bring the cure with him. We will be lying in wait and ambush him."

"The cure is a person—Able's brother, Aubrey. Able poisons, and Aubrey heals."

"Even better. Much easier to find than a small vial."

"What about the Supremacy cure?" Kale asked as Ginger made her way to the door.

"We must go through one door at a time, Kale. If Deznee doesn't survive the poison, then the Supremacy side effects won't matter."

And she was gone, followed by Mom, leaving me alone with Kale.

Kale took my arm in his hand, taking care to let the fabric slid back down over my skin. "He knew about this, and I didn't."

He meant Alex. "Yeah."

"Because I hurt you. Because you know it would hurt me?"

"Sorta—I mean, not really… It's comp—"

He was glaring at me.

Then his words really sank in. The bottom fell out from my stomach, and my newly formed, oh-so-fragile puff of hope disintegrated. "Wait—hurt me?"

"When I kissed Jade. I hurt you."

I didn't answer right away—I couldn't. My tongue felt heavy, and my throat was dry. It was like watching it happen all over again. In slow motion.

He understood my hesitation. Expression pained, he said, "You thought it was a hallucination."

"Guess it wasn't." Taking a deep breath, I answered his question. "And yeah, you hurt me, but I didn't tell Alex to hurt you back. Actually, I didn't *tell* Alex. He found out on his own. He saw it a few days ago, before it got this bad."

Kale's face darkened. "He saw it? How did he see it? Did you—"

It took me a minute to figure out what he was hinting at. "Oh, God! No. How could you even ask—" Then it *really* hit me. "And whoa—that reaction? Wrong on so many levels after what happened with Jade, Kale. You know, that thing that *wasn't* a hallucination?"

He was quiet for a minute, so I decided to keep talking before I chickened out.

"It's one or the other." I swallowed. The pain surged, and a wave of dizziness swept over me. A rush of heat, then an arctic chill, followed by a dull, all-over ache. "I tried to warn you this might happen. That once you were able to touch—"

He growled and stepped away. "You make me want to scream. It's very strange."

"Right back atcha."

His expression softened. "I have *no* feelings for Jade."

"You *kissed* her. Hell, you even asked first. And at the ice cream place—Jade's hand. You said it was different. Good different."

He smiled. "It was. It didn't come close to the feeling I get when I hold yours. I kissed Jade so you could stop worrying. About me. About us. About *her*. I had no intention of hiding it from you."

Time stopped. The air stilled, and the music downstairs quieted. "You—"

Carefully, he reached across and placed my hand over his heart. "My heart only beats like this for you. No amount of touching, no other girl, nothing will ever change that. I knew you didn't believe me. After what happened on the crane, when Jade took my hand in the conference room, I saw it in your eyes. Doubt.

It was hard for me to deal with that—having you feel so uncertain. I wanted you to feel as sure about me as I do about you."

I felt like there was an entire bag of cotton stuffed inside my mouth. "So you thought kissing her would get rid of my doubt?"

Kale took a step back. "Of course. I kissed her and have no desire to do so again. It fixes everything."

"So you're saying it was a bad kiss?"

"Bad," he mused. "Not bad. Enjoyable, actually. Although she's rather pushy. She kept trying to take her shirt off the other night."

"You're not winning the argument here…"

"I kissed her to prove to you that no one else matters. I've spent time with her. Held her hand. I've had something to compare you to, and it changes nothing."

Kale logic. Unique, and totally innocent. I was an ass for not realizing it from the start. "So you don't want her?"

"You thought I did? Is that why you've been avoiding me?"

"Losing my immunity to you, it screwed things up. I ran off like an idiot that night and dug myself a huge hole—only I didn't realize it at first. Then Jade got here, and she *so* obviously wanted you. By the time I realized I was in serious trouble, you and Jade seemed cozy with each other. I wanted to tell you, trust me. I wanted more than anything for you to hold me and tell me things would be fine—but you couldn't. Instead, I've been running around, terrified and alone."

He unzipped his hoodie and shrugged it off. Draping the hood over my head, he wrapped it around me from behind and wound his arms tight around.

"Everything will be all right," he whispered, his breath tickling my ear. "I swore nothing would ever make me go back to that place, but it was a lie. I will make sure you get better no matter what it takes. No matter what I have to do."

31

When we finally emerged from the room, Jade was waiting at the end of the hall.

She looked me up and down, eyes lingering on Kale's hoodie, and snapped, "What took so long?"

I stuffed my arms through the sleeves and pulled the fabric tighter. I knew it was over seventy in here, but according to my internal clock, it was going on forty. "Didn't realize we were on a time schedule. It's Friday, and we're at a party. No school till Monday."

"Whatever." She turned to Kale. "Shall we?"

He stared. "Shall we what?"

Clearly Jade was confused. "Go? I was thinking we could head downstairs. Maybe grab a drink and dance a little before we head back to wherever it is we're shacking up for the night."

"I'm not practicing tonight. I'm going to stay with Dez."

"Stay with—I don't understand."

If I hadn't felt so crummy, I would have laughed at her.

Wiggled my ass in its spectacular leather low riders, thrown an arm around my guy, and sauntered off while she drooled all over herself. I mean hell, I was literally knocking on death's door, and I still looked awesome. The way I felt, it just annoyed me. "Seriously? You thought he was in there breaking up with me?"

Kale glanced back at the door. "Breaking up?"

"Saying you wanted her instead of me," I supplied. "Stepping out permanently."

Kale shook his head. He even looked a little apologetic. "No. I'd never step out on Dez."

"But—the ice cream place—my hand. You told me things you never told her! You trusted me. You *kissed* me!"

Kale tilted his head, confused. "I would tell anyone who asked what I told you. It was because I didn't care what you thought of me. And the kiss wasn't for you, it was for Dez."

Jade's jaw dropped.

"There you are." Mom turned the corner just as Jade twirled on her heel to leave. She watched her go, trying to hide a smile. "I take it you two are fine now?"

"Now that little Miss Porn Star has been put in her place, yeah."

"Good. Kale, can you take Dez back to Meela's? She doesn't look well. Ginger thinks stress might be helping the poison spread faster."

Kale nodded, and I couldn't help but laugh. "Very good! That was a total mom thing to say! See? You're getting it."

She hesitated, then smiled. "There are a few more things to do here. After we're done, Dax will drop me off on the way back to his place."

"So, Dax?" I said as soon as Mom was out of earshot.

"He was holding her hand earlier. It made her smile."

"Well, then, good for them, I guess. Will you—are you staying at Meela's, too?"

His smile faded. "Do you want me to stay someplace else?"

"No," I blurted. "It's just—the last few nights you didn't exactly push to stay close…"

"At first Ginger didn't think it was safe for me to stay so close. She didn't think we could—keep our hands to ourselves?"

I snickered. "Valid point."

"Then she said she wanted me close to Jade so I could safely be around people." He shrugged. "She said spending all my time with you wasn't teaching me how to *properly* interact with others and that I was bound to pick up bad habits."

I snorted.

He draped his arm around my shoulder and steered me toward the stairs. "Sue is right. You need rest. How do you feel?" Palm pressed firmly into my shoulder, he frowned. "You seem warm. You have a fever."

"At the moment? Fine. It comes in spurts."

We made it down the stairs, people moving aside to give Kale a safe berth. When we reached the bottom, we wove around to the edge of the room. The dance floor was packed with bodies, all enjoying the music. In the far corner, several guys were scaling the rock wall. Someone had turned the surface to ice, and those climbing were forced to use their gifts to make it to the top. I knew we should go, but I couldn't help stopping to watch them for a moment.

One had it easy. I couldn't remember his name, but I knew he was an animal shifter who could shift specific body parts—kind of freaky. He'd shifted his hands into claws and was easily taking the lead.

The second, I couldn't remember seeing before. He was trailing just behind Shifter Guy, using some serious muscle to punch holes through the ice and grab the grips beneath.

The third—well, I had no idea. His gift obviously wasn't helpful in a situation like this because he was stuck on the ground, staring up at the other two. Every now and then he'd try to dig in a foothold, slipping back to the ground to a symphony of laughter.

I was just about to turn and head for the door when I saw Alex weaving through the crowd. I started forward but wasn't fast enough.

"Leaving?"

"Looks that way, doesn't it?"

He gave Kale a dismissive wave. "With *him*? Didn't you catch him trying to suck the tonsils out of Porn Star Barbie?"

It bothered me that news of the kiss had apparently made the rounds—Sixes were skilled in the game of telephone—but I merely rolled my eyes.

Alex shrugged. "Whatever. Keep forgetting you're into that weird shit now. Hang on, just lemme grab my jacket."

I stopped him. "Um, why?"

"'Cause I'm going with you."

"No, you're not."

He flashed me a wicked grin and pulled free. "Yeah, I am. Ginger *insists*."

"Bullshit."

His smile faded. "Look, I'm not trying to hassle you and the *cheater*—though pissing him off is a major perk. Since Denazen wants you both, it's safer to take along an extra body. Ya know, just in case."

Kale didn't try to hide the disdain in his voice. "You want to come to ensure both of us are protected?"

Alex straightened and squared his shoulders. Taking a step closer to Kale, he smiled. "No. I want to ensure that *she's* protected. Don't give a dead rat's ass about you, brother man."

Kale stood tall. "I am all the protection she needs."

"And who's gonna protect her from you? Or did you figure out how to pet puppies without murdering them?"

"Come just a little closer," Kale growled. "We can find out."

Shoving Alex, I grabbed the back of Kale's shirt. "He wants to tag along, fine. Whatever. Let's just go."

And with that, I left the party wedged uncomfortably between my boyfriend and my ex.

• • •

They went at it the entire way to Meela's house. Never came up for air. Before we even got off the block, I considered touching Kale so I'd have some peace and quiet.

"If you continue to push me, Alex, I'm going to touch you. I've counted to three hundred. Twice."

Alex snickered. "Counted to three hundred? What the hell is that supposed to mean?"

"It means you need to knock it off." I glared at Kale. "Both of you."

"Fact is fact. I knew what was going on. You didn't. She didn't *tell* you, brother man. What's that say?"

Kale stopped walking. We were standing in front of Meela's house now. The lights inside were off, but someone had left the one over the front door on.

"It says," Kale said in that dark, deceptively calm way of his, "that you are an annoyance. I don't deal well with annoyances. But it's a very simple fix. No one will miss you. Your kind are like vermin. Everywhere."

"I disagree. I think *Dez* would miss me." Alex winked. "A lot. And my kind? Dude, we're the same kind."

Fists clenched, Kale leaned closer. "We are nothing alike."

Alex lost his grin. Jaw tight, he nodded in my direction. "We're exactly alike. We both hurt her."

"Wow. And there it is. Your inner asshole just bled through." I turned away from them and stalked up the walkway.

I managed to get the key into the lock and turn the handle without strangling either one of them. As soon as I stepped through the door, I heard a muffled voice.

"I don't care. It's only a matter of time. I'm done. Get me the fuck out."

"That sounds like—"

Alex put his hand over my mouth. Eyes wide, he shook his head and pointed to the hall. Silently, we crept along the wall, stopping right outside the room. Kiernan was sitting on the couch, feet kicked onto the table, and talking into her cell.

"Does it matter who you get first? One pretty much guarantees the other—trust me. It's kind of pathetic."

"This *isn't* what it sounds like...," I whispered.

Kale's hand was on my shoulder, urging me back. "Dez."

Kiernan continued talking, oblivious to our presence. "No. There was no party tonight. The old lady said it was canceled."

And that's why she hadn't been at The Rockies. She didn't even know about the party because Ginger knew about her. I was guessing she and Jade didn't get a list of people to notify. That's what Jade had meant about wasting their time. Random errands. Ginger had kept them busy and out of the way.

"Okay, fine. One more night." A pause. "Okay. Night."

Alex tapped my shoulder and pointed to the door. I shook my head and pointed to the living room. "*Not a frigging chance*," he mouthed. "*Need to go*."

I put my hands up in surrender. Turning like I was about to head for the front door, I whispered, "But just one thing first."

Before either of them could stop me, I flew around the

corner and charged. Knocking her back against the couch, I pinned Kiernan down. "Lemme guess—ordering pizza?"

She dropped the cell. It bounced off the cushion and landed on the floor. "It's not what it sounds like, Dez! I can totally explain."

"Oh, so you weren't on the phone with Denazen?"

"Denazen? Those tools? Of course not. I was on the phone with my *dad*."

She kicked up, catching me off guard. I toppled to the side, allowing her to jump up. "Who just happens to work for Denazen. Oh. Wait. I guess it *was* what it looked like."

"It would be foolish of you to think you could fight both of us," Kale said, stepping up beside me. With a chuckle, he added, "It would be foolish to think you could fight Dez. Me, well, that would be ridiculous."

I rolled my eyes. Poor guy didn't have any idea how insulting that sounded…

"Fight you? I don't need to fight you." She snapped her fingers—purely for show—and disappeared. "I can do *this*."

"Shit."

Something slammed into my left side, knocking me to the ground. Vision blurred as my eyes watered, and I struggled to catch my breath. A few seconds later, the front door swung open.

"Oh, and Dez? There really *is* a cure for the Supremacy side effects—and it *does* work. They gave it to me first. Daddy always *did* like me better."

"Dax will be by to get us in fifteen. We're all going to shack up at his place."

I cringed, wrapping both arms around myself. I had the chills again. They were almost bad enough to take my mind away from the pain, which had gotten significantly worse in the last few hours. "Dax's apartment? That's insane. There probably isn't enough floor space."

Alex shook his head. "Not the apartment. The house."

I blinked. "He has a house?"

"He's got, like, four of them, actually."

"If he has *four* houses, why the hell is he living in a crappy apartment in the Parkview dumps?"

Alex shrugged and pushed aside the curtains to keep watch. "It belonged to a friend of his."

I sank onto the couch, pulling Kale's hoodie tighter. "I can't believe this. It's getting to be a seriously freaky trend."

Kale kneeled in front of me, hand resting on my knee. I

almost wished I'd kept the jeans on. The warmth from his fingers didn't make it through the leather pants. "What is?"

"Am I *that* easy to fool? I go how many years living in the same house as Dad, having no clue what he's about or the horrible things he does. This is like the same thing all over again. Kiernan and I were tight. How did I not see this?"

"No one saw this," Alex said.

"But my *sister*? How is that even possible?"

Alex sighed. "Well, when a man and a woman lo—"

One look and he shut up.

The chill started to fade, and I shed the hoodie. The heat was taking its place. Of the two, this was the worst. The chill eased some of the pain. Made everything feel somewhat numb. But the heat… The heat intensified everything. Each little throb, every single pang, all amplified. I gritted my teeth against the pain, and said, "I feel like Lois Lane. Completely oblivious."

Alex glanced over his shoulder from his post by the front window. "Lois Lane?"

"Sure. I mean she was the poster child for clueless. Clark Kent and Superman—the same dude, only without the glasses! Come on."

"Superman?" Kale asked.

"The ultimate comic book badass," Alex answered, turning back to the window.

I snorted and tried to flex my fingers. They wouldn't move. "Not even," I managed. "He got his powers from being an alien. Total cop-out. Frank Castle—he was a badass comic book guy."

Alex whirled around again. He looked annoyed. I should have known better. We'd had this debate a million times before. "The Punisher? Seriously? The guy was a pussy. When are you gonna get over that?"

Kale looked slightly annoyed. "This is what Jade meant?

Your history?"

Alex gave a satisfied chuckle and went back to watching for Dax.

"Sort of," I said as the heat faded. I pulled the discarded hoodie back over my head and welcomed the chill. Making sure my voice was loud enough, I finished with, "But don't stress over it. Alex's and my shared history doesn't have any bearing on *our* future."

Alex's shoulders stiffened. Fingers curling in irritation, he said, "Let's go. Dax is here."

When we stepped outside, Dax was in the driveway, behind the wheel of a jet black Hummer. With frantic motions, he waved us over. "Hurry. I doubt Cross will send someone here, but let's not take chances."

Alex took the front seat, while Kale helped me into the back. "Dax! Did you steal this Hummer?"

He glared at me through his rearview mirror. "I should really be offended. Your mother asked me the same question."

He threw the truck in reverse, and, with a surge of gas, we were flying into the darkness and down the road.

I must have dozed off because the next thing I knew, the Hummer was going down an unpaved driveway. When I glanced out the back window, I saw small pebbles bouncing through the trail of dust illuminated by the red gleam of the brake lights. It seemed to stretch forever into the night.

When we got to the end, a small log cabin came into view. "Where are we?"

"About ten miles outside town. We're safe here. The house is in another name, so it's not traceable to me." Dax killed the engine and climbed out of the truck.

We followed. For a few moments, the only sound was wind whispering through rustling leaves and the slight *slosh* our shoes made as we stomped through the mud.

About ten feet from the house, Kale grabbed my arm and froze. He pulled me back and stepped between me and the bushes. "Someone is here."

Dax waved him off. "It's okay. Shanna?"

"We're here," Mom answered, stepping from the shadows around the side of the house. Behind her, Ginger hobbled forward, flanked by Jade, Paul and several others.

"Find the place okay?"

She nodded as he pulled a set of keys from his pocket. Holding open the door, Dax smiled. "Welcome home, guys."

We stepped inside to a moderately furnished living room. To the right was a small eat-in kitchen. To the left was what looked like a small hallway. Judging from the outside, though, this couldn't be more than two rooms.

"This is nice, but it looks kinda small for all of us. Not a whole lot bigger than your apartment."

"It is. That's why we'll be staying downstairs. A little more room. Come on. Let's get everyone settled so we can all catch a few hours of sleep."

Dax started forward and disappeared around the corner, the rest of us trailing behind. In the first bedroom on the right, he opened the closet. He picked up several plastic bags that were sitting next to the door and tugged the sleeve of the only thing hanging in the closet—a bright yellow sweater.

Mischievous grin aimed at Mom, he said, "You're gonna love this."

Eyeing the small closet, she didn't look too convinced.

A few seconds later, there was a clicking sound, and the closet disappeared. In its place was a large white elevator. "All aboard."

Like Mom, Kale wasn't thrilled about getting into the elevator, but Dax assured them it would be a short ride. We didn't go down far. Two floors—possibly three. When the doors opened again, we stepped out into a much larger version of the upstairs living room.

"Someone slipped me something back at the party, didn't they?" I whispered.

"I started this three years ago with a slight nudge from Ginger. Did most of the work myself." Dax pointed down the hall to our right. "The common areas aren't quite done yet, but the kitchen is complete and stocked, and the bedrooms are all finished. There's some gym equipment in the room at the end of the hall if anyone needs to let off some steam, and the pool should be usable by the end of the week."

"Pool?" Jade breathed.

"This is all very Bruce Wayne of you, Dax." I scanned the room. There was a huge TV screen mounted on the wall across the room. Two large, fluffy beige couches and a matching chaise lounge were arranged in a semicircle around it. Shelves lined the entire wall closest to us, stacked with DVDs on one side and CDs on the other. Scanning the titles, I saw everything from *The Smurfs* to *Reservoir Dogs*. The CDs were the same. Everything from Disney tunes to Metallica.

Dax smiled. "We'll talk in the morning. Right now I think everyone could use some sleep. The rooms are down there. Sticky notes on each of the doors to tell you whose is whose." He turned to me as everyone filed into the hall. "You don't look good. Is there anything I can get you?"

"Maybe some Advil or something. I just hurt everywhere, and it's making it hard to concentrate."

He nodded. "Go get yourself settled. I'll see what I can find."

Kale and I followed the dwindling crowd, finding both our rooms toward the end. I was sort of relieved to see just my name on the door. Sharing a room with Mom for the last few months had been hard.

Pushing open the door, I didn't bother with the light. The thin strip coming in from the hall was enough to illuminate the way to the single bed across the room. Ten steps. That's what it took to get from the door to the bed. Ten agonizing, forced steps. The pain was constant now. Not very intense, but exhausting. Sleeping in leather pants wasn't one of the smartest things I'd ever done, but I didn't have the energy to worry about it. Changing or mimicking was just too much work. The door closed, and a few moments later, soft footsteps crossed the room.

Kale pulled the blanket up around my shoulder. "I should go. You need to rest."

I curled around the pillow, eyes closing despite my best efforts to keep them open. "You won't stay?"

"I'll be here until you fall asleep."

I frowned into the darkness. An invisible hand was already tugging me under. "That won't be long."

If he replied, I never heard it because suddenly I was back at the construction site. I was really getting to hate this place. At least this time I ended up closer to the building in progress than the crane. The crane hurt to look at.

"I'm worried about you."

Brandt-as-Sheltie was sitting on a large cinder block to my right. The building next door to the construction site was in ruins. I couldn't remember what it'd been, but I knew it was set for demolition in a few weeks. With all the debris and broken glass, I found it odd that Brandt—and I—were barefoot.

"I'm dying." It sounded like I was complaining about something as trite as math homework. But at least I looked good. It'd been awhile since I'd really had a chance to go all out like this. Since this was a dream, I was positive my subconscious was trying to tell me something.

Instead of Meela's horrible Marist sweatshirt, I had on my favorite eggplant-colored camisole and stonewashed jeans. I even had the set of necklaces Brandt gave me for my sixteenth birthday on, and my nails were done. An evil French, Kiernan had called it. Black with white tips.

"That thing on your shoulder?"

I nodded, fiddling with the long necklace. "I don't think I've got much time left."

"You're in good hands. They'll find a way through this."

"I'm scared." Brandt was the only person other than Kale that I'd admit it to. "There's a way to fix it, but the fallout won't be pretty."

"You'll manage. You always do." He looked like he wanted to say more but turned away.

"I wish you were here with us. I'd feel better."

Still facing away, his shoulders tensed. "I wanna come back to town, Dez, but I can't. Not yet. I'm in the middle of something."

His response stung a little. "In the middle of something? What are you up to, Brandt?"

When he turned back to face me, his mouth was open, lips moving, but no sound came out. Sighing, he pointed to the building. Mom was standing in front of the frame, two women I didn't know on either side of her. A man moved to the first one, giving her an injection.

"Next stop," Brandt said. The words came garbled and forced, but I could understand him. He pointed to a spot on the frame above Mom. The second floor. There was a man standing next to a barrel.

"I hate this cryptic crap."

Everything blurred, and suddenly we were in an elevator. Brandt grabbed my hand and mashed it against one of the buttons repeatedly. When I looked, it wasn't a floor number, but two words.

Next Level.

• • •

I opened my eyes to pitch black. Groping in the darkness, I finally found the lamp I'd caught a quick glimpse of before I crashed. The room was nice. Bigger than the one I'd stayed in at the Sanctuary and oddly more suited to my personality. The walls were dark gray, and the floor was carpeted in royal blue. I had to wonder if it was a funky coincidence, or if Ginger had a hand in it.

Sliding off the bed, I caught sight of a small note in front of the lamp. Two Advil sat on a paper towel. The note, in Kale's sloppy writing, said, *Dax left these.* I felt slightly better than before but downed the pills, anyway, just to be safe.

A simple wooden dresser sat in the corner, drawers empty. Next to the bathroom, there was a closed door—a closet, I assumed. When I opened it, I was a little surprised.

Unlike the dresser drawers, the closet wasn't quite empty. On one side, several pairs of jeans—size six—hung from hangers while a small collection of shirts hung from the other. Pulling one down, I smiled. Black stretch cotton tank with the Hot Topic logo on the bottom. Grabbing a pair of jeans, I took the tank and hurried to get out of the leather pants.

Once changed—and feeling much less chafed—I wandered into the hall. There was no way to tell for sure since I'd lost my cell again, but I didn't think much time had passed.

There was a sound coming from several rooms down. A soft, constant tapping. When I followed it around the small bend in the hall, I saw it was Kale. He was focused intently on the large white punching bag hanging from the ceiling in what I guessed was the exercise room.

For a minute, all I could do was stare. He was like a demon possessed. Feral and deadly. Beautiful. It was a side I didn't see often. His Denazen side, he'd called it once. All the rage and darkness channeled for the sake of one single goal. Survival.

Focused on the bag like it had personally been responsible for stealing his freedom, he let each blow scream a message in eerie clarity. *Never again.* He'd kill them all one by one if they ever got their hands on him—or he'd die trying. I'd never let that happen.

I was so lost in thought, I didn't realize he'd seen me.

He steadied the bag and smiled. "You're awake."

I stepped inside the room. "How long was I out?"

"Not long. I've been in here for two hours."

"You didn't get any sleep?" I could see he was tired. Dark circles hung like rocks under his eyes, and his posture was just slightly stooped. All little things no one else would have picked up on. To me, though, they screamed.

He stiffened. "I can function effectively on no sleep."

"This isn't Denazen, Kale. No one expects you to function on no sleep."

He slid down the wall. "You heard me talking to Jade earlier."

"I wasn't spying on you, I swear. If it'll make you feel better, when you were telling her all that stuff about Denazen, I felt guilty."

He cocked his head to the side. "Guilty?"

"You didn't want me to know any of that stuff."

"Jade asked me why. Did you hear my answer?"

Instead of answering his question, I sat down across from him and sighed. "My whole life, Brandt was there for me. He always had my back. No matter what. I needed to vent, he was there. I needed to cry, he was there. If I was being stupid or about to do something epically dumb, Brandt was there to stop me—or in some cases, drag my ass to the ER." I nudged his sneaker with my bare foot. "And then I met you. You're everything Brandt was—and more. Do you understand what I'm saying?"

"I will always bring you to the ER if you get hurt."

I sighed. "I mean, *you're* my best friend, Kale. My partner in crime. It's you and me against everything else, remember? There's nothing about my life that I don't want to share with you, and I want you to feel the same way. I know I didn't tell you about the poison, and I realize now how dumb that was. I was trying to protect you, and that was stupid. Jade was right about that. You don't need protection—but neither do I. I won't hide anything from you from now on, but you have to promise the same."

He didn't look convinced. "I love the way you look at me. There's purity in it, and I don't want to ruin it."

"You couldn't ruin it. There's nothing you could have done— or would do that could make me change what I see when I look at you."

"I think you underestimate Denazen."

"I have something for you," Kale said as we made our way down the hall toward the living room.

We'd talked for a little while, but in the end, we were both too antsy and headed off to see if anyone else shared our insomnia.

He pulled Kiernan's cell from his pocket and held it out. "She dropped this."

"Wow. I totally forgot about it." I remembered Kiernan dropping it but had lost track of it after that.

"Shouldn't you two be asleep?" Dax said, stepping out from one of the rooms.

"Too jittery," I said, wiggling the fingers on my left hand. When I'd fallen asleep, they'd started to tingle. Now I could barely feel them. It was kind of a blessing. If they were numb, then I couldn't feel the pain.

He sighed and pointed down the hall. "Everyone else is in the kitchen. Kale, can you give us a minute?"

Kale hesitated. He liked Dax just fine, but sometimes when he looked at the guy, I could almost swear he was hearing the angry things that were said when Dax first found out I was Marshall Cross's daughter. I couldn't blame Dax. Denazen had stolen his twin nieces, and he would have done just about anything to get them back.

After a few seconds, Kale nodded and disappeared around the corner.

"I need to talk to you." Dax leaned against the wall. "You might have noticed—"

"If this is about Mom, then no worries. You're both adults."

He nodded. "No. I know—but there's a slight age difference. I didn't want it to be weird for you or anything."

"I dunno. Might be weird if I didn't have a crap ton of other things to worry about."

He folded his arms. "You were really going to turn yourself in, weren't you?"

I opened my mouth, then closed it. Silence would confirm his suspicion as easily as talking would allow him to see my intentions. Lose-lose.

"Come on. We've already got a plan in the works. No one is going back to Denazen."

When we entered the kitchen, I saw Kale and I weren't the only ones who couldn't sleep. Ginger was at the table between two younger guys—both with their shirts on for once. Mom was sitting at the center island, a Coke in one hand and a cigarette in the other, while Alex sat across from her twirling napkins in the air just above their heads.

Kale was standing in the doorway. "You're okay?"

"Right as acid rain."

His forehead furrowed, but he didn't ask.

"Whatever the plan is," I said, turning to the rest of them.

"We need to do it soon." I held out my arm and tried not to gag. The spidery black lines were now almost to my wrist. I'd looked in the mirror before leaving my room and saw they'd also passed my neck. Any minute now, they'd start creeping up the side.

"How fast can we rally the troops?" Mom asked. She was slightly pale.

"Call Cross," Ginger said. "Arrange to meet him. Let him pick the place and time. He needs to think this is on his terms—that you're desperate."

I pulled out Kiernan's phone and thumped it on the table. "I am desperate, so, not a stretch there."

"Tell him your only stipulation is that he must bring Aubrey with him."

"We're a little short on manpower, Ginger." Alex snapped his fingers and the napkins fluttered to the table. "Don't you think Cross will bring back up?"

"Deznee is weak. He knows this. If she plays her part correctly, Cross will believe her to be scared and desperate. He won't see this as a trap."

Alex frowned. "That sounds a lot like underestimating the enemy."

"We'll bring everyone we can. Trust me, Alex. This will work out."

Something in her voice sent chills down my spine. Like there was more to the sentence. This will work out—*the way it was meant to.* It wasn't that I didn't trust her, but I knew where her loyalties lay. To her gift and the weird code that went with it.

Still, I didn't have a choice. I already had a backup plan if things went south. Picking up the phone, I scrolled through Kiernan's contacts until I found *Dad.* Pushing send, I hoped—for a reason I couldn't quite put my finger on—that it wasn't really *my* dad that answered.

"Hello, Deznee."

I sighed. And so went hope. "I guess my sister from the same mister told you she lost her phone, eh?"

"I'm surprised it took you this long. You must be in a great deal of pain by now."

I glanced around the room. Ginger nodded encouragingly. Dax, who'd been standing behind Mom's chair, was now beside me, bent close so he could hear Dad's voice.

"I don't want to die."

Dad chuckled. "What is it you're trying to say?"

"I'll do it. I'll turn myself in. Just swear to me that you'll bring the cure, and I'll do it."

"I don't know, Deznee. While Kiernan informed me that your abilities have progressed, I'm not sure we really have need of them. And to be frank, I haven't decided if I'm going to waste the last bit of Supremacy cure on you. It would be pointless to make you suffer if we choose to administer it to someone else. I'm not that cruel."

The room was starting to spin. The chill was back and tiny, pulsing barbs of pain trickled down my shoulder, spreading to every limb. "Please—"

"Now if you were to offer me 98, then we might have a deal. Your ability, as useful as it might be, isn't offensive. 98 is far more useful to me right now."

"No," I growled. I had to bite the inside of my lip to keep from screaming. "I'll suck it up and die slowly. Then you lose both of us. It's me or nothing."

Seconds passed, but they felt like hours. Possibly days. Finally, he sighed. "I suppose I can work with it. After all, the animal is so obsessed with you, it won't be long before he does something foolish."

"Where and when?"

"Next Monday. At Parkview Field."

"Next week? I won't make it till then, and you know it. Now. It needs to be right now."

Voice low, I could almost see the smile on the bastard's face. "Tomorrow. Eleven p.m."

"I don't know if—"

"Tomorrow. Eleven p.m. I'll see you then." A pause. "God willing." And the line went dead.

• • •

The poison had peaked. I could feel it, moving through my blood and under my skin. It was sapping up all my energy. Stealing my time away. When I came to around noon, I was positive I wouldn't make it to eleven p.m. Every nerve ending was on fire, and twice I started screaming, convinced Dad was standing over my bed. Since pills didn't really help anymore, I spent the majority of the day drifting in and out of sleep.

"How ya feeling?" Alex was in the corner, sitting in the chair Kale had been in each time I'd previously visited the land of the living.

"Remind me never to do this again."

He smiled, but it was forced.

"Where's Kale?"

He hesitated. "Ginger kinda had Jade drug him."

"What?"

"I'll give the dude this—he's got some amazing stamina. I don't think he's closed his eyes in over four days. He was getting snappy. Ginger thought it'd be dangerous, so she asked him to please get some sleep. When he refused, she took his choice away."

"Jesus."

"It was pretty funny, actually. You would've appreciated it. They sent Jade in to do it—for obvious reasons. He freaked. Tried to choke her."

"Of course. I always miss the good stuff. Is she dead?" I was sure he didn't miss the hopeful tone in my voice.

He frowned. "Invincible, remember?"

Silence.

"I have something I need to say," he blurted suddenly. "And it's not easy, and it sucks, so I'm hoping you'll just let me get through it, okay?"

I nodded. No reason to tell him he could stand there and sing show tunes, and I'd be in no position to stop him.

"I'm sorry. About what happened with that girl at Roudey's a few years ago. About what happened at Sumrun. I tend to be… impulsive. I don't think things through. At Sumrun, I wanted to hurt Kale. I wanted to show you he was weak, and I was strong. *I* could protect you." He sighed and lifted his head toward the ceiling. "But you have to believe I never meant to kill him—no matter what it looked like."

"But you *were* going to hand him over to my dad?"

He lowered his head to stare at me. "Absolutely. And that I won't apologize for. I thought I was doing what was best for you, Dez. Because you're the only one that mattered." Shoulders squared, he added, "*Matters*."

"Alex—"

"I get it. You love him. And ya know what? I can see he loves you. The way he refused to leave your side to sleep, the look in his eyes when he realized what Jade had done—he'd do anything for you. But I want you to know I would, too."

He stood and took two steps toward the door. "I'm not asking you to pick between us. You've made your choice, and I'll live with it. But you needed to know—*really* know—that everything I've ever felt for you has been one hundred percent real."

34

"Everyone is clear about their part, correct?" Ginger stood in front of the Hummer in a crisp blue housecoat with matching orthopedic shoes. I felt sorry for anyone on the street that mistook her for a helpless little old lady.

Parkview Field was a playground that had been under construction for three years now. The park was at the top of a hill and had cliffs bordering one side. They were in the process of putting in a six-foot fence around the property. Without it, it'd be too easy for some kid to chase his soccer ball right over the edge.

The plan was for Kale and me to enter through the front gate and head straight through to the other end. By the cliffs. The layout of the park made it easy for Ginger and the rest of the guys to watch from a safe point on the outside and fall in, surrounding the place when they saw Dad and Aubrey come through. The perfect bottleneck scenario.

I was originally supposed to go in alone—which honestly scared me a little but made total sense. Why waltz in with the two things Dad wanted most? But Kale, completely uncompromising, refused to let me go without him. He'd used my own words against me. *We're a team. It's us against everything else.*

After a while, it was obvious Kale wasn't going to budge. Ginger's options were limited. Either let him go with me or drug him again. In the end, I think she agreed because she knew she'd never fool him twice. He was staying clear of everyone— especially Jade—which kind of made me happy.

On the ride to the park, I drifted in and out. Watery images and strange sounds lingered on the edge of consciousness. Brandt was there again. He held my hand as Kale talked about what great humanitarians the people at Denazen were. At one point, Dad was there, Mom wrapped in his arms laughing and smiling in a way that made all the wrong things right in my world. It was a scene right out of my childhood wishes. A happy family.

By the time we arrived and I pulled myself from the backseat of the Hummer, I couldn't be sure what was reality and what was a hallucination. Everything was too loud. Too sharp. My legs were rubbery, and my muscles all ached like I'd been hit by a bus.

Sweat beaded across my forehead and dampened the back of my neck, yet I couldn't pull the hoodie tight enough. The ground was covered in a thick layer of fluffy snow. That would have been odd enough considering it was only September, but even stranger was the snow's color. Green and a bit stringy. Snow-grass.

"Ready?" Kale stepped up beside me.

I pulled the hood over my head and tucked the sleeves over my fingertips, nodding. Words were painful and took too much effort. I'd been sucking on razor blades. That was the only explanation. I forced myself to swallow, tasting their metallic tang. Like that funky aftertaste you get when carrots aren't quite ripe—only with razor-y sharpness.

Ginger stood in front of me. Her eyes seemed bigger than

normal, and her voice echoed just a little. "Jade will go in behind you. In case something happens, I want her there."

In case something happens. That must mean in case I didn't make it. I wanted to argue that Kale could easily carry my corpse back—but then remembered he couldn't. Not if they wanted something to bury. Somehow it wouldn't be fair to hand me over to Mom as a pile of ash. *Here's your daughter, Sue. Sorry about the mess—I should have brought a Tupperware container.*

The scene brought an insane giggle to my lips. They all turned to stare.

"We need to hurry," Mom said, reaching for my face. I batted her hand away. She was going to pull my hair out. I just knew it. I refused to die bald.

"Dez, can you walk?" Kale's voice.

Something deep inside me stirred. Kale wouldn't steal my hair. He wouldn't feed me razor blades. I nodded, letting him wrap his arm around my shoulders and steer me to the path.

The walk down the hill was surreal for some reason. It might have been trying to walk in the weird, sludge-like snow-grass, or it might have been the feeling that it wasn't really me. Like I was there doing it but also there watching it as a spectator. Like a movie with really bad camera angles. Several times my legs gave out. Kale caught me carefully just before I toppled into the snow-grass. I was thankful. It smelled bad, and I was sure it'd stain. I didn't want to ruin Meela's sweatshirt.

We made it down the hill to the cliffs in no time, which was a little disappointing. As I stood there, something poked me. Something I was supposed to remember. I'd caught a glimmer of it here and there as we made our way down the path, but no matter how hard I chased it, the thing always skated just out of reach.

Wrinkled hands. Green ink. Urgent teeth. No. That wasn't

right. Not urgent teeth. Urgent instructions. *Wait till you're there. Then look*. Shaking, I slipped my hand into the right front pocket of the hoodie, pulling out the small note Ginger had slipped me before we'd left the cabin. As soon as Kale turned away for a second, I flipped it open.

At first I couldn't read it. The words on the paper blurred and jumped around. When they finally stayed still for a moment, I saw two simple words. That's all. Two words that made my pulse pound stronger and the blood in my veins turn to ice.

I'm sorry.

"Kale," I whispered, swallowing the impossibly large lump in my throat. My voice sounded funny. Small. Garbled. I hoped he could understand. "Do you love me?"

He tensed. "You know that I do."

I held my breath for a moment to keep from panicking. Reality wasn't just fraying at the edges anymore, it was splitting right down the middle. I had to keep it together. Just a little bit longer. "If you love me, then you'll do something for me, right?"

He was cautious, eyeing me suspiciously. "I would do anything for you."

I nodded. "I'm going to ask you to do something for me. Something you're not going to like."

He dropped my arm and took a step back.

The tears fell. I couldn't hold them back. They slipped down my cheeks, leaving searing, possibly even smoking, trails in their wake. Beneath me, the snow-grass shuddered. The sky quaked. Time was coming to a stop. Now or never.

I had to concentrate on each word so hard, I thought my brain might explode. "It's something you swore you'd never do, but I'm going you to ask to—to do it anyway. Even though it will be hard. It will be horrible. I need you to do this."

Realization sparked in his face. "They're not coming.

Ginger's backup."

"Isn't this a surprise," Dad said.

I turned to see him standing on the path behind us, Aubrey on one side, Kiernan on the other. Somehow this time I knew he wasn't a hallucination. This was the real deal.

"Don't come any closer," Kale breathed.

"Do you really want to be the reason she dies, 98?"

I pulled back on his arm. "Remember what I asked you a few minutes ago?" Pale, he nodded. I let out a breath I hadn't realized I'd been holding. Or maybe, it had been holding me.

Turning to Dad, I said, "Deal's a deal. If you let Aubrey heal me, I'll go with you."

"*No!*" Kale roared. Blue eyes wild, he grabbed my face and turned it to his. I knew it wasn't real—*couldn't* be real—but I relished the sensation. "Me! I'm the one who will go. That's what you asked."

I should have known he didn't understand. He'd been too accepting of the whole thing. "It's not. I want you to *let me go*."

Dad cleared his throat. "This argument is really very pointless."

Kale's lips twisted, and he actually laughed. At least, I think it was a laugh. He could have mooed for all I knew. Everything was hollow and watery sounding. Staying on my feet was becoming close to impossible. The only thing keeping me up was the aversion I had to the funny snow-grass. It seemed to have gotten thicker. Deeper. It certainly smelled worse. Like death and decay. The smell that emanates from roadkill baking in the summer sun for days.

"You can't touch me," he said. "And if you try to touch her, I'll kill you."

Dad, unmoved by Kale's threat, smiled. "Your backup appears to be—late."

He knew. Never try to lie to a liar. Dad was one of the best.

Hell, he'd fooled me into thinking he was a normal lawyer for seventeen years.

"Where are they?" I managed to spit. To me, it sounded something like, *Werarhtha*, but I hoped the insinuation was clear.

Dad laughed. He obviously understood. "They're fine, don't worry. I have employees preventing them from entering the park." He added, "In a very peaceful manner. I'd say it was very generous of me considering my mood.

"You see, Deznee, I've changed my mind. I know if I left here with you now, 98 wouldn't rest until you were free. Eventually, he'd slip up, and I'd have you both—but that's too easy as you've managed to destroy what little patience I had with you." He folded his arms. "98 will come with us, and Aubrey will cure you. Those are the terms. If you decide you want the Supremacy cure, you may seek me out, and we'll discuss it."

I opened my mouth to object, but a series of earth-shattering coughs shook my entire body. Despite my disgust for the snow-grass, I collapsed. Fluffy, my ass. I landed on the ground with a jar, the stench of rot triggering my gag reflex.

"I need weapons, Deznee. To fight the war *you* started. Had you not been whoring yourself out to the neighborhood the night 98 escaped, none of this would have happened. I could have happily shipped you off to college, gotten you out of my hair, and moved on with my life. This will solve two problems. I will get my favorite weapon back, and you will learn not to piss me off." Dad took a step closer. "A lesson you will need to learn if you hope to get the Supremacy cure."

"No deal," I snarled, grabbing Kale's arm and getting to my feet. "Let's go. We'll find another way." Lies. Bitter, rotting lies. But I would have said anything to get out of there. To get Kale away from Dad. To get myself away from that smell. Anything. But Dad wasn't letting go.

He'd never let go.

"The *only* one who can stop the spread and reverse the poison is Aubrey," Dad pushed.

The toxic twins. He had a creepy obsession with *touching* Sixes. I tamped down another inappropriately timed giggle.

Waving a hand in front of my face, he chuckled. "She doesn't look good. If you don't hurry, 98, it will be too late. You'll be responsible for yet another death."

Beside Dad, Aubrey flashed a feral smile. "So what'll it be, 98? Dez—"

"Or Denazen." Kiernan smiled, revealing several rows of jagged, deadly looking teeth. Her jaw was longer than I remembered, and her skin had a slight sheen to it. Almost scaly.

Hallucination. It was just a hallucination. Not real.

Notreal. Notreal. Notreal.

My stomach rolled—and this time it wasn't the poison. This is why I hadn't told Kale to begin with. Obviously I didn't want to die, but no way in hell did I want him going back to Denazen.

Kale was staring at me. Leaning close, he brushed the softest of kisses across my lips. With his thumb, he skimmed my cheeks, wiping away the fire-tears. More hallucinations—but this kind I was okay with. My memory deserved some serious kudos. It was almost as good as the real thing.

"I love you, Dez," he whispered. Turning to Dad, he said, "Make her better."

"We have a deal, then?"

"Anything. As long as you fix this."

"No!" Jade came tearing down the path. It pissed me off to see she had no trouble navigating the snow-grass. Even more of a reason to hate her.

"Jade Banna," Dad said. "Formidable. I take it you dispatched my employee?"

She put herself between Dad and Kale. "Sending a telekinetic to keep me grounded? Someone hasn't done their homework."

I wondered what she'd done? Bitched him to death? Maybe there was more to her.

Dad chuckled. "Indeed. What would you say if I were to offer you a job, my dear?"

Jade didn't answer right away. When she finally made her choice, the movie in my head had her shaking hands with Dad and high-fiving Kiernan and Aubrey right before running a victory lap around us.

In reality, she flipped him off.

"Are you certain?" Dad pressed. "I could offer you more than you can possibly imagine. You'd never want for anything again. Your family could come out of hiding, free to live a normal life."

"No, thanks."

"Your choice—for now." Dad snapped his fingers, and Kiernan took a step toward Kale. She'd pulled on a pair of dark gloves, and there was a set of shiny silver handcuffs dangling from her pointer.

Kale's hand shot up. He took a step back, glaring from Kiernan to Dad. "Fix it first," he demanded.

"You should know better, 98." Dad clucked his tongue and gestured to Kiernan and Aubrey. "Let's face it. We all know you could run circles around these two. I'd wager even Ms. Banna could give them a proper run for their money. I'm not foolish enough to underestimate you. When you are safely bound, Aubrey will help Deznee."

"You have no honor. How do I know you'll keep your word?"

The floor spun, but I managed to stand and keep from toppling down again by grabbing Jade's arm. "Don't do this, Kale."

He didn't budge.

"He's full of crap." Despite the poison speeding through my veins, the thing I was most scared of at that moment was losing him to Dad. "Don't fall for it. We can find another way."

"Are you sure this is what you want?" Jade's voice was low, but I heard her as though she'd screamed in my ear. God. Even with me at death's door, the bitch was trying to change his mind about me.

"I am trusting you to make sure she is okay. Please. Don't let me down." Kale kept his eyes on her, refusing to glance my way. Me? I couldn't look away. "Watch over her."

Nodding to Dad, he held out his arms. Clinking metal and an almost deafening snap as the cuffs locked into place.

Kiernan glanced from me to Kale. She looked almost sorry. *That* had to be a hallucination. "Don't give me any crap. If we don't make it out and into the car, he won't let Aubrey help her."

"I won't fight you," he said, turning.

"Please," I begged. "Don't do this. It's not worth it."

Kale froze and turned back. It had to be the poison. His expression was all wrong. Happy. Serene. "Knowing you'll be okay is worth anything I could possibly go through. Please remember that."

He held my gaze for a moment before turning to Kiernan. She led him around Aubrey and up the path. Dad followed without as much as a word.

Once they were out of sight, Aubrey took a step back. "He of all people should know Cross has *no* honor."

Jade was pale. In fact, her skin looked a little green. Like she'd been rolling around in the snow-grass and gotten it all over her face and arms. "You're not going to heal her, are you?"

Aubrey watched us for a moment, then frowned. "My instructions were to bring her with me or let her die."

This was it. After all I'd been through. After all I'd seen. I was going to bite it in the middle of a cold, empty field surrounded by two of the most annoying human beings ever to walk the earth.

Seriously. Karma must've had it in for me.

Everything was getting colder. The air I forced in and out of my lungs. The snow-grass soaking through my jeans. It was so cold, I couldn't feel my arms anymore. In fact, I couldn't really feel anything. The pain was gone, and while that should have made me happy, it scared me. The pain had been real. Tangible. It was something to hold on to in the middle of everything breaking apart. Without it, I'd lose hold of reality.

I don't know where he came from, but Able appeared in front of me. He hopped from foot to foot, chanting, *Too far gone to feel it, yeah?* I turned away, not wanting to see the smug satisfaction all over his face.

Something blurred in front of me, then a puff of warm against my neck and ear. Able's voice again. "Cross has no honor. *I*, however, do."

No. Not Able. The pitch was the same, but the words were wrong. Able's weird, almost unnoticeable accent was gone.

Aubrey.

He reached out, cradling my face in his hands. Something inside me broke. Whatever biological or chemical wall that had been holding the poison at bay. The thing that had blissfully numbed the pain. It finally gave out, shattering to let a rush of agony roll over me like a rogue tsunami. I'd jumped from a moving car, lost my footing while train surfing, and now I'd lost Kale. At that moment, though, none of that pain could come within a ten-mile radius of the agony ripping me apart.

A scream tore from my throat. I didn't hear it, but I felt it work its way through my body and explode from my mouth. The sound of it—of everything—was sharp. Like every noise was amplified by a thousand speakers all aimed at my head and backed with white noise. Muscles itched, blood boiled. And just when I was sure he'd killed me, the painful fog cleared. Like someone magically snapped their fingers or flipped a switch. It was all just…gone.

When I opened my eyes, Aubrey was kneeling in front of me, face impassive. "Why—"

He stood. "I believe in what Denazen stands for. They want to better the world through our gifts."

Jade snorted. "If you believe that, then I bet Cross has a golden goose to sell you, too."

Aubrey held out his hand. I took it and let him pull me to my feet. It was clammy and cool, like Able's, but I didn't care. It was nice to *feel* it.

"Cross is no Mother Teresa. His methods are—unorthodox."

I snorted. "You consider allowing his own daughter to die *unorthodox*?"

"That," Aubrey said with a frown, "has given me something to think about." He turned and started up the path.

"Wait."

He stopped, but didn't turn around.

"You were supposed to bring me back, but you're empty handed. He's going to find out I'm still alive. Won't you get in trouble?"

Back to us, Aubrey shrugged. "You agreed to come with me. My brother hit you hard. It was obvious you weren't going to make it, so I had no choice but to heal you first. We were on our way to the car, and there was an ambush. I was lucky to get out." He took several steps forward and stopped. Turning, our eyes met. "I'll watch out for 9—Kale."

35

Six days had passed since Kale had chosen my life over his freedom.

At first, I didn't feel anything. I was numb again. There was an icy hole where my heart used to be. A black void covered every hour of every day. Then the five stages of grief set in. First was the denial. Wake up. Go about my morning. Knock on Kale's door and wait for him to answer.

He'd answer. He wasn't gone.

That only lasted two days.

Next came the anger. I'd smashed the few pieces of furniture in my room at Dax's underground cabin to pieces—screaming until my voice was long gone. He was a saint. Everything was replaced the next day without a word.

The bargaining stage was over almost before it even started. Several hours of crying and pleading to any higher power that would listen. I'd done the unthinkable once—infiltrated Denazen and broke him out. I could do it again. I'd do anything—*give* anything—if I could just make that happen one more time.

But as the hours ticked by, I saw the situation for what it really was. Impossible. That's where the depression stage started to bleed through. Dad would be expecting me to charge in. He'd be waiting. Hoping. And even though I seemed to have gained a little momentum and control over my gift, I couldn't fool myself—or the others—into thinking I could slip in and out unnoticed. Getting tossed in a cage at Denazen wouldn't help Kale. Or the underground. And now, more than ever, Dad needed to be taken down.

And that's where I hovered. Stuck somewhere between bargaining and depression—because acceptance? That was never going to happen. This wasn't a situation I could live with. As soon as my head cleared, things were going to change.

I slept long hours curled in the middle of Kale's bed waiting for Brandt to contact me. He'd come back. Just as soon as he found out what had happened. He'd drop whatever it was he was doing and back me up. That's how it worked.

But he never showed.

"I thought I'd find you here," Jade mumbled as she settled beside me. "Sitting in the dark in his room isn't going to change anything, you know. When the lights come on, he'll still be gone."

"Whatever." Lame, I know. But what else could I say? You couldn't argue with fact.

Well, you could, but where does it put you?

It puts you in the dark in someone's room. Someone who wasn't coming back.

"Not me, because I think you're vile—and a raging bitch—but everyone else is worried about you."

"And they sent *you* to give me the message?"

"I volunteered. As much as I *enjoy* seeing you miserable, this is ridiculous. And Kale wouldn't want it."

They'd all pretty much left me alone. Even Mom. Food was left in a plate on the counter in the kitchen with my name on it. Pots of coffee would mysteriously appear outside Kale's room at all hours of the night. Along with a plate of cheese sticks and piping hot marinara sauce. That was hard. They only knew I liked them. They didn't understand the meaning they held or the memories they sparked.

But Jade was right. This was ridiculous. "You were wrong."

Her brows rose, interested. "About what?"

"You said Kale was toxic. To me, to other people—but you were wrong. Kale isn't the toxic one. *I* am." I thought about Brandt and how his life had been turned upside down for helping me. And Curd, who'd gotten a nice fat concussion back when all this started. Mark Oster, Rosie, Alex… "Everyone in my life gets hurt. This is my fault."

Jade snorted. "As much as I'd love to pin this all on you, I don't see how you could be to blame. Because you didn't see through Kiernan? No one did. She had everyone fooled—though you still owe me a pretty sizeable apology."

"That," I sighed. "I still don't get. How I didn't know… But that's not even what I mean. If I hadn't gone back to the old house that night, Able never would've touched me. There wouldn't have been anything to hold over Kale's head."

"That's crap," she spat. "For someone so smart, you're kinda thick, you know? If it didn't happen that night, it would've happened another. Walking down the street. At the restaurant. You're the only one they could use to get to him and vice versa, and they knew it."

Even though she was probably right—a thought that, while depressing, still made me smile on the inside—I couldn't acknowledge it.

"I'd like a few moments alone with Deznee, Jade," Ginger

said from the door. Jesus. That woman was like ninja granny. Must have been where Kale got it.

Jade gave me one last, semi-irritated look and let Ginger take her spot next to me. I knew I owed her an apology—and a couple of hard-core rounds for trying to *really* steal my boyfriend—but it would have to wait.

Ginger didn't waste any time. "This is not productive."

"Can't say I care."

"You should care. I know this is painful for you, but there's a bigger picture here."

"Bigger picture?" I balked. "You've gotta be shitting me. Kale is your *grandson*. You knew this would happen. You put that damn note in my pocket and let us walk right in. You *let* him get taken by Denazen. *Again*."

"We've been through this before, Deznee. Destiny is not something to toy with. Things are what they are."

"That sounds like an excuse to me."

She didn't respond. Instead, we sat there in silence for a bit, and a helpless, desperate feeling started creeping up on me. It reminded me of the night at the crane. Which for some reason, reminded me of the night I met Ginger.

"When we first met, you said you were sorry. For what was coming. This was it, wasn't it?"

Standing, Ginger placed a wrinkled hand on my shoulder. "I did know this would happen, but no. This wasn't what I apologized for."

The knot of grief twisted into something else. Something worse. I remembered what she said to me the first night at Meela's. Alex and I would pay the biggest price.

She squeezed my shoulder and hobbled toward the door. Without looking back, she said, "The worst is yet to come."

Acknowledgments

/mushy on

First and always—thank you to my family. It's their unlimited love and support that make it possible for me to do what I do. My husband, who is the most loving and patient man on earth, and my parents, who, simply put, are just frigging awesome. I love you guys.

My CPs, Heather, Katy, and Christa—thank you for your thoughts, ideas, and friendship. I consider myself extremely lucky to have you guys in my life!

Liz, my editor-of-epic, and Entangled Publishing...there will never be a limit to my appreciation and thanks to you for taking a chance on me. I look forward to the many good things I know are in store.

To my agent, Kevan... Thank you so much for believing in me!

A huge thank-you to Dani, my publicist, who works her magic to make some of my crazy ideas a reality...you're awesome, and I'd be lost (and much less sane) without you!

And lastly (but far from leastly—yes, I'm making up my own language here), to the readers and bloggers. You made the release of my first book, *Touch*, a dream come true. I am eternally grateful for the support and am in awe of your love and dedication to Dez and Kale. You guys are the sugar *and* cream in my coffee!

/mushy off

Keep reading for a bonus scene from TOXIC, as told in Kale's point of view...

Jade's Dream Come True

Jade and I went back to the house as instructed. I hated leaving Dez but trusted Ginger knew what was best. Besides, it gave me more time to work on my control. We'd been at it for a while now with no success.

It was starting to wear thin.

"Here," Jade said, holding out another plant. I didn't know where they'd come from, but someone had left several dozen potted plants for us. There were only a few left. "Try this one."

I took the plant by its plastic holder, wondering what she meant by 'this one.' It had white flowers on it. Did she think that would make a difference?

When she nodded, I stretched a finger out, hesitating for only a moment before touching one of the delicate white petals. For the briefest moment, it was soft beneath my fingers and reminded me of the satiny smoothness of Dez's skin. Then it evaporated into a pile of dust and dried dirt.

I dropped the pot and kicked it hard across the room. That could be her. Dez. Nothing more than memories and dust, all because I couldn't do this.

"Hey," Jade said, coming up behind me. She was standing very close. I could smell the sweet scent of her perfume— something fruity that would have given Dez a headache. "Look at me. You can do this."

I turned to face her. She'd moved even closer and was now nearly pressed against me. Her eyes kept fluttering. It was understandable. The dust in this house was thick. "Did you get something in your eye?"

She seemed surprised by the question. Stepping back and giving me an odd look, she said, "I—you—no."

I sighed and fell back against the wall. "Maybe if Dez had come with us, I'd be able to concentrate."

"Just the opposite," Jade snapped. "Besides, I think this space is good for you. It's giving you a chance to find out who you are without someone telling you."

Unfortunately, I knew who I was. And I didn't like it. Jade didn't understand that the only time it was bearable was when Dez was with me. When she looked at me. In her eyes, I was perfect and pure. Not the dark thing I knew myself to be.

This girl didn't like Dez. That much I could see—and the feeling was mutual. It was amusing to me. Neither would admit it, but they had a lot in common. Both stubborn and strong, they'd each been forced to face horrible things much too early in life.

"Did you ever stop to think that maybe your inability to touch Dez was a sign from the universe?"

"The universe? You mean, like God?" That worried me. I wasn't sure I believed in a higher power, as Ginger put it, but if he was real, surely I was on his bad side because of all the things I'd done.

"Let's move out to the backyard," Jade said, taking my hand. Her skin was warm and soft, but there was no comparison to

Dez. Still, I didn't pull away in fear that it'd hurt her feelings. "It's a beautiful night, and there's plenty of green out there."

She was right. The night air was cool and relieved some of the tension I felt. I was frustrated, and there was no way I could concentrate. Not when I knew Dez was hiding something. It involved those twins—mainly Able—and that worried me. "She's lying to me."

Jade picked a leaf from the tree to her right and stepped into my path. Holding the leaf out, she asked, "Who?"

I knew what would happen, but I took it from her anyway. The minute my fingers—thumb and pointer—closed around its thin stem, it shriveled and blew away, tiny bits catching on the edge of Jade's hair. "Dez. There's something she's keeping from me. She told me earlier."

"*This* is why you're making no progress. I told you, this is all tied up in emotion. You need to clear your mind. Let it all go."

Why didn't she understand that it was impossible? This was Dez. How could I let it all go when there was so obviously something going on? "She said it was to protect me."

Jade looked annoyed. "Protect you? Unlikely. Someone like *you* doesn't need protecting. Personally, I think it's something else."

"Something else?" It took a moment, but I realized what she was going to say before she spoke the words out loud. And even though I knew it wasn't true, anger bubbled in my gut.

"I'd be a really horrible *friend* if I didn't point this out, Kale. But really, don't you see the way she looks at Alex? They've got history together. He's obviously still got a thing for her, and I've seen the way she looks at him. She feels the same way."

I flexed my fingers. Pointer. Middle. Ring. Pinkie. Thumb. Then I counted to five. There would always be a small amount of concern for Alex. Dez denied it, but I knew it was true. I could see it when she looked at him. Even the most fleeting glance spoke volumes, but that's where it ended. She'd told me I was her future—and Dez had never lied to me. "You're wrong. He hurt her."

Her lips twisted downward, and I didn't appreciate the look she gave me. Pity. "And you did, too. You almost killed her."

All the air expelled from my lungs like I'd been kicked. "I didn't—" Suddenly there wasn't enough air. I knew what I'd done. I'd relived the moment a thousand times since that night on the crane. "That wasn't my fault. I would never—"

Jade came closer and took my hand in hers. "I know you didn't mean it, but Dez runs on pure emotion. She's an all-or-nothing kind of girl. She can't touch you, and maybe that's just too much for her. Alex is available, interested, and she can touch him."

She was wrong. "You don't know her."

"She saved you from Denazen. I get it. It's totally natural to feel attached to her because of that—"

"I *love* Dez," I said. I'd told Jade this countless times over the last few days. I wasn't blind. It was obvious that she was attracted to me. But I'd made it clear.

"Are you sure? Maybe you should take a break from the Sanctuary. Go out and see the world. Get to know yourself. I'm not trying to confuse you, but Kale, if you've only been able to be with her, how do you know there's not someone else out there?"

"Dez said that to me once."

She put her hand on my shoulder and nodded. "See? She knew it, too."

I loved Dez. With all my heart and every part of my mind, body, and soul. But looking at her lately, I could see her doubt. I'd catch her watching me with Jade, and I recognized the look that sparked in her eyes. I recognized it because it's what I felt when she looked at Alex. Jealousy.

All the tension drained away. Suddenly it was all so clear to me—what I should do. What I *had* to do. In the beginning, Dez had doubts about our relationship. She worried that if it ever happened that I could touch someone else, maybe I'd realize I didn't want her. That I stayed for the wrong reasons.

Jade reclaimed my hand, and I felt a smile overtake my lips. "I think you need to consider—"

"Can I kiss you?"

"What?" It's what she'd wanted—which confused me. It seemed most everything about me irritated her. The things I said confused her, and the way I acted seem to insult her. Yet she wanted to kiss me. To do other things with me. The look of surprise on her face almost made me chuckle.

"Can I kiss you?" I said again. Maybe she hadn't heard me—I was speaking quietly. An old habit. When the lights went out at Denazen, a strict silence policy was enforced.

Stepping closer, I wrapped my arms around her waist and pressed my lips to hers. She was different than Dez. For one thing, she was taller. She didn't need to rise up on her toes to meet me, and I kind of missed that. For another, there was less to her. Jade was beautiful and delicate. Like a piece of porcelain— something you'd be afraid to break. Dez, in comparison, was strong. A beautiful warrior. My equal.

I worried, thinking maybe I'd done something bad by simply leaning in and getting right to it because Jade didn't respond at first. But after a moment, a bubbly laugh slipped free, and she grabbed me tight, dragging me close until we were pressed up against each other.

The kiss wasn't long. Fifty-seven seconds, to be exact. I knew because I'd counted.

When she pulled away, her cheeks were pink, and her expression was smug. "Oops."

I followed her gaze. Dez and Kiernan were standing a few feet away, the look on Dez's face unlike anything I'd ever seen before.

A horrible sound escaped her lips. "Some ninja, huh? I was standing here a whole twenty seconds."

She was upset—that much was clear—and I understood. But as soon as I explained things, she'd be happy again. She'd never have to worry again. "Dez, I—"

"No. Seriously. It's cool, right? You guys are great together. You know, 'cause you can grope each other without all the death and pain and shit."

She started to back away as I advanced. That's when I realized the mistake I'd made. "Wait. Dez, it's—"

She was laughing as the tears fell down her cheeks. They pooled at the bottom of her chin for a moment before falling onto her borrowed shirt. "Not what it looks like? Is *that* what you were gonna spew? Did you know that's what Alex tried to say to me? Or maybe you were going to tell me this was all some kind of setup? An act played out to shield me from something big and bad? Guess what? *Alex* said that to me, too. Matter of fact, for all the bad blood between you two, you have a hell of a lot in common all of a sudden. You both fucked me over for some cheap-ass whore."

Jade snickered. "See? Notice how she keeps bringing up Alex?"

It took every ounce of self-control not to hit Jade in that moment. I'd kissed her to prove a point to Dez. She was worried that I'd never been with anyone else. Now I had. It was an experience I would never forget.

One that was completely unremarkable.

One that didn't come close to what I felt when I was with her.

To me, it was the most logical way to quell her fears. But sometimes it was easy to forget that other people didn't see things the way I did. Alex had done exactly the same thing to her years ago. In her eyes, I'd just done the same.

I tried to reach for her, but I was too slow. She turned on her heel and bolted into the darkness.